Talk of the Town

Also by Karen Hawkins

To Catch a Highlander
To Scotland, With Love
How to Abduct a Highland Lord

KAREN HAWKINS

Talk of the Town

Pocket Books

New York   London   Toronto   Sydney

Pocket Books
A Division of Simon & Schuster, Inc.
1230 Avenue of the Americas
New York, NY 10020

Cover design by Min Choi.
Cover photo of woman by Shirley Green Photography; photo of dog by Veer

Manufactured in the United States of America

ISBN-13: 978-1-60751-401-5

To Nate:

Thanks for fixing the printer all 1,981.5 times it stopped "communicating" with my computer. My method (yelling at it from across the room) just wasn't working.

acknowledgments

SPECIAL THANKS TO MY agent, Karen Solem, who has deftly guided my career through the rocky shoals of a very uncertain business. Thank for your belief in me and all I do. I can't tell you how much that means.

And extra-special thanks to my editor, the divine Micki Nuding, who gets my "process" (to use the term loosely). Micki, you are an editing GENIUS!

I LIVED IN NORTH GEORGIA for seven wonderful years and I often drove through the gorgeous mountains of North Carolina to visit my family in East Tennessee.

I always drove the exact same route. Along the way, near a rather hasty looking exit, there was a cute, flower-surrounded assisted living center across from a rather tired looking strip mall. According to the map, they were located on the edge of a tiny town, though you couldn't see the town from the highway.

Every time I drove by, I'd notice how the stores in the strip mall would change. Over the years, that mall housed a taxidermist, a ballet studio, an auto parts store, a church, two hair salons, a used electric appliance dealer, a gun shop, and more. Even the U.S. Post Office temporarily occupied a section.

While the strip mall was a harbinger of change, *nothing* ever changed at the assisted living center. For the seven years I drove by that place, it remained exactly the same, even to the same cars parked in the same spaces in the same lot out front.

This tickled my imagination and, over the years, as

I drove past that same exit, the idea of a story grew beyond the strip mall and into the quirky town of Glory,
North Carolina.

   I hope you enjoy visiting my imaginary town as
much as I've enjoyed creating it. And if you are ever
in the mountains of North Carolina and see an assisted
living center across from a strip mall, smile a little; you
might be in the birthplace of Glory.

Talk of the Town

chapter 1

Dear Bob,

My new girl cheated on me with the guy who came to check the perk on our septic tank. That's the third girlfriend I've had who's done me wrong.

Where can I find one who won't?

Signed,

Ain't Perking No More

Dear Ain't Perking,

First you need to find yourself a new plumber. A man who'd steal your girl will just as soon cheat you on your pipe work, too.

When you get done missing your girl, join the bowling league. It's where I met Mavis and I've never been sorry. A woman who can bowl without making a single gutter ball will be true to the end.

Signed,

Bob

The Glory Examiner
Aug. 6, section B3

⌐⌐⌐

On MONDAY, ROXANNE LYNNE Treymayne Parker bleached her hair blonde, had her navel pierced, and got a tattoo on her right ass cheek. And that was all before noon.

It wasn't every day a woman could celebrate shedding two hundred and fifty pounds of worthless husband. Today was Victory Day, and in honor of the occasion she'd ditched her sober navy blue suit and sensible pumps for a pair of dangerous, four-inch do-me heels, black miniskirt, and low-cut top.

She straightened her shoulders before she marched up the courthouse stairs. For once, prim and proper Roxanne Lynne Treymayne Parker wasn't going to stand meekly aside and let life hand her leftovers. This time, she was going to take life by the throat and choke its scrawny ass until it cooked her a four-course meal.

She grabbed the heavy glass door and heaved it open, stepping into the courthouse foyer. She was immediately rewarded when the security guard's eyes widened appreciatively.

She flicked him a smile as she whisked through the metal detector, collected her purse, and headed for the elevator. She'd been sensible her whole life, and look what it had gotten her—a cheating husband, a boatload of pain, and the loss of her sense of femininity. With one bold, selfish move, Brian had snatched it all away while she'd been busy being a "good wife."

To hell with being good. She'd tried it and had gotten nothing in return, so now she was going to be bad. No, bad wasn't enough. She was going to pass bad and jump right into *wild*. Even better, she was going to do it in a court of law.

The elevator opened and she strutted into the final hearing to end her marriage. Head high, she hid a satisfied smile when her lawyer gasped at the sight of her. Her whole body tingled with bitter happiness when Brian and his lawyer stopped talking in midsentence to stare at her and her *incredibly* naughty Dolce & Gabbana heels. She took her seat, adjusted her short skirt to an even more scandalous level, and then winked at the judge.

Judge Kempt, who looked to be all of a hundred years old, turned a pleased pink and within twenty minutes had granted her the lion's share of her requests, leering at her greedily while ignoring Brian's lawyer's endless objections.

For Roxie—once Glory High School's most popular Homecoming Queen, the first Glory resident to be voted Raleigh's Debutante of the Year, and current Chair of the Raleigh Lakes Country Club Women's Organization—it was further proof that good girls finished last, while bad girls got whatever their little hearts desired.

As they all waited for the final signatures to be added to the piles of paper that represented the rubble of her marriage, Roxie crossed her legs to make sure Brian saw exactly how short her skirt was, how great her do-me pumps made her calves look, and how her scanty stretch shirt lifted just a bit to reveal her new navel ring.

Maybe she should have gotten her tongue pierced, too. It would have been priceless to stick it out at Brian and see his reaction. But she'd been afraid a tongue-piercing might have made her lisp, which wouldn't have fit with her "badass" image at all.

She sent Brian a glance from under her lashes. He sat rigidly, his manicured hands gripped together in his lap, looking so startled that one good puff of air might topple him over—Armani suit, Prada shoes, Rolex watch, and all.

Good. It was about time someone other than her got shocked by life.

After the last signature had been added to the towering pile of papers, Roxie's lawyer took her arm and practically waltzed her out to the hallway.

There, she turned down a not-very-subtle pass from the heavily cologned man, then clickety-clicked down the hall on her to-die-for heels to the waiting elevator.

She drove straight home, an odd whirling noise in her ears. *I've won,* she told herself. *Soon I'll feel it, and things will be better.*

She parked her car, went inside, closed and locked the door, stopped in her huge, Italian marble kitchen to collect every bag of chips in the cupboards, then climbed the grand stairway to her bedroom. Once there, she stripped off her new, uncomfortable clothes, kicked off her tippy shoes, and yanked on her favorite jersey sleep shirt. Then she unplugged the phone from the wall, fell into bed, and piled the bags of chips around her in a protective wall. She ripped one open and ate a handful, savoring their salty comfort.

Somehow she didn't *feel* like a winner. During the last few weeks, as this day had approached, she'd thought the moment of release would lighten her painful sense of failure. She'd thought that when she won the huge settlement, she'd be vindicated and would no longer feel so . . . empty.

Instead, sitting in her bed in the middle of her huge, silent house, all she felt was lonely.

A tear landed on her wrist. It was followed by another, and then another. Suddenly the enormity of the last few months hit her, and she pushed away the chips, curled onto her side, and sobbed into her pillows, weeks of anguish pouring out.

Finally, her face salty with tears and chips, she fell into a deep, dreamless sleep. She slept for the rest of the day and the entire night. She might have slept for most of the next day, but at ten in the morning she was awakened by the insistent doorbell.

She slowly opened her eyes, aware that something was wrong . . . oh, yes. The divorce. Her heart sank again, but she refused to cry anymore. She scrubbed her face with the edge of the sheet. The doorbell rang again and her heart leapt with hope. Perhaps one of her neighbors had come to check on her! But no, that would never happen. She might have "won" the divorce and gotten a very generous settlement, but that meant nothing to the inner sanctum of Raleigh society. To the socially elite that made up her snooty neighborhood, Brian was a man with a future, while she was nothing more than an "ex."

Damn it, she had a degree in political science and could have gone to law school herself if she'd wanted; she'd had good grades. But that would take years—and in the interim, she was positioned for a painfully slow social exorcism. Besides, after three months of emotional upheaval, she didn't have the energy to start again. Right now, she barely had the energy to eat chips. Thank God the bags were easy to open.

The doorbell rang again, even longer this time.

Roxie pulled the blankets over her head. *I don't need them anyway. I have friends like . . . like . . .* She bit her lip. The closest thing she had to a friend was her housekeeper, Tundy. Roxie had been too busy being Brian's chief cheerleader to find any real friends.

She swallowed the lump in her throat. "Screw the lot of them!" she told the ceiling defiantly. "Tundy's always been better company than the Raleigh Wives, anyway." Thank God for Tundy. The housekeeper was always cheerful, always ready to help, and—right or wrong—always willing to give her honest opinion. Tundy's frankness was a trusty compass while navigating the unpredictable ocean of guile and Southern politeness that made up the Raleigh Wives.

Brian had snickered when Roxie had named the aimless, avaricious women who populated their exclusive subdivision "the Raleigh Wives." From the tops of their salon-colored hair to the tips of their perfect nails, the Raleigh Wives were worse than Stepford Wives: they were Stepford Wannabes. At first Roxie had avoided them, until Brian had pointed out that it was her duty to help his budding legal career by accumulating "useful friends." Pasting a smile on her face, Roxie had submerged yet another part of her pride and made an entire subdivision-worth of false friends. Mother would have loved every minute of it; they were her sort of people.

But Roxie knew what a vicious gaggle of griping, sniping geese the Raleigh Wives could be. After Brian's defection, far from rallying around her, they had collectively ignored her, all the while continuing to invite Brian to their houses, where, she was sure, they'd cooed over him and offered their "support." She shouldn't have been surprised; they went with the money, and despite the generous settlement, in the long run that would mean Brian.

The doorbell annoyingly rang again. "Go away!" Roxie snuggled deeper into the womb she'd created with 600-thread-count sheets, an embroidered silk comforter, and her wall of chips.

But the doorbell didn't stop. It got more insistent, then *more* insistent. Roxie glared at the ceiling. Didn't anyone respect anyone's privacy anymore? Didn't people know she had A Situation on her hands that required complete and total despair?

If she left the house from the terrace door, she could drive into town and buy a gun. It was only a fifteen-minute drive. Then she could put a final end to the annoyance.

There was a long silence, then she heard the click of a key in the lock and then her brother's voice, calling from the foyer, "Roxie, I saw your car in the drive! Are you here?"

Damn it, Mark must have heard about the divorce. She hadn't told anyone—not Mark and certainly not Mother. Mark might get angry at Brian, but Mother would have a cow. Treymaynes did not get divorced. Why, when Arlene left Mark, Mother had almost disowned him, saying that if he didn't find Arlene and patch things up, the family name would be "smirched." Though, if anyone had besmirched the family name it was Arlene, who'd ridden off into the sunset with a rodeo rider.

"Roxie?" Mark's voice was on the stairway now.

She struggled to sit up and yelled, "I'm up here. What do you want?"

She should have left straight for Paris yesterday and had a passionate rendezvous with a mysterious Frenchman in a dark café. Or perhaps found a bedroom-eyed Italian to sip wine with in a trattoria in Florence.

Mark appeared in her bedroom doorway, his clothes rumpled, his hair mussed, his tie askew.

He opened his mouth to speak, but his gaze locked onto her hair. He just stood there, mouth ajar.

She frowned. "What?"

He rubbed a hand over his eyes. "You're *blonde*."

"Did you come to compliment my new 'do, or did you want something?" She dug through the bags of chips, opened a fresh one, and munched a handful. "I suppose you've heard about what's happened?"

He ripped his gaze from her hair with obvious difficulty, coming further into the room, looking relieved. "You already know? That's good."

"Of course I know. How could I not?"

"I don't know. I've been trying to call you since I found out, but no one answered." He frowned. "You seem very calm."

"I am. I'm glad it's over."

He paled. "*Over*? Mother didn't—"

"Please don't bring Mother into this! It was hard enough going through a divorce, without knowing how Mother was going to take it and—"

"Divorce?" Mark gaped at her. "But . . . why? You and Brian were the perfect couple!"

"Someone forgot to tell Brian." Roxie forced the words from her stiff lips. "He fell in love with someone else."

Mark winced and suddenly looked exhausted. "Jeez, Roxie. I don't know what to say. I'm so sorry."

"That's OK." Though nothing was OK anymore. She rubbed her forehead with a weary hand. *I should miss Brian, but I don't.* She frowned. *Is that normal? Maybe I don't miss him because I was already sad and lonely when*

I lived with him. Now I feel angry and betrayed, but that beats sad and lonely by a huge, scary margin. She cleared her throat. "Since you didn't know about the divorce, why did you come?"

Mark rubbed his eyes. "Oh, God. You don't need to hear this, but—Roxie, it's Mother."

Time shuddered to a halt. Roxie clutched her bag of chips like a shield. "What happened?"

"She had a heart attack, but Doc Wilson says she'll be fine."

Roxie breathed a relieved sigh. "Thank God!"

"No kidding. It happened yesterday."

"Why didn't someone call me?"

"I tried! Your phone just rang and rang."

She looked at the cord, where it hung over a chair in the corner of the room. "Oh, yeah. I never thought something might happen."

"None of us did. Doc said it was a very mild attack, but you know how Mother is." Mark sent her a grim look. "Rox, we have to go home to Glory and get her back on track."

Roxie looked down. This certainly put a crimp in her budding plans to be bad, but that was what she got for hesitating. She shoved the chip bags aside and climbed from her bed. "It'll just take me a few minutes to pack."

Mark smiled tiredly. "I don't know how we're going to do this. Mother'll want someone with her night and day, and—" He blinked. "Hey, do you think you could talk Tundy into helping us? She's got more sand than any woman I know."

Roxie paused with one hand on the closet door. "That just might work. Tundy'd do anything if you paid her enough, and she knows Mother from the times she came to visit."

Mark fished his cell phone out of his pocket. "I'll give her a call. What's her number?"

Roxie let Mark make the call. Tundy was a sucker for a smooth man, and when Mark was on his game, no one was better.

Roxie threw clothes into a suitcase; sensible, sober clothes for "With Mother" and fun, playful clothes that showcased the new Roxie for times "Away From Mother."

Frowning, she looked with distaste at a high-necked yellow dress suitable for an episode of *Father Knows Best*. She set her jaw, then pulled out every last sober and sensible thing she'd packed, leaving nothing but her flirty new clothes. Then, chin high, she zipped up her suitcase. Like it or not, Mother was just going to have to adjust.

It was time someone other than Roxanne Treymayne compromised on life.

chapter 2

*S*HERIFF NICK SHEPPARD KNEW the little town of Glory better than any human should. He knew every car and pickup, every house and shed, and every last tree for a ten-mile radius. He could recite names, relationships, and even the birth dates for most of the citizens. He should have been able to—he'd been born and raised in Glory and, except for a twelve-year move to Atlanta, he'd never lived anywhere else.

Glory, North Carolina, was the exact opposite of his experience in Atlanta. Here, being sheriff was a personal sort of job. Just this morning, he'd had to *personally* unwedge the head of Mrs. Clinton's fat pug from between the spindles of her front porch railing, then he'd *personally* investigated a report of a stolen lawn mower over on 5th and Elm, which had turned up in a neighbor's garage, having been borrowed but forgotten. After that he'd very *personally* answered yet another emergency call from Deloris Fishbine, the city librarian, about a supposed noise she'd heard in her attic late last night.

That was the third call she'd made this week, and

he'd already half-decided that the old woman had a thing for men in uniform when he'd caught her at the bottom of her attic ladder, shining a flashlight up at his ass. It didn't get much more personal than that.

The distant sound of a car approaching fast made Nick lift his radar gun and look down the road.

A red-hot '68 Mustang roared into view. Oh, yeah. That was a good one. He clicked the trigger and was rewarded with a rising squeal. Twelve miles over the limit.

He reached into his squad car and flipped on the lights, then waved the car over. The Mustang's rear lights flashed on and the car whipped to the side of the road, spraying gravel. Nick caught a glimpse of the driver, a hot blonde wearing huge hater-blocker sunglasses that would look less out of place in L.A.

Well! That was a sight he hadn't seen in his two-year tenure as town sheriff. And a good thing, too. If he knew anything, it was that women could be trouble, especially hot blondes who thumbed their perfect noses at the law. He'd seen the damage a woman could do if a man got too mixed up and lost his objectivity. He'd sworn to never succumb to such dangerous temptation.

He approached the car, noted the Raleigh plates, and counted at least two other occupants besides the driver. To keep his hands free, he tucked his ticket book into his back pocket and walked to the open window. The driver was turned away from him as she dug through her wallet, obviously looking for a license. His gaze dropped to the space between the woman and the door, instinctively looking for a weapon—old training from when he'd worked somewhere far busier and far more violent.

As he expected, he didn't find anything of interest. Well, that wasn't entirely true. That long expanse of smooth, tanned thigh and, at the curve of her hip, the hint of a tattoo peeking from the edge of her white shorts were very interesting.

His gaze lingered appreciatively.

Whoever she was, she definitely wouldn't fit in with the grayhairs and shiny domes who sat around Micki & Maud's Diner, complaining about the weather.

Nick bent down to the open window. "Ma'am, I'm going to need to see your driver's license and registra—"

The woman looked up and flipped her sunglasses to the top of her head. In one blinding moment, Nick forgot everything he was going to say. Sitting before him was the reason he'd left the idyllic little town of Glory in the first place—Roxie Treymayne. "You changed your hair color!"

It was a stupid thing to say and her reaction was immediate.

Hot color flooded her cheeks, but her chin immediately notched up a level as if ready for a fight. "You think?" she asked in a cool, faintly sarcastic way he immediately recognized.

Nick flicked a glance at the creamy blonde hair lifting

up into a ponytail, hair that had once been such a deep brown that it had bordered on black. He might not know that new hair, but he did know those wide, pale blue eyes, thick black lashes, and pouty, kissable mouth, just as he knew that too-stubborn chin. At one time, he'd showered them all with kisses. "Roxie Treymayne."

"Nick Sheppard." Her gaze flicked over him before she met his gaze, humor lurking in her expression. "A cop. I never saw that coming."

"Yeah, well, neither did I. Though my mother's glad I'm in charge of the jail rather than residing in it." Though he tried not to, his gaze drifted, noting the low-cut halter top and . . . the twinkle of a navel ring above the waistband of her short shorts.

Once a too-good-for-anyone brunette ice queen, Roxie Treymayne had returned to town as a hot, sexy blonde. A hot, tattooed, navel-pierced blonde, at that.

Hot damn.

Nick's mind reeled. Growing up, he'd watched little Roxie Treymayne prance about Glory, so pure and perfect that it had almost hurt to see her. He'd watched her grow from a leggy sprite wearing a Peter Pan collar to a supremely confident homecoming queen with a large blue satin bow on her shoulder. Just breathing, Roxie had kept every male for miles around panting. Except him.

He hadn't panted. He'd dreamed, desired, longed for . . . and had had the good sense to make a run for it before he'd made even more of a fool of himself.

Now, he met her icy blue gaze and realized just how

much things had changed. At one time, she'd been the town's hottest and most unavailable virgin, while he'd been Senior Most Likely to Be in Jail During the Reunion. Now he was a by-the-book cop, while she, by all appearances, had returned a sultry scofflaw, the exact sort of woman he avoided like the plague.

"Well, Officer?" Roxie's voice traced across his skin like warm fingers. "Am I getting a ticket?"

Nick shoved away his far-too-strong reactions and pulled his ticket book from his back pocket. "You were going twelve miles over the posted speed."

A snicker from the other side of the car made Nick look across Roxie. In the passenger seat sat a rotund, squat woman dressed in a pink velour sweat suit that clashed with her short, curly red hair. She gripped an oversize bag of barbecue pork rinds in one hand, her fingers orange from the rind dust. She pulled her heart-shaped neon-pink glasses to the end of her freckled nose, and flashed an orange-tinted smile. "Well, hello there, Officer."

Nick blinked. Had she just winked at him?

He grinned and tipped his hat, then glanced in the backseat and saw a familiar man with tousled dark hair and blue eyes, who was hiding a smile.

"Mark!" Nick exclaimed.

Mark grinned. "Nick! I haven't seen you since . . . I don't know when."

"Your wedding."

A shadow crossed Mark's face.

Oh. So it was like that, was it? "What are you doing back in tow—oh, right." Everyone knew Mrs. Treymayne had taken ill, and he should have realized what that would mean. "Sorry about your mother."

"Me, too." Mark glanced at Nick's uniform. "I thought you were in Atlanta."

Roxie glanced his way, but Nick kept his attention on Mark. "I came back here a couple of years ago."

"Not paying enough?"

"Not enough peace."

A question flickered through Mark's eyes, but all he said was, "I suppose that's as good a reason as any."

Nick thought so, too. He was glad Mark didn't ask any more questions; he wasn't ready to talk about Atlanta. That was a time best forgotten, just like he should forget Roxanne Treymayne. Only . . . it wasn't Treymayne now, but Parker.

Which was a good thing. He wanted to stay in Glory and make a life here. He didn't want any trouble, and the new Roxie Treymayne looked like trouble with a capital *T.* But at least she was someone else's Trouble.

Nick opened the ticket book. "I'm afraid I'm going to have to issue you a warning."

"Roxie, how fast were you going?" Mark asked.

"Oh, she was flyin'," the redhead in the front seat said. "Just flyin'! I warned her, too, but she wouldn't have none of it. No, sir, she told me she *knew* the speed limit and—"

"Thanks, Tundy," Roxie said through clenched teeth.

Nick raised his brows. "Tundy?"

Roxie showed him her teeth in a saccharine-sweet smile. "Nick, this is Tundy Spillers. Tundy, this is Nick Sheppard. He used to be one of Mark's friends back in high school."

He'd been Roxie's "friend," too, if four weeks of mindless, all-absorbing passion warranted the term. But Roxie hadn't been willing to publicly claim him as such, of course.

To his surprise, the old hurt returned and, jaw tight, he touched the brim of his hat. "Nice to meet you, Miss Tundy."

The redhead grinned. "Nice to meet you, too. I'm Miz Parker's maid."

Nick sent a quick glance at Roxie. Who in the hell would come to Glory with a maid?

"Tundy's come to take care of Mother," Roxie said impatiently, her blue gaze pinning him in place, as if she'd been able to read his thoughts. "She has a lot of experience tending older folks."

Tundy leaned forward to tell Nick in a confidential voice, "I make corn bread and soup beans, and they like that. Keeps 'em regular and—"

"Tundy," Roxie interrupted, "Nick's not here to hear about your recipe for staying regular."

"No," Tundy said, crunching on another pork rind. "He's here 'cause you were drivin' like a bat outta hell."

Roxie sent an accusing look at Nick. "Someone changed the speed limit."

"The city council did it last month because we've been getting a lot of vacation traffic whizzing through here on weekends. I've been giving out warnings ever since."

"Lovely. Just give me that warning and we'll be on our way. We've things to do." With that, Roxie settled her hater-blocker glasses back onto the bridge of her patrician nose and effectively relegated him to the level of security guard at Costco.

Nick took his time finding his pen. "I'll be glad to give you the warning, Mrs. Parker."

"I prefer Treymayne," she said tersely.

Nick lifted his brows, but before he could speak, Mark sighed. "Rox, just pay attention to the signs next time, will you?"

Tundy snorted. "I tried to tell her, but you know how stubborn she can be. How completely pigheaded and—"

"Thank you, Tundy," Roxie said abruptly before saying to Nick in a voice most people reserved for repelling telemarketers, "Can you hurry, please? Mother's expecting us."

Heaven forbid anyone keep Lilah Treymayne waiting. If there was one thing Nick disliked about Glory, it was the fact that Roxie's mother, the widow of and mother to the sole descendents of the town's founding father, General LeeRoy Treymayne, thought she owned the whole place. And Lilah wasn't shy about invoking the spirit of her long-dead husband whenever she felt she wasn't being treated with enough deference.

Nick refused to treat Lilah Treymayne any differently than he did anyone else, which was one of the many reasons she couldn't stand him. "I'll need your license and registration, and then you can be on your way."

Nick filled out the warning while he tried not to stare at Roxie's smooth, tanned thighs and remember the time when he'd kissed his way up them to— He blinked at the ticket and scowled. He'd written his name in the date slot, and he'd be damned if he'd let her see it. He flipped the page over and started a new one, hoping she didn't notice. It took all his concentration, but he filled it out correctly. "Here you are."

She reached for it and their fingers met. For a long moment, they stared at each other, their fingers clenched over the same paper. Nick's heart gave an odd gallop, and then, with a wince, as if she'd burnt her fingers, Roxie snatched the paper from his hand, almost tearing it in two.

Nick stepped away from the car. "Watch the signs from now on," he said in a voice that matched hers for terseness.

She threw the car into gear.

"See you around, Nick!" Mark called as Roxie hit the gas and wheeled onto the road.

"Bye, Officer!" Tundy yelled out the window, waving a pudgy, orange-fingered hand.

Nick watched the Mustang until it disappeared and the gravel dust settled into a low haze.

"I'll be damned," he said aloud. Glory was definitely less predictable than it had been a few minutes ago—and all because of a hot blonde in a red Mustang.

Nick jabbed his pen back into his pocket and turned toward the squad car. If Roxie Treymayne had returned to town as she'd left it, innocent and pristine as the rising sun, he might be worried. Fortunately for him, she'd come as the one thing he was now immune to—a woman in trouble. He didn't know what kind of trouble, but he recognized the signs, every tempting, tattooed one.

He tossed the ticket book onto the car seat, lifted his hat, and raked a hand through his hair, realizing his shoulders were as tense as if he'd been facing an armed murderer. "Hot damn," he told the warm breeze that ruffled the trees overhead.

Once again, Roxie Treymayne was off limits. Only this time, it was for an entirely different, and far more interesting, reason.

chapter 3

*T*UNDY TWISTED IN HER seat and watched Nick's retreating figure. "Uhm-mmm! They sure do know how to grow cops here in the mountains! If they had cops as looked like that back in Raleigh, I'd have shoplifted more."

"More?" Mark's voice rose in surprise.

Tundy blinked, then stuffed her mouth full of pork rinds.

Roxie hoped Nick hadn't noticed the way her heart pounded in her throat. She didn't think so; he'd looked at her exactly the way he'd always looked at her—as if she'd had a smudge on her nose. It irked her that he could still make her want to check a mirror.

She couldn't believe he was back in town—and a policeman, of all things! The wild, rebellious nineteen-year-old she'd known would never have gone that route. How had he gone from Town Bad Boy to Top Cop? It was a little like finding out the devil drove a minivan.

Tundy finished chewing. "Mr. Treymayne, what did Officer Hottie mean about wantin' more peace?"

Mark shrugged. "When Nick went to Atlanta, he

made sergeant within eight years. He was on the fast track to be named captain, but something happened. Some sort of corruption investigation."

Tundy's brows shot up over her heart-shaped glasses. "Was he on the take?"

"No, but his captain and some others were involved in some sort of unethical practices. Nick testified against them. From what I heard, he was pretty much ostracized for it."

Roxie blinked. "That doesn't sound like the Nick we knew."

"No, he was headed for trouble back then. I don't know what turned him around, but from what I've heard, he's really changed."

Roxie thought of how Nick's hot gaze had noted her blonde hair and navel ring. He wasn't *completely* different.

Tundy munched a pork rind reflectively. "I've heard the police are tough on their own kind if they snitch."

"Which is probably why he jumped at the chance to come to Glory," Mark said. "It took nerve to do what he did."

"I like a man with balls." Tundy's sharp gaze suddenly locked onto Roxie. "Miz Roxie, you said Hot Cop was a friend of your brother's, but you sure looked like you knew him, too."

Oh, she knew him, all right. She knew how his eyes crinkled when he laughed, how he always smelled like soap and mint, how he liked to spoon up behind her right before he fell asleep and would stay like that all night, snuggled together in a way that left her feeling loved and cherished.

It had been an illusion, of course. Those four glorious weeks during her senior year, when she'd thought they'd found something special, had merely been a notch on Nick's worn belt—a belt with so many notches, it had barely kept his pants up.

"I saw him at school now and then," Roxie said. And after school, though no one had known. And on weekends, between cheerleading practice and singing lessons for her pageants. And late at night, when she'd finally gotten the courage to slip out her window, where Nick's warm hands and hot mouth had made her forget everything except him.

Even now, if she let her mind drift back to that time, her body tightened and a low heat began to burn in her stomach. There was no denying that the physical aspect of their brief fling had been satisfying, though every other part of it had been filled with pain and teenage angst. For a few brief weeks, she'd been all of the things she'd never dared before—impulsive and bold and wild. Seeing Nick again had brought back the taste of those wanton weeks, a spicy and tantalizing tang in her otherwise bland memories.

Nick had kept his dark, sensual looks over the years. He was still lean, though more muscled than before. He still had thick dark hair and gray eyes that heated to silver when he was interested in something or someone. Worse, he still had the same sensually masculine mouth that promised untold pleasures and made her shiver with memories.

It was yet another reason to get Mother back on her feet quickly so Roxie could head for the Riviera on the first possible plane. All she had to do was avoid being drawn into Mother's drama and keep the sleepy town of Glory from draining her desire to change things.

Roxie didn't just want change. She *needed* it. Her fingers tightened over the steering wheel. People were going to talk about her; they always had. Well, if they didn't like the new Roxie, they could all take a hike. She was thirty-four years old, and if she wanted to dye her hair purple, then what could anyone do about it?

Roxie sighed. She knew exactly what Mother'd do. She'd stage a scene. She'd tell Roxie about the sacrifices she'd made. About the opportunities she'd missed for her sake. About how she'd struggled after Father's death to provide her children with the things that befitted a Treymayne. Then she'd talk about the pain of childbirth, which seemed to have indebted Roxie to her mother for life.

The bag of pork rinds rattled. "I suppose it's too much to hope you know the color of Hot Cop's Underoos?"

"No, I don't," she said shortly.

Tundy sighed. "Lord, you ain't had a sense of humor since the divorce."

Tundy said the word "divorce" as if the first syllable couldn't bear to be beside the next syllable. Dee-vorce.

"Tundy, I'm fine. The divorce is over and done with."

Tundy peered over her heart-shaped glasses. "Not that I blame you for bein' out of sorts, what with findin' your husband cheatin'. Men with little peckers can be vindictive."

Mark snorted a laugh while Roxie tried to keep the car from swerving off the road.

"Yup," Tundy said, unaware she was causing turmoil. "I see'd it when he was swimming. He wore them little bitty Brazilian trunks that don't cover nothing." She wrinkled her nose. "I felt sorry for you. And that's all the more reason to go out and get yourself a new man like Hot Cop. Think about it: W.W.O.D.?"

Mark leaned forward from the backseat. "What's W.W.O.D.?"

"What Would Oprah Do," Tundy replied. "Oprah's got it all. She's wealthy, has her own show, and a man dyin' to marry her, but she won't have none of him. That's the way to be. Make your own money, and tell all the Steadmans to kiss your ass."

If only Roxie had a Steadman. Someone who loved her for who she was, not for what she could do for his social aspirations and career. By the end, that had been all she had been to Brian—a pass into the social set that doted on young, attractive, well-monied couples.

Roxie blinked back sudden tears, surprised. She would *not* cry for that jerk. Never again.

Tundy shoved her pork rinds back into the grocery bag at her feet. " 'Course, if you want a man, you're gonna have to do something about that DayGlo hair of yours. The belly ring, I understand. Wouldn't mind having one of those myself." Tundy slapped her stomach, leaving orange pork-rind prints on the pink velour. "Though I don't know what in the hell you were thinkin' gettin' a tattoo."

"A *tattoo*?" Mark's voice had a bit of a yelp to it.

"Hell yes, she has a tattoo," Tundy said. "But why she wanted a goose put on her ass is beyond me!"

"It's an eagle," Roxie said in a firm tone. "Not a goose."

"Humph. Whatever it is, it's missin' a leg."

"The leg is tucked up under it. It's a perfectly fine tattoo, and you know it!"

"I think the boy who done that was high."

Roxie was fairly sure he had been. "He did an excellent job and I refuse to hear another word about it."

Perhaps she'd gone a bit overboard with the tattoo, though at the time it had made perfect sense. She wanted to feel bigger, stronger, *badder.* If she could grow a hard-enough shell, betrayals wouldn't hurt so much.

In truth, the hardest part about Brian's defection hadn't been the leaving. If she was honest, there'd been a void between them for a long time, though she hadn't wanted to admit it. No, the hard part about Brian's defection was how it had changed the way she saw herself. She'd always been successful, capable, and smart. In one fell swoop, she'd found out that she could be deceived, and by the one person she'd trusted the most. She'd been duped and she hadn't seen it coming.

She glanced at herself in the rearview mirror and was comforted to see that her brassy blonde hair made her look harder, tougher, as did the huge hater-blocker sunglasses. She would never again be blind. She'd hone her lie-detecting skills until no lie, no matter how small, escaped her notice.

Tundy licked her fingers. "I can't imagine what yo' momma's goin' to say about the divorce."

"She doesn't know, and you're not to mention it."

Tundy's eyes widened. "You want me to keep quiet about the divorce, and how Mr. Parker cheated on you and how you got arrested—"

"Tundy!"

Too late.

"*Arrested?*" Mark leaned over the seat. "For what?"

Roxie flashed a glare at the maid.

Tundy sniffed, suddenly prim. "He would have found out sooner or later. Lies always come home to roost, Miz Roxie. You should know that."

"I wasn't going to lie. I just wasn't going to mention it."

"Damn it, Roxie," Mark said. "What's she talking about?"

"It wasn't anything," Roxie said through her teeth. "No one was hurt and Brian dropped the charges. It's really not worth mentioning—"

"My ass!" Tundy said. "You ran a car into that floozy's trailer and almost killed him . . . her . . ." Tundy frowned. "What *do* you call a transvestite?"

"*Transvestite?*" Mark's voice cracked.

Roxie winced. "I didn't want to get into all of this right now, but . . . Brian's lover is Larry, his law partner."

There was a moment of stunned silence, then Mark roared, *"What?"*

"That was pretty much my reaction, too," Roxie agreed. "I suspected he was cheating, because he kept coming home later and later, and I found blonde hairs on one of his jackets. But I didn't expect to find him with a six-foot-three blonde in a sequined negligee and an Adam's apple the size of Virginia."

"Good God." Mark shook his head. "You had no idea . . . you didn't know . . . there were no signs that—"

"Not a one," Tundy said before Roxie could answer. "Mr. Parker always seemed like a man's man. Guess he was, in a way."

"I can't believe it," Mark said weakly. "Brian?"

"I never saw it coming, either, and I worked for the man," Tundy said. "Though now that I think about it, I once caught him watching an ice skate show on the TV."

"Incredible," Mark said. "I thought I knew him."

"Tell me about it," Roxie said in a hard voice.

Tundy shook her head thoughtfully. "I don't know what Mr. Parker was thinking. It wasn't like this Larry was any good at being a woman, either. That man was hairy. Never saw so much curl sticking out of a negligee. Someone needs to give him a good wax job."

"Good God," Mark said faintly.

Roxie clenched the wheel tighter and stared straight ahead. There was a special sort of pain that followed a betrayal, one that went deep and made one doubt one's worth. Worse, it had made her doubt her own femininity, which was why her newly blonde hair and short shorts felt right in so many ways. Brian might have forgotten that she was an attractive woman, but *she* hadn't.

Mark let out his breath in a long sigh. "Roxie, I'm so sorry you went through all of that alone."

"I wasn't alone. Tundy came and stayed with me."

"Yup!" Tundy fished in her shopping bag and brought out a jar of picante sauce and some meat sticks. "I stayed at her house for a week, mainly 'cause I was afraid she might shoot someone and I wouldn't get to watch."

"I'm glad Mother doesn't know any of this," Mark said fervently.

Tundy dipped her meat stick and munched thoughtfully. "I suppose. Not to say anything against yo' momma, but she is a bitch."

"Tundy!" Roxie said reprovingly.

"Well, she is, though not one of them loud ones. She's more of a soft-spoken bitch, which is the worst kind of all." Tundy patted Roxie's hand. "But don't you worry none, I won't say nothing ugly to Miz Treymayne. Not to her face, anyway. I'm here out of the goodness of my heart to help a poor, old, sick woman."

"You're here because I'm paying you three times your salary."

"There's that, too," Tundy said cheerfully.

"So when we reach Mother's, not a word about Brian or my divorce. OK?"

"Humph! I'm a lot of things, but a snitch ain't one of them. Did I call your mother when you set your house on fire?"

"Wait a minute," Mark said faintly. "Roxie, you set your house on fire?"

Roxie glared at Tundy again. "That was an accident. I piled Brian's golf clubs in the front yard and set them on fire. Somehow it spread to the house."

"Right up the yard to the front door!" Tundy twisted in her seat. "There was more than golf clubs in that fire, too. She done put in all of Mr. Parker's clothes and his favorite pictures, two chairs he liked to sit in, his framed law degree, and the bed from the guest room because she found out he'd gotten jiggy in it with that hairy boyfriend of his."

"Good God," Mark said feebly.

"Uh-huh! Why, the paint melted right off the front shutters. Took the fire department two hours to put it out. The president of the homeowners association threatened to sue Miz Roxie, but she told him to go blow himself." Tundy beamed. "I was never more proud of her in my life."

"He asked for it," Roxie said defensively. "It wasn't as if there was any permanent damage. I had the shutters repainted and the yard resodded, and it was as good as new."

Mark groaned.

"But that was before, when I was angry."

"That was Saturday," Tundy said. "*Last* Saturday."

Mark put a hand on Roxie's shoulder. "Why didn't you tell me what was going on? You were there for me when Arlene left. I would have been there for you, if you'd let me."

For a horrible instant tears threatened again, but she fought them off and clasped his hand gratefully. She was through with tears. Tears were for wimps and Momma's girls; not women who had the guts to have their navel pierced *and* get a screaming eagle tattoo, all in the same day. She was the newer, improved Roxanne Treymayne. All she had to do was remember that fact, and her life was bound to change for the better. "Thank you, but there was nothing you could do." She returned her hand to the steering wheel. "I'm fine now. Better than ever."

Tundy snorted. "You'd best be finding yourself a way to be angry that don't include settin' things on fire. Just think W.W.O.D., then make yourself a plan of action. You'll feel better, I promise."

"I'll remember that." What *would* Oprah do? Roxie didn't know, but a small part of her hoped it involved her ex-husband's large ears and a red-hot blowtorch.

Sighing, she turned the car into a long, flower-edged drive that curved up a hill to the front of a wedding-cake Victorian manor with a wide porch. Inside, reclining in a lace-covered bed and probably scheming madly like a spider in an iced web, was Mother.

"Hot damn!" Tundy stuck her head out her window. "Is this the house from *Gone With the Wind*?"

Mark snorted. "More like the house from *Bride of Frankenstein*."

Roxie parked the car and climbed out, then glanced up at Mother's window, filled with white lace curtains. A shiver of apprehension tickled her neck, and she tugged her shirt down to keep it over the winged edge of her tattoo.

She heard the strains of a song from the open window and tilted her head. "She can't be feeling too bad; she's listening to music."

"Show tunes," Mark said disgustedly. "*Fiddler on the Roof* is not music."

Tundy had reached down to gather her bags, but she straightened suddenly. "*Fiddler on the Roof*? I saw that on the Turner network."

"It's Mother's favorite movie."

Tundy gawped. "Miz Roxie, I didn't know yo' momma's kosher!"

Roxie shook her head. "Mother likes the movie, but—"

"*And,*" Tundy warmed to the subject, "Mr. Treymayne called her the Bride of Frankenstein. Anything ending with *stein*'s a Jewish name. I know, 'cause I saw a show on cable about that."

"Mother's not—"

"I wished I'd known yo' momma was kosher." Tundy collected her bags. "I'll leave my pork rinds out here."

"You don't need to—"

It was too late; Tundy was already out of the car, exclaiming over the height of the azalea bushes.

Roxie watched the maid waddle to the front door before she turned to her brother. "Mark Treymayne, you are a troublemaker."

He offered her a sweet, sincere smile. "Whenever I can be, sis."

She sighed. She'd never been able to take Mother as casually as Mark did. Though she knew they loved each other, they clashed fiercely, which left Roxie to maintain the peace. "We should have brought Mother flowers."

"Yeah," Mark said, opening the trunk and unloading an assortment of luggage, followed by Tundy's Piggly Wiggly bags, which seemed to be filled with stretch pants and a particularly large lime green thong. "Because uprooting our lives and coming to wait on her hand and foot just isn't enough."

"Mother will expect more."

"Roxie, she always expects more." Mark handed her two suitcases. "It never ends."

She took them and headed for the porch. He was right; Mother was never satisfied. Roxie paused at the foot of the steps and looked around. It was hard to believe she was back home. The shadow of the house rested heavy on her shoulders and made her chest ache. She got this feeling every time she came back to Glory. One time she'd made the mistake of mentioning this to Mother, who'd gotten so offended that Roxie'd never dared bring it up again. Fortunately, Mother had loved their house in Country Club Estates. It had suited her *Southern Living* standards to a tee.

Mark passed Roxie on the sidewalk. "Stop dawdling. Mother's bound to have heard our car."

Just as they reached the foyer, Dr. Wilson came walking down the stairs.

The doctor, now in his sixties, was tall despite his perpetual stoop. His once brown hair was now white, but his blue eyes were the same as ever, quizzical and steady.

He set down a small black backpack. "Mark Treymayne! Wondered when you'd arrive."

Mark smiled and offered his hand. "How are you doing, Doc?"

"Good, good." The doctor's gaze drifted to Tundy. "I was just checking on—" His eyes widened as his gaze landed on Roxie.

"Hi, Doc. How's Mother?"

Doc pulled his gaze from Roxie's hair, his expression immediately sobering. "Your mother couldn't get worse if she tried." At Roxie's gasp, he waved a hand. "No, no! Her *condition* is good. Very good, in fact. It's her *disposition* that's worse."

Roxie winced. "Mother can be demanding."

"Young lady, that is so much of an understatement that it borders on being a lie. Your mother called me at three this morning and said she was gravely ill. I raced over here only to find her out of bed eating ice cream, which I'd expressly forbidden."

Mark sighed. "She needs a keeper."

"Which she'd have, if she'd stop accusing every nursing assistant who steps over the threshold of trying to kill her. She's already chased off four, and those women talk. Now I can't get anyone to come."

Tundy *tsk*ed. "Someone ought to horsewhip that woman."

Doc started to nod, but hesitated.

Roxie introduced them. "Tundy has come to keep Mother company, so there's no need to find a nursing assistant."

"Yup!" Tundy puffed out her impressive chest, her girth puffing right along with it. "Don't you worry none, Doc. I got a way with spoiled bitches. I provide maid service to a lot of them."

Mark snuffled a laugh. "Are you including Roxie in that?"

"Nah. She watched Oprah with me every week."

Doc smiled reluctantly. "Do I understand that you're a maid and not a nurse?"

"I'm better than a nurse," Tundy said confidently. "I'm a Red Cross–trained candy stripper technician. Got my certification and can do CPR, too. Why, I was so good at giving those CPR breaths that I cracked the head on the CPR dummy."

Roxie caught the doctor's startled gaze. "Tundy won't let Mother bully her. *No one* bullies Tundy."

Doc Wilson eyed Tundy with interest.

"No, sir!" Tundy said, grinning. "Where I come

from, all the old women are like Mrs. Treymayne. My aunt Lilah was the meanest bitch this side of the Riverdale Trailer Park, and I took care of her for two years." Tundy leaned toward Mark and said in a low voice, "She left me two antique Coke bottles as had never been opened and her favorite velvet Elvis painting. That painting is something else. I didn't have no wall space left, so I hung him in the bathroom right over the toilet."

Mark's lips twitched. "I'll have to come and see that sometime."

A faint smile curved across the doctor's face, deepening the lines at his eyes. "Miss Tundy, you might be just what the doctor ordered."

"Why, thank you! Now, what sort of things do I need to know about Miz Treymayne?"

"She should be kept quiet, but she should also get up and walk a little every day. It's good for her lungs to move around, and she might develop pneumonia if she doesn't."

"Keep her quiet and walk her. That all?"

"That's enough, trust me. I'll be back the day after tomorrow to see how you're getting along."

Tundy picked up her Piggly Wiggly bags. "Don't you worry none, Doc. I'll have her up and about before you can say Tom Kister!" She looked at Roxie. "Where's the kitchen? Got to put my salsa in the fridge."

Roxie pointed to a door down the hallway and Tundy headed in that direction.

Doc Wilson watched the kitchen door swing shut. "Mark, as capable as Miss Tundy might be, she'll need some help."

"That's what I'm here for."

"Good. And Roxanne, maybe you could ease your mother's mind that her charity work is being seen to. I'm sure the Women's Auxiliary would be glad to pitch in if you need them."

"That's an idea," Roxie said doubtfully.

Mark read her mind. "Mother won't let anyone touch her charity work—maybe not even Roxie."

"She'll have to." The doctor picked up his backpack. "As much as your mother irks me at times, I can't think of a person who's done more for Glory. She's on every committee in town." His gaze rested on Roxie, and he smiled tiredly. "You look a bit like a young Marilyn Monroe."

Roxie took the doctor's arm and walked him to the door. "That's exactly the look I was going for." She patted his arm. "Thank you for being here for Mother, Doc. Now get home to Mrs. Wilson. Mark and I will keep Mother from bothering you after hours."

The doctor pushed open the screen door. "Call if you need me." The door closed behind him.

Mark looked up the stairs, then back at Roxie. "Are you ready?"

There was no "ready." Roxie grasped the banister and began to climb, Mark following after.

A loud thumping sounded behind them as Tundy clambered up the stairs after them, puffing loudly. "Had to throw out some sort of white stuff to make room for my salsa."

Roxie bit her lip. "Was it in a green jar?"

"Uh-huh. Don't worry, though; it was no good." Tundy scrunched her freckled nose. "I tasted it, and it was rancid."

"That was Mother's face cream. She says it works better if it's cold."

"Uhhhgh!" Tundy stuck out her tongue and scrubbed it with the back of her hand.

"Roxanne? Is . . . is that you?" The feeble voice drifted out the open door, through the air like a gossamer spider's web, and wrapped around Roxie's throat.

Mark glanced at Roxie, sweeping from her hair to the navel ring barely visible under her shirt, a grin spreading over his face. "I can't wait to see Mother's expression when she sees the new you."

Roxie straightened her shoulders. "I am who I am, and Mother will just have to deal with it."

"Oh Lordy," Tundy breathed. "Yo' momma's gonna have a cow."

Mark's smile broadened and he waved Roxie to the door. "After you."

Roxie turned toward the door, pasted a smile on her face, and walked in. "Hello, Mother!"

chapter 4

"THANK GOD YOU WAS near, Officer!" Tundy batted her eyes at Nick as he bent over Lilah Treymayne's unconscious form and took her pulse.

Roxie stood at the foot of the bed, the cordless phone still in her hand after calling 911 when her mother collapsed.

Nick released Mother's wrist. "Her pulse is normal. I think she just fainted."

Roxie studied her mother. Her eyes were closed and her hands were crossed over her chest, but her color seemed good and she was breathing with reassuring regularity. Even sick, Mother managed to "dress." She never allowed a hair out of place and prided herself on always looking like "a lady." Her nightwear, which consisted of layers and layers of gauzy material, did a silent homage to every Audrey Hepburn movie made.

Tundy *tsk*ed loudly. "I didn't know people still swooned in this day and age."

"Or could scream that loud." Mark sat in the overstuffed chair by the window and watched Mother as if she were a strange species on display at a zoo. "Scarlett O'Hara rides again. Whoever gave her that book when she was a child should be shot."

Roxie stole a look at Nick and then wished she hadn't. His gray eyes were dark, his police hat cocked at a rakish angle. Though his manner was cool and professional, she couldn't help but wistfully note the way his neat uniform hugged his hips and clung to his broad shoulders. No uniform could disguise his faintly bad boy air. In fact, he could easily pass for a faux cop stripper.

To shake off the unwelcome thoughts, she asked, "Isn't an ambulance coming?"

Mother's eyes flickered, but she didn't open them. *Hmm. That's odd.*

"They're on their way," Nick said. "I just happened to be closer."

Tundy leaned over Mother from the other side of the bed. "Personally, I think she's playin' possum. Ain't never seen a real sick person who held their hands on their chest. Looks like she's dying on a stage."

Mother's hands relaxed, one sliding to her side.

Roxie's gaze narrowed. Surely Mother wasn't pretending. That was too much, even for her. Wasn't it?

Nick's gray gaze narrowed, too. "Mark, could you fetch a pitcher of water? *Ice* water?"

Mark grinned and jumped to his feet. "Sure! I'll be right back." He looked at Mother and added, "I'll bring a *big* one."

Mother's lips were now pressed into a thin line, but

she didn't move otherwise. *Darn it, Mother! What are you trying to do now?*

Mark went downstairs, and they could hear the freezer door opening and closing. Roxie crossed her arms. "Nick, what are you going to do with that ice water?"

He grinned, looking devastatingly sexy as he leaned against the post of the elaborate bed, one hand resting on his hip. "I'm going to throw it on your mother, of course."

"That will revive her?"

"Like nothing else. It's just a pity it'll mess her hair."

Mother's lips were white, they were pressed so tightly together.

Despite herself, Roxie grinned. It would serve Mother right for being such a ham.

Tundy blinked. "Ice water? Can't you put one of them defibrillator paddles on her chest and ZAP!" She pretended to flop around. "I saw one of those on *ER*. That'd revive her!"

Roxie turned her laugh into a cough.

"The zapper is next." Nick smiled when Mother's brows snapped to the center. "First we'll try the ice water."

Tundy looked at him admiringly. "Did they teach you that trick in one of them emergency training classes?"

"Actually, no. I saw it in a movie."

"*Three Stooges,* no doubt," Roxie murmured.

Tundy didn't hear her, but Nick's grin widened. "It's

standard procedure in a case like this." His gaze locked with hers and he added softly, "Trust me, Treymayne."

Roxie's skin tingled hot and prickly, and her mind filled with the memory of Nick's muscled body beneath hers in the backseat of his car, of awkward elbows and frantic passion, of an urgency so bittersweet that it had threatened to burn her alive and make her forget everything.

Even now, her body hummed with awareness just because he was in the room.

Mark thundered back up the stairs, a pitcher of ice water in his hand, a wet spot on the front of his shirt. "I spilled a little, but here it is—"

Mother moaned loudly, moving her head from side to side. "Roxanne," she said weakly. "Where is Roxanne?"

Mark's face fell, and he looked at the pitcher with evident regret.

"Save it," Nick suggested. "You can always use it later." He moved from the bed and began to repack his emergency kit.

Roxie walked to the other side of the bed, as far away from Nick as she could, and took Mother's hand. "Mother, I'm here."

Mother's eyes fluttered open. "What happened?"

"You fainted."

"Did I? I seem to remember—oh yes, I was saying hello to Mark and you when—" Her gaze fixed on Roxie, then her hair. Mother closed her eyes as if in pain. *"Ohhhh!"*

"She's fainting again! Give me that pitcher!" Tundy reached for the pitcher in Mark's grasp.

Mother's eyes snapped open and she glared at Tundy. "*Who* are *you*?"

Tundy set the pitcher on the nightstand, wiped her hand on her sweatpants, then grabbed Mother's hand and pumped it in a friendly shake. "My name's Tundy Spillers. I suppose you don't remember my face, as you didn't ever look directly at me when we crossed paths before, but I'm Miz Roxie's maid."

Mother pulled her hand free, staring at Tundy as if she was an apparition.

Unfazed, Tundy grinned. "You can call me Tundy. Only time I ever fainted, I was pregnant." She leaned forward. "You carrying?"

"Tundy!" Roxie said in a choked voice.

Nick's laughter filled the room, followed by Mark's.

Mother tilted her chin to a pugnacious angle. "I am *not* pregnant!" She reached for Roxie's hand and held it between both of hers. "Roxanne, please. I'm ill and I don't want a stranger in my room." Her gaze found Nick at the foot of her bed, and her pained expression grew stronger. "*Or* a policeman."

She said "policeman" as if the word might bite her back.

Tundy blinked. "Stranger? Why, when you stayed with Miz Roxie afore, I washed yo' underwear!"

Mark made a noise that sounded like a cross between laughter and snorting.

Roxie hoped Nick was enjoying the show. She usually sympathized when faced with Mother's dramatics, but this time she felt a strong sense of impatience. Thanks to Brian, her Bullshit Meter was now working overtime.

Roxie gently disengaged her hand. "Mother, Tundy has come to watch over you. Doc Wilson said he couldn't find any more nursing assistants for you."

Mother sniffed. "I don't need anyone, now that you're here."

"That's too bad." Mark rubbed his chin. "There's not another woman in all of Glory who has a maid of her own."

"That's true," Roxie said quickly. "Tundy's an amazing cook, too. I was lucky to even bring her. All of the women from Country Club Estates have tried to steal her away."

Mother regarded Tundy up and down. "Really?"

Tundy chuckled. "As if I'd work for those prissy, stuck-up, tennis-addicted freaks! Why, that Miz Silvers, the doctor's wife, has enough silicone in her body to caulk up every leak in yo' attic. And Judge Turner's wife's done wrecked three BMWs and a Lexus, on account of her martini hour lasting for most of the day. She offered to double my salary right there in Miz Roxie's kitchen, too."

Roxie frowned. "When did that happen?"

"About six months ago, before Mr. Parker decided he was—"

"Right," Roxie said hastily, sending Tundy a warning look. "I remember that dinner party." She didn't, of course. There had been so many.

Mother sighed weakly. "I don't want a maid; I just want Roxanne." She took Roxie's hand again more tightly this time. "I don't need anyone else."

The woman should have been an actress. Well, more than one person could play this game. "Mother, you're right," Roxie said.

Mother beamed.

"Mark and I will stay with you while Tundy takes on your charity work."

Mother's smile sputtered to a halt. "My . . . my charity work?" She looked at Tundy, taking in the pink velour sweat suit and red, red curls.

Tundy grinned, her teeth faintly orange from the pork rinds.

Mother straightened. "Tundy most certainly will *not* do my charity work!"

"Then perhaps someone at the Women's Auxiliary could help. Doesn't Dot Weaver—"

"That woman is a vile, vindictive, hard-hearted—do you know she tried to unseat me from my position as chair of the Garden Club? She called for a special election, saying I had misused funds for buying tea cakes without a vote! I was never more furious in my life."

"Not Dot Weaver, then. How about Brenda Sullins? She could—"

"No, she could not. Brenda is a sweet soul, but she

couldn't plan an ice party in the dead of winter. She was in charge of last year's Cake Bazaar, and I can't recall a bigger mess in my life. There weren't enough tables, none of the judges showed up on time, she forgot to order ribbons—just forget it! She won't do at all."

Roxie lifted her brows.

Mother sent her a hard glance, then sighed. "Oh, very well. Miss Tundy can stay with me while you *and Mark*—"

Mark sat straight up. "Hey, wait a minute—"

"—*and Mark,*" Mother repeated, "attend to my volunteer duties. I'll write up a list."

"Great!" Roxie said.

Nick, who'd quietly watched the drama, now turned toward the window, where the faint wail of a siren could be heard. "The ambulance's close." He collected his things and headed for the door. "I'll send them up to make sure Mrs. Treymayne has completely recovered from her attack."

Roxie glanced at Mother, expecting a thank-you, but Mother's lips were pressed into a straight line, her gaze fixed on a distant point just beyond Nick.

Roxie was embarrassed, but Nick didn't seem surprised. He tipped his hat to Tundy, nodded to Mark, exchanged a quiet look with Roxie, then walked out the door.

"Mother!" Roxie said. "You should have thanked Officer Sheppard."

Mother sniffed. "He just did what he is paid to do."

Roxie spun on one heel and marched to the door.

"Roxie! Where are you going?"

"To tell Nick you're thankful, whether you are or not!" Roxie was out the door and down the steps, thudding her feet loudly so she wouldn't hear Mother's reply.

She found Nick beside his car, loading his kit into the trunk, the ambulance wail very close. He closed the trunk lid and caught sight of her.

Roxie took a deep breath. "Nick, I wanted to—"

Siren blaring, the ambulance wheeled into sight and turned into the drive, lights flashing. The siren flipped off, and a man and a woman jumped from the vehicle, then rushed to the side panels, where they pulled out several boxes of equipment and stopped to check in with Nick.

Nick gave them a brief report about what had occurred, and Roxie was again struck with the differences between this Nick and the old one. The old Nick hadn't known the meaning of the word "professional," except in the sense of being a professional hell-raiser. He'd raced his car at dangerous speeds, smoked, drank whenever the opportunity arose, slept with every attractive girl in town, stayed out too late, and refused to accept authority. He argued with his teachers and skipped school regularly, though he never missed a football or basketball game. He was known as Trouble and seemed proud of the fact. He'd been the absolute last boy Lilah Treymayne deemed good enough to date her daughter.

But Roxie had been flattered when Nick had noticed

her; he was a legend in town and was known to only go after the prettiest girls. Later it had been something else, something far more basic—primitive, even—that had kept her attention. No one had *ever* made Roxie feel the way Nick had made her feel for those few brief, passionate weeks. Even at nineteen, he'd been darned good at lovemaking. She shivered a little to think how good he'd be at it now.

The EMTs thanked Nick and entered the house.

As soon as they were inside, Roxie turned back to Nick. "As I was saying, Mother meant to thank you."

He eyed her dryly. "No, she didn't."

"Well, she would have, if she wasn't so upset at us foisting Tundy on her."

"Tundy or no Tundy, your mother dislikes me. She always has."

Roxie sighed. "She thought you were trouble."

"I was, sixteen years ago. I was headed for jail and she knew it. Everyone knew it." His silvered gaze raked across her, and she felt it as if it had been a touch. "Even you knew it."

She had. It had been one of the things that had attracted her to him from the beginning—his disregard for all of the proprieties that held her down. Things were different now, though. Now she was no longer weighed down by anything. She was free and . . . well, she didn't know what else she was, but she was determined to find out and now seemed as good a time as any.

She closed the gap between them and brushed a finger over the badge clipped to his chest. "You don't look like you're such a bad guy now."

"I'm not. Now I'm the law, and I don't 'do' trouble anymore." His gaze flickered over her, and to her surprise, she saw a touch of regret in his expression. His hand closed over her wrist, his long fingers warm on her skin as he slowly pushed her hand away.

Roxie couldn't look away from his gray eyes, a mix of silver and slate with flecks of blue. "Nick, I—"

"No. Roxie, don't—" He dropped her wrist and stepped back, looking anything but happy. Before she could speak again, he turned and walked toward his car, putting even more distance between them. "I'd better get back to the office. I hope your mother is better soon."

Just like that, he was leaving.

Darn it, this isn't the way things are supposed to go! I'm taking chances, being bolder. Maybe I haven't been bold enough. Roxie stepped forward until she was even with him. "Nick."

He paused, one hand on the door, his gray eyes shadowed. "Yes?"

Her mind raced. "Do you, ah, do you think you could leave the defibrillator with me? In case we run out of ice water?"

Nick's look of surprise dissolved into a deep laugh. His eyes crinkled, and his smile grabbed at her heart and sent it beating wildly. She'd always loved his laugh. Loved it as a girl and loved it now, as a woman.

What am I waiting for? No more hesitating; no more

rules. All I have to worry about is being happy and feeling good, and I know exactly what would feel good right now.

Without another thought, Roxie stepped forward, threw an arm around Nick's neck, and pulled him into a kiss.

The second their lips touched, the low heat that had simmered between them roared to life. Suddenly the new Nick was just like the old one, hot and ardent, possessive and wildly passionate. He delved into the kiss, holding her so tightly that she could feel his instant erection.

She raked a hand through his hair as Nick's hands slid down to her ass and cupped her to him, sending tremors of pleasure through her.

The sound of a door slamming in the distance brought Nick to his senses. What the hell was he doing? One touch from Roxie, and he was back to being nineteen and crazed for her. He'd forgotten how potent a turned-on Roxie could be. Worse, he'd been totally unprepared for how potent she was now, her eyes full of fire, her body so temptingly close, a challenge in her every gesture.

He stifled a groan and fought for control, his breath harsh between his teeth. Damn it, he wasn't the same reckless kid who followed every impulse no matter where it led. He was a man now, one with responsibilities and a life worth living right. He didn't have to follow his libido every time it sat up and howled for notice. It was time to put that wolf back in its cage.

He collected himself and released her, stepping back, his body aching from the unfinished embrace.

Roxie's hands dropped from his shirt, and she shivered. *"Wow."*

"Yeah, wow." He couldn't stop looking at her mouth. Soft and pink, it begged to be tasted again.

She smiled, her cheeks flushed. "Just like old times."

She couldn't have said anything to bring him back to reality faster. It *was* like old times. He'd been playing with fire then and he'd be playing with fire now.

She grinned at him mischievously. "But this time, you're not the wild child. I am." She reached forward and slowly ran a hand down his shirtfront. Nick's mouth went dry. This was where a stun gun could come in handy—to use on himself, to bring his howling libido back to heel.

Just as her fingers reached his belt, he let out his breath. "No," he said grimly. "Roxie, I have to go."

Her blue eyes widened, surprise evident. "Now?"

"I have to get back to the office."

"Can't you just take off for an hour or so? We could catch up on old times," she coaxed.

"I have responsibilities."

She smiled seductively. "That doesn't mean you can't kiss a woman now and then."

"I can't kiss *you*," he said firmly. *Especially not you.*

"Why not?" she asked indignantly. "I'm no longer married."

"That doesn't have anything to do with it." It had

to do with his ability to maintain his control, to make coolheaded and well-thought-out decisions. And it had everything to do with the way Roxie's breasts pressed against her shirt, her navel ring winking wickedly at him from the gap above her low-cut shorts.

Nick turned and climbed into his car. He slammed the door closed and brought the engine roaring to life. He didn't dare to even look at her one more time. "Good-bye, Treymayne. Tell your brother I'll look him up sometime."

With that, he left Roxie in the driveway, her gaze ice cold, her lips still swollen from his kisses.

It was *exactly* like old times.

FROM UPSTAIRS, AS THE EMC workers repacked their kits, Mark watched his sister spin on her heel and march into the house. *That's interesting.*

Though he'd never expected Roxie and Brian would divorce, he couldn't think of better news. He wouldn't tell Roxie that, though. Many people had tried to cheer him up during his divorce by telling him how much they'd hated Arlene, pointing out all her flaws and imperfections as if they'd been doing him a favor. None of it had helped.

It wouldn't help Roxie, either. She'd have to find her own path to peace. Although . . . he glanced down the road where Nick's car had disappeared. He only hoped she didn't cause herself more pain on the way.

The EMTs finished up. Mark thanked them and escorted them to the bedroom door, where Tundy took them downstairs, talking loudly about a kosher diet and how she needed to buy a cookbook.

Mark turned back to Mother's bedroom, glancing around in annoyance. The entire thing was done in white. Not cream or off-white, but blindingly pure white, and straight off the set of a clichéd Southern movie. The canopied bed, sheets, down comforter, dust ruffle, curtains, carpet, dresser, and bookshelves were all ruffled and white. The room was even accessorized in white—candles, picture frames, pillows piled on the bed. Only a few books, some landscape pictures (though replete with white, fluffy clouds), and Mother's face splashed any color in the room.

Mark looked at her now. "I hope you're happy."

She avoided his gaze, picking up a mirror and a tube of lipstick from her nightstand. "I don't know what you're talking about." With a few practiced swipes, she applied the lipstick.

"You should be spanked for causing such a scene, just because you didn't like Roxie's hair."

Mother replaced the lipstick on the nightstand and picked up a compact. "I didn't cause a scene. I fainted. I've been very weak, and I was shocked when—"

"You staged that whole thing. I bet you saw Roxie when we were in the driveway and plotted this while we were talking to the doc."

Twin spots of color stained Mother's cheeks. "I didn't do any such thing."

"I bet."

"Not that it matters. Poor Roxie! I'm surprised Brian let her ruin her hair. He's always been good about curbing her impulsive nature."

Mark shoved his hands into his pockets. "Mother, leave Roxie alone. She doesn't need your 'help.' You need hers."

"I can't just stop worrying about my own daughter! I'll call Teresa at the Stuff 'n Fluff and get Roxie an appointment. I'm sure it can be fixed."

"You aren't going to do any such thing," Mark said levelly.

Mother stiffened. "Her hair is a mess."

"It's the way she wants it. If she decides to change her hair, her clothes, or her life, it's her own choice and not yours."

From the stubborn tilt of his mother's chin, he could tell he was wasting his time.

He headed for the door. "If you'll excuse me, I'm going to get unpacked. Roxie and Tundy can take the two rooms up here. I'll take my old room downstairs."

"The one as far away from me as possible," Mother said waspishly. "Some things never change."

He stopped and looked back at her. "No," he said slowly. "Some things never do. Even when they should."

Mother frowned. "You've always been a difficult child. Roxie never tried my patience the way you do."

"She never said no to you before. But I have a feeling that's about to change."

"What do you mean by that?"

"Nothing. Would you make a list of what needs to be done for your charity work? Roxie and I will start tomorrow."

Mother pulled open the drawer of her nightstand and removed a small notepad. She filled the page, then ripped off the top sheet. "These are my weekly obligations."

Mark crossed to the bed and took the list. He whistled silently. "Good God! You're never home."

"Why should I be? No one is here." Mother clamped her lips together and dropped her head back against the pillows. "I'm alone almost every day, though I don't suppose you care."

There was a faint sheen of perspiration on her upper lip, and for a moment she looked every one of her sixty-two years. Mark glanced down at her hands. They were as colorless as the white comforter they rested on, the skin wrinkled and sagging.

She wasn't the iron maiden he'd always thought her. She was flesh and blood, and right now, though she did not want anyone to know it, she was as weak as a kitten. Somewhere in the region of his heart, something beat against his chest and softened the rock that pumped his blood.

Mark reached over and patted her hand. "I'm sorry, Mother. You do a lot for this town. Roxie and I will do your volunteer work while we're here."

She gave him an uncertain smile. "Thank you. I

will get Roxie's hair appointment right away, before she goes about representing us. What was she thinking? It must be a new fashion in Raleigh." Her lips pressed together. "I never wanted her and Brian to move there. He could have set up his law practice here and done quite well."

"You didn't expect that when you pushed Roxie into his arms, did you?"

Mother blinked. "I don't know what you're talking about. Brian and Roxanne love each other."

"Right." He lifted the list. "Roxie and I will get to work first thing tomorrow morning. Meanwhile, you get some sleep." He returned to the door.

"Mark?"

He paused and looked back.

Anger and something else fought in Mother's gaze. Finally she sighed, her shoulders slumped like a bent butterfly wing, and her eyes filled with tears. "Thank you," she choked out.

"You're welcome." Mark managed a smile. He might be a sarcastic ass at times, but he wasn't completely unfeeling, even though Arlene had ripped out his heart and stomped it into a grease stain—all without the benefit of anesthesia, too. That had made him tougher and less easy to fool; but it hadn't deadened him to a woman's tears, especially when he suspected they were real. This time. "Go to sleep. We're right here if you need us."

He softly closed the door, then stood leaning against

it. In the last twenty-four hours, the world had gone topsy-turvy. His perfect, shy little sister had turned into a blonde bombshell intent on seducing the town sheriff, while his heart-of-stone mother had become a fragile, weeping bundle of uncertainty.

God, he needed a drink.

chapter 5

Dear Bob,
  I'm a forty-seven-year-old woman with six children. I've been divorced for four entire months now and want to step out with a nice man I met at a PTA meeting.
  My sister says it's too early. My mother says a divorced women hasn't any business hooking up at PTA. And my two daughters think I should take the chance and run with it, though they might be prejudiced because this gentleman runs the local skating rink and promised them free passes.
  When is it OK for a divorced woman to move on?
Signed,
Hankering to Move

Dear Hank,
  If I were you, I'd see if the gentleman in question is really good for those free skate tickets and THEN I'd decide.
Signed,
Bob

The Glory Examiner
Aug. 8, section B3

OXIE SLAPPED THE NEWSPAPER onto the table. "Who is this 'Bob' and why does he think he knows so much?"

"I read that." Tundy put a glass of orange juice on a tray. "I thought he made sense. You wouldn't believe what a man will promise to get into a woman's thong. I once't dated a man who owned a junkyard, who offered to give me a free muffler for my Pinto if I'd let him watch me undress."

"I hope you turned him down."

"Yep. I made him give me a new muffler *and* a carburetor. A woman has to know her price." Tundy picked up the tray and headed out of the kitchen. "I'll be back to make more coffee." Her voice faded as she tromped upstairs to Mother's room.

Roxie stabbed her spoon into her oatmeal and let it go. It stood straight up for a long moment before slooowly falling to one side.

That summed up her entire day so far. She'd woken up with a headache, had helped Mother get dressed (which had taken awhile since Mother had been so busy suggesting helpful hints about how to deal with Roxie's "hair problem"), had argued with Tundy over the necessity of playing Christian polka music loudly at the ungodly hour of eight in the morning, had hit her head on the low beam in the hallway, and then had burnt her toast—the very last slice of whole wheat in the house, which was why she was now eating icky oatmeal.

She stabbed her spoon into the bowl again and scowled at the congealing mass, her gaze distracted by her left hand. Damn it, one of her nails had chipped. When had *that* happened? She absently put her finger in her mouth and grimaced at her reflection in the window over the sink. Her hair stood around her face like the rays of a yellow sun.

She closed her eyes and dropped her head to the table, ill humor washing over her. The truth was, her mood wasn't just about her hair or Mother or even the beam in the hallway. She'd been in a horrid mood since yesterday, when she'd kissed Nick.

When one idolized people from high school, one rather wished that when they met again, the person would be ... fat. And round-shouldered. And balding. Instead, Nick Sheppard had turned into a sexy, hard-bodied cop every bit as mouth-wateringly sexy at thirty-six as he had been at nineteen. More, even. Now he exuded confidence and success in addition to raw sexual appeal.

Life wasn't fair. She sighed, lifted her head from the table and stood her spoon back in her oatmeal, and watched it slowly slide to one side again. "I know exactly how you feel," she told her sad spoon.

"Still talk to your food, huh?" Mark breezed into the kitchen and poured himself the last bit of coffee.

She sniffed. "No. If you must know, I was speaking to my spoon."

"Unhealthy." He sat across from her and placed his cup on the table, then reached into his jeans pocket and pulled out a slip of paper bearing their mother's elegant scrawl.

"What's that?"

"Our volunteer assignments. You do this one"—he ripped the list across the top and placed a small slip in front of her—"and I'll do these." He stuffed his much-longer list back into his pocket.

"Great. Assignments."

"It'll get us out of the house."

Volunteer assignments meant smiling. And being nice. And pretending to listen. Roxie didn't much feel like doing any of those things, but the alternative was staying here, so she'd go and make the best of it. "I hope Mother gets more comfortable with Tundy and stops calling her 'that girl.' "

"Mother wouldn't be comfortable with the pope." Mark grinned. "Especially now that Tundy thinks Mother is Jewish."

"I tried to explain the whole Frankenstein connection this morning, but Tundy wouldn't listen. She told me I should be proud of my heritage."

Mark chuckled. "And so you should be! I know I am." He hopped up, humming "Hava Nagila," and opened the pantry door to stare at the cereal selection, all the while looking annoyingly chipper.

"Don't you have tax preparations or something to worry about?"

"Yup, but I can't deal with them now, so I'm not going to worry."

Roxie looked at the scrap of paper on the table before her. "This only has one assignment."

"Yes, but one *big* assignment." He pulled a box of Froot Loops from the pantry and kicked the door closed, grinning smugly. "You get to babysit a batty old-folks group at the Pine Hills Assisted Living Center."

She squinted at the list. "The Muddy Mustard Club?"

"Let me see that." He squinted at the paper, too. "Ah. Murder Mystery Club." He returned the paper and fished in a cupboard for a bowl. "There are three members, and she visits them for an hour every day and tries to get them to go on outings and such."

"An hour every day? That's not bad."

"Yes, but Mother said they'll hound you to come more often." Mark grabbed a spoon and sat across from her. "A word of warning: Mother said they were difficult. They were forced by the activities director to join some sort of club, and they didn't want to. Eventually they came up with this Murder Mystery Club, but all they really do is sit around and watch *CSI*." Mark opened the box of cereal. "They just *love* that sexy Gil Grissom. Apparently one of them has a picture of his naked ass on the back of her door."

Roxie dropped her head into her hands.

Mark chuckled. "I thought you'd like that. Mother says that if left to their own devices, they'd never get out of their chairs. She makes them move around, get some exercise, visit the park." He reached past her for the milk.

"I bet they hate that."

Mark smiled smugly. "Which is why you have only one item on your list. My list may be longer, but it's much easier. I'm to deliver items for the church yard sale, meet with the pastor about the flowers for every third Sunday, inform the Baptist Ladies' Organization that Mother will be out for the next few weeks, and on and on and on. Fortunately, unlike you, none of *my* activities begin before nine."

"Nine? In the *morning*?"

"Yup. If you don't like it, take it up with the Murder Mystery Club. Maybe you can move it to a later hour."

She sighed and pulled her coffee closer, staring morosely into the cup. She loved coffee, but this morning it didn't seem to be "talking" to her.

Mark's blue eyes twinkled. "Hey, it could be worse. They could be into *Barnaby Jones*."

"You're killing me."

"I'll drop you off at the assisted living center and come back in an hour and rescue you. By the way, Mother says they meet in Doyle Cloyd's old room."

Roxie put down her coffee cup. "He died a few years ago and he still has a room?"

"Things are probably pretty slow at the assisted living center." Mark dunked his spoon into his cereal. "Doyle's death always bothered me. It was a hit and run, but they never caught who did it."

"He was run over at The Pig." The Piggly Wiggly was their local supermarket.

"Sounds like a mob hit to me."

"In Glory? If you'd seen the number of half-blind customers with bottle-glass-thick spectacles coming out of the Piggly Wiggly parking lot on a daily basis, all of them driving big old tanks, you'd know it was an accident. Whoever did it probably thought they'd run over a curb and didn't think twice about it."

Mark took a big bite of Froot Loops and mumbled, "I haven't thought about Doyle in years. He used to sit in the town square and spit at people." He chuckled. "When Arlene came to town the first time, he pinched her while she was standing in front of Micki & Maud's Diner. She wanted me to challenge him to a fight, but I was laughing too hard." Mark's smile dimmed, then faded away. After a painfully silent moment, he sighed. "That was a long time ago."

Roxie began to say something about his ex, but she caught his expression and wisely said instead, "I can't take those old people around town; they won't fit in the Mustang."

"There's a van with your name on it. Mother says you should go to the center and introduce yourself today, which means you have"—he glanced at the red rooster clock over the door—"about ten minutes to get dressed."

Roxie carried her oatmeal to the sink. "It won't take me that long; there's no reason to dress up for an assisted living center. I'll shower when I get back."

"That's the spirit! I'll be busy this morning, too. I'm to deliver a bag of clothes from Mother's car to the Salvation Army. Then I'm to find Mrs. Clive and see what—"

A loud crash sounded from upstairs, followed by Mother's raised voice.

Tundy could be heard replying; all too soon, the maid's heavy tread stamped down the steps.

"What was that?" Mark asked when Tundy entered the kitchen.

"Yo' momma wanted bacon with her breakfast. Bacon!" The maid snorted and set down a tray on the counter. "As if that was on her heart diet!"

"She loves her bacon in the morning," Roxie said.

"She can love it all she wants." Tundy's cheeks were flushed, and there was a militant sparkle to her eyes. "Bacon's not kosher, and I ain't going to have no biblical curses brought down on *my* head."

"Tundy," Roxie said, "Mother isn't—"

"Rox," Mark said, a wicked light in his eyes, "we'd better leave Tundy to work her magic."

"That's right, Mr. Treymayne. It's a good thing I worked with my mean old aunt and I've seen it all, and so I told her."

Roxie blinked. "What happened?"

"She pretended to choke, and tipped her coffee into her oatmeal." Tundy's eyes sparkled dangerously. "Now I have to clean it all up. But I'll take care of that, wait and see. I didn't learn to play checkers at my daddy's knee for nothing! It's time for strategy."

She tossed a dishtowel onto the counter. "You all had best skedaddle. They's about to be some changes which yo' momma might not cotton to."

Mark finished his cereal, then put his bowl into the sink and rinsed it. He grabbed the dishtowel, dried his hands, and dropped a kiss on Tundy's red curls, which made her anger melt into a red-faced grin. "Tundy, you are a saint."

Tundy snorted and snatched back the dishtowel. "You pay me enough to be one. Just hope things don't get worse, or I'll be asking for a raise."

A high, insistent ring tinkled in the distance.

"What is that?" Mark asked.

"Yo' momma found a bell somewhere. She says she'll use it to call me."

Roxie whistled. "You are so going to hate that."

"I already do," Tundy said grimly.

The bell rang again.

"Let's go, Rox," Mark said. "I want to stop at Micki & Maud's on the way and get some *real* coffee." He looked at Tundy meaningfully.

"Don't look at me! Doc's instruction sheet said no caffeine, and no caffeine it is."

Roxie glared at her cup. No wonder the morning was feeling so dismal.

"More reason to get out of the house. C'mon, Rox, I'll buy you a cup of the real stuff."

The bell jangled oddly now, as if it was being waved in a wide arc.

Tundy rolled up her sleeves, her jaw set. "I don't know where that bell came from, but it's going back."

Mark clapped Tundy on the shoulder. "You're a brave woman, Tundy."

"Yes, I am." Tundy turned to the stairs. "You all need to get goin'. Yo' momma is gonna vent her spleen once I de-bell her ass, and whoever is closest—"

The bell began to clunk now, as if it was being slammed into a night table. Tundy grunted, then marched up the steps.

Roxie shuddered. "Let's go. I don't need any makeup, and I can wear my hair in a ponytail."

Grinning, Mark immediately opened the door. "After you."

"YOU'RE GOING TO GET a crick in your neck."

Nick straightened, hitting his head on the top edge of the windowsill. "Ow!" He lifted a hand to his head and tangled it in the blinds. "Damn it!" He stepped away and yanked his arm free, the blinds following, piling onto the floor with an impressive crash of cheap aluminum.

He dropped into his seat and glared at them.

Susan Collins stood by his desk, her brows so high they were almost hidden by her hair. Besides being the county dispatcher, she was also his secretary, the closest thing he'd ever get to a deputy. Over the last two years, she'd become one of his best friends.

Nick rubbed his face, which felt brighter than Susan's auburn hair. "Sorry about that. You startled me."

"No!" She walked around his desk, her lithe form encased in jeans and a dusky green shirt that matched her eyes. "What were you looking at? I cleared my throat three times, but you were engrossed."

Nick moved so she didn't have a clear view out the window.

Her gaze narrowed. "Oh. So it's like that, is it?"

"I have no idea what you're talking about." He crossed his arms and silently dared her to look around him.

She looked around him, standing on tiptoe. "I see—ah! A red Mustang!" She dropped back onto the balls of her feet, a smug smile on her face as she crossed her arms and pretended to ponder. "Let me think . . . who do we know who drives one of those? Hmmm! I heard something about a red Mustang. Who told me—wait. It was you. You told me you pulled Roxie Treymayne over in a red Mustang just two days ago."

Nick pulled his chair to the desk, opened the closest folder, and stared at it. "I wasn't looking at the red Mustang." For very long.

She snorted. "I think you *were*—or more importantly, who was in it."

Nick flipped a page in the folder. He liked Susan. She was a great dispatcher, had terrific investigating instincts, could cook a mean gumbo, and understood the intricacies of football better than any guy he knew. Unfortunately, she also possessed a biting sense of humor that would take a piece of your hide if you weren't careful.

Susan placed her hands flat on his desk, leaned forward, and said in a teasing tone, "You won't admit that you've still got a thing for Roxie Treymayne, will you? Some things never change."

Susan hadn't cared for Roxie Treymayne in high school; few girls had. Of course, she didn't know Roxie the way Nick did. Or rather, had. Beneath that cool exterior had beaten a shy, wild heart. Like everyone else, he'd first mistaken her aloof demeanor for disdainful superiority. When he'd finally realized that behind that picture-perfect façade was a terrified girl, his heart had melted into a puddle.

He—rough, tough, nobody-told-him-what-to-do Nick Sheppard—had fallen head over heels for the girl no one could have. In the end, he'd discovered that he couldn't have her, either. It had been one of the blackest moments of his life.

But the few weeks between those two discoveries were still crystal clear in his mind, which was why he was so aware of her now. The chemistry that had raged between them then hadn't abated one bit, but they were now on opposite ends of the spectrum.

Now, he was the one who knew who he was and knew where he was going. And Roxie seemed lost somehow; searching.

Something had changed her. For better or worse, he had yet to discover. But he would. That was his job: to watch over the inhabitants of Glory, even the ones who rolled back into town determined to stir things up.

And stir things up, she had. Nick hadn't slept a wink last night, remembering the feel of her lips on his, the delicious pressure of her body against his—

He stirred in his chair and caught Susan's amused look. "What?"

"Want to talk about it?"

He scowled. "There's nothing to talk about. Roxie is back in town. You know it. I know it. All of Glory probably knows it by now, too."

"Oh, yes. Everyone is commenting on how much she's changed. I never thought Roxie the type to go blazing blonde."

He shrugged. "You can't keep anything quiet in this town."

"I don't know about that." Susan perched on the corner of his desk and twiddled with a cup of pencils. "I know several 'secrets' that most people don't know."

"Like what?"

She sniffed. "They wouldn't stay secrets long if I blabbed them to everyone, would they?"

Nick lifted a brow.

She lifted one back at him. "You *also* answered a 911 at her house, and you've yet to mention that, either. You must have spoken to her then."

Yes. And been kissed so passionately that he'd had a hard-on for so long afterward that if he'd been on Viagra, he'd have had to make an emergency call. "I spoke to her, but don't worry. I'm immune." He was probably the only man in Glory able to claim that. Not physically, of course; no man breathing could claim that. But emotionally, Roxie Treymayne would always be off-limits.

"She's divorced, you know."

He looked up from the file, then realized his mistake when Susan's smile widened. "That's too bad," he said blandly. "Is there any coffee left?"

Susan crossed one leg over the other and swung her foot back and forth. "Of course there's coffee. Fix me a cup while you're up, will you?"

Nick reluctantly grinned and stood. Susan did a lot of things in the office, but fetching coffee wasn't one of them. He didn't blame her; she had too many duties as it was. "I'll be glad to fix you some. Two creams and one sugar—I could make it in my sleep." He strode to the coffee table and fixed them each a mug, then brought them back to the desk.

Susan held her mug with both hands and sipped, a thoughtful expression on her face. "The divorce thing might explain Roxie's hair. It means Brian must have cheated on her." A troubled look flickered over Susan's face. "I never thought he was that sort, but apparently so."

Nick debated not asking Susan what she meant, but the room was painfully quiet. He sighed and placed his mug on the desk. "OK, I'll bite. How does the divorce explain Roxie's hair?"

"When someone cheats on you, it's a harsh blow to your sense of self-worth, even for a woman like Roxie. There's a tendency to want to change things: your hair, your job, whatever you can."

Even for a woman like Roxie . . . interesting that Susan had put it that way. There weren't many women like Roxie, with that strange mixture of strength and fragility. "So a woman might not only change her hair, but get her navel pierced and maybe spring for a tattoo, as well?"

Susan's mouth dropped open. "Roxanne Treymayne has a *tattoo*? Wow. I never thought I'd hear that." Susan pondered this a moment, then shrugged. "Not that she couldn't carry it off." Susan left her perch on his desk and walked to the window, now that Nick was no longer blocking it. "Most women I know couldn't get away with going from brunette to blonde like that and still look—well, like Roxie. She's beautiful."

"I hadn't noticed."

Susan made a rude noise. "She's one of those women who can go around without any makeup and still look perfect." Susan shook her head regretfully. "Makes it hard for a woman to like her."

Nick pushed back his chair. "Susan, did you come in here for something, or did you just want to pester me?"

Susan turned to lean against the window. "Both. You got a call from the mayor. More budget cuts."

"You have to be kidding! We already gave back twelve percent; we can't give back any more."

"That's what I told him, and he said we all had to tighten our belts. I told him we didn't have a belt, as we gave it up in the last round of cuts, but he didn't seem impressed—" Susan broke off and looked over her shoulder. "There goes Roxie and her brother."

Nick flipped a page in the file and gritted his teeth. Damn, he hadn't seen her. Then his neck tightened with irritation at himself for being so juvenile.

He didn't care; he was merely curious. One of the bonds he and Roxie had shared had been their dislike of this town. Here, everyone was firmly shelved, labeled, and limited by name and reputation. Roxie had been imprisoned by her mother's expectations and her own desire to be perfect, just as he'd been imprisoned by the town's belief that he was trouble and nothing could ever change him.

But someone had. Actually, two someones. Roxie's defection had hurt. It had hurt so badly that it had given Nick a burning desire to take his floundering, directionless life and fix it. He soon came to the blunt realization that if he wanted to change, he would have to do it himself and ignore what everyone else thought. So he'd left town the second he'd graduated and moved in with an uncle in Atlanta, where he'd found a job delivering pizza and enrolled in a two-year college. On a whim, he'd taken a criminal justice class.

That was where he'd met a detective named Lee Parsels, who was teaching night classes. Lee was a tough cop who'd taken an interest in a troubled youth, and it was Lee who'd suggested that perhaps Nick's true path was in law enforcement.

Lee had been right. Following his advice, Nick transferred to a four-year college and majored in criminal justice. The day he graduated, he'd joined the Atlanta Police Department, determined to be the best cop who'd ever walked the streets. He'd lived and breathed the job, working every hour he'd been able to and listening to the radio when he'd been off duty. Eventually he'd been assigned to Lee's squad, and Nick had thought things couldn't get any better.

Through it all, Lee had been there, offering sage advice and helping Nick navigate the sometimes complex waters of law enforcement. All had been going very well until Lee had met a woman by the name of Barbara Thomas.

At the time, Nick had thought it was like any other bust: a patron had roughed up a twenty-two-year-old blonde stripper in front of a belligerent crowd. Nick had answered the call and had contained the situation fairly easily, arresting the suspect after a short fight. Just as Nick had wrapped things up, Lee had arrived. It had been routine for a supervising officer to drop in, so Nick hadn't thought much of it at the time. Later, he remembered that moment with painful clarity.

He remembered how Lee had looked at the victim, and how she'd played up to him, exaggerating the attack far beyond what she'd reported to Nick. Lee had lingered, then offered to drive the victim to the ER while Nick had taken the suspect downtown to book him.

It wasn't until several months later that Nick would remember any of it as special. But it had been. Lee, hardened and grizzled, a one-hundred-percent by-the-book cop whose wife had recently left him, had fallen hard and fast for a beautiful, trouble-seeking woman. By the time it was over, Lee was charged with tampering with evidence, interfering in an investigation, and perjury.

When it was discovered that Nick had assisted Internal Affairs in the investigation, he'd been ostracized by his fellow officers and rotated to the night shift to the roughest part of town. Every time he'd called for backup, his fellow officers had taken their sweet time arriving. After a narrow miss with a crazed drug addict, Nick had walked into his commander's office and turned in his badge and gun. He'd been damned lucky Glory's old Sheriff Thompson had been considering retirement at the same time.

Nick rubbed his eyes and shut the folder on his desk. That was all in the past now. He'd left his old friendships with his old job, buried under bad feelings and the bitterness of betrayal. Now he just wanted to learn to relax, be a human again and not just a cop, and enjoy the little bit of the magic that was Glory, North Carolina.

"Not that you're interested, of course," Susan said, her tone thoughtful, "but Mark was driving." She turned and leaned against the window, much as Nick had done before. "He's looking quite fit, isn't he?"

"Mark?" Nick shrugged. "I guess."

"He's looking very tasty this morning. I was never into the nerdy accountant type, but he has the sexiest smile. I wonder why I never noticed that in high school?"

"Probably because you were too busy chasing Brian Parker."

Susan grimaced. "Good thing I didn't catch him." She looked slyly at Nick. "By the way, Todd at the Fast Mart said Mark mentioned where Roxie's going to spend her mornings for the next few weeks."

A long silence ensued, the cheap wall clock the only sound. He gathered the folder and began paging through it again.

Susan sighed. "You aren't going to ask, are you?"

"Nope." He turned a page of the report, even though he hadn't read a word yet.

"Fine." She stepped over the fallen blinds and marched to the door. "You're a stubborn man, Nick Sheppard, which is a good thing: because a woman like Roxanne needs a stubborn man. She took over her mother's place at the Pine Hills Assisted Living Center, working with Rose Tibbons's little group."

Nick just couldn't hold it in—he smiled.

"I thought you'd like that," Susan said in a smug voice. "Perhaps it's time you visited your great-aunt Clara."

It had been a while. Almost a week. Nick prudently kept his gaze on the folder.

Susan sauntered toward the door. "Don't forget to tell Roxie I said hi. I didn't like the old Roxie very much, but a woman with bleached hair *and* a tattoo here in Glory is just the sort of woman I'd like to call friend."

chapter 6

_ _ _ _

"*P*ARDON ME. I'M LOOKING for a club."

The pretty, dark-haired nurse, whose name tag read Becky, looked up from her clipboard. "Which club? We have a gazillion now that Miss Moore is in charge of activities."

"My mother visits with—" Roxie checked the scribbled words on the paper Mark had handed her. "—Mrs. Tibbons and her Murder Mystery Club."

"You must be Lilah Treymayne's daughter. How is she?"

"Fine. She's not very happy about having to stay home."

"Your mother isn't the type to take bed rest well. Or anything else, for that matter." Becky turned to the desk behind her. "Maggie, do you know where Rose Tibbons and her posse have run off to this morning?"

The harried-looking nurse behind the counter slapped two folders onto the desk. "No, I don't."

Roxie cleared her throat. "They may be in Doyle Cloyd's old room. My mother seems to think they meet in there."

Becky pointed to the Mickey Mouse watch on her wrist. "I bought this at the garage sale after Doyle died. The whole town turned up for that, didn't they, Maggie?"

Maggie clicked a pen and began marking a chart. "Yup, I bought a boatload of Christmas ornaments there myself. Who'd have thought a sourpuss like Doyle would have had so many Christmas ornaments?"

Becky grinned at Roxie. "You'd be hard-pressed to find a person from Glory who doesn't have something from that sale; his sister sold everything he owned. Why, there were even unopened packages of underwear."

Roxie tried to look impressed.

"It's kept him in everyone's mind, in a way," Becky said. "I always liked the old coot."

Maggie closed a folder with a snap. "You like all of the weird ones."

"I like people with personality—including you."

"Ha!" Maggie's grin surprised Roxie. "Becky, before you track down Rose's gang, can you take the incident reports to the supervisor's office? Two more visitors smelled weed in the 200 wing." She grimaced and handed Becky a blue folder. "It has to be the new cleaning service."

"I wouldn't be surprised." Becky placed the folder on the shelf of a small trolley filled with plastic cups and an assortment of colorful pills. "I'll just take Miss Treymayne to— Well, well! Speak of the devil." Becky nodded toward an old man pushing an even older woman in a wheelchair down the hall. "There are two of your characters right there."

"Mrs. Tibbons?"

"No. Those are Rose's minions, Clara and C.J. Clara's sweet-natured but stubborn as the day is long; once she gets an idea into her head, you can't get it out. C.J. is nice enough when he remembers who he is." Becky used the tip of her shoe to unlock the wheel on the medicine cart. "Come along; I'll introduce you."

Roxie followed Becky across the hall, where a stooped-shouldered, white-haired man dressed in a navy housecoat, the belt dragging behind him, was leaning with all of his might against a wheelchair that enthroned a tiny woman who looked as if the slightest puff of smoke might blow her away. She made up for her size with a brightly flowered housecoat and a thick application of silvery blue eye shadow accented with the longest false lashes Roxie had ever seen, all magnified by huge glasses so thick they made her eyes look like saucers.

The old woman's hands were covered with gaudy jewelry and protectively cupped about something that rested on her knees, covered with a blanket.

"Well, what have we here?" Becky parked the cart and looked from C.J. to Clara to the lump on Clara's lap.

Clara hugged the mound a little closer. It crackled loudly. "We don't have a thing! Just going for a walk, ain't we, C.J.?"

"What?" he said, blinking with confusion. "I thought we were raiding Doritos from the cafet—"

"*We,*" Clara said loudly, "are taking a *walk* on our way to our *meeting*."

Becky eyed the lump in Clara's lap. "Just one bag of Doritos?"

"Yes!" Clara nodded so hard that her huge '80s-style glasses flopped up and down on her nose. "One bag, no more."

"All right, then. None of you are on a restricted diet, but you'll owe me for this."

"Deal," Clara said with a quickness that was disconcerting.

Becky grinned. "All right. I'm off to deliver the morning meds to the 100 wing. You two behave yourself and keep Rose out of trouble."

"We will," Clara said.

"Who is Rose?" C.J. asked.

As soon as the nurse was gone, Clara looked at Roxie. "Who are you?"

"I'm Lilah Treymayne's daughter, Roxanne."

"Ah!" The old woman smiled kindly. "Your mother's told us all about you. How you live in a huge house in Raleigh and have the perfect husband and live like a queen—" Clara's smile faded. "I didn't know you was blonde, though. Seems the pictures she showed us were of a brunette."

"Yes, I changed my hair."

Clara brightened. "Oh! It's like a disguise."

"Exactly." She was growing to love her new hair more and more every day. It could use a touch of lowlights, but it definitely made her look and feel younger.

Nick's kiss from the day before had made her feel

younger, too. In fact, it had taken her all the way back to high school.

But why had he ended it so abruptly and then run as if his tail was on fire?

Perhaps his tail was *on fire. Perhaps he liked it as much as I did and couldn't handle the heat.*

She slowly smiled. Perhaps, in some odd way, their positions over the years had changed. Now *she* was the one who caused people to be nervous because she wasn't bound by the rules.

Clara peered up at her. "How's your mother?"

"Better, I think. She has to stay in bed for a few weeks."

"Pity. She was here when she fainted away. Said she'd been dizzy off and on for a few days." Clara looked around, then said in a low voice, "Rumor has it she's hooked on cough medicine, but I think she might have a bun in the oven myself."

Roxie blinked.

C.J. added in a helpful tone, "That means 'having a baby.' "

"I know what it means," Roxie laughed, "but it's not true."

Clara and C.J. looked disappointed. Clara recovered fastest. "Oh. Well, then. I suppose you're here to visit?"

"Actually, I'm supposed to take you on an outing."

C.J. shook his head. "We can't go out today. There's a *CSI* rerun on in"—he looked at his watch, suddenly all proficiency—"twenty-two minutes."

"Yes, but my mother said I—"

"Your mother isn't here," Clara said in a firm voice that belied both her age and her diminutive size. "Besides, it takes us thirty minutes to get loaded into the van, and that's if we're dressed, which we're not." A note of triumph entered Clara's voice. "So I guess we won't be going on an outing this morning.

"Besides, your mother thinks we shouldn't do anything but drive across town and look at roses and that statue in the park." Clara's voice dripped with disrespect. "Who in heck wants to look at a statue over and over? It ain't like it's gonna change or anything."

"Not me," C.J. said.

Clara sniffed. "I tried to explain that to your mother, but she wouldn't listen. I hope you're not going to force us to do something we don't want to."

Roxie found two sets of hopeful blue eyes fixed on her. She said mildly, "I just thought you might enjoy getting out."

Clara brightened immediately. "Watching that sexy Gil Grissom solve a murder on *CSI* does me good! Makes my heart pound and my—"

"I couldn't find my shoes." C.J. held out a foot shod in a purple sock.

Clara scowled. "C.J., we was talking about *CSI,* not your shoes!"

He looked at his watch. "It comes on in nineteen minutes."

"Then we'd better hurry! Miss Roxanne, since you're here, I suppose you can come to our meeting."

"In Doyle's old room, right?"

Clara and C.J. exchanged a startled glance before Clara said cautiously, "Your mother must have told you about that. We, ah, decided to have meetings in my room and save Doyle's room for special occasions. C.J., let's go! You know how Rose gets when she gets hungry."

C.J. nodded. "Twitchy and mean." He took two shuffling steps forward, then paused. "Where are we going again?"

"To my room. Our meeting, remember?"

"Oh yes." He took two more steps, then stopped. "Where is that?"

Clara sighed. "Straight forward, second left, third door on the—"

"That's right."

Roxie followed as they set in motion at a shuffling pace.

Into the quiet, C.J. suddenly blurted, "Doyle has a still."

Clara glared at him. "C.J., darn it! Keep your mouth shut!" Clara looked at Roxie nervously. "You ain't a snitch, are you?"

Roxie threw up her hands. "Not me."

"Your mother is," Clara said sourly. "I had a pack of Marlboro Lights and she told Nurse Becky about 'em as fast as she could."

"Yeah, she caught me smoking once when I was in high school. She still brings it up."

Clara grimaced. "She's that kind."

"So Doyle has a still in his room?"

"Yup," C.J. said. "We had to stop having our meetings in there because it gets too smoky."

"Bummer. It's not dangerous, is it?"

Clara waved a thin, liver-spotted hand, her faux jewelry glittering brightly. "Naw. It's not exactly a still, anyway. A still makes liquor. This just makes it better."

C.J. pushed Clara's wheelchair around a corner. "Doyle used to make his special bourbon all of the time. We lit it up this morning and started emulsifying a new batch." He paused before a door marked Room 210.

Clara leaned forward and knocked once. Then twice. Then four times in rapid succession.

The door slowly creaked open, and a tall, cadaverous woman wearing a red wig glared down at them, a cane clutched in one hand, a long, hot pink caftan fluttering over the tips of brand-new running shoes. "Who the hell are you?" she asked Roxie.

Clara wheeled past the woman and into the room, C.J. huffing behind her. "Rose, don't get your dander up. This is Miss Roxanne, Mrs. Treymayne's daughter."

Rose looked Roxie up and down, suspicion evident in every line of her body. "How do we know you are who you say you are?"

"You want to see my driver's license?"

Rose's lips thinned. "You don't look like your mother."

"Thanks."

"Yes, well, I'm the president here, and I can't just let every loose wheel roll in and out of our meetings without a by-your-leave."

Clara put the brake on her wheelchair and pulled the shawl off the Doritos. "C.J. spilled the beans about the still to Miss Roxie."

Rose sent a hostile glare at C.J., but he just smiled benignly. Cheated of her quarry, she turned on Roxie. "You won't tell?"

"Nope," Roxie said. "Providing no one is in danger, I promise not to reveal a single thing I hear or see in this room."

"Very well," Rose said grudgingly. She jerked a thumb toward an empty chair. "You'd better sit down. We're about to begin."

Roxie took a chair, glancing around. It was a fairly typical room, with a hospital bed, a plain brown night-stand, two plastic chairs, a plastic-covered lounger—all of it very institutional. But Clara had covered most of it with a blinding assortment of afghans, pictures, potted plants, and candles.

A candle burned in the corner of the room, which Roxie was fairly sure was against regulations, but the warm vanilla scent mixed with something else . . . a faint, vaguely familiar aroma that tickled her nose.

Suddenly it hit her; she knew that scent from college. It was weed. The nurses had been right about the clean-ing personnel.

Clara ripped open the Doritos. "Time for the club snack!"

Rose took her seat and leaned forward, looking uncannily like a caftaned vulture perched for an attack. "Good work, Clara! Did anyone see you?"

"Only Nurse Becky and she didn't care. I just went into the kitchen and told the cook I thought I needed to have a BM right *now*. Next thing you know, she'd scampered away to find a nurse. C.J. and I snatched the bag and took off."

Rose dived into the Doritos, and the others did the same.

Poor things! The food here must be horrible. Maybe I can bring them some snacks, Roxie thought.

Rose licked her lips. "I don't usually like these, but they taste mighty good today." She eyed Roxie a moment. "What did your mother tell you about us?"

"I am to help with your club activities and drive you on outings and such."

"Humph. You're here to keep us from watching *CSI* is more like it." Rose took another Dorito. "Your mother never told us you turned your hair yeller."

"She didn't know until I arrived."

Clara paused, a Dorito halfway to her mouth. "Why not?"

Roxie shrugged. "It's my hair."

Rose's angular face held grudging respect. "Bet your mother didn't like that."

"Not one bit," Roxie agreed.

C.J. pointed to his watch. "Only fourteen minutes until *CSI*. We'd better start the meeting."

"Right!" Rose hopped up, pulled a Pepto-pink bedpan from under a laundry bag, poured an inch of liquid into a Styrofoam cup, and shoved it into Roxie's hand. "Here. This'll clear your head."

Clara grabbed another cup from a side table and slapped it on the arm of her wheelchair. "Hit me, Rose!"

Rose obligingly poured an inch of amber liquid into Clara's cup.

Roxie eyed the liquid with mistrust. It was as if she'd come to babysit, only to find her charges at a frat party. Should she say something about the deleterious effects of alcohol? Hope someone volunteered the information that the bedpan had been thoroughly washed and disinfected before it had been used?

Rose looked at Roxie suspiciously. "Aren't you going to drink it?"

"Are you all sure this is safe?"

Clara cackled. "Honey, we drank Doyle's bourbon every Saturday for eight years before he passed on. It ain't going to hurt us none now." She lifted her cup in a toast. "Cheers! Here's to doing what we want!"

And what they wanted was *not* to get out for some fresh air and exercise, but to sit in their room, drink bourbon, and watch Gil Grissom solve murders.

Roxie sighed and took a sip of the bourbon. It was . . . not bad. She took another sip. Not bad at all.

Rose nodded her approval. "Doyle starts with Maker's Mark. Then the emulsifier does its magic, and there you have it."

Roxie took another sip. And then another. The bourbon tanged on her tongue and made her pleasantly warm. "Whatever that emulsifier does, it's pretty good." The room seemed filled with a gentle golden glow, and she suddenly felt an inexplicable friendship for these dear old people. She'd never known her grandparents, but if she had, she'd bet they'd have been just like Rose and her gang.

She giggled at the thought of Nick seeing her drinking bourbon with her senior citizens. A slug or two might loosen him up and get him to relax a bit, might mentally get him out of that uniform.

She wouldn't mind helping him physically get out of it. That tailored green shirt conformed lovingly to his chest and shoulders, stirring her . . . imagination. And the way his belt rested on his hips made her hands want to do the same.

Was it hot in here? Or was it just her?

She took a final gulp.

Rose stomped her running shoe on the ground. "Time to come to order! This here is the twelfth meeting of the Murder Mystery Club. Is there any old business?"

Rose and Clara looked at C.J.

He blinked.

Clara reached over and pulled a notebook from his shirt pocket and placed it in front of him. "You wrote the minutes down last week, C.J. Check your notes."

"Oh, yes!" He slowly thumbed though the notebook. After a moment, he shook his head. "Nope. Don't see any old business."

"C.J. has the best handwriting," Clara confided to Roxie.

Roxie smiled, though she was hard-pressed not to giggle. She felt like Alice in the rabbit hole; everything was surreal and so brightly colored.

She absently munched a Dorito, amazed at how good it tasted. Things weren't as bad here in Glory as she'd thought they'd be. In fact, things could be much, much worse. She could still be married and not know about Brian's betrayal. She remembered how he'd looked when she'd found him with Larry, and for the first time, a grin tickled her lips. Larry. In drag. Roxie giggled a bit. It *had* been funny, though until now she hadn't been able to admit it. Hurt pride tended to filter out all of the funny from life.

"Good Doritos, huh?" Clara asked.

"The best I've ever had," Roxie said truthfully. "May I have some more?"

Rose handed her the bag. "Take as many as you want. Clara can always filch another bag."

Clara grinned around a mouthful of Doritos, her eyes owlishly large behind her glasses. "Last week I stole a whole pie."

"Butterscotch," C.J. said in a blissful tone.

Rose stomped her foot again. "Back to the meeting

and this week's *CSI*. Boy, was it hot! That Gil Grissom can bed down in my room any day he wants."

C.J. looked at his watch. "Eleven minutes. We should hurry."

"Yup," Clara agreed. "Before we go any further, we should show Miss Roxie the box."

"Clara!" Rose snapped.

Clara blinked. "What?"

"You weren't supposed to mention that."

"Why not? Roxie might be able to help us." Clara looked at Roxie. "Your eyesight's pretty good, isn't it?"

"Yes."

"Good. C.J., get the box." Clara pushed her huge glasses back on her button nose. "We found this with the still under the bed in Doyle's old room."

C.J. reached under Clara's bed, pulled out a small cardboard box, and reverently handed it to Roxie.

Clara bent closer and said in a stage whisper, "This is the *real* secret stuff!"

"*And* a mystery," Rose said, her eyes shining. "A real, live mystery, although . . ." She frowned. "We haven't quite decided what we should do about it yet."

Curious, Roxie put aside her empty cup and dug into the box. Twenty or so different lighters filled the top. There were Winston Cup lighters, Playboy lighters, and even an American Eagle lighter. "Too bad these weren't in the yard sale."

"Doyle loved his lighters," Clara agreed.

Roxie pushed the lighters aside to find a layer of papers. She picked up the top one, trying to decipher the writing. It was a shopping list with a recipe for quiche, of all things.

Not much of a mystery. She picked up another piece of paper, a Christmas list from the looks of it. Apparently all of Doyle's beloved friends and family received socks that year. Cheap bastard; Doyle'd had a bank full of money when he'd died, much to everyone's surprise.

She fished out another piece of paper and squinted at it, trying to decipher the squirrelly handwriting. Slowly, it began to make sense.

She dropped the paper and picked up another. And then another. "This looks like—" She stared at the mass of papers as her heart thudded against her chest. "Have you all looked at these?" Her voice echoed oddly in her own ears.

"I did," C.J. said cheerily. His expression clouded over. "But I don't remember what they said."

"I do," Clara said. "They're blackmail notes."

"*That* is our mystery," Rose said, obviously satisfied with Roxie's reaction.

Roxie stared at a paper. "His handwriting is atrocious." She frowned and slowly read, " 'Received two—' Hm. Is that 'thousand' . . . I think it is. 'Received two thousand dollars from Mayor Harkins—' " Roxie squinted. "It's either 'March' or 'May,' I can't tell. 'The third, 2006.' "

Rose nodded. "There are receipts for almost everyone in town: Mayor Harkins, Mr. Kimble at the post office, even Pastor Rawlings! The only problem is, he doesn't say what the secrets were, just the amounts collected."

It was certainly surprising and interesting, but not much more. Still . . . Roxie looked at the mass of papers, a thought slowly settling. "If you'd all like, I could take the box and catalog the blackmail notes for you."

Rose brightened. "You'd do that?"

"If I can decipher this writing."

"That would be helpful," Clara said. "It'd give us a list of suspects." She added in a loud whisper, "We think this might be the reason Doyle was *murdered*."

"I thought Doyle's death was an accident."

"He was run over in the parking lot of the Piggly Wiggly. I'd call that murder!"

Rose shook her head. "Everyone said Myrtle Thorton must have done it and not known, as she has that huge car and can't see over the steering wheel, but I heard that a test revealed that the blood on her car came from a dog, not a human."

Roxie looked at the box. "I wonder how Doyle came to be blackmailing so many people."

"Sounds just like something he would do," Clara said, munching on another Dorito. "He was an ass."

"Yup," Rose said. "Couldn't stand him, myself."

"We liked his bourbon, though," C.J. added.

"He kept a lot of friends with that bourbon," Rose said. "I went to the garage sale after he died." She pushed back her sleeve to reveal a large Sears watch. "Got this for two bucks."

"I got underwear from there." C.J. stood. "Want to see?"

"*No!*" Rose and Roxie said at the same time.

"I'll take a gander," Clara said. "Are they boxers?"

"May I remind you two that this is our *meeting*?" Rose said in a strident voice. "C.J., sit down and take some notes. If we have a real murder to investigate, this will be just like *CSI*."

Roxie pursed her lips. "Tell you what . . . I'll decipher these notes and make the list, *if* you'll all come out with me to investigate."

Clara blinked. "Investigate?"

"Yeah. Drive into town and interview people. Maybe even question some suspects. How else are you going to gather clues?" Roxie patted the box. "I can't see Gil Grissom passing up a chance to investigate such a fascinating mystery."

There was a moment of stunned silence, then Rose said in a breathless tone, "She's right! We could go undercover and investigate, just like Gil!"

Clara clasped her hands together. "We could even have a *stakeout*!"

"Hot damn!" C.J. said brightly. "I'd like that!"

Sweet success! Roxie grinned. "I'll reserve the van." Looking for clues would be a heck of a lot more interesting than debating episodes of *CSI* or dragging the old folks out to look at flowers. Plus, it wouldn't hurt them to work on Doyle's really-not-so-mysterious death, either; it would stimulate their minds. Heck, even she was wildly curious about the blackmail notes. "Excellent. Should we—"

A knock sounded on the door.

The Murder Mystery Club froze in place. Rose gripped the arms of her chair and yelled, "Who is it?"

"It's Nurse Becky. What are you all doing in there?"

"Meetin'! What do you want?"

"I came to tell Clara that her nephew is here. Should I send him in?"

Clara's eyes widened hideously behind her thick glasses. "It's the fuzz! Hide the liquor!"

There was a mad scramble as Rose jumped to her feet and carried the bedpan of bourbon back to the closet, while Clara rolled around the room gathering cups.

"Clara will be out in a minute," Rose shouted at the door. "Tell the sheriff she'll meet him in the lobby."

Roxie looked at Clara. "Sheriff?"

"My sister's grandson, Nick. Normally I'm glad to see him, but I do wish he'd waited until later. Our meetin' was just getting interesting."

C.J. tsked. "*CSI* starts in four minutes. You're going to miss it."

"I'll hurry." From her wheelchair, Clara looked up at Roxie. "Can you take me to the lobby? If we don't get a move on, he'll come lookin' for us here, and he might find our bourbon stash."

How could she say no to a frail old lady with such ridiculously large glasses? "Sure. No problem." *Besides, it might be interesting to surprise Mr. Starched Shirt.*

"Here." Rose handed Doyle's box to Roxie. "Take the shortcut through the atrium." Her caftan fluttered around her as she marched to the door and threw it open. "We'll see you tomorrow for the first day of our investigation!

chapter 7

"*Let's go!*" Clara ordered. "And make it snappy!" Grinning, Roxie settled Doyle's box in Clara's lap, took the wheelchair handles, and jogged down the hall and across the atrium to the lobby.

Clara's housecoat fluttered around her stick-thin legs. She held onto the box, cackling madly, and Roxie had to laugh.

As they turned down the atrium path, she caught a glimpse of herself in the mirrored windows. Good God, why hadn't she worn makeup this morning? Or at least combed her hair? The last thing she wanted to look was pale and mussed when she saw Nick.

Worse, she was sure she reeked of bourbon. She pulled Clara's chair to a halt and hurriedly pulled the tie from her hair, smoothed the strands with her hands, then replaced the tie.

"What are we stoppin' for?"

Roxie pinched her pale cheeks. "I need a breath mint." And a comb. A little rouge. Perhaps a lobotomy, if there was time.

Clara pushed the box to one side, dug into a deep pocket, and produced a half-wrapped mint. "Aha! Here's one!"

Too desperate to question it, Roxie accepted the mint. Thankfully, it was strong and sweet and made her entire mouth tingle.

Clara waved a hand in a forward-ho motion. "Come on, Miss Roxie, give this chair a push! We gotta get rid of my grandnephew so we can get to detectin'!"

The idea *was* rather exciting, though that could still be the bourbon talking. As Roxie pushed Clara's chair down the path, a sense of expectation enveloped her. Her body tingled with a breathless euphoria, almost of invincibility.

That's not because you know Nick's waiting; it's because of the bourbon. Don't forget that!

Rose hadn't poured more than an inch into their cups, so it was ridiculous to think it'd had *that* much effect. But still . . . *something* was making her feel as if she was capable of doing anything she wanted. Maybe it was her success in finding the right incentive to get the Murder Mystery Club out into the community. Whatever was lifting her spirits, she planned on savoring it.

Just as she'd savor running into Nick more often, since Clara was his great-aunt. She felt more alive around him, and not just because she enjoyed mentally undressing him—

"Hold it!" Clara hissed.

Roxie stopped Clara's chair just outside the lobby door. "What's wrong?"

"Nothing. Just want to be sure I cover the scent from the still. It gets smoky, and that Nick's a sharp one. I don't want him busting me." She reached into her many pockets again and came out with a small bottle of perfume, then liberally doused herself with Eau de Church Lady.

Roxie winced, waving the air around them. "Good Lord, that could kill these plants."

Clara's owlish eyes glinted amusement through her glasses. "Good. Now, let's go."

Roxie opened the heavy door, hoping that they didn't both smell like French prostitutes. "It must be nice to see Nick more often, now that he's in Glory," she said casually.

Clara reached down and threw on the hand brake, her eyes shining with a militant light. "I don't care what the gossips say, my nephew is *twice* the sheriff this town has ever had!"

Roxie blinked. "I'm sure he is."

"Why, Nick got a stack of commendations from his job in Atlanta. The only reason he returned to Glory is because—" Clara clamped her mouth closed. "Never mind that. He was a crack officer. It's a pity about what happened in Atlanta, but who could have foreseen that?"

That was the second time someone had mentioned Nick's troubles in Atlanta. That was interesting.

"So . . . how often does Nick come to visit you?"

"Every other day or so. He's a good boy. But don't worry; I know how to get rid of him."

"How?"

Clara cackled. "I tell him about my medical conditions. When I get to my BM schedule, he can't get away fast enough."

Roxie grinned.

"The quicker we get rid of him, the quicker you can get to Doyle's box." Clara unlocked the brake and wheeled across the lobby, narrowly missing Roxie's feet.

The lobby was bright and airy, decorated in subdued pinks and blues with tasteful groupings of chairs and potted plants. Standing to one side, looking devastatingly sexy in his tailored uniform, was Nick. Becky and another nurse gazed at him as if he were a juicy turkey leg and they hadn't eaten in weeks.

Nick smiled. "Good morning, Aunt Clara. You look rested."

"Slept like a rock," Clara said. "Had my morning BM right on time, too."

Nick winced. "That's nice." His gaze flickered past Clara to Roxie and then away, as if he couldn't have cared less that she was there.

She stiffened and the bourbon suddenly boiled in her veins. He was going to ignore her? And after such a hot kiss?

Roxie thought she detected the faintest hint of a superior smile on the second nurse's face, along with a commiserating one from Becky. Both fanned Roxie's sense of ill usage all the more.

"Why, there's Mayor Harkins." Clara waved. "Yoo-hoo!"

Across the room, a tall, rather paunchy man paused. Floridly handsome, he was dressed in a dark suit and didn't look happy about being seen, though he hid his impatience behind a bland smile. "Good morning, Miss Clara."

Becky said in an undertone, "He's here visiting his mother."

"The old biddy," Clara said back without losing her smile as she waved at the mayor. She sent a sidewise glance at Roxie and said out of the corner of her mouth, "Our first suspect, eh?"

Roxie nodded. So this was Mayor Harkins. She vaguely recognized him from years ago, when he'd been an alderman.

Clara called across the lobby, "Nice seein' you, Harkins! How is that wife of yours?"

The mayor flushed, his eyes narrowing, but as quickly as the expression crossed his face, it disappeared. He gave a patently false laugh before crossing the lobby. "Miss Clara, I got divorced over two years ago. You know that."

"Oh, yes. That's right. I should have asked how your *bimbo* was doin'. She still your secretary?"

Becky made a choking noise. The other nurse suddenly became very busy with her clipboard. A few other visitors in the lobby looked on with interest.

Harkins's smile never wavered, though his eyes narrowed with unmistakable venom. Aware of the potential voters in the room, he said in a falsely cheerful tone, "I wish I could stay and chitchat, but I have to go." He started to turn, but his gaze locked on Clara, and his florid skin flushed a deeper red.

Roxie frowned. Was the man ill?

The mayor's gaze flickered to Nick. "Sheppard, your aunt is quite a character."

Nick shrugged. "She can be."

Mayor Harkins smiled at Clara. "Have a nice day, ma'am." With a nod, he left.

"Good riddance," Clara said.

Roxie could hear the desire to spit in the old woman's tone. "Is he such a bad character?"

"Left Tammy Jo after forty-one years of marriage for a bimbo."

Nick shrugged. "It could be love. He's been with Robin since before the divorce."

"Robin?" Roxie asked.

"Robin Wright. You might remember her from high school."

Roxie most certainly did. Robin had been two years behind her, and a more avaricious, conniving cheerleader hadn't existed. "She's a bit young for him, isn't she?"

"Twenty-seven years," Becky said.

The other nurse added, "It's a disgrace."

"That man ought to be shot," Clara said, not bothering to keep her voice down. "After leaving his wife like that and spending all of his retirement money buying his little bimbo that BMW and those breasts, he deserves to be shot like the dog he is."

Becky looked interested. "He bought her implants?"

"For Christmas," Clara said. "Tammy Jo told me all about it. She said that snake has gone through their entire retirement fund, buying that slut all kinds of plastic surgeries and—"

"Clara!" Nick interrupted, looking slightly harassed. "You shouldn't spread rumors."

"Ain't a rumor if it's true."

"Well, your heart would fail if you got mad at every man who'd ever made a fool of himself." Nick bent to kiss Clara on the forehead, pausing a fraction of a second and frowning. "Clara, you smell like—"

"I knew it," Clara said in a dramatic voice, the picture of sudden outrage. "The perfume your mother got me is crap."

Nick blinked. "Clara, I didn't say—"

Clara sniffed her arm and wrinkled her nose. "Gerbils, that's what it smells like. The next time your mother comes to see me, I'll tell her you said that her crappy perfume smells like gerbils, and that I don't want any more."

"No, no," he said hastily. "I didn't say that and you know it."

"You like my perfume, then?"

Nick managed a perfunctory smile. "I love that perfume. I was going to ask where you got it so I could buy some for Mom. Guess I'll have to ask her."

Coward, Roxie mouthed from behind Clara.

Nick's gaze narrowed, but he couldn't say anything. Clara was all over him like a rash.

She was already wheeling toward a side door that led to a small patio. "Ditch those nurses," she called over her shoulder, "and come sit outside in the sun."

Nick flicked an apologetic smile at the nurses and went to open the door for his great-aunt.

As she wheeled past him, Clara jerked her head toward Roxie. "By the way, this is Lilah Treymayne's daughter, Roxie. She's visiting now that her mother's sick, which suits us all fine since her mother is a sanctimonious witch."

Nick met Roxie's gaze. "Sorry."

"Don't be. It's true."

Nick looked surprised, but she just smiled. She didn't know if it was the bourbon or her lifted spirits, but she was liking it either way. There was freedom in being honest.

"Now Miss Roxie's going to take us for rides and things," Clara continued.

"Oh? Going to see the statue in the park?"

"I don't *do* statues," Roxie said. At Nick's raised brows, her cheeks heated. "You know what I mean."

He grinned and helped Clara outside. Roxie removed Doyle's box from Clara's lap and set it on a nearby table. She took a seat a short distance away to give Nick and his great-aunt some privacy.

For the next twenty minutes, Roxie was treated to

an increasingly personal recital of Clara's medical conditions. The more Clara talked, the quieter Nick got,
though he didn't budge from his seat. Which gave her
plenty of time to admire how his uniform accentuated
his God-given assets, like his broad shoulders. He still
had the shoulders of the football star he'd been.

Nick caught her gaze. For a long moment, he
stared back. Roxie's body heated immediately. There
was something hypnotic about his eyes—the gray that
seemed to heat into molten silver, or the way he had
of looking directly at her without looking away—that
made her knees weak.

The pre-divorce Roxie would have blushed and
looked away, but the new Roxie met him gaze for gaze.
Then, to spice things up a bit, she even winked.

His eyes widened, but he gave her an intimate smile
and winked back.

A flush of pleased excitement raced through Roxie.
Flirting with Nick was easy. Too easy. It was like those
little candles on the table at so many restaurants. You
knew that if you played with it, you'd burn your fingers, but somehow, as it glowed and flickered, teased
and taunted, you were compelled to stick the corner of
the menu right into the flame.

More than one eating establishment had been brought
to its knees by the lure of a forbidden candle, just as
more than one female had been put in a similar position
by a flirtatious wink from Nick Sheppard's fascinating
gray eyes.

He was still incredibly handsome, his hair still thick and dark, his eyes just as mysterious and challenging, but life had made him rock-hard and even more focused.

Better yet, he could still turn her bones to water with just one hot look. And though she had initiated the kiss yesterday, he'd responded with all of the passion and skill she remembered. And oh, how skilled he was! Nick had elevated kissing to an art: his were neither too hard nor too soft; too wet nor too dry. When he finished, you were a trembling mass and only wanted *more*.

Clara began to hint that she was about to embark on a litany of her "woman troubles" and Nick stood. "Aunt Clara, I hate to interrupt, but I need to be going."

Clara looked even more relieved than he did. "Good!" At his raised brows, she added hastily, "Glad to know you're out keeping us safe." She wheeled around and headed for the door. "Come back tomorrow and we'll talk again. Come on, Miss Roxie!"

Nick didn't leave. He just looked at Roxie, as if he was . . . *interested*. Suddenly she didn't want to go back inside. She wanted to stay here, in the sunshine, and enjoy the warm bubble of bourbon sloshing through her veins while Nick looked at her and made her feel attractive and fun and sexy.

The safe Roxie, who'd left Glory as an ambitious, picture-perfect wife, would have clung to Clara's safe presence. The Wild Roxie, who'd faced the harsh reality of rejection and discovered her tough inner core, decided one wink wasn't enough. She wanted more. More winks.

More Nick. More . . . everything. And if she burned her fingers, so what? She'd gotten her fingers burned with Brian, too. This time at least she'd have the thrill of the moment, the excitement of sensual kisses, the taste of real passion—that was worth a few burnt fingers, and perhaps more. "Clara, I think I'm going to go now, too."

Clara looked over her shoulder. "Really?"

"Really. I'll be back tomorrow, though, *with* a full report on these notes." Roxie patted Doyle's box.

Clara brightened. "Do you think you can get through all of them tonight?"

"I can try."

Clara threw her a thumbs-up. "Works for me! Now I can go and watch my show. See you tomorrow!" With amazing alacrity, she whipped her chair around and disappeared back into the center.

Nick looked curious. "What did you do to her? That group never wants to go out."

"I found something they're all crazy about."

"Other than *CSI* and Gil Grissom?"

"Actually, it has a little to do with both of those. I think I might get the group out and about more."

"Thank you. I try to take her to the movies and whatnot, but she's pretty stubborn." His eyes twinkled and he added, "You know how women are."

She eyed him. "Are you trying to rile me?"

His gaze flickered over her, resting on her lips, her breasts, then her hips. "Oh yes," he said softly. "Is it working?"

"Not one bit." She settled the box on her hip. "If you'll excuse me, I'll go and wait for Mark out front. He should arrive soon." Or not. She was supposed to call him when she finished, but she didn't really want him to show up yet.

Nick followed as she went back through the lobby. Nurse Becky and her companion sent covetous glances her way, quite making up for their earlier pity.

It felt good to be queen again. And for the moment, walking outside with Nick, she felt as if she was queen of something far more important than the homecoming parade.

She turned her face to the sun and closed her eyes. A faint breeze wafted over her, lifting her hair a bit. She felt the sun warm on her skin, and she could hear birds chirping, a lawn mower whirling lazily in the distance, the whoosh of the door as it closed behind Nick. "I'd forgotten how much you could hear in the country."

"I thought you lived outside of Raleigh?"

"Our neighborhood was well inside the city limits. The lots were huge and made it seem like the country, but you could hear the highway all of the time."

"Sounds idyllic." Nick leaned against his car and crossed his arms, his gray eyes glinting down at her.

She'd always had a soft spot for a man with gray eyes.

Nick made her aware of how her cotton T-shirt rubbed her shoulders. The way her jeans hung loose on her hips. The way her naked toes were curling inside

her Keds. Even more, she was aware of how good it
would feel to have Nick's hard, warm mouth on hers.

Nick shook his head. "I can't believe you're here. I
never thought to see you in Glory again."

"Neither did I." She tilted her head and regarded him
for a long moment. "What are you doing here? Clara
mentioned that something happened in Atlanta—"

The friendly expression on Nick's face disappeared.
"That's past history."

Something about his expression reminded her of her
own when people asked about her divorce. "You know,
it helps if you talk about it."

Nick's brows rose.

"That's what people say when they find out I'm divorced."

"Ah." His eyes flickered over her face, lingering on
her lips. "I take it you agree with them."

"Not particularly. But I figure that if you tell me your
painful story and I tell you my painful story, we'll be
spared having to find out the truth in bits and pieces
from the town gossips."

Nick's lips twitched. "You have gotten more direct."

His appreciative gaze made her feel even bolder.
"Meanwhile, you're still reticent about anything that
matters."

He shrugged. "I don't like reliving the past."

"Most good stories are about things that happened
long ago—even fairy tales."

He laughed. "You won't quit, will you?"

"Nope. Here, I'll even go first. I met Brian, fell in love, went to college, got married, became a very busy social wife, then found my husband in bed with his law partner."

Nick winced. "Damn."

"Yup. And his law partner's name is Larry Berkowitz."

"*Larry?*"

"Yes. In addition to being the best man at our wedding, which is a betrayal in itself, Larry didn't look particularly attractive in pink satin lingerie."

"Double ouch!"

"No kidding. I got divorced, won a boatload in the settlement, and was on my way to Paris when Mother had her attack."

"Why Paris?"

"Or Italy. I just want to go away and start over."

Nick's gaze flickered over her. "You can start over here."

"In Glory? No, no, no. You've forgotten something. This is *Glory*. Last night, I ran into Mrs. Klutchton at the gas station, and she told me I had the highest kick of any cheerleader she'd ever seen. Nick, it's been sixteen *years* since I kicked in front of a crowd." She shook her head. "If I want change, it's not going to happen here."

Nick glanced at her hair. "A friend told me that women who'd been cheated on always want to change things. And you certainly have."

She laughed. "This was a compromise. You'd be horrified if you knew what I *really* wanted to do." She crossed her arms and smiled up at him. "So? What about you?"

Nick hadn't told anyone about Atlanta since he'd returned, though the papers had carried the stories. Still, Roxie had shared her tale, so he could do no less. "Long story short, after high school I went to Atlanta to live with my uncle and start fresh. I got a job and went to college. I ended up enrolled in a criminal justice class taught by a real cop—a detective, in fact. He didn't teach a dry, boring class but slid in a bunch of real-life experiences—'war stories,' he called them.

"I did something I'd never done before—I studied and asked a lot of questions during class. I even started hanging out afterward. Eventually, Lee gave me an application for the force and suggested I apply after I graduated. I did." He shrugged.

"That was it?"

Nick wished it had been. "Not quite. I got the job and Lee became my mentor. For about eleven years, I ate, drank, and slept that job. I was being promoted very quickly because of Lee's recommendations and because I worked hard—damned hard."

Roxie's pale blue eyes never wavered from his.

Nick wondered why he was telling her all of this, but she was right—it was better she heard it from him and not the gossips. "One day, I noticed something odd about some paperwork I'd submitted. Someone had altered it, changed the date and time." He stopped, his voice suddenly catching in his throat.

"Lee?" Roxie asked, her eyes soft with sympathy.

He nodded shortly. He so rarely spoke about Lee that the knot of emotion caught him by surprise. "A few years after I met him, he went through a very painful divorce. I guess he was lonely, because he became involved with one of our sources—a very beautiful but very troubled woman with a long history of using and abusing men. I guess he thought he could take care of her and turn her around. That's the trouble with cops: they're innately chivalrous, sometimes to their own detriment. She'd convinced him that she was innocent, saying she'd gotten involved in a drug deal by accident. Lee fell for both her and her lies."

"I'm so sorry. That had to hurt."

"Lee was the most ethical man I knew: the reason I stopped fighting authority, and started understanding why it exists, why our civilization needs it. To see him brought so low . . . it was painful. I challenged him on it, but he denied it all. I really wanted to believe him. But though he swore it was a onetime thing and would never happen again, it did. Eventually, others started to notice, and Internal Affairs came to me and asked me to wear a wire."

"Oh no!"

Nick nodded. "I wasn't going to, but they told me that if I didn't help stop Lee now, he would be sucked into even stupider stunts. So I did it and discovered that Lee was on the verge of stealing evidence and destroying it. A policeman in jail is as good as dead, and everyone knows it. So IA agreed that if he'd resign, they would halt the investigation and wouldn't press charges."

"So you saved his life."

At a hell of a price. "To a lot of people, *I* was the real traitor."

Roxie bit her lip. "Nick, I'm sorry you went through that."

He shrugged. "It is what it is. I discovered that ambition isn't all it's cracked up to be. Now I know what's important—which is why I returned to Glory, and I don't plan to leave."

"What? You want to stay here? *Forever?*"

He smiled at her surprise. "Why not?"

"I just never thought you'd bury yourself in the middle of nowhere." Roxie looked him up and down. "When you left Atlanta, you didn't bump your head on anything, did you?"

He laughed. "No. But I did learn that you can't find peach cobbler in Atlanta that's half as good as what's served at Micki & Maud's Diner."

Her eyes twinkled. "Ah, my kingdom for a peach cobbler!"

Suddenly the sunshine seemed a bit brighter to Nick, the day a little more carefree.

"You're not mocking peach cobbler, are you?" He leaned forward and captured a golden curl that had escaped her ponytail and now cupped her face. "I know how much you like it, Treymayne."

Roxie flushed, but she didn't move away. Years ago, she'd have been stiff with trepidation. He'd never met a person more afraid to enjoy life. But whatever had held her back then, she'd clearly conquered it. And he found it damned intriguing.

He leaned forward, his face only a few inches from hers. "Don't forget that when you mock my peach cobbler, you're also mocking the law. Things could get"— his gaze dropped to her lips—"serious."

The warm morning sun caressed her cheek, and he realized that she didn't have a stitch of makeup on. He could see the smooth line of her skin and the faint dusting of freckles across the bridge of her nose.

She met his gaze, her pale blue eyes shimmering with laughter. "I *live* to mock the law."

Nick's body heated immediately. He looked at her a long moment, then he turned abruptly. "One minute." He leaned in the open window of his squad car and picked up his radio. "This is Sheppard. I'm 10-81."

The radio crackled, then Susan's voice came over the radio. "Now? It's not even ten yet."

"My muffin didn't last. I'm 10-81 for another hour."

There was a long silence. "OK. I got it."

He dropped the radio onto the seat.

Roxie frowned. "What did you just do?"

He took her hand and led her down the sidewalk to a large tree, then tugged her behind it so they were no longer in sight of the many windows of the assisted living center. "I called in for lunch. I'm officially off duty."

"Because?"

"Because I wanted to do this." With that, he pulled her hard against him and kissed her.

Roxie instantly melted, feeling alive, and hot, and out of control.

As his warm mouth covered hers and his hands slid down to her hips, she stopped thinking and soaked in the wildness, the naughtiness, the pure wrongness of it. Moaning, she pressed closer, deepened the kiss, and slid her hands to his firm ass. God, he felt good, and oh, how she wanted more and more and—

He stepped away, breathing hard, bewilderment in his warm gray eyes. "Hot damn."

"Is . . . is that a good 'hot damn'?"

He gave a shaky laugh. "Oh yeah. It's *real* good."

She laughed and moved closer, but Nick shook his head. "We need to do this somewhere else. I'm in uniform."

She traced a finger around his badge. "We could fix that." She grinned wickedly.

He laughed and pulled her close once more, his delightful mouth moving toward hers—

A car whizzed by and Roxie caught sight of the Mustang.

Nick sighed and straightened. "Your brother's here."

Damn it. Roxie wanted to wail and stomp her foot like a child. She wanted another kiss. After all she'd been through, she *deserved* it. Why was Mark here anyway? She hadn't called him.

Nick took her elbow and led her from the tree just

as Mark hopped out of the Mustang. "Well! Hello, you two! I was passing on my way to the church to talk to the pastor about the flowers, so I thought I'd go ahead and pick Roxie up."

She didn't *want* her brother to pick her up; she wanted more of Nick's kisses!

Nick handed her the box of letters she'd left on top of his car, his fingers warm as they brushed hers. Her nipples went to immediate Red Alert.

"What's that?" Mark asked, eyeing the box with interest.

She patted the box. "Doyle Cloyd's blackmail notes."

Nick's brows shot down. *"What?"*

"Doyle was being blackmailed?" Mark asked.

"No, he was blackmailing others. Almost the whole town, from the looks of it."

"Where did you find that box?" Nick's gaze was narrowed.

"Your aunt and her friends found it in Doyle's old room." She settled the box on her other hip. "Once I decipher Doyle's atrocious handwriting, I'm going to make a list of suspects."

Nick frowned. "Have you read them?"

"A few. I'm hoping this will get your aunt Clara and her friends out some."

"Roxie," Nick said slowly, "I think I'd better have a look at that box."

"Sure. Once I make my list—"

"No, I think I should take it now. If those really are blackmail notes, it's possible they're a clue."

She was stunned. "A *real* clue?"

Mark laughed. "Rox, you should see your face!"

"I didn't believe Doyle had been murdered!" she replied. "But you don't have clues in accidents."

"Sure you do," Nick said. "How else do you know it's an accident?"

Her face fell. "Oh. I hadn't thought of it that way."

Nick shrugged. "I'll go back through the records and see what's in the case file."

"Yes, but . . ." Her hands tightened on the box. Damn it, if the clues were real, then she *really* wanted to keep it. "What if I photocopy the notes and—"

Nick's face turned hard as stone. "Roxie, that's evidence. You aren't suggesting I pretend that it's not?"

Her jaw tightened. "I didn't suggest any such thing."

"Good. I'm asking you now to hand over the box."

"I'm asking you now to hand over the box," she mimicked, frustrated. "Your aunt and her friends are going to be upset."

Nick shrugged, his expression still closed.

"Fine!" She handed him the box.

Nick turned to Mark. "I need to go, but it was good seeing you."

"Good to see you, too," Mark said, opening the door for Roxie.

Nick turned to her. "See you around, Treymayne."

His peremptory manner in taking possession of the box still stung, so she merely shrugged.

He waited an awkward moment, then said in a cool voice, "Good-bye, then." He turned and walked toward his car.

Roxie watched him from under her lashes. God, his ass was perfect, even encased in dark blue polyester.

Mark frowned at her. "What was that all about?"

"Nothing." She slid into the Mustang, feeling oddly bereft. Somehow, every time she and Nick parted ways, there always seemed to be so much more that should've been said. It was as if he was waiting for her to say or do something . . . but what? The fact that he could switch gears so seamlessly between hot-and-bothered potential lover to cool, calm, and collected cop had really stung. Damn it, they had just shared some bone-melting kisses—her knees were still quivering from the last one—when he'd gone all Mr. Professional Cop on her and demanded Doyle's box.

But that was the way Nick was. Even in high school, he'd been amazingly single-minded once he'd focused on something—or some*one*. But now, something had changed. While she was quite capable of catching his attention, she couldn't seem to keep it.

She ground her teeth as, discouraged, she waited for Mark to climb into the driver's seat. "Off to the pastor's then," she said with false cheerfulness. Anything rather than sit and think.

chapter 8

Dear Bob,

My fiancé, "Roger," and I have been engaged for over seven years now. Last Christmas, I told "Roger" I was ready to set the date. Since then, he's found a hundred and one reasons not to do so, saying that September is fly fishing month and October's good for turkey hunting, and November's deer season—you see what I mean. I've offered to have a camo theme wedding, but even that didn't take.

Short of dressing up like a doe for deer season, how do I get "Roger" to step up to the plate like a real man?
Signed,
Dying to Wear White

Dear Dying,

A man who is unwilling to set a date is a man who is getting his "pie" for free. It's time you started charging for the "pie," and if he doesn't want to pay up, tell him to get his "pie" from another "baker."
Signed,
Bob

⌐⌐⌐

"*Ahem*."

Nick lowered the newspaper to find Susan standing on the other side of his desk.

"Are you done yet? I want to see my horoscope."

He folded the newspaper and handed it to her. "I was checking the crime report. I don't know where Pat gets her stats, but they sure don't come from us."

Susan opened the paper. "She probably makes 'em up. I hear Ty is a pretty lax editor and she can do what she wants." She flipped the page. "Not that it matters to me; the only parts of the paper I like are the horoscopes, the sports section, and 'Dear Bob.' "

" 'Dear Bob?' No one reads that."

Susan's brows shot up. "What's wrong with 'Dear Bob'? Or perhaps you already know everything you need to know about the opposite sex."

Nick opened the budget printout and pretended to be absorbed in the numbers.

She lowered the paper, tilted her head to one side, and stared intently at him. "You're upset."

He frowned. "I am not."

"Yes, you are. I can tell."

"How?"

"Your neck is red."

He touched his neck before he caught her grin. He scowled. "Don't you have some work to do?"

"Sure, but this is more fun."

Nick returned his gaze to the budget summary, hoping to discourage her.

But Susan was made of resilient stuff. She tossed the paper aside and perched on the edge of his desk, her long, jeans-clad legs crossed at the ankles. "If you don't tell me, you're going to explode."

He lowered the report. "Get off my desk. I don't want the mayor coming in here and thinking we have more than a professional relationship."

"We have much more than a professional relationship. We watch football together every Monday night."

"Yes, but he'll assume we're sleeping together."

"That's because the mayor has a guilty conscience from sleeping with *his* secretary." Susan curled her nose. "I have no idea what he sees in Robin Wright. She's a gold digger and worse."

"I have no idea what Robin Wright sees in that paunchy, greedy old man. She's an attractive woman and reasonably intelligent; she could do much better."

"Not in Glory. I'll tell you what she sees in Mayor Harkins. Just by lying on her back and reciting the names of our presidents, Robin's managed to weasel out of him a brand-new, powder-blue BMW convertible, a little house on the lake, and breasts large enough to give her black eyes if she ever bends over to pick up her own laundry."

Nick grinned. "She doesn't do her own laundry?"

"The house on the lake comes with maid service."

"You sound bitter."

"I'd like to have maid service, but the black eyes I can do without." Susan looked down at her chest. "I'm perfectly happy with the girls the way they are now. Any bigger and they'd sag as I got older."

He held up a hand. "Susan, do you remember the other night, when you told me it was hard to get more than one or two dates out of a guy before he starts making excuses and refusing to return your calls?"

"Yes."

"And then I told you it's because you tend to say things that make a man uncomfortable?"

"Like yesterday, when I mentioned that I prefer Always to Kotex?"

He winced. "Exactly like that. This conversation regarding your 'girls' is in the 'too much information' category, as well."

"Oh. Sorry. I forgot I was talking to a guy for a moment."

He threw the budget file on the desk. "Did you just come in here to insult me?"

"No, I came to see why you've been in such a horrid mood for the last two days. Not only have you been snapping at me but Mr. Thomlinson said you stopped by the hardware store and didn't ask once about the fishing, and Mrs. Clinton said you barely said two words to her when you came to rescue her pug this morning."

"You are in the know, aren't you?"

"I'm the county dispatcher; I know everything. Plus,

Mrs. Clinton wanted to know if I thought she should send some cookies."

Nick sighed. "I'll call her."

"Don't bother. I told her I thought you had a heat rash and it made you surly. She said her husband had the same problem every summer for twenty-two years before he died."

Nick looked at Susan.

She grinned. "OK, maybe I didn't tell her that, but I will if you don't explain what's got you in this mood."

Nick wished he could; he could use some advice. He'd spent the last two days in a funk of frustration for once again making a fool of himself over Roxie Treymayne. He just couldn't seem to stay away from her. Each time, he swore he'd keep his distance, but he wasn't capable of it once confronted with her delectable presence. If she was close, he made sure she got closer, and if her lips were involved, all the better.

But there was a new complication; he *liked* the new Roxie. More than once, she'd made him laugh with her dry humor. Had she always had that? The physical heat that flared to life whenever she was near fogged his earlier memories.

But telling Susan such a thing was tantamount to asking a bull to fetch a piece of china from the back of the china shop: the outcome was guaranteed to be sensational and messy.

Instead, he tapped the budget printout. "If I seem to be in a bad mood, it's because the mayor sent out a memo that said that if I don't find a way to reduce expenses before the next county meeting, not only will you be county dispatcher but you'll also be doing the billing for the water department."

Susan stood so suddenly that she appeared to have leapt off the edge of the desk. "He wouldn't!"

"He's threatening. I told him you're too busy to do another job, but he won't listen."

She scowled. "That damn jerk!"

"Yeah. I've been avoiding him."

"I know. He's called three times. Said he was expecting you at three."

"You didn't tell me that."

"Did you want to know?"

Nick grinned. "No."

She sniffed. "See how efficient I am?"

"You're the best dispatcher I've ever met," he said with complete honesty.

Susan cocked a brow. "And you're the best officer this town's ever had. Of course, that doesn't obscure the fact that you still haven't answered my original question: what's got you riled?"

"I'm not riled."

"You've been a bear for two days and I'm tired of it. When you came in today you didn't even say hello to me."

"I said hello."

"No, you grumbled something that sounded like, 'Go to hell.' "

"I said '*What* the hell' because there was no coffee."

"I rest my case."

Nick rubbed his face with both hands. He liked Susan, but sometimes she could wear a man down until all he wanted was a nice piece of tape for her mouth.

"This is about Roxie, isn't it?"

Nick dropped his hands and stared at Susan. *"What?"*

"You heard me. Does your foul mood have anything to do with Roxanne Treymayne?"

"This has nothing to do with her, although—"

Susan's gaze sharpened.

Nick threw up a hand. "Never mind."

"Come on, Nick." Susan crossed her arms. "If you want advice, it's either me or 'Dear Bob.' "

Nick sighed. She wasn't going to let up—ever.

"Save us both some time and just spit it out."

"OK, OK. When I went to see my aunt Clara, Roxie was there and—" He rubbed his neck. "I kissed her."

"Really?" Susan sat on the edge of his desk again.

"Yes. It wasn't the first time, either."

"Hmmm. Did she like it?"

"Yes." Nick eyed Susan defiantly. "I could tell."

"That's a good sign, then. What happened afterward?"

"I came to my senses."

Susan frowned. "What does that mean?"

Nick tightened his jaw. "Look, Susan, I don't need the complication of a woman like Roxie Treymayne in my life."

"A woman like Roxie. What does that mean? A *sexy* woman? A *beautiful* woman? An *intriguing* woman? What kind of woman is she?"

"She's just gone through a divorce. You were right about her hair—Brian cheated on her."

"I know, I know. With his law partner, Larry." At Nick's surprised look, she shrugged. "I got my hair done yesterday. If you ever want to know anything in this town, you'll find out at the Stuff 'n Fluff."

"Do they talk about me there?"

"They talk about *everyone*. Nick, what's your biggest problem with Roxie?"

"I just can't seem to keep my perspective. And in this profession, that's important. *Damned* important." He rubbed his forehead. "Roxie just—when I see her, I can't—it's as if— Oh, to hell with it! I just need to stay away from her, and that's that."

Susan pursed her lips. After a moment she said, "Let me get this straight. You kissed her and she enjoyed it."

"Yes."

"And so did you."

"Yes."

"But . . . you're not sure you're *really* interested in her?"

"Susan, she's the wrong woman for me on all levels. She always has been."

"Nick, you don't know that."

He sighed. "No, I don't. But it doesn't matter, because Roxie's not long for this town. As soon as her mother's better, she'll be on her way to Paris. She told me so."

"Right now, Roxie doesn't know what she wants. I know just where she is. At least, I think I do."

Sadness darkened Susan's eyes and Nick wisely didn't say a thing. Once, Susan had been engaged to the man who'd owned the largest grocery chain in Asheville. They'd broken up after Susan had caught the man sleeping with one of his employees. Though Susan wouldn't admit it, Nick was certain that was why Susan chased off every guy she met.

"There are stages to getting over a cheater." Susan counted down on her fingers. "First, there's disbelief and denial. Then there's hurt, and last, there's anger."

"Aren't those the stages of grief?"

"Very similar. Stage one was when she didn't want to believe Brian was capable of lying. Stage two comes after The Reveal."

"Reveal?"

"The day you find them in a position even you can't justify, like in bed with another woman. Or in Roxie's case, with a guy in a negligee."

"Oh."

"Then there's hurt, where most women want to change everything about themselves. That's where Roxie is right now. Her divorce is brand-new; it'll take time for her to figure out who she is and what she really wants.

"And Roxie has the added complication of being raised by that poisonous Lilah Treymayne, who always made you feel as if you weren't good enough." Susan shuddered. "Imagine growing up with that."

Lilah was even worse than Susan imagined. He'd been the recipient of the woman's poison often enough, and it had changed him and his life forever.

Suddenly unable to sit still with his thoughts, Nick stood and collected his hat.

Susan smiled brilliantly. "Going to see Roxie?"

"No, I'm going on my rounds. If what you say is right and Roxie's going through those stages, then she's off-limits and probably always will be." That was where Lee had messed up: he'd fallen in love with a woman who hadn't been able to love him back. Nick would never go there.

He checked the safety and clip on his 9 mm and tucked it back into his holster. "By the way, did you finally finish cataloguing everything in Doyle Cloyd's box?"

Susan brightened and hopped off the desk. "Yes, I did. It took forever too. His handwriting was horrible." She reached for a blue folder on the top of a file cabinet. "I cleverly disguised it in this folder marked 'Doyle Cloyd's Notes.' "

"Smart-ass." He flipped it open and read. After a moment, he gave a low whistle. "This looks like the entire Elks Lodge!"

"And that's only about half of them. I couldn't read the handwriting on the others." Susan frowned. "Do you think this means something? I've always thought his death was an accident."

Nick closed the folder and replaced it on his desk. "I don't know. Would you mind pulling all of the files on Doyle's death?"

"Sure! This could be a real case. It's about time!" She tapped a slender finger on her chin, her eyes bright. "I'll also gather whatever public information on him is available—birth and driving records, real estate transactions, that sort of thing."

"Good idea." He looked at the box where it sat on a long worktable by the door. Doyle's name had been written down the side in large block letters, probably by Aunt Clara. "If you're done with that, lock it in the evidence room."

"OK." She collected the box and walked to the door. "Nick, if you're going out, would you do me a favor?"

"What?"

"Could you stop by the Stuff 'n Fluff and ask Teresa if she'd look in on my dad this week? He needs a trim, and she's been coming out to the house now that he can't get out of bed."

Nick hesitated. The last place he wanted to go was a salon where a large contingent of women might be gathering. But one of the things he liked about Susan was that she possessed a sterling character. When he'd run off to Atlanta to make his own life, she'd stayed in Glory to take care of her father, an alcoholic who deserved a lot of things, but not a devoted daughter like Susan.

He set his hat on his head. "I'll stop by there first."

Susan smiled. "Thanks. Tell her Tuesday will be fine, if that works for her."

"OK." He headed to the street, mulling over what Susan had said about his reaction to Roxie. Susan made sense, as she usually did.

It was too bad there was no chemistry between him and Susan. He liked her uncomplicated style, though he thought she hid her own issues behind a flippant façade. Since they were just friends, those issues didn't come into play, and for that he was forever grateful.

Still, Susan had given him some new insight into the shimmering and tempting waters that were Roxanne Treymayne. She had a myriad of layers, each more complicated to decipher than the last. He felt like a blind man in a maze who he knew that treasure lay at the center, but who was becoming more and more doubtful that he'd be the one to discover it.

He gritted his teeth, disgusted at his runaway imagination. If he kept this up, he'd be picturing himself riding in on a white steed and trying to rescue Roxie from a tower or some fire-breathing dragon. He'd tried that once, and all he'd gotten for his trouble had been a sharp rebuke that had taken years to heal.

Perhaps in a few years, after Roxie had healed from her divorce, she might be ready for a relationship. It was funny, but men approached divorce from an entirely different angle than women did. While there might be some hurt pride, it was usually quelled with some hard drinking and some mindless sex. Some women might use the same method, but others built walls around themselves and then stood there, daring anyone to even try to connect with them.

Shaking his head, Nick headed for the Stuff 'n Fluff. Better to get through this unavoidable dose of estrogen, then head over to the mayor's office and see what Harkins wanted. The man was a fool six ways to Sunday, but he was also still "the boss."

After that, he'd do his rounds, and this evening he'd retreat to the safety of Kenny's Bait Shop to see if there were any minnows. Fishing was the best way to rid his mind of unwanted thoughts. He'd found that it was hard to be irritated while floating in a boat on a peaceful river.

If there was one thing Glory had, it was some very good fishing. It was too bad Roxie Treymayne didn't fish.

chapter 9

"THE WAY YOU WERE yawning at dinner, I thought you'd already be in bed."

Roxie smiled at Mark, who stood in the doorway to the porch. "I'm going to bed soon." She tucked her feet under the cushion on the porch swing and leaned back to rock it again.

Mark came out onto the porch, letting the screen door swing closed behind him. "It's peaceful tonight."

"Is Mother asleep?"

Mark took a chair nearby and unfolded his long legs. "Not yet, but she should be soon. Tundy wore her out today. She told Mother she'd accidentally spilled candle wax on Grandma's antique rug in the living room. Mother wouldn't rest until she'd gotten out of bed and seen the damage herself."

"That's *brilliant*!"

"That's Tundy."

"Was the rug really damaged?"

"No. Tundy put a dried piece of wax on it, though, to make it look real. Then she 'scrubbed' it out using

Mother's miracle baking soda solution." He linked his hands behind his head. "What are you doing out here?"

"Contemplating change."

"Your own?"

"All of ours. Mother has to change things because of her heart. You and I are facing change because our marriages ended." She sighed. "I never understood why Mother liked Brian so much."

"I did," Mark said promptly. "He was tall, handsome, had a good career, was a town hero, but most importantly of all, she never thought he'd leave Glory."

Roxie blinked. "But that's all he ever talked about doing."

"To you. To Mother, he said whatever she wanted to hear." Mark shrugged. "That's probably how Brian coped with being both ambitious and having a secret life. He simply became whoever he needed to be to keep everyone happy."

Roxie toyed with the worn edge of her cushion. "That had to have been difficult for him."

"Yeah, I think Arlene was the same, in some ways— though that doesn't make what they did hurt any less." Mark was silent a moment, staring down the street as three young boys rode by, the fading sunlight glinting off their bikes. "I thought I loved Arlene, but now I'm not so sure."

"Really? I always thought you were crazy about her."

"But was I crazy about who Arlene really was, or who I thought she was? Sometimes those two things can get so tangled up, you can't tell them apart."

"Do you regret it?"

"Nope. The worst thing you can do is live your life for the 'what ifs.' They'll seduce you into making even bigger mistakes. I'm done making mistakes."

"Me, too. So what do we do now?"

"Start being honest about 'what is,' then deal with it head-on and with no excuses. One of the problems of being raised by a mother who excels in burying her head in the sand is that we've learned to do the same ourselves."

Roxie pondered this a moment, then sighed. "I'm afraid I'll make the same mistake again. What if next time I *really* fall in love, and *then* find out it's the wrong guy? I don't think I could stand the pain."

"Then don't," he said simply.

"Don't what?"

"Don't fall in love with the wrong guy."

"That's about as useful as Tundy telling me to do what Oprah does," she scoffed.

He chuckled and plopped his feet on the wicker ottoman. "Well, she might have something there. Oprah seems pretty spot on about a lot of things."

At Roxie's surprised look, he shrugged. "She's an advocate of change, and that's what we both need. Look at this house: from the street, it seems idyllic, perfect even." He dropped a leg from the ottoman and slid it over the porch, his shoe scraping across a loose floorboard. "But if you look close, it's in bad repair and needs several thousands of dollars' worth of work. Mother pays to have the thing painted every year, but God forbid she fix something that's not visible from the road."

"You think we did that in our marriages? Bought a house because it was painted well?"

Mark met her gaze evenly. "Didn't we? You married the high school quarterback well on his way to becoming a polished, successful lawyer. Since he looked like Clark Kent, you and Mother were certain he was Superman."

"And Arlene?"

"I was the rebel, remember? I could tell Arlene's paint was peeling, and that's what I liked about her; I knew Mother would hate her. But I should have checked to make sure the house beneath that peeling paint was sound." He shrugged. "It wasn't. Arlene's the sort of person who'll reel from mess to mess, leaving a trail of broken hearts behind her."

"I'm sorry," Roxie said softly.

"Me, too." He slapped his hands onto his knees. "But enough of that! I should check my messages and make sure everything is OK at the office." He stood and placed a warm hand on her shoulder. "Roxie, I know it's not easy. But if we set good standards—more than just a good job and a perfect physique—then all we have to do is sit back and wait for the proof."

"What proof?"

"Proof that the person is as good as they look. Think about it: if you'd dated Brian for a couple of years instead of a few months, do you think you'd have married him?"

She thought about it, then reluctantly shook her head. "No. We didn't really have a lot in common, so our entire marriage became based on furthering his career."

"Arlene was the same for me. We had a great time in bed, but that was about the extent of our relationship. Unfortunately, I didn't realize it until after we were married."

Could Mark be right? She and Brian had never had much in common, either—something she hadn't discovered or admitted to herself, until well after the wedding.

Their only common interest had been a desire for a better life away from Glory. In that they'd been united, and for a while it had been enough. But there'd been one more thing, too. After living with Mother's drama, Brian's quiet and reserve had been a welcome haven. She didn't realize until much later that his reserved nature hid a somewhat passionless soul.

She curled her fingers into her palms. At the time, she'd consoled herself that at least he cared about her and respected her, and that was enough. It had worked for a while, too. Despite the fact she lived in a gorgeous house complete with a two-story library and a bathtub big enough to do laps, as she'd grown older and spent some time with other couples, she'd seen and hungered for a taste of the passion missing in her own marriage. Yet the harder she'd pressed Brian to change things and spice up their relationship, the more distant he'd become.

At the time, she'd been frustrated and irritated by his lack of enthusiasm, but after she'd realized he preferred men, it all made sense. In some ways, it had even been a relief.

She looked at Mark. "Let me know how your plan works, will you? I'm not sure it's that easy."

He moved to the door, his long shadow cast across the porch by the lamplight through the lace-curtained window behind him. "It's going to take time. By the way, the next time you see Nick, would you tell him that if he'd like to go fishing, I'll be free Saturday?"

"Why would I be seeing Nick?"

"It's a small town. It could happen." He winked and said, "I'd better get up to see Mother."

Moments later, she heard his voice drifting down from Mother's room.

Roxie stayed where she was, watching the night creep in. So she needed to set some standards, did she? She could do that. Let's see . . . honesty was essential. So were maturity and openness. She loved a man with a good sense of humor, too. There also had to be a certain amount of physical attraction—no relationship could work without that. It would also be necessary for her guy to share her newfound desire for adventure.

All in all, she'd just described the opposite of Brian.

Nick, on the other hand, seemed to have it all—
except the desire for adventure. He was as deeply
embedded in Glory's soil as the huge oak in the town
square, and just about as likely to pick up and walk
away.

The thought depressed her. He had so much potential, but was that enough? And did it even matter? Because he certainly didn't seem all that interested in her.

Every time they were together, he pulled away. She
thought of their last kiss and shivered. They certainly
had the physical attraction down. It was unfortunate
they were speeding down opposite sides of life's highway: she to Paris and a life of excitement, and he to his
desk overlooking the town square.

Sighing, she stood and stretched. She didn't want to
settle down yet, anyway. She'd had that, and it had stag-
nated her spirit until she'd almost lost sight of who she
was.

Never again, she vowed. Never, *ever* again. She left
the porch and went inside.

"How dare the pigs confiscate our box!"

Roxie sighed. "Clara, it's not polite to call your
nephew a 'pig.' "

"He stole our box!"

"It's not 'our' box. It was Doyle's box, and technically
it now belongs to his sister. Didn't she inherit all of his
stuff?"

Rose scowled fiercely. "She died. Besides, Doyle left

a boatload of money in the bank; she wouldn't miss one measly box."

Clara sighed. "What are we going to do now?"

They were silent for a long minute. Finally, Rose said, "We'll just have to do our investigation without the notes."

Everyone nodded enthusiastically except Roxie.

"No," she said. "If Nick is right and this is a real murder, then it's possible the murderer is still here. I couldn't take the responsibility for putting you all into harm's way."

Clara scowled. "Damn it, I told everyone at the Stuff 'n Fluff yesterday that we were hot on the trail!"

"So did I," Rose said, her angular frame slumped. At Roxie's bemused gaze, she added, "We go to the hair salon every Wednesday afternoon."

Roxie glanced at the glum group. "Perhaps we could find another mystery to investigate."

"Where?" C.J. asked.

"Yeah," Rose chimed in. "Where are you going to find another great mystery like this one? I've lived here all my life, and I can count on one hand the number of odd occurrences that have happened within the city limits."

C.J. sighed, clearly disappointed. "I guess we'll just watch our shows."

Clara stared morosely into her cup. "And drink our bourbon."

Roxie shook her head. "We can still do lots of fun

things. We could . . . We could . . ." Damn it, what could they do? "We could go to a park—"

"No, thank you. I'd rather have my bourbon," Rose said in a waspish tone.

"What about a craft class?"

Clara drew herself up, affronted. "We are not 'crafties.' "

"Besides," Rose added sullenly, "there's already a Craft Club. We can't copy them."

C.J. glared at Roxie. "I can't believe you'd suggest that."

"Hey, I didn't know." Roxie tapped her fingers on her knee. She had to think of something they could do, something fun and different and—"What about starting a fishing club?"

"No!" Clara, Rose, and C.J. said at the same time.

Roxie waved her hands. "OK, I'm sorry I mentioned it! You know, the fact is that you're too good."

Rose's eyes narrowed. "What do you mean by that?"

"Nick agreed with your assessment of Doyle's situation right away. You all have great instincts."

"Some good that did us." But Rose looked a bit mollified. "What else did he say?"

"He said the box could be evidence and he should take a look at it."

"I *knew* it was important," Rose said, sniffing.

"Yes, and I—" A loud snore cut her off. Roxie frowned and looked at C.J.

He met her gaze and flushed. "Ah. Sorry. My stomach is a bit upset. The eggs at breakfast are powdered, you know. Sometimes they don't sit well and—"

Another snore sounded. This time, Roxie could tell it came from the bed behind C.J.

She jumped up and headed for the bed. It appeared empty, though there were a lot of pillows piled up on one corner.

Clara unlocked her wheelchair and swiftly cut Roxie off. "You don't need to go there!"

This time the snore was accompanied by the movement of the pillows. Not much, but a little, as if someone had stirred in their sleep.

"Oh, my tummy!" C.J. called. He patted his stomach harder. "Yep, that was me, all right—"

Roxie leaned past Clara and grabbed one of the pillows.

There, sound asleep, was a huge beagle, its white muzzle resting in a puddle of drool.

He stirred, opened his eyes, lifted his head, and looked at Roxie.

She stared back.

His eyes slowly closed, his head flopped back on the bed, and he snored again.

Roxie replaced the pillow.

Clara sighed. "Pumper's my brother's. He just got moved to an assisted living center and can't keep him, the poor baby."

"Clara, you're in an assisted living center, too."

"Yep. Same one, in fact."

"Then how can you keep him if your brother can't?"

"Because he has a roommate. I don't, so I can keep Pumper all I want." She grinned at Roxie. "Pretty dog, ain't he?"

"Ah, yeah. He's quite a specimen. Clara, I—"

"Enough about Pumper," Rose snapped. "That old dog won't be alive much longer, anyway. All he does is eat and sleep."

"Well," Clara said honestly, "that's not *all* he does."

"No, he goes out, too, twice a day." Rose looked at the pile of pillows with grudging respect. "That's the most regular dog I've ever met."

Roxie laughed. "I never know what you guys will be into next. First it's Doyle's murder, then the bourbon, and now this dog—sheesh! Next you'll want to go *bird-watching* or something."

Rose's gimlet gaze locked on Roxie. "Bird-watching? That's an idea."

Clara scowled. "I don't want to watch no birds—"

"Miss Roxanne," Rose said in a rushed voice, "would you please step outside a moment? We need to discuss some private business." She stood and swept the door open.

Sighing, Roxie stepped out. The door closed. The low murmur of voices could be heard inside, followed by the crackle of Clara's laughter.

What were they doing in there? She leaned forward to see if she could hear—

The door opened and Rose stood in the doorway in

her flowing caftan. "We've decided to change the club name."

"We voted!" C.J.'s voice floated from behind her.

She grimaced at him over her shoulder before saying to Roxie, "We're now the Pine Hills Assisted Living Center Bird-Watching Club."

"But—"

"And we want to go and watch birds *now*."

Clara rolled up to the door and peered around Rose. "Can you wait for us in the lobby? We've got to dress."

"Sure. But won't we need binoculars and a book—"

Rose waved a peremptory hand. "We already have binoculars and we can stop at the library for a book. Meet you in the lobby in ten minutes." She slammed the door closed.

What the heck is going on? Roxie stared at the closed door for a long time. Well, at least they were going out. And if they were up to trouble, she'd figure it out. They weren't exactly subtle.

She turned and wandered out to the lobby. Nurse Becky was nowhere to be seen, so Roxie found a chair by the door and plopped into it.

What would the center do when they found out about the dog? Banish Clara? Or just the dog?

Roxie shook her head. So long as no one expected her to take the mutt. She'd never had a pet. Mother had always said they were too much trouble, and Roxie had been too busy with Brian's social demands to get one herself.

She wondered if Nick had a dog. She could picture that. He'd probably have a large golden retriever with soulful eyes, one that would snuggle up against his feet on cold nights. Then she wondered what Nick looked like wearing something other than his uniform. She could see him in worn jeans and a T-shirt, the soft material draping over his hard chest and hinting at his iron-flat stomach beneath.

He'd been a bit on the thin side in high school, but he'd filled out nicely, muscles on muscles broadening his shoulders and arms, thighs, and that very fine ass.

She closed her eyes a moment. She'd groped that ass right here, behind an oak tree by the parking lot. If she curled her fingers right now, she could almost feel those hard muscles curving—

"There she is!" Clara's voice rang across the lobby.

Roxie sighed and reluctantly let go of her pleasant daydreams. "That wasn't ten minut—" Roxie frowned at the new Bird-Watching Club. "Why are you all dressed in black?"

"We're undercover," C.J. said happily.

"For birds?"

Rose nodded. "You wouldn't believe how smart some birds can be."

"Yup," Clara agreed. "Almost like *humans*."

If they thought the birds wouldn't see them coming because they were wearing black, they were sorely mistaken. Clara had a sequined Christmas elf on her black sweatshirt, while Rose's sported a Pittsburgh Steelers logo, and C.J.'s a KISS emblem.

Clara fished in a bag that hung from her chair and pulled out a set of binoculars. "Let's go."

"Where are we going?"

Clara and C.J. looked at Rose.

"Well," she said, "there are a lot of birds that sit on the statue in the town square."

Something wasn't right here. "I thought you all hated going to look at the statue."

Clara held up a pair of binoculars. "That was before we became bird-watchers! I know there has to be a lot of birds near that statue because it's covered in bird crap. The FBI would call that a clue."

Roxie supposed it was better than sitting in Doyle's room, sipping bourbon, and watching reruns of *CSI*. "If that's where you want to go, we'll go. I'll get the van."

A few moments later, she was locking Clara's chair in the van when she realized that C.J. was missing. She looked for him and caught sight of him staggering up the walk, carrying a sagging pillowcase over one shoulder. "C.J., that can't be—"

C.J. set the pillowcase on the seat.

A tail wagged against the fabric.

"No," Roxie said.

Clara blinked at her. "We can't leave Pumper in the room by himself. Someone will find him."

"I can't let him roam about the van while I'm driving."

They all looked at the pillowcase. It didn't move. Even the tail had stopped wagging.

Rose flipped back the opening so Pumper's nose stuck out. He snored gently.

Roxie sighed. "Fine. But Rose, you're in charge of him. I've got my hands full with the three of you."

Rose grinned and covered Pumper's head. "Let's go then! Birds don't wait for no man."

chapter 10

*R*OXIE PARKED THE VAN near the statue across from City Hall. She could see the sheriff's office down the street, though it was almost hidden by large, leafy trees. Not that she was looking.

Clara, Rose, and C.J. lifted their binoculars and stared intently.

Roxie turned in her seat. "Hey, guys?"

Rose lowered her binoculars. "What?"

"The statue is that way." Roxie pointed.

"Oh. Right." Rose frowned and looked at the statue through her binoculars. Slowly, she turned back to her original position.

Roxie undid her seat belt. "All right. You all can just put your binoculars down. I know what you are doing."

Clara lowered her binoculars. "You do?"

"We're not bird-watching; you're staking out the mayor's office." She scowled. "You didn't listen to me at all!"

"You look mad," C.J. said, his binoculars now turned her way.

"I *am* mad! I asked you all to let this go, and you agreed."

"Miss Roxanne," Rose said primly, "it's obvious that the sheriff needs our help."

"He doesn't think so."

"Oh, child, they *never* do," Clara said. "They always think they can solve the cases by themselves. Just look at that nice sheriff on *Murder, She Wrote.* Why, he couldn't solve a case if it happened right in front of him and the murderer left their driver's license on the floor beside the body."

"Yup," Rose said. "Some men don't know when they need help. Look at C.J."

"That's true." He nodded so vigorously that his teeth clicked. "I never think I need help, but Rose and Clara assure me that I'm not able to do half the things I think I can."

"You can't," Rose said shortly.

"Especially not the climbing part," Clara added.

"Climbing?" Roxie asked.

"C.J. thinks he can climb to the top of City Hall without a ladder."

Roxie looked at the imposing, marble-faced, two-story building. "Why does he think that?"

"Because he did it once."

Roxie looked at C.J. in amazement. "When?"

Rose snorted. "When he was sixteen. When you're sixteen, you're too stupid to know what you can and can't do. Sometimes that'll work in your favor, and sometimes it won't."

"Oh," Roxie said. C.J. looked sad, so she added, "I bet he was a good climber when he was sixteen—"

A knock sounded on the van door, and Roxie turned to see a tall, angular woman with an iron-gray pageboy haircut standing in the sun, her hand shading her eyes as she stared in the window.

"Who's that?" Roxie asked without moving her mouth.

"Her name's Pat Meese," Clara answered. "She's with the newspaper."

Rose looked as if she'd like to spit. "That woman writes trash. Why, she wrote a piece on how the Kennedys were cursed after John-John went down in the plane crash!"

"Pah!" Clara said. "Everyone knows it's the mob who's been knocking off the Kennedys. There's no curse involved."

Rose eyed Pat narrowly. "What you think she wants?"

"I don't know," Roxie said, "but she can hear every word you say."

Pat nodded. "Yes, I can." Her voice, though muffled, was easy to hear.

"She wants in," Clara announced. "I don't want her to come in."

"I'll see what she wants." Roxie unlocked the doors and climbed out, then went to the other side of the van. "Hi! My name is Roxie Tr—"

"Treymayne," the woman finished in a brisk tone.

"Lilah's daughter and married to that lawyer up in Roanoke—"

"Raleigh."

"—whatever, though people say you're getting a divorce." Pat flipped open a notebook that had appeared almost magically. She pulled a pen from behind one ear, and stood poised to write down Roxie's every word. "So? Are you getting a divorce? And why?"

"Ms. Meese—"

"Call me Pat." Her gaze flickered past Roxie to the van. "So this is the Murder Mystery Club that the whole town's talking about." Pat's pen began to flick across her notebook. "Let's see . . . that's Rose Tibbons, I'd know her anywhere. Don't know the old man—who is he?"

"Ms. Meese, I'm not going to—"

"Fine, I'll find out myself. And there's Miss Clara, the sheriff's great-aunt. That's an interesting connection, wouldn't you say? I bet that gives you access to all sorts of records."

Roxie stiffened. "No, it doesn't. The sheriff has made no secret of the fact that he doesn't wish the club to pursue this case."

"Oh! You call it a 'case,' do you?"

Drat! Whatever this woman is writing, it isn't going to be to the good. "Look, this is a just a club outing. We're bird-watching. That's it."

"Bull," Pat scoffed.

"I don't think you underst—"

"Hello."

Roxie turned. Mayor Harkins stood smiling down at her. Until he stood beside her, Roxie hadn't realized that he was so tall. He was dressed in a polyester suit with lapels that bespoke a fascination with the '70s. Beside him, her chin at a pugnacious angle, her skirt as short as her temper, stood Robin Wright.

Oh great. The whole world knows we're here. "Mayor Harkins. Robin. Nice to see you again."

Mayor Harkins smiled, revealing a row of false white teeth. Roxie almost recoiled. She'd never seen anyone smile quite like that, so wide and yet so insincerely.

"Mrs. Parker—that *is* what you go by, I presume?"

"Actually, I prefer Treymayne."

His smile grew unctuous. "Oh, yes. You're *divorced*."

"As are you, I believe," she pointed out with a sweet smile.

Pat's pencil flew over her notepad.

The mayor's gaze flared, but his smile didn't budge an iota. "I don't mean to intrude, but I couldn't help but wonder if perhaps your van was broken down? Should I call in a tow truck?"

"No, my seniors are bird-watching. Thanks for your concern, though."

Robin leaned in. "Charlie, don't let her get away with her lies! Everyone in town is talking about how she and these loonies think Doyle was murdered, and how they think you did it, and now here they are, staring into our windows with binoculars and—"

"Robin!" Charlie made a faint move of his head toward Pat, who was eagerly writing every word.

Robin flushed scarlet and muttered, "It's no secret."

The mayor glanced back at the van, his gaze hardening.

Clara, Rose, and C.J. all had their binoculars up, but they were trained on the group. Roxie gave a quick shake of her head and the three immediately swung their binoculars to the trees overhead.

"I'm so sorry about this misunderstanding." Roxie lowered her voice. "Actually, the poor dears can't even see well enough to identify a bird. Here at the city park, they can watch all sorts of interesting things instead. In fact, there's a statue they are particularly fond—"

"Pardon me, is there a problem?" Nick's rich voice washed over Roxie like a cooling spring rain.

She gave a silent quick prayer of thanks before turning to face him. He stood with his arms crossed over his broad chest, looking so solid and invincible that she grinned like a loon and had to force herself to keep from sprinting to his side.

"Nick! I brought the gang out for some bird-watching, and the mayor thinks the group has been staring into his office windows instead. I'm sure he and Miss Wright are just confused, and—"

"They were too looking into our windows!" Mayor Harkins's face was red.

"We both saw them," Robin snapped.

Nick shrugged. "It doesn't matter if they did. They're

on public property and so were the both of you. There's no law to prevent them." As he spoke, Nick glanced at the van behind him. His aunt and her two friends had their binoculars pinned right on him. He frowned, and all three binoculars swung back to the trees overhead.

He slanted a glance at Roxie, who shrugged.

"What's this? A town meeting?" A tall man with tousled blond hair crossed the road toward them.

Roxie blinked. "Ty?"

The man's eyes widened. "Roxie Treymayne! As I live and breathe!" He stepped forward and scooped her up into a hug.

Up until that moment, Nick's primary emotion had been irritation tinged with amusement. But the sight of Ty's enthralled expression made him forget why he was here and sent a surge of pure, hot male hostility through his veins.

"Ty, I haven't seen you since high school!" Roxie laughed, the sound as delicious as the way the wind was ruffling her hair around her face.

Nick scowled.

Ty shook his head ruefully. "Roxie Treymayne! I can't believe it. After all these years. And look at you! You haven't changed a bit, except that you're more beautiful than ever."

Roxie's face pinkened, and she tucked a strand of her hair behind one ear. "Some things have changed."

Ty grinned. "Some things look even better."

Nick's jaw tightened. Since they'd first met in second grade, Nick and Ty had had a shared antipathy. Ty came from the richest family in town. His father owned most of the buildings on the square, and they ran the local newspaper, while Nick's mother was divorced and had spent every last dime keeping dinner on the table.

Nick always thought it had been Roxie's indifference to Ty's money that had made her the target of his attentions in high school; he was used to being thought of as the town prince, and he'd exploited it every way he could.

Ty had had everything handed to him on a silver platter, but he'd never appreciated it. In high school he'd run wild, and many people said he'd done that and more at college, spending his father's money faster than the old man could make it.

Eventually Ty had flunked out of college, and his father had announced that he'd had enough. From then on, he'd refused to even speak his son's name. When the old man had died, he'd left his son only the family house and the town's newspaper, and the latter had been known to be deeply in debt. The rest of old man Henderson's assets had been distributed among various charities.

Rumor had it that Ty had been furious when he'd discovered that his father hadn't left him anything of real value. But several months after his father's death, Ty had returned to town and taken his position as owner and editor of *The Glory Examiner*. He'd continued to live in town and had apparently made the paper far more lucrative, for his lifestyle had been, and still was, quietly affluent. He'd slowly won over the town, one citizen at a time. Even Roxie's mother had been known to refer to him as "that nice Ty Henderson."

Now, Ty beamed at Roxie. "I'd heard you were back in town, but I didn't believe it. Are you staying long?"

"A few weeks. Mother's still ill."

Ty instantly looked concerned. Nick wondered if Roxie could see through that phony expression, but one glance at her made him realize she was falling for it lock, stock, and monkey barrel.

Ty took Roxie's hand between his own. "Roxie, I'm so sorry! I've wanted to visit your mother, but I'd heard she wasn't seeing anyone. Will you tell her I asked after her?"

"Sure. She's seeing visitors now, if you'd like to stop by."

Nick seethed as Ty continued to hold Roxie's hand.

"Excellent. I'll try and make it tomorrow." Ty grinned. "Will you be there?"

"I'm usually gone in the morning, but—"

"Pardon me," Robin snipped, glaring at Roxie. "If you two are through with your little reunion, the mayor and I would like to speak to the sheriff about the *invasion* of our privacy by those old loons!"

Roxie pulled her hand from Ty's and moved between Robin and the van. "Whatever your problem is, it's with me, not my club."

No one could mistake the challenge in Roxie's voice. Nick almost swelled with pride. So she had a protective streak, did she?

Robin's gaze narrowed. "If you won't listen to reason, then I'll tell those old farts a thing or two—"

"No, you won't." Roxie plopped her fists on her hips. "Back off, Robin."

Nick stepped forward. "Robin, that's enough."

She glared at him, her lips thin. There was a cold, cruel quality to her, and her ginormous breasts did little to soften her image. "If you were doing your job as sheriff, we wouldn't be having this sort of lawlessness."

"No one is breaking the law."

"So they can just stare into our windows all they want?"

"That's right. It's a public office and they're not harming anyone."

Pat's pencil flew over her notepad.

Ty captured Pat's pencil. "That's enough. There's no story here."

The mayor paled when he glimpsed Pat's notes. "Robin," he said in an uneasy tone. "Let's just leave this be. We can talk to Nick about it later." He sent a scowl toward Nick. "Be in my office at three."

Nick shrugged. "Sure."

"No story?" Pat said, outraged.

"No story," Ty said firmly.

Pat's face grew red and she said through clenched teeth, "Your father would have covered this."

"My father is dead. If you haven't yet realized that, perhaps you aren't capable of reporting the news anymore. Our advice columnist has been clamoring for more responsibility."

Pat stiffened. "I'll have you know that I have my associate's degree in journalism!"

"If you don't recognize a weak story when you see one, it doesn't matter what degree you have." He turned his shoulder on her outraged expression. "Mayor, I think these elderly citizens could use some ice cream, don't you?" Ty winked at the mayor. "*That* sounds like a front-page story to me."

The mayor's gaze brightened. "The front page?"

"Oh yes. You, handing out ice cream to some of Glory's most venerated citizens? Great front-page copy!"

Pat snorted rudely, but the mayor beamed. "Ice cream! Certainly! Robin, go to Micki & Maud's and fetch some soft serve for these deserving bird-watchers."

Robin stiffened, her brand-new breasts jutting like German helmets on a coat rack. "I am not going to 'fetch' anything for these old ba—"

Mayor Harkins forced a laugh. "Never mind. You have plenty to do in the office. I'll get the ice cream." He favored Ty with a nod, then sent Roxie a triumphant glance before scurrying across the square.

Ty quirked a brow at Pat. "You might want to get the camera."

"For *this*? Mr. Henderson, I've been at the paper for twenty—"

"Twenty-three years. I know; you tell me all the time. But that doesn't make you the boss. *I* am the boss."

Pat's sticklike form was so upright that she almost bent over backward. "You aren't the man your father was."

"Thank God for that or you'd still be using a manual typesetter. Now, are you going to get the camera, or should I call our advice columnist?" Ty pulled out his cell phone.

Pat made an infuriated noise, then turned on her heel and marched away.

Ty turned to Roxie. "So, are the rumors true? Are you and that crazy group really investigating Doyle Cloyd's death?"

Roxie laughed lightly. "Us? No, we're bird-watching."

Ty's gaze narrowed. "People are saying he left—a notebook, I think?"

"No, not a note—"

"Roxie," Nick said firmly, taking her elbow, "we should get your bird-watchers out of the van for the picture."

Three pairs of binoculars were now greedily pinned on the soft serve cones in the mayor's hands.

Roxie nodded and turned toward the van.

Robin stood in her way. "I don't know what you and those crazy old coots are doing, but you'd better stop. This is a small town and people talk. Charlie and I've had enough talking, and we don't need any more, so keep your binoculars to yourself. *Or else!*" Robin spun on one heel and marched back to City Hall.

"Well," Roxie said. "That went well."

Despite himself, Nick laughed.

She shot him an amused look, but before he could speak, Ty slipped his arm around Roxie's shoulders. "Robin Wright is a harpy. You're lucky I was here to rescue you."

Nick's amusement disappeared. "Roxie didn't need rescuing. She can handle herself."

Roxie's cheeks pinkened. "Indeed I can."

"Here we are!" The mayor rushed up, ice cream dripping over his knuckles as he tried to hold all three cones upright. "I didn't get sprinkles. Thought it might make the ice cream melt faster." Mayor Harkins looked around, a sudden frown between his brows. "Where's Robin?"

Nick went to open the van door and help an eager Rose down the steps. "She went back to the office."

The mayor fixed Roxie with a hard stare. "I'm not surprised."

"I have the camera," Pat said sulkily, arriving just then.

Nick escorted the Murder Mystery Club from the van, including Clara and her wheelchair. To Nick's surprise, Roxie then dragged out a very sleepy looking, very chunky beagle who tottered to the grass, peed, and then lay down and fell asleep.

"What in the hell is *that*?" Nick demanded.

Roxie grinned at him. "Ask your aunt."

"Oh God. I don't want to know."

"Probably not." Roxie went to help Rose, who was complaining that her white sneakers would get grass stains if she had to cross the park.

Meanwhile, Ty seemed to be everywhere, making everyone but Nick laugh at his good-natured sallies. He even had Pat smiling reluctantly when he teased Clara for taking the biggest ice cream cone.

Soon the picture was taken and Pat went to download it. Nick watched, his humor gone, as Ty said a lingering farewell to Roxie before strolling with the mayor toward City Hall.

Nick helped Aunt Clara back into the van and locked her wheelchair into place. "I hope you're happy now, troublemaker."

Clara glared at him through her bottle-thick glasses. "We would have been fine if those two from City Hall hadn't shown up."

"Clara, you all *cannot* continue this investigation."

"But, Nick, what if—"

"If those blackmail notes mean anything, then someone in this town *might* have a motive for murder."

She lit up and grinned. "I knew it!"

"I said 'might'. I don't want to believe that, but it's possible. Meanwhile, I'm responsible for the safety and welfare of all of our citizens, even stubborn ones like you. So *leave the investigation to me.*"

Clara frowned. "I'll think about it."

"No, you'll do what I ask or I'll lock you in the hoosegow."

"You wouldn't! I'm seventy-three!"

"You're eighty-three, and yes I would, if it meant keeping you safe."

She sniffed.

He checked her chair to make sure it was secured and then stood back. "I'll be by tomorrow to visit. Do you need anything?"

"More chocolate," she said grudgingly. "Oh, and can you bring me a new housecoat? Mine got singed."

"Singed? How'd that happen?"

"I don't know, but—" Her gaze locked onto something past him, and she smiled sweetly.

He turned to see Roxie standing outside the van door, reaching in to help C.J. adjust the buckle.

"That's a good woman," Clara said. "A real good woman."

Nick nodded, unable to stop watching. The sun was shining on Roxie's hair, and she was laughing at something C.J. said. She replied, and he cackled loudly and patted her cheek fondly. She squeezed his hand, then moved on to help Rose.

Nick's throat tightened. The Roxie he used to know had been an ice queen, afraid to show emotion. It was only in the dark backseat of his car that she had been able to let her feelings flow. That secret side of their relationship had been flawless, but the public side—or rather, the *lack* of a public side—had torn them apart. He'd believed that she'd been unable to share her true emotions because living with her mother had frozen her heart in some way.

Now there was something more genuine about her, and he found himself wanting her even more than he used to.

"She's a hottie, isn't she?"

Nick reluctantly turned from Roxie to face his aunt. "I don't know what you're talking about."

"Sure you do." Clara smiled knowingly. "She's the best thing that ever happened to our club."

"Yeah, well, no more stakeouts. You got that?"

"OK," she said in a grumpy tone.

Nick kissed her cheek, then stepped back and secured the door. Roxie was closing the side door as he walked to the front of the van.

"I'll drive the club back to the center." She bit her lip. "We didn't get you in trouble with the mayor, did we?"

"I'm always in trouble with the mayor, so it's nothing new. He and I don't agree about much of anything."

"That must make your job hard."

"Not really. I'm very good at ignoring stupidity, and he's very good at getting too wrapped up in his secretary to remember half the meetings he's supposed to have."

Roxie rolled her eyes. "How did he get elected?"

"No one else ran."

"I guess that'd do it." She slipped her hand into her jeans pockets and shifted from one foot to the next. Nick tried not to stare, but he couldn't help it. She looked so young, standing there with almost no makeup, half her hair in a ponytail, the other half falling down around her face. What would she do if he tucked a strand behind her ear and let his fingers slide along her smooth skin?

She smiled awkwardly. "I guess I'd better be going. After all this excitement, the gang is going to need a nap. Oh—I almost forgot!"

She disappeared behind the van, then reappeared carrying the huge, fat beagle. He wagged his tail twice when he caught sight of Nick, but the efforts seemed to drain him, for he went back to sleep after that. "Can you get the door?"

"Sure." He opened the door and reached to take the dog. "This dog must weigh a hundred pounds."

"There's Pumper!" Clara said. "I almost forgot him, poor thing!"

"I don't blame you." Nick set the dog on the floorboard behind the passenger seat. Pumper didn't open his eyes, but his tail thumped once in thanks. "I guess he won't bother you when you're driving."

Roxie shut the door. "He won't bother anyone, anywhere. I've never seen a dog sleep so much."

"Only my aunt Clara would have a narcoleptic pup."

She grinned, a tantalizing dimple appearing in one cheek. "Thanks for helping out, Nick."

"No problem, Treymayne."

"It could have been. I'm glad you were here."

So was he. "Yes, we're going to have to do something about—" He frowned. "Clara, put the binoculars down! There's nothing to see here."

Roxie smothered a giggle. "There is no controlling them. They were very invested in helping find Doyle's murderer."

Here's your chance. "Roxie, would you stop by my office this evening? We should probably talk about that."

She sighed. "Yes, we should."

"Maybe at five? We could even get a bite to eat if you want." *What are you doing?* his brain asked. *You know that you'll just want her more if you see her more.*

The sunlight gleamed on her cheek and the tip of her nose, and he could almost count the freckles that dusted that cute nose.

He also liked the way her hair curved against her cheek, how her thin cotton T-shirt clung to the slopes of her full breasts, and how her—

"I'm busy tonight. Could we discuss this now?"

He forced himself to shrug. "Sure. I don't want this gang out stirring up things. Not until I've been able to do some investigating myself."

"I know. I've tried to tell them." She sighed. "But I'm afraid they'll just get other people to help them."

"Who?"

"A nurse, or some of the cleaning staff. With the right contraband, you can get about anything you want. And your aunt is the *queen* of contraband. If she wants someone to take her and the gang for a ride, she'll just bribe them."

He sighed. "Great."

They were silent a moment as they each pondered this.

"Nick? What if . . ." Roxie glanced toward the van, then leaned forward and said in a low voice, "What if the club agrees to only investigate already dead suspects?"

"What do you mean?"

"They only know a few names from the box. The old preacher, for example, died four years ago."

Nick rubbed his neck. "I don't know—"

"If we don't throw them a bone, they'll just get some guy from the cafeteria to drive them all over town. At least with a limit like that, they couldn't cause any real harm."

He looked at the van. Three pairs of binoculars followed his every move. "We do need to keep them out of trouble. OK, Treymayne. I'll go visit Pastor Rawlings's widow this afternoon, and then you all can have it."

Roxie smiled, and it was as if the day had gotten a little warmer, the sky definitely bluer.

"Perfect! Thanks, Nick. I'll keep them in check as well as I can." Roxie turned and climbed in the van. As she slid into the seat, he caught a glimpse of the tattoo on the smooth skin of her lower hip, and a flood of hot, primal urgency flashed through his body.

The force of it shocked him. *This was what Lee must have felt like when he first met Barbara. No wonder he fell so fast.* Fortunately, Nick already knew where this road would go, and he was determined not to take it.

The thought dashed the cool water of reason over his fevered imagination. *She's not the girl for you. She wasn't before and she isn't now, and that tattoo is just one sign that that's so.*

At least he'd been able to see her this time without kissing her. That was some improvement.

Maybe a good five-mile run would keep him focused. He'd make sure he was good and tired from now on, and hopefully that would keep them both out of trouble.

The exact curve of Roxie's ass in her low-cut jeans flashed through his mind, and he decided a five-mile run might not be enough. A five-mile run *and* two hundred sit-ups *and* fifty chin-ups might do the trick. He'd be too sore to move if he did that every day.

But whatever it took, he'd do it.

chapter 11

Dear Bob,
   The 29th Annual Kiwanis Dance and Pig
Roast is coming up. This year two different gentlemen asked me to go.
   I really want to go because I bought
a new dress at the JC Penny's. How do
you think I should handle this without
an ugly incident occurring? I don't
want to cause no fights.
Signed,
Torn Between Two Lovers

Dear Torn Between,
   Whoever you are, you're no Scarlett
O'Hara and the chance of "an ugly incident" breaking out is pretty slim.
I know the boys over at the Kiwanis
pretty good and they're all fairly
mild-mannered.
   I suggest you go with whomever you
want. Personally, I'd make a comparison
chart and pick the guy with the most
horsepower and funding. You can never
go wrong with a man who knows his way
around an engine and a debit card.
Signed,
Bob

The Glory Examiner
Aug. 14, section B3

"THAT BOB'S A REAL smart-ass," Mark said to no one in particular as he spread the newspaper on the porch steps and taped it down. Then he grabbed his paintbrush and began to finish the new railing he'd just nailed into place. Dear Bob obviously knew the town pretty well. It would be worth buying a ticket to the Kiwanis Dance just to watch the carryings-on of Torn Between and her two beaus.

The morning sun warmed his shoulders and he glanced at his watch. At noon he'd head over to the Baptist church and pick up the donations from the Women's Auxiliary's Clothing Drive for Goodwill. After that, he needed to stop by Micki & Maud's Diner to finagle a contribution to the Rotary Bake Sale.

Mother seemed to be on every committee, volunteer and otherwise, that Glory had. No wonder she'd succumbed to an attack. Before the month was out, he'd probably fall ill too, exhausted from toting and carrying for every women's group in town.

The front door opened and Roxie tottered out onto the porch.

Mark looked her up and down. "Somehow I don't think you're going to church."

She was wearing a bright yellow halter top that ended beneath her breasts. Below that, a low-slung, spectacularly short blue jean skirt exposed her long tanned legs.

Her sparkly heeled sandals didn't look as if they'd been designed for walking, much less standing.

"If I wore this to church, the roof would probably fall in. And if it didn't someone would hit on me. Those men in the singles group are terrors."

Mark laughed. "I've heard that. Still, that new preacher's supposed to arrive soon and the Women's Auxiliary say he's a real looker."

"They say the same about you."

He grinned even wider. "I know."

"Mrs. Nabors said you were the cutest thing she and the girls had ever seen."

He placed the paintbrush on the newspaper and used his T-shirt to wipe his brow. "I'm handsome, charming, and I can carry a *lot* of boxes. What's not to love?"

She returned his smile and tottered down the stairs toward the car.

"So where *are* you going?"

"To town." She smirked over her shoulder as she pulled her sunglasses from a huge blue purse and put them on. "I've already completed my chores. The Murder Mystery Club was busy putting together a surveillance chart when I left them this morning."

"Surveillance?"

"Yup. They're going to investigate a real murder." She frowned. "Well, maybe it's not a murder, but it *is* a mysterious death. Doyle Cloyd's, in fact."

"Good for you. Hey, you're not taking the Mustang, are you?"

"Yup."

"But that means I'll have to drive Mother's boat-car!"

"Sorry!" she chirped in a singsong voice that said she was anything but. She slipped into the car and, with a glance up at Mother's window, put the car in neutral.

"Ah!" Mark walked to the car and leaned in, forcing her to stop the car from rolling backward. "It's like that, is it?" He knew just what she'd been about to do. Back in the day he used to do the same thing—release the clutch and let the car drift to the bottom of the drive before starting it so their mother wouldn't hear.

She shot another glance up at the window. "Keep your voice down, will you? Mother wants to talk to me about my hair. I've been avoiding her all morning."

Mark held his tongue. His once prim, never-do-anything-wrong sister was still going through her metamorphosis from starchy Mother's little girl to . . . well, he wasn't sure where she was heading. It was hard to tamp down his protective instincts, but she wouldn't accept his interference and it might push her to do more.

Mark had done the same after Arlene had left, though his debauchery had been more private and had consisted of rum, wearing beach clothing to the accounting firm instead of his usual suit and tie, and letting his beard grow to scruff length.

He guessed Roxie was bursting with the desire to be someone different from the woman who hadn't kept Brian's interest, which could be dangerous. Thank goodness she was in Glory, North Carolina, where it was unlikely her attire would do more than raise the brows of the Women's Auxiliary, send Mother's control gene into Über-Twitch Mode, and maybe drive the town sheriff crazy. Mark was just the tiniest bit sorry for Nick.

Still, he wished she didn't look quite so . . . *available.* "Where are you going?"

"To town. Tundy asked me to get a pecan pie from Micki & Maud's Diner for our supper."

Mark nodded and stood. "All right, just—" He caught the flash in Roxie's eyes and amended his sentence from "be careful" to "—bring me back a latte."

"From Micki & Maud's?"

"Micki's daughter, Connie, has been sprucing up the menu. She used to be a chef in New York, and she let me sample her latte yesterday—wow."

"That explains the pecan pie. Even Tundy thought it was out of this world. See you soon." As she spoke, she let the car go.

It was either move or lose a toe. Mark stepped back and watched as his sister rolled the car down the drive, hitting the engine just as she reached the main street. She seemed to know exactly what she was doing.

Sighing, he turned back to the porch and began to clean up. He needed to let Roxie find her own way.

He removed the taped newspaper that had kept him from dripping paint on the steps. Then he collected his tools and headed for the garage. One good thing about asking Roxie for a latte was that she couldn't stay in town for long or it would get cold.

Mark grinned as he put the paint can back on the shelf and went to rinse the brush in the utility sink. That should keep Roxie out of trouble for today. He'd deal with tomorrow then.

ROXIE PULLED THE MUSTANG into the gas station. Two retro-looking pumps adorned the front of the Safe-Co, a large plastic bin between them sporting the faded words "Red Hand Beef Jerky, a Real Man's Jerky!" Beside the words was an equally faded picture of a Cary Grant look-alike, his lips pulled back in a handsome-man grimace. Some local joker had placed a large wad of gum over one of his eyes.

"Welcome to Glory," Roxie said under her breath as she undid her gas cap and turned to the pump. As she lifted the handle, the wind fluttered a white paper that someone had taped to the pump. "YOU PAY BEFORE PUMP," it read, "THE MANAGEMENT" scrawled beneath. Someone—probably the same person who'd so carefully applied the wad of gum to the ad—had marked out the signature and replaced it with a smug "SATAN."

She chuckled, replaced the nozzle, and headed for the store. Inside, a blast of cool air hit her. This had once been the only gas station in town; now it was one of three. Having lost its supremacy, the owner now offered not only the usual gas, milk, and bread, but also rows and rows of pink shell wind chimes that read "Welcome to Paradise!" hanging over crude pink pottery pigs with "Yeehaw, it's Paradise!" written on their rotund little backs.

Roxie blinked.

Not that she had anything against pigs or chimes, it was the sheer magnitude of the pinkness. Chimes hung from every slat of the dropped ceiling. Spray-painted shells clacked and clattered in the fierce breeze of the air-conditioning. Between the strands of shells were crystals and beads, these painted pink and beige and occasionally, as if one had spoiled, a dark brown.

Roxie blinked around at the assortment, remembering the half empty store from her childhood. It used to astound her that Mr. Rickers ever made enough money to support himself and his family.

She turned in a slow circle, looking for other changes, and her gaze landed on an ice cream display. *Ice cream would be good with pecan pie. Especially* warm *pecan pie.* She picked out two pints of French vanilla, then saw a display of Sweet Donna's Crème Cakes. She might as well get some of those, too. She'd just grabbed a box when a familiar voice stopped her cold in her tracks.

"Roxie! I was wondering when I'd run into you!"

Roxie turned to find a tall, red-haired woman with pale skin, blue eyes, and incredibly high cheekbones holding two boxes of chocolate chunk cookies. Beautiful in a who-needs-makeup way, the woman exuded

casual chic in her jeans and T-shirt in a way most of the
Raleigh Wives would have paid to possess.

"Susan!" Roxie juggled her two pints of ice cream
and box of crème cakes into a better position. "I haven't
seen you since—well, forever."

"It's been since high school. In fact, the last time I saw
you, we weren't speaking because of Brian."

Susan had been Roxie's archrival in high school and
had gone after every guy Roxie'd ever wanted to date,
sometimes with alarming success.

Roxie said, "Well, I certainly won the booby prize
there. You haven't lived until you've caught your husband in bed with another man—especially a man who
looks *far* worse in a pink negligee than you do."

For an instant, Susan looked surprised. But on catching Roxie's wry expression, she laughed, her eyes spar-
kling. "You've changed."

"I hope so," Roxie said fervently. "I daresay we all
have."

Susan chuckled. "We can only hope." She regarded
Roxie frankly. "Now I see why Nick's so fascinated."

"Nick?" A surge of something painfully close to jealousy raced through Roxie.

*But Susan said Nick seemed "fascinated." That isn't
something a girlfriend would say. Not that I should be surprised if Nick did have a girlfriend—should I?*

As if she could read the confusion running through
Roxie's mind, Susan added, "I'm the county dispatcher.
As bosses go, he's pretty laid-back."

The casual note in her voice made Roxie relax. "Oh. So you two work together."

"Yup." Susan's eyes twinkled. "He's been running in circles since you came back to town. I don't think I've ever seen him so flustered."

About *her*? Surely not.

Susan tilted her head to one side. "I never pictured you as a blonde, but it works."

Roxie grinned. "Thank you. It's my Rebel With a Cause look."

Susan chuckled. "Roxie, I'm glad I ran into you."

"Me, too. While I still know a lot of people here in town, I've been gone a long time."

"Lucky you." Susan looked at Roxie for a long time and then set her cookies on a nearby shelf. "Roxie, let's start over. I was a bit of a bitch in high school, and you were a bit of a snob—"

"I was not!"

Susan quirked a brow. "Oh?"

There was something so infinitely *likable* about the way Susan said it, that Roxie found herself laughing. "OK, maybe I was a *little* snobby."

Susan beamed and held her arms wide. "Roxie! I didn't know you were back! How *are* you?"

Roxie dropped her purchases on a nearby shelf and hugged the other woman, laughing. "I'm doing great. So, what are you into these days?"

Looking absurdly pleased, Susan collected her cookies. "As you might remember, I had planned on doing the same thing you did—leaving Glory the second I could."

"Didn't you?"

"No, I stayed to help Dad. I got my associate's degree in journalism, but couldn't find the money or the time to go on for my four-year degree, so now I'm the county emergency dispatcher. It's not much of a job in terms of pay, but at least I'm doing some good for the community."

Roxie remembered how often Susan had announced to the entire cheerleading squad that she planned to "shake the dust of this place" if it was the last thing she did. "A dispatcher? That must be exciting at times."

"Oh, it's a great way to stay in the know," Susan said blithely. "Though between Bertha Clinton's pug, who gets his fat head caught between the porch rails of her house every ten minutes, to Lanie Boswick's husband coming home drunk every Friday, Saturday, and Sunday, I never get to watch TV."

Roxie grinned. "I see some things never change." She collected her ice cream. "Well, I need to check out. I've been ordered to get some pecan pie and a latte from Micki & Maud's."

Susan's eyes brightened. "They have latte?"

"Yup. Mark said Connie gave him a sample the other day."

"Connie's done wonders for the diner." Susan followed Roxie down the aisle. "Hey, if you're free for lunch one day, I'll regale you with all of the scandal that's occurred since you left town."

"I'd really like that." Roxie placed her items on the front counter.

The tall, skinny gentleman behind it was bald and sported a sparse goatee, his arms covered in tattoos.

Roxie blinked. "Where's Mr. Rickers?"

The man looked Roxie up and down and apparently liked what he saw. He leaned forward on one arm and grinned, showing two missing teeth as he said in a broad New Jersey accent, "Mr. Rickers retired. I'm Tony, the new owner."

"Rickers retired about two years ago," Susan added. "No one in town had the money to buy the station, so he sold it on eBay. Tony here bought it."

"Yeah. I bought this place eighteen months, three days and—" He turned to squint at a huge pig clock that hung over the counter. "—six hours ago."

She glanced around. "You've changed some things."

Behind her, Susan said in a low voice, "Oh man, you're going to regret saying that."

Tony beamed and rocked back on his heels. "Yeah, I did. We added that there rack and—" He droned on and on, pointing out each feature in minutia.

Susan giggled.

The second Tony paused to take a breath, Roxie said, "Before I forget, I need some gas, too. Fifteen should do it." She whipped out her credit card and placed it on the counter.

Tony rang up her purchases and the gas. "That'll be twenty-four forty-two." He gestured toward the credit card. "But we don't take those. It's cash only."

"What?"

He pointed to a sign in the front door. It was huge, about the size of her car hood, but somehow the astounding array of wind chimes and pink pigs had blinded her to it.

She replaced the card and began to dig in her purse. Finding a twenty, she waved it in triumph. "Now, I just need four dollars and forty-two cents more."

Tony leaned over the counter, peering into her purse with her, as if his sharper eyes might detect the gleam of a quarter first.

Susan came to stand beside her. "Roxie, do you want to borrow—"

"No, thanks. There's some money in the car. My brother keeps a slew of change in the ashtray." She looked at Tony. "I'll be right back."

He shrugged. "OK."

Roxie hurried out to the car, the heat hitting her in the face as she left the chilly comfort of the store. This was what she got for impulse shopping in a Safe-Co. Sheesh! Next she'd be fishing pennies out of the fountain on the town square.

She'd almost reached the car when a movement to her left made her glance that way. Nick was standing on the sidewalk. He'd apparently been jogging, for he wore loose shorts and running shoes. The hot wind was molding his T-shirt to his muscular arms and chest. *He looks good enough to lick.*

The thought made her shiver, which caused her to stumble, her high heels pushing her forward.

In less than a second, Nick was there, catching her against him.

They stood there, chest to chest, his face inches from hers. Heat radiated from his skin, the damp fabric of his T-shirt sending a primal thrill all the way to her bones.

Roxie's heart pounded in her throat; her skin tingled where his hands gripped her. She couldn't breathe without her chest rubbing against his.

When Roxie slowly stepped out of Nick's arms, he reluctantly let her go. Damn it, he'd run five miles to forget her, and what did he do but find her at the store where he'd stopped for a bottle of water? That was the problem with a town the size of Glory: the only way you could avoid someone was to move away.

She was past him before he knew what to say. She hurried to the Mustang, which was parked at one of the pumps. Though he told himself he should hurry inside, grab a bottle of water, and leave, he lingered on the sidewalk, admiring her trim legs and the shape of her ass under her jeans skirt.

Damn, some things never lost their "good." Like the taste of hot coffee on a cold morning. Or the wonder of the first beam of morning light when it broke over the still waters of a prime fishing pond. Or the tantalizing sight of Roxie Treymayne's legs. He'd followed those legs down the halls of Paradise High School and had felt this same exact heat rising from his—

No. He shouldn't be thinking such things. *Play it cool. She's not for you.*

Yet as he clung to the thought, Roxie leaned in through the window of her car, and dug in her ashtray for change.

She was bent at the waist, her ass lifted by the edge of the door, her feet barely touching the ground. One shoe had fallen off; her foot aimlessly searched for it. Her thighs were smooth and tanned, as was the rest of her. It must have taken some work to get a tan like that. But then, what else was a lawyer's wife to do besides tan and play tennis?

His gaze narrowed as he noticed her hand clutching the car door, defining her arm muscles. She played a *lot* of tennis. He wondered what she'd look like naked now, for she seemed more toned than when they'd been in high school. Toned, slim, and more wanton—every short inch of her skirt held out a promise.

Nick unconsciously moved a little closer, gritting his teeth against the wave of lust that hit him. She'd been too damn hot for her own good before, and now she was downright irresistible. She unconsciously called him and sent him away at the same time.

She wiggled a bit and he caught a glimpse of the top of her tattoo over the band of her skirt. Hot damn, what *was* that tattoo, anyway? He stepped closer still, tilting his head to one side. Was it a tu—

"Got it!" Roxie pushed herself out of the car, her shoulder almost banging into Nick's chin.

She held up a fistful of change and beamed. "Four dollars and forty-two cents!"

Susan came out of the store carrying two bags, Tony following her.

Roxie grinned and crossed to hand her change to him. "Here you go—exact change."

"Great." Tony took the money, though Nick noticed the man didn't bother to count it. His gaze was stuck on Roxie's cleavage. "Susan here said you were Mrs. Treymayne's daughter and—" Nick's impatient move drew Tony's gaze away from Roxie's chest.

Tony's cheeks reddened and he grinned sheepishly. "Oh, uh. Hi, Nick. Out running?"

"Yes," Nick replied smoothly. "I was out running."

Susan smirked. "You seem to be doing a lot of that lately." A blue BMW swung into the parking lot and she winced. "I knew it was too good a day to last."

The BMW pulled up to the store, the door swung open, and Robin stepped out.

"Oh no!" Susan breathed and grabbed Nick's arm tightly.

"What?"

"Look at what she's *wearing*!"

He looked at Robin and shrugged.

"Nick, she has on a blue jean skirt *and* a yellow tank top. *Just like Roxie.*"

Nick glanced over at Roxie, who stood as if glued in place. "Roxie has on a halter top."

"It's the same color, though. *Someone* will have to go home and change."

Robin's gaze locked on Roxie and her stance stiffened, her hands balling into fists at her side.

"What's happening?" Nick asked Susan in a low voice.

"I have no idea," she returned, looking from Robin to Roxie and then back.

Robin suddenly straightened her shoulders and stuck out her chest.

Tony's eyes widened until they looked as if they might pop out of his head.

"Whoa!" Susan breathed.

Even Nick recognized the challenge.

Roxie smiled smugly and threw back her own shoulders. Her full breasts strained the thin yellow fabric of her halter top.

Tony made a *gack* sound deep in his throat, his mouth now hanging open.

Nick's body tightened even more.

Robin's mouth thinned. She deliberately reached down and adjusted her skirt, yet more of her legs appearing. She had nice legs, but they didn't compare to Roxie's.

He swung his gaze toward Roxie. Her entire attention was focused on Robin.

"Zowee," Susan breathed. "I hope Roxie's wearing panties."

Panties? The world stood still. As if in slow motion, Nick watched as Roxie adjusted her own skirt, moving it until the tops of her thighs showed. She didn't expose her panties—or lack thereof—but the sight was as tantalizing as if she had.

Nick wished he had a newspaper or something to hide his reaction, but fortunately for him, all eyes were on Roxie and Robin.

Robin sniffed, apparently unimpressed. She reached up and undid her hair, the long, dark length falling around her, a cloud of black silk that clung to her shoulders and caressed the curves of her breasts.

"Dios mio!" Tony breathed.

Nick barely managed to keep his own heavy breathing under control.

Everyone looked at Roxie. She reached up and pulled her ponytail holder from her hair. Blonde tresses tumbled down to her shoulders. She reached up and, with a casual flick of her wrist, mussed her hair.

"Ahhhhh," Tony breathed, entranced as the sun gleamed off Roxie's golden hair, which now artfully suggested the effects of early morning sex.

"Oooo," Susan said. "That was a good move."

Robin's gaze narrowed. She placed her hands on either side of her breasts and slooooowly slid them down to her thighs, caressing every curve.

Roxie did the same, though she began at the bottom.

Her hands slowly moved from her trim thighs, up her narrow waist, to her full breasts. Then she gave a little hop that made her breasts jiggle so enticingly that Tony gasped aloud.

Nick deliberately stepped hard on his own foot, the pain focusing his fuzzy mind. Broken toe or not, it was worth it not to make a total fool of himself.

Her face storm dark, Robin glared at Roxie, then whirled on her heel, threw herself back into her car, slammed the door, revved the engine and, tires squealing, zoomed out of the parking lot.

"What . . . ? I don't understand," Nick said.

Susan looked at him as if he was a half inch from stupid. "Robin's breasts are fake. They don't *bounce*."

"Ah." Nick watched as Roxie, grinning proudly, accepted the bag of groceries from a now-stuttering Tony.

After pumping the gas, with a quick wave and glance at Nick, Roxie hopped into her car and left.

Susan sighed. "That was priceless. I've wanted to see Robin put in her place so many times." She grinned. "I'm damn glad Roxie came back. We needed her here."

Nick wasn't so sure of that. "I'd better finish my run."

Susan looked surprised. "It's about four miles to your house."

Four miles wouldn't be far enough, but it would be a start. "See you tomorrow." He gathered himself and took off.

"Nick!" Susan called after him. "Why are you limp-ing—"

"Tomorrow!" he returned, continuing grimly on. Foot hurt, thirsty as hell, he still couldn't stomp out the images burned into his brain.

Susan might be glad Roxie had returned to Glory, but Nick only wished things would go back to normal—slow, peaceful, and safe.

chapter 12

WHEN ROXIE TOOK CLARA and the others to visit Mrs. Rawlings, wife of the late Pastor Rawlings, the gang was on their best behavior.

It helped that Nick had already been there. In smug tones, Mrs. Rawlings told Clara how she'd snubbed "the law." Apparently she was under the impression that anything she said to Nick might "besmirch" her husband's name.

Clara and the others exclaimed over the effrontery of present-day law enforcement, fondly remembered old Sheriff Thompson, who had taken up fly-fishing since his retirement, and wondered about the town's safety without an older, more mature man wearing the badge.

Roxie had to hide a giggle at how willing Clara was to throw her nephew under the bus, but the ploy worked. Within an hour, Mrs. Rawlings disclosed the reason for Doyle's blackmailing the pastor: Rawlings had been addicted to bingo and had gamed away not only his wife's retirement fund but also a good chunk of the church's building fund.

No wonder the Baptist Church used to have bingo six nights a week.

Roxie asked if it was possible for them to look at the pastor's old bank records for the last year he was alive and Mrs. Rawlings agreed to call when she found them. She was almost pathetically eager to help once Clara promised to mention Mrs. Rawlings if they ever made a movie of the club's exploits.

"You know," Mrs. Rawlings said, pink with pleasure, "when I was younger, I do think I looked a bit like that nice Angelina Jolie!"

Eventually the tea grew cold, C.J. ate the last cookie, and it was time to leave. Roxie drove the club back to the assisted living center, where she spent another hour locating Styrofoam cups for the club's evening bourbon tasting and then "walking" Pumper. This consisted of putting him in a big box marked Rice Pudding that C.J. had stolen from the cafeteria, carrying the dog outside, dumping him out of the box, letting him relieve himself, rolling him back into the box, then carrying him back inside to sleep away the rest of the day. Using their special bourbon stash, Clara paid one of the cafeteria workers, a very helpful ex-con by the name of Elbow Jones, to take Pumper for his evening "walk."

By the time Roxie left, a nursing assistant had come to take Clara to her daily physical therapy, Rose was off to a knitting class, and C.J. was sound asleep in a chair by Pumper's bed.

A bit tired herself, Roxie climbed into the Mustang

and headed home. The tires scrunched the graveled country road, the engine whining softly.

What a day! Who knew that her wheelchaired, slightly paranoid, and snippy friends were natural interrogators? Mrs. Rawlings hadn't been able to talk fast enough, and C.J. had had the dickens of a time taking notes.

Clara still thought the mayor was the #1 suspect, saying there was just "something" about him. Rose and C.J. had readily agreed.

It was possible, though Roxie had trouble imagining the weak-chinned mayor having the balls to do away with someone.

Robin Wright was another story. Hard-eyed and tough, she gave the impression that she'd do anything in order to protect the mayor and their secrets.

But what secrets could they have? Everyone knew they were having an affair; it was old news by now. But they had to be hiding something.

Roxie shook her head and turned her car onto a back road that would take her home without having to go through the town square. At this time of day, it would be clogged with the lunch crowd all trying to park at the diner.

As she turned onto the road, a wisp of smoke seeped from her hood. "Oh, no!" The little wisp was not alone for long; soon clouds of smoke bellowed from the engine. Roxie glanced down at her dash and saw the ominous red engine light glaring at her. She swung the car onto the side of the road just in time. The car wheezed, gurgled, then made a loud *BANG!* as smoke poured from under the hood.

Roxie flung open the door and got out, glaring at the cloud of smoke as the engine hissed. Darn it all! She'd have to call someone and get a ride home. She plopped back into the car and slammed the door, then began fishing in her purse for her phone. She flipped it open and glared at the screen. "And of *course* there's no signal." She tossed the phone back into her purse, mumbling, "Oh, you'll work every time I'm upstairs with Mother and you're downstairs, won't you? And every time I dash outside to get the mail. And if I happen to go to the bathroom. But work when I need you? Ha!" She slapped her purse closed and eyed her high-heeled sandals with a dubious gaze. "I guess I'm going to have to walk my way out of this one."

The sound of a car approaching made her look up. In her rearview mirror, a green-and-white squad car came into view. "No!" She slid down in the seat until she wasn't visible from the road. *Please keep going. Please keep going. Please keep going. Please keep go—*

Gravel crunched behind her car as Nick pulled in behind her.

Great! Now here she was lying down in the seat. If she sat up, it would look odd. If she stayed where she was, it would look odder yet. Maybe Nick wouldn't get out of his car. Maybe he'd just call in the apparently abandoned car and—

"Are you sleeping in there?"

Damn it, she hadn't heard his car door. Grumbling to herself, she sat upright. "I was looking for my cell phone."

Nick rested his folded arms on the open window and smiled, his eyes crinkling agreeably. "Looked to me like you were hiding."

"I," she said loftily, "do not hide."

"Then why were you hunkered down on the seat?"

"I don't hunker, either."

He sent her a disbelieving look that she pointedly ignored. With a grin, he gestured to the smoke pouring from her hood. "So the Mustang finally gave up the ghost?"

"I hope not. I don't want to drive Mother's boat of a car on these narrow roads."

"Let's take a look at her, then. Pop that hood."

She bent and did as he asked, then went to join him at the front of the car. As soon as he lifted the hood, clouds of smoke roiled into the air.

Nick walked past her to the other side of the car, glancing at her sideways from beneath his lashes. It was a trick he used to do when passing her in the hallways at high school, and it had always left her breathless and aware. That same glance had an even stronger effect now.

Her entire body tightened; her skin prickled; her nipples hardened. She caught his gaze on her thin shirt, and her cheeks pinkened still more. She reached into the car to open the trunk. "There's a rag in a box back here. I've seen Mark use it when he changes the oil." She fished around until she found it, then brought it to Nick, who stood looking under the hood, smoke drifting around him.

On its own, her gaze was drawn to his ass. Her fingers itched with the urge to touch him. *Get a grip, Treymayne!*

He straightened and wiped his hands on the rag. "Your water hose broke. That happens in these old cars. I'll call Dan's Tow and Mow to pick it up."

"Tow and Mow?"

He grinned, looking too appealing by far when the wind ruffled his hair. For a cop, he certainly didn't wear his hair military style; she rather liked that.

Nick closed the hood. "In a small town like this, it sometimes takes more than one angle to keep your business in the black."

"Shouldn't we let the smoke out?"

"It's just steam. I'll have Dan tow it to the gas station on old 41. They still do repairs, and this shouldn't take too much."

"And?"

He raised his brows. "And what?"

"Well, it's Dan's Tow and Mow. The hair salon's the Stuff 'n Fluff. What's the gas station?"

He grinned. "Bob's Engine Repair and Ballet Studio."

"You're kidding me."

"Actually, yes. Bob's Engine Repair is beside Claudia Banks's Dance Studio. The building's owned by Claudia, if you remember her?"

Roxie had an instant memory of a small brunette with big brown eyes. "I do; she used to be captain of the school's dance squad."

"That's her. She bought the old Ford place when it closed. It's a pretty big structure, so she turned half of it into a dance studio and leases the other half of the building to Bob Little for automotive repairs."

Roxie laughed, and Nick's eyes crinkled. "Come on; I'll give you a ride. You headed home?"

She hesitated. The last place she should be was in a car with Nick Sheppard and his cute ass.

He flashed a grin. "Come on, Treymayne. It's on my way."

"Nick, you were going the opposite direction."

"I was going to the assisted living center to find you. So if you're going this direction, so am I. Hop in the car and I'll explain."

Sighing, Roxie collected her purse from the car and locked it up, handing the key to Nick.

He placed it on top of the front tire away from the road. Then he followed her to his car, reaching past her to open the door. "Your chariot awaits."

Roxie slid into the seat and looked around with interest. It was an older car, surprisingly similar to her mother's. The seats were cheap vinyl, the floor mats generic, and the dash faded from years of being parked outside. The dash had a radio and a number of switches, one of which had to be for the police lights. The surprising thing was the computer sitting on a docking station and pushed against the dash.

Nick climbed behind the wheel.

"What's the computer for?"

"To check tags, send information to the office for Susan to look at, and see what's happening in other parts of the area. I can send an alert out if I have an emergency, too, and get some backup if I need it."

"Wow. That's impressive."

"It's not my Camaro, but it'll do."

Her heart thundered a bit louder. "You still have your Camaro?"

His gaze slid over her. "Of course. It has too many memories to let go of it."

Her nipples tightened. Lord yes, that car had memories.

"I came close to selling it once. I almost got married, and it seemed a waste of garage space. But it didn't work out, and I was glad I'd kept it after all."

She couldn't help herself. "You almost got married? When? What happened?"

He turned the car down a narrow road. "A long time ago. There's a very high divorce rate among cops. I didn't want to be a statistic, and there were some signs that it wasn't the right thing so . . . I ended it."

He'd almost *married*. She didn't know why that bothered her—she'd gotten married and divorced, for heaven's sake—but the information was an unpleasant surprise. Beyond shock, she also felt something far less attractive. Not quite jealousy—more like bitter envy that someone had gotten that close to him. "You always said you'd never marry."

"I also used to say that the Buccaneers would never win a Super Bowl, and look where that prediction ended up."

She tried not to notice his hands on the wheel, but she couldn't help it. Lean and strong, they were unmistakably masculine and all Nick. Darn it, she wanted control, discipline, power—not tingling awareness and flashbacks to a youthful crush.

"Do you always clench your fists when someone is giving you a ride?"

She flattened her hands on her knees. "No, I was just thinking about something. I'm sorry to hear about your breakup."

"In a way, I think we were both relieved. Besides, she got over it quick enough. She got married less than a year later to a buddy of mine on the force."

"Another cop?"

"I think she was something of a badge bunny, though I didn't realize it at the time." He slanted her an amused glance. "Anything else you want to know? I might still have a picture of her somewhere, if you want me to look."

Her cheeks heated. "I'm sorry. I didn't mean to pry."

"Yes, you did, but that's OK. The cop world is a small, tightly knit community. I call it 'As The Blue Light Turns.' "

She smiled. "Lots of drama?"

"More than there should be. Citizens aren't always comfortable socializing around cops, and frankly, after a while you get tired of every John and Jane telling you about the time they got a speeding ticket they didn't deserve, or asking for legal advice as if you were a free attorney. Add to that all of the people who can't go out for drinks with you without saying loudly to the waiter, 'Oops! Better check my ID or Nick here might have to arrest you.' "

"Real jokers, hm?"

He shrugged. "People get nervous. Anyway, add all of that up, and after a while you stop associating with non-cops. Once that happens, you tend to feel like part of an exclusive club and that no one on the outside understands you. It's only natural that there's a lot of hooking up within that world."

"I would imagine so," Roxie said.

"But that's all old history. I was coming out to see you because I've received a complaint."

"About *me*?"

"And Aunt Clara's club. An hour ago, the mayor stormed into my office. He says you and the gang went to see Mrs. Rawlings this morning and announced that he was your number one suspect."

She blinked. "Wow, word gets around fast."

"Yep. Widow Rawlings and her cronies play bridge at Micki & Maud's every Wednesday, and she informed the entire place—including the mayor's aunt—about the club's suspicions. The mayor and his aunt have never gotten along, and she latched onto the club's suspicions and began to remember all sorts of discreditable stories from the mayor's youth that might be interpreted as signs that he suffers from severe depravity."

"Family can be so cruel."

Nick shot her a hard look. "The mayor says that if you all don't stop, he'll sue the lot of you for defamation of character."

"He's getting nervous," she said with satisfaction.

"Roxie, this could be serious. I'm going to talk to Clara, but I need your promise not to rile things up more, and to keep a check on what they say while you're taking them around town."

"I'll try, but I can't promise anything. You know your aunt."

"Yes, I do," he said grimly.

"I hate that the mayor's on a tear. We got a ton of info from Widow Rawlings. She was very talkative."

"Talkative?" He shot her an astonished glance. "I couldn't even get her to tell me the weather!"

"That's because she was sure you'd tarnish her beloved Harry's good name."

Nick grimaced. "Being a cop in Glory is like being the only dog at a cat party. You'd think they were all still making moonshine and I was a revenuer."

She chuckled and fished in her purse for C.J.'s note-book. Somehow, she'd become the official notebook keeper. "Here's what she told us. We asked Suspect #2's wife—"

"Suspect #2?"

"Pastor Rawlings." She returned to her notes. "We asked the widow of Suspect #2 what Doyle might have on her husband—" Nick made a small noise, and she frowned at him. "What?"

"Nothing. Go ahead."

"OK. The widow told us that Pastor Rawlings was addicted to gaming. He'd stolen from their personal re-tirement account and had tapped into the church build-ing fund."

"That's interesting. Did anyone know?"

"Just Doyle. At the time of Pastor's Rawling's death, his improprieties with the building fund were just com-ing to light."

"That explains why he tried to make the church bal-lots look like bingo cards. Other than that, I don't know what it might prove. Not yet, anyway."

"Doyle wrote that he'd received money from the pas-tor."

"So?"

"His widow is going to give us her husband's old bank records to show all of his withdrawals. If you can get Doyle's bank records, and we can match the with-drawals to the deposits, then we'll know for sure if the pastor is a possible suspect in Doyle's murder."

Nick slowed the car down and turned into the parking lot of the First Baptist Church.

"What are you doing?"

"I don't want to drive into a ditch while you explain how you and that group of crazies have made the jump from blackmail to murder without any evidence whatsoever." Nick pulled the squad car into a space under a tree, put it in park, and turned to face her. "Go ahead."

"But the bank records will be evidence!"

"Of blackmail. Not murder."

"Motive is a key component."

"So are many other things, like opportunity. Pastor Rawlings had nothing to do with Doyle's death."

"*Suspicious* death."

"Whatever you call it, the pastor wasn't involved. He was in a coma in the hospital when Doyle died, and had been for weeks."

Roxie looked down at her notes. "Oh." And he'd made such a good suspect. She found a pen in her purse and crossed the preacher's name off her list.

Nick rubbed his face. "Roxie, I thought it would be OK if you and Clara's group just puttered about and asked a few questions, but that's not what happened."

"It is too what happened. I was there!"

"No, what happened is that Clara rolled into Widow Rawlings's house and announced there'd been a murder—which we don't even know is true, as it's very possible Doyle's death was a simple hit and run. But then Clara proceeded to question people with one object in mind—to prove that her theory is true, that Doyle was murdered because of this blackmail scheme. When you look for evidence to support one theory, you're very likely to misinterpret information and miss the truth. Worse, you might unwittingly lead others into giving false witness."

Roxie bit her lip. He had a point. Some of Clara's questions might have been a little leading. Well, OK, more than a little. "I suppose that's true."

"Everyone in town is talking. And as these things get repeated, they get changed and exaggerated and told with such authority that people begin to accept the rumors as fact. It's no wonder the mayor feels he's been violated."

"He used that word? Violated?"

"Repeatedly. Worse, he might be on to something. His complaints might bear fruit in a civil court."

Nick regarded her solemnly, his gray gaze locked on her face. He had the most beautiful eyes. She didn't know if it was the rich, shimmery color, the shape, or his long lashes, or all three, but the combination was potent.

Suddenly breathless, she said, "Yes?"

"I need your cooperation in this case, but more importantly, I want you to be careful. I don't want any of you on the wrong side of a lawsuit."

"I agree, but there *are* questions that need to be asked. Someone should ask the mayor where he was the night of the murder—"

"Death."

"—and did he have any reason not to want Doyle alive—"

"Roxie!"

"—and did he know why he was listed in Doyle's blackmail notes."

"That's another thing. When you have evidence, you don't *tell* everyone about it."

"That's not my fault. Before I could say a word about how important Doyle's notes might be, Clara and Rose had already gone to the hairdresser's and told everyone."

"I wish I could close that place down just for passing incorrect information, gossiping, and starting hysteria," Nick said disgustedly. "It would solve a lot of this town's problems."

Roxie sighed. With the car turned off, the warm sunshine spilling in, and birds twittering in the tree above, the setting was idyllic. Her conversation with Nick, not so much. "I'll try to keep Clara and Rose from ruining things."

To her surprise, he reached over and brushed her cheek with the back of his hand. "Thank you." He gave her a lopsided smile that made her all warm and snuggly.

She had to fight the urge to lean into his hand. The feel of his skin against hers sent her emotions tumbling, and she looked at him, wanting much more than he offered.

He froze, and his eyes flared with something. Then his jaw hardened and he dropped his hand and straightened in his seat. "We'd better get going. Mark will think you've been kidnapped."

He started the car.

Roxie hid her disappointment with a shrug. "I have a lot to do, too." For a heart-stopping second, she'd been certain Nick had been about to kiss her.

She cleared her throat. "About the case—I don't know if it matters, but there is one more thing I figured out."

He turned the car back onto the road. "What's that?"

"I know how Doyle found out the information for this blackmail scheme."

"How?"

She opened the notebook to a page in the back. "You know Tick Hamlin?"

"Sure. He ran that bait shop for years."

"His son is in prison."

"Tick told me that Herb's got a job as director of some fancy resort in the Bahamas."

"That's what he's telling everyone, but Herb's in for grand theft auto in Alabama and has twenty-four more months to go."

"That's interesting, but I don't see how—"

"Do you remember old Preacher Duncan?"

"From when we were kids? Barely."

"Round, fat man. The church didn't like his style

and they sent him packing after only a year. He was moved to Ohio, and last year his wife was arrested for making online pornographic movies on a site named preacherswife.com. Fortunately, she'd made so much money that they could afford a good lawyer, who got her off on a technicality. Somehow the church never found out, and he's now in a church in Alabama." She looked at Nick. "Do you want to know more? Because I have a whole page of it."

"Roxie, how did you find all of this out?"

"Every time I go to the cafeteria at the center to fetch snacks for your aunt and her friends, I walk by all of these hard-of-hearing folks who are speaking at the top of their voices to their friends and telling every family secret they can think of."

Nick looked stunned. "Good God."

"I heard Clara tell Rose that when you were six, you used to like to play with—"

"I'm sure you did." Nick's ears were red. "My aunt has no sense of decorum."

"She's a bit deficient in that area."

Nick frowned, seeming to think her hypothesis through. "So you think Doyle—"

"Was gleaning information from the old people at the center, and maybe blackmailing their family members." Roxie frowned. "Or maybe he thought he was blackmailing them—I'm not sure about his mental abilities. I don't remember a lot about him, but he didn't seem to be all there."

Nick sent her a hard look. "You knew Doyle?"

"He was one of Mother's pet projects for a while. He'd come to dinner now and then, and was always making odd comments. She couldn't stand him, but . . . well, you know Mother."

"She thought she could force him into more acceptable behavior."

"I believe the term you're looking for is 'browbeat.'"

"I can imagine. What I can't imagine is that someone could actually collect enough information at the assisted living center to be a successful blackmailer."

"Who said he was successful? The information you'd hear at the center wouldn't all be true, of course, but if you knew your sources well enough, you could dig up enough information to make a run at it."

"I'd say he was pretty successful. We added up all of those receipts, and if they're true, then over three years, Doyle Cloyd collected over $420,000 from various members of the town."

Roxie gawked. "You're kidding me!"

"Nope. There's not a person of influence in this town who hasn't been touched by Doyle."

"I can't believe no one knew."

"I've got the old case files, but they're sketchy so I'm going to talk with Sheriff Thompson this evening and ask about the investigation. Perhaps people did know, but no one would make an official complaint."

"I could see that. Appearances are important in a small town."

"Especially Glory."

"Especially with my mother." She sent him a look from under her lashes. "So . . . what other names are in that box?"

He turned the car into her driveway. "A lot."

She didn't move. "Nick, that's not the way things work."

He parked the car. "Oh? And how do things work?"

"Like this: I told you everything I know, so now you have to tell me everything you know."

"No."

Irritation flashed in her eyes.

"Why not?" she demanded.

"Because I'd rather work this alone." One of the benefits of coming to Glory was that he had free rein over his work. "It's for your own safety."

"Some of it has to be public record!"

He shrugged. "If you stop by the office, I'll have Susan hook you up with the request to see the ME report."

"ME?"

"Medical examiner."

"I'll come by tomorrow morning and pick up what's available." she said stiffly, throwing open the door.

"OK. It's not much, but you and any other citizen who requests reports are welcome to them." He came around the car as she was gathering her purse. "If you make it by eight, I'll take you to Micki & Maud's for a cup of coffee before you head out to the assisted living center."

She flashed him a hot, disbelieving look. "No, thank you."

Nick sighed. "Roxie, there are other issues beyond confidentiality." *Like how hard it is for me to keep my hands off you, even though you're angry at me.*

She stepped up to him, her toes almost touching his, her breasts brushing his shirt. "The truth is that you don't trust me. Well, fine! But don't expect me to share any more information with you."

The brush of her breasts against his chest flooded his body with pure, hot, lust. In that instant, he forgot everything—where he was, what they were doing, why she was angry. Without another thought, he slid his hands about her waist and jerked her forward against him, then he kissed her with every ounce of passion that pounded through his veins.

For a second she remained stiff and unwelcoming, but then she gave a muffled moan and arched against him, her arms twining about his neck, her hips pressing forward.

Passion and heat, fate and fury poured into the kiss, melding them exquisitely. Nick's hand traveled over her back, slipping down to her ass as he lifted her against him. God, she was so sensual, so perfectly made, filling his hands and making him crazed.

Suddenly Roxie stiffened, and Nick reluctantly released her.

Roxie stepped back, her cheeks flushed, her lips swollen from his kiss. "You shouldn't have . . . I mean, that should never have happened," she stammered.

Her words hit him like a bucket of ice water. She was right. He was in full uniform and on the clock, not to mention the fact that he was also in full view of the entire neighborhood.

Nick's stomach tightened. It was yet more evidence of why Roxie Treymayne should be off limits.

She wet her lips nervously and began to back up the walk. "Nick, I . . . Thank you for the ride."

"Roxie, I'm sorry—"

"So am I," she said, seeming to recollect herself as her eyes sparkled with anger. "Let me give you a little advice, Sheppard."

"What's that?" he asked, knowing he wasn't going to like the answer.

"Don't kiss a woman you don't trust enough to share an investigation with. She'll just tell you to keep your wandering tongue to yourself."

"Roxie, look, I didn't mean to—"

But she'd already turned and was halfway up the walk, her shoulders back. Despite himself, he found himself watching her ass as she marched away, a tantalizing bit of her tattoo once again peeking between her waistband and her shirt where his wandering hands had rumpled it.

One day, he'd have to check out that tattoo up close. Perhaps with his lips—

Damn it, that's the sort of thinking that'll make a mess of your life! Just let her go.

She stomped up the stairs and into her house. When the door slammed behind her, he returned to his car.

Furious with himself for his lack of control, he slid behind the wheel.

The problem was that he was only human, and she was a thoroughly tantalizing woman. Every time they were together, the pull of attraction grew stronger.

As he sat there lost in thought, a sleek Audi pulled up and Ty Henderson got out dressed in one of his Italian suits. Ty walked around Nick's car as if it hadn't been there, flicking a faint smile Nick's way as he made his way to the front door, the sun glinting off his titanium watch and cuff links.

"Jackass," Nick spat, putting his car in gear and backing out of the drive.

As he did so, the front door opened and he caught sight of Roxie before Ty disappeared into the house and the door closed.

"Way to go, Sheppard," he told himself bitterly. "You're the king of smooth. Not only have you made her furious, but now she's going to continue investigating the stupid case."

He'd seen the flash in her eyes and knew exactly what she was thinking; she'd show him.

The problem was, he was beginning to think she already had.

chapter 13

"Mmm, mmm. Miss Roxie's done got herself a beau!"

Roxie turned from peeking out the curtains at Ty's retreating figure. "I do not."

Tundy chuckled, her plump figure encased in a lime green velour jogging suit. In Raleigh, Roxie had only seen Tundy in the uniform provided by the maid service. She was now profoundly grateful for that fact.

Tundy pulled back the curtain and waved. "Bye, Mr. Not-No-Beau!"

Roxie grabbed the curtain and yanked it closed. "Tundy! Will you stop that?"

"I don't know why you're so shy. He's a hottie!"

Roxie had to agree. Ty also seemed like a genuinely nice guy, and not once had he touched her beyond a lingering handshake when he'd first arrived—which was a nice break after Nick's too-physical presence.

She couldn't believe he'd kissed her, and with so much passion that her skin still quivered with the memory, as if his large, warm hands were still stroking her back and molding her to his hard body.

She shivered. It was a good thing Ty had come. Not only had his presence forced her to calm down but he'd also soothed her vanity.

Why couldn't Nick be more like Ty, who'd spent a good hour recalling past times, asking her about her activities since she'd arrived in Glory, and paying her extravagant compliments? Not once had he treated her like an imbecile or suggested that she couldn't be trusted. In fact, he'd looked at her as if he thought she could do anything she wanted.

"Yo' momma sure likes that Mr. Henderson. She said he was a catch."

"Which is a good reason to be leery of him." After all, Mother had liked Brian, too.

Tundy beamed. "You are coming along nicely, Miss Roxie. Mr. Blondie-Locks can't compare to that hot cop."

"Nick is not hot."

Tundy lifted her brows so high that they almost disappeared into her red curls.

Roxie sighed. "Oh, all right. He's hot! But at least Mr. Henderson doesn't act like I can't *do* anything—like, oh, conduct an investigation. I bet Clara and the Murder Mystery Club would have better luck solving this case than anyone else in this town, including Sheriff High-and-Mighty Sheppard!"

"Miz Roxie, you done gone *CSI* on me and I didn't

even know it!" Tundy shook her head. "Not that I'm surprised. You was like a bulldog once you got wind that Mr. Parker was cat walking on you. I never seen such a determined woman in my life."

"You think I could be a good investigator?"

"The way you nosed out Mr. Parker and his shenanigans? Honey, you're a natural."

Roxie sat a little straighter. "Thank you, Tundy. I appreciate your confidence."

"That Mr. Henderson seemed to think you could do it, too. Or he did when he wasn't busy tellin' you about how runnin' the newspaper was puttin' him on good footin' with all the local power people, and soon he'd be runnin' for election himself." Tundy stretched, her pale, freckled stomach showing between her velour top and sweatpants. "It's almost four, isn't it? Yo' momma and I are making matzo ball soup."

Roxie gaped. "You're kidding."

"Nope. The only way to get her out of bed is to convince her that the whole house is going to rack and ruin without her, and that includes meals. Four days ago, I stopped cooking good stuff and started making the worst crap you ever tasted. Now she's coming downstairs to show me how to do it right."

"But she's never made matzo ball soup."

"That's what she tol' me, too, but she says she has a recipe in a book, and if she sits with me in the kitchen while I make it, I might not mess it up too bad."

"Tundy, you're amazing."

"I think so, too, seein' as how I'm handmaiden to the devil. I don't know whether to call a doctor or an exorcist, though I'm leanin' toward the exorcist." Tundy grinned and headed for the kitchen.

Chuckling, Roxie sat by the window and picked up one of the old yearbooks she'd dug out at Ty's request. She began to flip through the pages, stopping when she came to a picture of Nick. He was nineteen, leaning on his Camaro in the school parking lot, scowling at the camera. It was a very James Dean pose, and the black-and-white photo played it up.

His hair shadowed his gray eyes, his jaw was angular as only a youth's can be, and he looked dark and sullen—the kind of bad boy mothers warned their daughters about.

"He's no good, that one," Mother had warned her. "He'll pretend he loves you but will be on to the next girl so fast it'll give you a whiplash."

For once, Mother had been right. Roxie and Nick had shared four glorious weeks of forbidden passion. Incredible, romantic, intimate weeks during which she'd shared herself as she'd never shared herself before. Then they'd had an argument, and within one day, he was with another girl.

Roxie had been devastated as only a love-struck teen could be. She flipped a page in the yearbook and found a picture of herself, dressed in her cheerleading uniform and a fake smile. Mother loved that picture, but Roxie couldn't stand it.

She slammed the book closed and stood, replacing it

and the other albums on the shelf. *Enough of this! Stop moping. What you need is a good dose of chocolate.*

With that thought, she wandered into the kitchen, only to pull up short when she saw Mother sitting at the kitchen table reading through a recipe in her tattered old cookbook. Though still attired in a housecoat, her hair was perfectly coiffed, her red lipstick applied with a careful and expert hand.

"Mother, you're up!"

"Yes, dear. Why? Did you need something?"

Tundy removed a chicken from the fridge shelf and closed the door with a flip of her foot. "Maybe Miss Roxie came to get me something to drink to help me numb the pain of this experience?"

Mother flipped a page in the cookbook. "You don't need a drink. I'm going to help you with the matzo ball soup, and then you'll be able to make it anytime you want. Before we start our chicken stock, reach in the cabinet by the sink and find that large iron pot."

Tundy's answer was lost in the melee of pans as she dove under the counter for the requested pot.

Roxie dropped into a chair beside Mother. She leaned over and said in a low voice, "Matzo ball soup?"

To her surprise, there was a twinkle in Mother's eyes as she whispered back, "Somehow Miss Tundy is under the impression that I'm Jewish."

"Didn't you correct her?"

"I was going to, but she's had such a good time trying to cook kosher and using Yiddish that—"

"Yiddish?"

"Oh yes. She managed to work the term 'schmaltz' into a sentence twice today. I decided this might be a learning experience for her." Mother eyed Tundy with a surprising amount of determination and—was that *affection*? "She's a lovely woman, but she could use a little polishing."

Poor Tundy! Roxie'd had that same polishing when she'd been a child. She wondered who would win.

Tundy found the pan and set it on the stove, then pulled a saltshaker from the cabinet.

"What are you doing?" Mother asked.

"I'm gonna put salt in the water for the chicken stock."

"You don't know how much yet."

"I don't need a recipe for how much salt goes in chicken stock. I've been makin' that since I was a babe."

"But," Mother said in a precise voice, "we are making it the way the *recipe* tells us to."

Tundy opened her mouth but then clamped it closed. She banged the saltshaker onto the counter and plopped a hand onto her hip.

Good God, it's Godzilla meets Momzilla. Roxie hid her eyes and waited.

"Miz Treymayne, if you wasn't a sick woman, I'd—" Tundy seemed to struggle in silence a moment before she snapped in a tight voice, "Very well, how much salt does that recipe of yours say?"

Mother looked at the recipe. "One half teaspoon, but we don't add it until later. For now, you should chop two cups of carrots."

Tundy harrumphed but found a knife and pulled the carrots from the fridge.

Mother turned to Roxie. "Did that nice Ty Henderson leave? I was hoping he'd stay for dinner."

"No. He was on his way to a meeting at the newspaper office."

"It was very sweet of him to visit." Mother slid a glance at Roxie. "When you were in high school, I always wondered why you and Ty didn't make a go of it."

"Because I couldn't stand him. He was so conceited."

Mother smoothed the page in the recipe book. "He doesn't seem conceited now. Perhaps you should call and ask him to dinner?"

Roxie gaped. "Mother," she said slowly. "Are you suggesting that I should be interested in Ty *now*?"

Mother's cheeks pinkened. "Why not? You're not married."

Silence met this, followed by the busy thunk of Tundy's knife. Roxie glared at Tundy's back, but the maid had suddenly become very busy chopping carrots.

"I see," Roxie said loudly.

Tundy flinched but didn't turn around.

Roxie turned to her mother. "I suppose you know all of it."

"I do now." Mother offered a tight, unhappy smile. "I had the basics, but no details. So I called Brian and spoke to him."

"You did *what?*"

"What else could I do when you wouldn't even mention it to me! It was obvious something was wrong; you've been here more than a week and he didn't call once. I was worried, so—"

"You badgered Tundy into telling you what happened, and then you called Brian. Why, Mother?"

Mother lifted her chin. "Because I care about you, that's why."

"It has nothing to do with me. You just can't keep out of other people's business, as usual."

"Roxie," Mother said in a voice that quivered with emotion, "whatever you may think of me, I am not an uncaring mother. If anything, I care too much."

It was such an honest statement that Roxie was left with no answer. Since she'd been a child, she'd seen her mother put her and Mark first. When times had been lean, Mark and Roxie had still had new shoes and nice clothes while Mother had worn the same dress year after year. And when times had gotten better, Mother had spared no expense on making sure Roxie and Mark had everything a kid could have wanted and more.

Roxie caught her mother's eyes and was surprised by a look of uncertainty. "You're right; I should have told you. I was too embarrassed to tell anyone. Later, you were sick, and it didn't seem as if you needed a shock."

Mother patted her hand. "Roxie, it wouldn't have been as bad of a shock for me; I wasn't married to the fool."

Roxie's lips twitched. "I never thought I'd hear you call Brian 'fool.' "

"Under the circumstances, you're lucky I'm not calling him something else," Mother said tartly. She gave Roxie's hand a final pat and returned to her cookbook.

"What did he say?"

"What could he say? He admitted that it was all his fault. That he wasn't truthful with you, and he didn't blame you for being angry. I told him we were all disappointed in him for lying." Mother snapped her lips together for a moment before she took a calming breath and said, "I'm glad I found out, so we can deal with it."

Roxie blinked. "What do you mean?"

"Just what I said," Mother replied in a bracing tone. "We need to get you back out there, finding a man. You're not young anymore, you know."

"No! Thank you for caring, but this is something I need to handle on my *own*."

Mother frowned. "There's no need to yell."

Tundy snorted. "Just this morning, *you* was yelling at me at the top of yo' lungs sayin' you wanted eggs and no more of that nasty oatmeal. I'm sure Miz Roxie done heard you. Why, you yelled so loud, I'm surprised you can talk right now."

Mother shot a reproachful look at Tundy. "Perhaps my throat wouldn't be so sore if I hadn't spent all morning calling for a glass of water."

"The pitcher and glass was right there in yo' room. I don't know why you wouldn't get it yourself."

Her expression tight, Mother tapped a finger on the recipe. "Next, chop one cup of celery."

Tundy went to the fridge. "I'll chop it, all right."

Mother turned back to Roxie. "My dear, I won't pretend I wasn't horrified at Brian's revelation, but there's no sense crying over spilled milk. He wasn't the man we thought he was, but that doesn't mean you need to go completely"—Mother's gaze flickered to Roxie's hair—"*wild.*"

"I'm not—though I wish I could have."

Mother sent her a hard look. "If you don't want people to think you've gone wild, then you should monitor your behavior in the driveway a bit more carefully."

Oh God, she saw the kiss. Damn!

Tundy whirled, a package of celery dangling from one hand. "Nuh-uh! Say you didn't kiss Sheriff Hottie!"

Mother ignored the maid. "Roxie, really. You must show more decorum. Worse," she continued, "of all the eligible men in town, that was *Nick Sheppard!*" She wrinkled her nose as if she smelled something unpleasant.

Tundy lopped the top off a stalk of celery. "Pshaw! Mr. Barkins says Nick Sheppard is the best thing to happen to this town since he can remember."

"Mr. Barkins? *Todd* Barkins? The owner of Glory National Bank? The president of the Kiwanis?"

"I don't know about no Kiwanis nor nothin'. I see him at the bank whenever I use my ATM card."

"Tall man? Very genteel looking? Gray hair—"

"Cleft in his chin, looks like an older George Clooney? That'd be him." Tundy paused in her chopping. "He has a great butt. You can tell it even in those business suits he wears."

Mother winced. "You've been talking to him?"

"Pretty near every day."

"Lovely," Mother said in a tone that implied otherwise.

Tundy grinned at Roxie. "Barkins said he likes a woman with a nice 'cushion,' and don't you know," she said as she slapped her own rump, "I happen to have one that is better than average."

Mother set aside the recipe book. "I am going upstairs to find some aspirin. My head is throbbing."

Tundy waved her knife in the air. "You go ahead, Miz Treymayne. They're on the top shelf of the medicine cabinet."

"I know," Mother said frostily. "I put them there. Roxanne, when I get back, we'll talk about this turn of events and come up with a plan to deal with it." She rose and swept from the room.

As soon as she left, Tundy grabbed some salt and gave the pot a few hard shakes. "What that woman needs is a man. One who wouldn't put up with no lip from her, neither. Has yo' momma had a date that you know of?"

"No, I don't think so."

"Well, she needs one. Bad. But then, so do I." Tundy put down the salt and came to the table to plop down in Mother's abandoned chair. "Miz Roxie, tell me something. In all the time you was growin' up, did you ever have a wild hair? Even once?"

"Well . . . there was one," Roxie admitted, but added hastily when Tundy looked as if she might ask more questions, "when I was in high school. A long, long time ago."

"Uh-huh," Tundy said, plainly disbelieving. "I suppose you drank a thimbleful of beer or something piddly like that."

"No."

"Drugs?" Tundy said hopefully.

"No."

"Pshaw! If you didn't drink and didn't do drugs, then how was you bad?"

"I sneaked out at night and had a relationship with someone Mother didn't like." It had been Roxie's one lone act of defiance. Even now, she shivered a bit when she thought about it, about Nick Sheppard's dark, wild-boy looks, his silver-gray eyes, his hands as they—

"Lordy, not the *cop*!"

"No! Of course not." Roxie's face heated until she knew it must have been bright red. How had Tundy guessed *that*?

Tundy's eyes narrowed. "How bad was this boy,

then? Was he the 'I might say a naughty word' bad, or was he bad-bad?"

"He spent his entire youth in and out of the local detention center. He was so bad that when Mother found out, she refused to allow me to talk to him again."

"And you listened to her?"

"Of course I did. She was right; he was trouble." Plus, immediately after their fight, she'd watched Nick walk right into the arms of another girl. It still made her chest ache with pain. At the time, she'd thought she'd die, though she'd covered her hurt with cool pride.

"What I want to know is, was he *good* at being bad?"

"I told you, he was—" Roxie caught Tundy's meaningful gaze and said, "Ooooohhhh. You mean was he good at *that*?"

"Hittin' it," Tundy supplied in a helpful tone.

"Yes," Roxie sighed. "He was *very* good."

And probably still was, if his kisses were any indication. He was every bit as sexy and dangerous, even with a badge.

"And you just walked away from it?" Tundy shook her head. "Uh-uh, girl. We got to work on you some. There's times when bad's the best you'll ever get. That's why tonight, we're going out and we're gonna let off some of this steam we've got buildin' up inside us."

"Oh yeah?"

"Yeah. I saw a honky-tonk on the other side of town

called Bigger Jigger. I drove past it while lookin' for a store that might keep their beer in a cooler." She gave a disgusted snort. "This is a backwards place here, Miz Roxie, it surely is."

As Tundy rambled on, listing all of the imperfections she'd found in Glory, Roxie listened with half an ear, wondering what it would be like to meet Nick wearing jeans and a T-shirt, maybe drinking a beer or playing pool. Just being Nick, not Sheriff Sheppard.

Tundy sighed. "I think a kiss from that Sheriff Hottie is a divine gift from above. Why, I'd *pay* the man to lay one on me. I'd even—"

Roxie stood with resolve.

"Where you goin'?"

"To get ready for our night out."

Tundy jumped up, grinning. "That's the spirit, Miz Roxie! We can dress up, have a couple of brewskis, maybe even flirt a little. That'll get you back into spirits." She glanced up at the ceiling, where Mother's footsteps could be heard. "It would definitely do *me* a world of good, too."

Roxie's spirits lifted. It *would* be nice to enjoy some male attention. Perhaps her reactions to Nick were so strong because she hadn't spent any time with other men. Except Ty, but he didn't really count. Nice as he was, there was no chemistry there. But tonight, she'd give the world a chance and see if it came up to her expectations.

Her decision must have shown on her face, for Tundy

gave a little hop of delight. "Give me a few minutes to get yo' momma frustrated enough to stomp off to bed. Mr. Mark is due back soon, so go put on something pretty. We are catchin' The Party Train tonight!"

NICK CAST HIS LURE from the dock, the light from his lamp flickering over the still water. Crickets chirped in the soft evening breeze, punctuated by the ribbits of frogs. Here and there, the water splashed as the fish stirred to life. The scent of damp wood mingled with the briny smell of the bait bucket.

This was pure paradise. If only he could stop thinking about Roxie. She permeated every thought, every waking moment. It was damned annoying and only getting worse.

Nick looked over at his companion. "So? What do you think?"

Old Sheriff Thompson had retired, but everyone in Glory had gotten so used to calling him Sheriff Thompson that they couldn't bring themselves to call him anything else.

Everyone but Nick. He understood more than others how precious the concept of "time away from the job" could be. The man had worked hard and deserved the right to retire in peace.

Tom sent him a glance now. "What do I think about our chances of catching a fish tonight? Or what do I think about your blackmail theory on Doyle Cloyd's death?"

"Both. Were you aware of Doyle and his little scheme?"

Tom cast his line. "There were rumors for years, but I never could get anyone to make a complaint." He smiled wryly. "That's the nature of blackmail. It has its own built-in security."

"I've noticed. I've tried to interview people all over town and everyone just closes up."

"No one wants their secrets revealed to their family and friends."

"I don't care about people's secrets; I just want to find out what's going on with the blackmail. Most of all, I want to know if Doyle might actually have been murdered."

Tom reeled in his line and recast it. He was a tall, lanky man with grizzled gray hair and warm brown eyes. Nick had liked him from the beginning. "It's possible either way," Tom said. "He was known to wander around after dark. I almost hit him a time or two myself. As for the blackmail scheme . . . I don't know. Do you think Doyle was capable of running it?"

"No. I think Doyle was the courier."

Tom's eyes narrowed. "That's interesting. One reason I hesitated to claim Doyle's death anything other than accidental was because of his bank records. I'd heard rumors of blackmail, but he never made any deposits larger than his government checks."

Nick lowered his fishing rod and looked at Tom. "I don't think Doyle was smart enough to pull off a stunt like that on his own. He always seemed burnt out on weed half the time, and drunk the other."

"True." Tom slowly reeled in his bait. "So someone else was involved with this blackmail scheme, someone local."

"Someone who probably kept the lion's share of the money."

"That makes sense. I daresay Doyle's cut wouldn't have been big enough to be unusual, *and* it was probably paid in cash."

Nick nodded. "Giving cash to a pothead is one of the best ways to launder money. Within twenty-four hours every dollar is gone, resting briefly in the pocket of every lowlife in town, only to surface at Waffle House or the gas station."

"Exactly. Sounds like you have the strong beginnings of a case. *Oh!* I got a hit!" He reeled in his line. "It's a little one, but a fighter. I think I . . . Nope. He got loose."

"You always get the first strike."

"And you always get the biggest fish, so quit bitchin'."

Nick chuckled. He liked Tom, and appreciated his calm good sense and strong instincts. It had been that, more than anything else, that had led him to accept the job in Glory.

Tom shot him a side glance. "How are you liking the job?"

"I like it just fine. It's been a bit of an adjustment for

us all, but the town is slowly coming around. My biggest problem is my aunt and her club."

Tom chuckled. "I saw your aunt last week at the Stuff 'n Fluff. She and that Rose Tibbons are quite the characters."

"You can say that again. And now that Roxie Treymayne is back in town, they seem to have a new lease on creating havoc."

"Roxie? Lilah's daughter?"

"That's the one. She's home now, and divorced." *And more beautiful than ever.*

Tom opened an old folding chair he kept on the dock and sat, stretching his long legs out before him. "I always liked Lilah."

Nick turned an amazed gaze on his friend. "*Liked* her?"

Tom nodded. "And admired her. She raised those two kids on her own and struggled for every bite of food or piece of clothing she gave them, yet not once did I see her ask for help from anyone."

"She loves Roxie and Mark. You can't question that."

"She loves them, but she also has her pride. I like that in a woman." Tom chuckled. "Don't look so surprised. You know I like a feisty woman."

"Feisty yes, but bitchy, no."

"Trust me. Lilah Treymayne may be prickly with pride, but underneath it you couldn't find a more true, giving woman."

Nick considered this a moment. "Roxie never mentions her dad."

"She never knew him. He died when she was knee-high to a grasshopper. Lilah speaks well of him, though."

"I never knew you were so close to Lilah."

"Me? Hardly. She's always been polite to me, but nothing more. I heard it all from Teresa at the Stuff 'n Fluff."

"That place is a gossip pool."

"Son, if you haven't learned one thing about being the only cop in town, it's that the whole world becomes your deputy."

Nick frowned. "You let other people in on investigations?"

"Under the right circumstances, yes. You can't do everything yourself, and in a small town like this, it helps to have extra eyes and ears." Tom jiggled his fishing pole a bit, then began to reel it slowly in. "Otherwise you might miss out on something significant."

Nick hadn't thought of it that way. In Atlanta, with over two thousand officers, you never jeopardized your case by sharing information with others. He had to stop thinking like he was still there. Glory was a whole different story.

Tom frowned. "Is that your phone ringing?"

"Yes, damn it." Nick crossed the dock to his tackle box and snapped the phone open. "Hello?" A brisk voice spoke and Nick listened a moment. "Got it. Thank you." He closed the phone, stuffed it into his pocket, and reeled in his line.

"That the new alert system?"

"Yes. It patches the 911 switchboard directly to whatever phone I tell it to." He set his fishing pole aside and began to collect his things.

"Gotta leave, hm?" Tom didn't look surprised.

"Yeah."

"Mrs. Clinton's pug?"

"No, Mrs. Freemont thinks she heard a noise in her attic." Nick closed his tackle box and secured the hook on his fishing line. "Again."

Tom grinned. "Better you than me." He reached into a cooler at his side and pulled out a frosty can of beer. "Pity you can't stay. Guess I'll have to drink these all myself now."

"You're a cold man."

"And here I was going to offer to keep an eye on Lilah for you. And her daughter, too, if you want me to."

"I don't think either Lilah or Roxie would allow that."

"Oh, I won't tell them." Tom took a deep drink of beer, obviously enjoying it. "I'm not a fool, you know."

Nick laughed and settled his fishing pole over one shoulder. "Sure, look in on Lilah and Roxie if you've time. It can't hurt." *And it might give me an idea how much time Ty Henderson is spending there, too.* Suddenly, Nick felt much better. Until that moment, he hadn't realized how much Ty's visits were bothering him. It'd be good to have some inside information.

"I've nothing but time," Tom said. "I'll drop by to-morrow and see what's what. Meanwhile, you go and do your"—he waved his beer can—"thing."

Nick strode to his car. "If I get done in the next hour, I'll come back." He tossed his fishing gear into the trunk and slammed it closed.

"Take your time." Tom grinned. "I'll try and leave you some fish."

chapter 14

*T*HE NEXT MORNING CAME way too early for Roxie. Her night out with Tundy had left them both bleary-eyed and wincing at bright lights and sudden noises. Mother seemed more strident than usual, and Roxie was desperate to slip out at the first opportunity available.

She drove to town and pulled up outside of the sheriff's office, noting that Nick's cruiser wasn't in the parking lot. To counteract her faint disappointment, she said aloud, "Good. I'm in no mood to speak with him anyway."

Truth be told, she wasn't really in the mood to speak with anyone. Tundy was a fun companion on many levels, but karaoke night at the Bigger Jigger was something else altogether. Roxie wasn't sure how it happened, but between margaritas, Tundy had talked her into taking the stage and embarrassing herself with an impossibly bad rendition of "Do That to Me One More Time."

"That's what you get for singing a Captain and Tennille song, you fool," she sighed. What in the hell had she been thinking?

Roxie flipped down the visor mirror and lifted her sunglasses to squint at her bloodshot eyes. "Pathetic, Treymayne. You look like you went on a bender." She winced and dropped the glasses back into place, then flipped the visor up. If she wanted to get that medical report before Nick returned, she'd better get a move on.

Sighing, she slowly climbed out of the car and made her way inside. Susan was more than helpful and Roxie managed to get the report and leave.

Unfortunately, the report had been a disappointment. As everyone knew, Doyle had died from injuries consistent with being struck by a vehicle. Still, Clara and the gang had pored over the document as if it were a map to a buried treasure. Over the next few days, Roxie had been able to use it to encourage several away-from-the-center trips, including a visit to the "crime scene." There, Clara had made C.J. lie in the parking lot in the approximate place Doyle had been found so she could get some "good pictures" for the file.

As the week passed, Roxie busied herself in visiting the assisted living center and helping at home. She almost managed to not think about Nick—almost. The moment she sat down, or got bored, or tried to go to sleep, her unruly mind would zone right in on the memories of hot kisses that had left her panting, the seductive feel of his warm, possessive hands as they slid over her skin—

She scowled now and impulsively pulled into a parking space by Micki & Maud's diner. *Peach cobbler. That'll do the trick.*

If she couldn't forget Nick by staying busy, then she'd do it via pure sugar. The peach cobbler Micki's daughter, Connie, kept warm at the diner was beyond heavenly—its flaky, cinnamony goodness was so delicious that it was impossible to think about another thing while eating it.

Over the past week, Roxie'd become a fixture at the diner. For one thing, there was nowhere else to eat unless one counted the hot dogs at the Quickly-Stop-Mart, which looked and smelled like burned rubber. For another, it was right across the square from the sheriff's office and, if one sat at the right table, one might see "various people" coming and going.

Not that she engaged in such activities. She just went for the cobbler.

She entered the diner now. The entryway held a battered coatrack and opened into two cheaply paneled rooms that were once segregated into smoking and nonsmoking areas. Along one wall of the first room ran a long counter with barstools attached to the white speckled linoleum floor. Each white speckled Formica table had four red plastic covered chairs and a bud vase holding a fake, yellowing daisy.

The kitchen area, visible through the order-up window, was large and as dated as the rest of the restaurant. In its fifty-two years, the diner had served as the favorite meeting spot and date night rendezvous for high school students, the VFW, Glory's many bowling leagues, the all-powerful Kiwanis Club, the chess club, and every other group in Glory.

As Roxie entered the diner, she paused by the small table placed beside the coatrack. A huge framed picture of Maud was in the center, with several smaller pictures to either side, along with a memory book that was yellowed with age.

"Micki won't let anyone take that down."

Roxie turned to find Susan standing behind her dressed in jeans and a crewneck shirt of deep blue that made her eyes look twice as vivid. "How long has it been since Maud died?"

"Twenty, twenty-one years." Susan looked around the diner. "Whew, it's almost full."

"I was going to have a latte and some peach cobbler. Want to join me?"

"I'd love to. There's room at the counter." Susan led the way. "I saw you pull in just as I was leaving the office. Been to see Clara and the gang this morning?"

"Yup." Roxie perched on a stool beside Susan and picked up the menu. "They are gung-ho on investigating Doyle Cloyd's murder—"

"Death."

Roxie rolled her eyes. "You're as bad as Nick."

Susan chuckled. "How's your investigation going?"

"OK, considering we haven't seen any evidence other than the ME report."

"In Nick's defense, he can't give information out randomly."

"If he's just going to let the case sit, then he should let the club take a stab at it. What can it hurt?"

Susan tilted her head to one side. "You're serious about this, aren't you?"

Roxie set down the menu. "The more I hear about Doyle, the more I think his death was unusual. Clara certainly thinks so."

"Nick says Clara's a sharp lady."

"She is. Even though we can't fully investigate the case, it's been a huge help in getting the club out of the assisted living center. This morning I convinced them to take a walk through the neighborhood Doyle grew up in, telling them we could get a 'feel' for our victim that way." She laughed as she caught Susan's disbelieving gaze. "You wouldn't believe the mileage I'm getting from this."

Susan grinned, her cheeks dimpling. "Clara can be a sweetie, though she certainly runs Nick in circles at times."

Maybe he deserves it, Roxie thought, but she held her tongue. "Have you tried the latte?"

"Yes," Susan said in a voice of deep reverence. "I've already had two today."

The front door opened with a jingle and they both turned to look.

Mayor Harkins came in, his navy suit accented with a hot pink tie.

Susan turned her shoulder and scowled as he made his way to the furthest table. "The City Council's after Harkins to cut the budget, which he does by trying to cut *our* office staff."

"But there's only two of you working there!"

"Yeah. As we've pointed out." Susan shook her head. "We stay on budget, too, while *his* side of the office always goes over. He has Robin *and* a full-time assistant just to do his typing."

"What's Robin do, then?"

Susan gave her a flat look.

Roxie chuckled. "I didn't realize it was part of her official job description."

A small sprite of a woman with dark brown curly hair and bright brown eyes fringed with ridiculously thick lashes came out of the kitchen. On seeing Roxie, she grinned. "Back again?"

"I'm a slave to your peach cobbler."

"Good," Connie said. "Then I'm doing my job."

"Connie!" A plump woman, her gray hair in a bun, poked her head out of the serving window. "That chicken soup is getting cold and— Oh, hello, Roxie! How's your mother?"

"Better, thank you."

"Good. I'll bring her some corn bread. She's always loved it. Connie, about your soup. Do you want me to put some potatoes in it?"

Connie looked horrified. "No!"

"I always put potatoes in *my* chicken soup."

"Mom, it's not chicken soup; it's shiitake *consommé*."

"Shitwhat?"

"Shiitake. It's a mushroom."

Micki sniffed. "I don't know anything about shitarc mushrooms."

"That's shii-ta-ke."

"Whatever it is, you turned off the burner and it's growing cold."

"You serve consommé cold."

"*Cold?* No one will want that."

"I will!" Susan said brightly.

Micki didn't look reassured. "Connie, what's wrong with the chicken soup I taught you to make?"

"Nothing. I just wanted to spruce up the special and I thought—"

"Fine, then! You do it. Just get it off my stove. I want to make my green bean casserole." She wheeled away, her face red.

Connie looked heavenward and counted to ten. At ten, she took a long, deep breath. "There. I am now calm. I am not going to kill my mother. Nor am I going to explode because she put dumplings in my beef Stroganoff." Connie shook her head. "Mom's not much for change, but I'm working on her."

"She's fortunate you're here." Susan glanced at Roxie. "Connie hasn't told a lot of people, but she's a genuine Cordon Bleu chef."

Connie paused in making Susan's latte. "Who told you that?"

"I Googled your name," Susan said smugly.

"Good job," Roxie said admiringly.

Connie gave mock scowl. "Is that part of your job as county dispatcher?"

Susan grinned. "No, but it *is* part of my job as county busybody. I personally think—"

The door opened again and they all turned. Robin came in, dressed in a red suit with a very short skirt. She paused when she caught sight of Susan and Roxie. Lips pressed into a tight line, she whirled on her heel and crossed to where the mayor sat. He brightened when he saw her and made a show of helping her into her seat, beaming eagerly.

"Pathetic," Roxie said.

"Delusional," Susan agreed.

"A total ho, fo' sho'." Connie handed Roxie her latte, then fixed two warmed bowls of peach cobbler and placed them on the counter.

Roxie leaned over the bowl and let the rich, cinnamony goodness fill her head. "Someone should bottle this."

Susan licked her spoon. "Or just make a face paste out of it so you can smear it all over and then lick it off."

"Or a body butter. Although that might be more like a body batter—"

The door opened again and this time a tall man in a black leather motorcycle jacket and gloves walked in. He was well over six feet tall, his shoulders broad, his jeans hugging his lean hips. His face was chiseled and handsome, his dark hair just brushed his collar, and his blue eyes were arresting.

Connie's eyes widened and she froze, hand on the coffeepot. "*Who* is *that?* I've been in town for three months and I thought I'd met everyone."

Susan licked her spoon. "That, my dear, is what we in Glory call Bad News. His real name is Ethan Markam. He's a wild man, a lawbreaker, and a preacher's kid."

"He doesn't *look* like bad news," Roxie said.

"Sure, he does." Connie shivered. "That's what makes him so delicious."

He pulled off his leather coat and gloves before sitting down. His gaze flickered around the room, almost immediately returning to Roxie.

"Wow," Susan breathed. "I wish someone would look at me like that."

"Me, too," Connie agreed.

Roxie colored and turned her attention back to her peach cobbler. *Why doesn't Nick look at me like that more often?*

"He's still looking at you," Connie said enviously.

Susan nodded. "Very, very hard."

"I don't care," Roxie said, though her heart thudded. She couldn't help but enjoy the envy of her gal pals, but she wished Nick were nearby to see Ethan's obvious appreciation. That would have really made it sweet.

Connie sighed. "I always attract the stodgy and

boring types, never the fun types." She pulled a small container from under the counter. "Since you're here, would you mind trying out my bourbon balls? I'm trying to get Mom to put them on the dessert menu, but she's resisting."

Susan popped one into her mouth and chewed, her eyes slowly closing. *"Mmmmmmmmmm!"*

Roxie took one as well. She bit into it; the mellow flavor of bourbon mixed with the sweet pastry melted onto her tongue. She finished it off and licked her fingers. "Connie, that's *incredible.*"

"May I have another?" Susan asked.

Connie grinned, looking pleased. She placed the entire container on the counter and dusted her hands. "You guys need anything else? I have to rescue my consommé before Mom adds something horrible to it."

"We're good," Roxie replied.

"Perfectly," Susan said, helping herself to another bourbon ball.

"All right then. Off to battle." Her shoulders squared, Connie left.

Susan pushed the container toward Roxie. "Have another."

Roxie did. "That's soooo good," she moaned. "Like a buttered doughnut covered in bourbon syrup. It's better than—"

"—sex!" Susan ate another. *"Wow."*

Roxie ate another, too. "I wonder how much alcohol is in these?"

"They're cooked, so most of the alcohol should have evaporated."

That was true. Roxie helped herself to another. She and Susan continued to talk about the weather, the new shoes displayed in Paula Beth's Boutique, and various other topics while they kept an eye on Bad Boy. He'd just ordered his lunch and had then reached into his pocket to pull out a book. Before long, he seemed lost within its pages.

Never breaking stride in their conversation, Susan and Roxie exchanged a surprised, approving glance.

Absently, Roxie ate another bourbon ball. The sun from the window glistened across the room and engulfed her in a warm haze. Though she had no desire to live the rest of her life here, she had to admit that it had its charm.

She was just embarking on her sixth or seventh bourbon ball when Connie reappeared. She looked around. "There it is!" She flashed a grin at Roxie and Susan as she scooped up an unlabeled bottle of spice. "I left my special herb mix and— Good God!" She picked up the near empty container. "Did you eat *all* of those bourbon balls?"

Susan peered into the container. "Nope. There's— let's see—one, two, three—" She squinted. "Yup. Three left."

Connie slapped the lid closed. "That's almost eight each!"

"I only had six—" Roxie began but her lips felt funny.

She pressed her fingers to them. "My lips are numb."

Susan tapped her own. "So are mine."

Connie laughed. "That's because there's a half cup of bourbon for every six balls! You two are looped."

"But you *cooked* them." Susan looked outraged. "How could we be looped?"

"Because I cooked them and *then* drizzled the bourbon over them."

Roxie and Susan blinked at the container.

Finally, Roxie turned to Susan. "You're drunk."

Susan considered this. "I suppose I am. But if I'm drunk, then you're tipsy."

Roxie ran her tongue over her lips. Still nothing. "I guess you're right."

Connie regretfully put the container back under the shelf. "I guess bourbon balls aren't such a good idea after all." She glanced over her shoulder, to where her mother could be seen scurrying around the kitchen. "Look, you two, I hate to say anything but ah . . . I don't want my mother to see you like this or she'll blame me."

Roxie stood. "It's time for us to go, anyway. How much do we owe—"

"Just go." Connie grinned. "We'll consider being guinea pigs for my new recipe sufficient payment."

"Works for me." Susan stood and made her way outside, swaying slightly. She wiggled her fingers at Bad Boy, who watched as they left.

Once outside, Roxie looked around. "How am I gonna get home?"

"I dunno. I just know I won't be going back to the office. Nick'll be mad."

Roxie grinned. "Serves him right."

"Damn straight. If he was any kind of boss at all, he'd make sure there were bourbon balls in the office. Now *that* would be a good boss!"

"I'd say."

Susan sighed. "But with Nick, it's by the book or not at all."

"He's changed a lot. Of course, so have I."

Susan tilted her head to one side and regarded Roxie through squinted eyes. "You and Nick can't ever seem to get on the same page, can you? First he was wild as a wombat while you were a complete prude—"

"I was not!"

"—and now he's a by-the-book sheriff while you're a hot sexpot."

Roxie hesitated, distracted. "Does Nick think I'm a sexpot?"

"*Hell,* yes—that's why he's running scared. And Bad Boy keeps sneaking glances at you as if you were on the menu."

Roxie looked behind her and, through the diner window, caught the blue gaze of Bad Boy himself. He winked, making her cheeks heat, but she smiled at him anyway. She turned back to Susan. "I *like* being a sexpot. I don't know why Nick would have a problem with that."

"Poor Nick. He's determined to be a superman and

resist emotional entanglements that could cloud his judgment, and then you come along, looking all sexpottish—" Susan frowned. "Is that a word? Sexpottish?" She waved a hand. "Either way, you knocked Nick for a loop."

Roxie couldn't help but feel the faintest hint of triumph. "You really think I've knocked him for a loop?"

"Sure. Of course, he'll resist it and you two will never be together, which is a damn shame if you ask me."

Roxie's nascent euphoria evaporated.

"If Nick ever decides to have a long-term relationship, he'll look for a prim, perfect, unemotional type." Susan rolled her eyes. "I've never seen a man so determined to avoid being swept away by emotion."

"But isn't being swept away sort of the whole point?"

"It won't happen if you've got your heels dug in, and Nick's are buried to his knees. There's no hope there. None at all."

She yawned. "Those bourbon balls made me sleepy. Guess I'll walk home and take a nap. What about you? Want to come over to nap on my couch until you can drive? It's only two blocks away."

"I didn't have as many bourbon balls as you did; I only had six."

Susan shook her head. "That's still too many. You'll get a DUI and Nick will have to lock you in the county jail."

Being locked in the county jail *with* Nick was tantalizing, but being locked up *by* him wouldn't be nearly as much fun. "I'll just go and sit in my car until I can drive."

Susan didn't look happy. "Are you sure?"

Roxie nodded.

"OK, have it your way. Just don't drive until"— Susan looked at her watch—"three, anyway."

"Deal." Roxie waved good-bye to Susan and made her way back to her car. She'd just reached the Mustang and had unlocked it when she realized that it was listing to one side. Grumbling, she tossed her purse inside and went to examine the problem. "Damn it, a flat tire! How did—"

"Excuse me."

The deep voice came from directly behind her, rich, low, and indescribably husky. She knew exactly who had spoken. Slowly, she turned to find herself facing Bad Boy.

He was a bit younger than she'd first thought, probably in his late twenties, but there was nothing "boyish" about him. His thick black hair was long and parted on one side; it swooped over one eye and brushed the collar of his white T-shirt. His face was covered with a sexy scruff of whiskers that outlined his sensual mouth. His shirt clung to his broad chest and muscles, while his jeans clung to his hips and thighs in a way that almost made her blush.

He quirked a brow at her. "It looks as if you have a flat."

"And no spare."

He flashed a lopsided grin. "Not one for planning, are you?"

"No," she said regretfully. "Though I do plan on making a plan very soon."

He laughed, his eyes crinkling. "There's a gas station a few blocks away that has a tow truck. I could give you a ride."

Her gaze flickered past him to the motorcycle parked a few cars down. "On *that*?" Excitement stirred deep inside her.

His brows rose. "Yeah. You have a problem with that?"

She grinned. "No. I was hoping you'd suggest it." She was a woman of passion, tough and cool, capable and strong, and high on bourbon balls and life. Nick would just have to live with that.

She smiled at Ethan. "Let's go."

His blue gaze warmed and he waited for her to lock her car before walking with her to his bike. It was low-slung and powerful, all shiny black paint and blindingly bright chrome. He opened a saddlebag and pulled out a helmet for her, then slung a leg over the machine and secured his own helmet. With a flick of his thumb and a twist of his wrist, the machine roared to life.

Ethan grinned at her. "Climb on."

She did so, glad she wasn't wearing a skirt, then set her strappy sandals on the foot pegs and hoped they'd stay on.

Once she was settled, she went back to work on the helmet straps, nervous excitement making her fumble. Just as she started to ask Ethan for help, she saw Nick come out of the sheriff's office.

He stopped in his tracks when he saw her sitting behind Ethan on the motorcycle. Then he marched her way, his jaw set, his eyes steely hard.

"Damn, what's he want now?" Ethan muttered.

Now? A flutter of warning tickled her stomach but Roxie pushed it away, hoping *she* was what Nick wanted. For a fleeting moment, she thought about jumping off the back of the bike and running toward Nick, yanking off his sunglasses, then wrapping her arms and legs around him and—

VARRRROMMMMMM!!!! Ethan cranked the engine.

Roxie clutched Ethan as the bike jerked. "Ethan!" she yelled. "My hel—"

The back tire spun, sending gravel flying, then the motorcycle leapt to life. Roxie pressed against Ethan's back and closed her eyes as the wind whooshed by. As they whipped by Nick, Roxie's undone helmet flew off. It hit the pavement and bounced, landing at his feet where it spun on its back, a single high-heeled sandal beside it.

Roxie had a fleeting impression of Nick's stormy gaze before reality hit her: she was riding a motorcycle with a sexy, hot biker who was mad, bad, and dangerous to know.

A wave of excitement rushed through her and she held Ethan tighter, letting the wind ruffle her hair and blow away her fears. *This* was what it felt like to be wild and crazy! A little scary and a whole lot exciting.

Then she heard the unmistakable wail of Nick's siren, and realized she was riding a motorcycle with an outlaw *while* running from the hottest cop in town. Life didn't get any more exciting than that.

NICK SNATCHED UP THE helmet and shoe on his way to his car. He tossed them onto the seat, jumped in, and was off within seconds, his siren screaming. *Damn it to hell, what was Roxie thinking? She could end up injured, or worse.*

Nick had ticketed Ethan going over 130 just last week, and there Roxie was, perched on the back of that monster bike without a helmet. Nick zipped down a side road, passing Susan, who appeared to be walking home and not to the office.

Her startled glance poured cold water over the blazing emotion that had sent him chasing after Roxie.

What in the hell was he doing? He grimaced and flipped off the sirens and lights, pulling to a stop at a red light.

He forced himself to breathe slowly, deeply, calming himself by force. Giving chase to a wild man on a motorcycle, who was no doubt spurred on by an even wilder and sexy Roxie hanging on the back, was *not* a good idea. It not only violated the county's "no chase" policy, which he'd written himself, but it could force Ethan to act in an even more dangerous manner.

The light had just changed when Mrs. Clinton stepped onto the road with her walker. She slowly tottered across, pausing to wave at him. Nick forced a smile, desperate to hurry on, but there was no hurrying Mrs. Clinton. She finally cleared his path and he wiped a hand across his damp forehead.

Now it was too late. He couldn't see the motorcycle at all; Ethan was long gone. Nick pulled his car into an empty lot down the road and parked it, rubbing his face with hands that shook.

She's going to be OK. Ethan won't drive like a maniac with Roxie onboard even though I hit the siren for a moment. And if he does— Nick slammed his fist into the steering wheel. *This* was what happened when a cop lost perspective. He didn't follow the rules, didn't think things through, he just reacted. And reaction without thought could get a person killed.

Even more reason to stay away from Roxie. No matter what Tom said about using the community as a tool and including Roxie in the Doyle Cloyd investigation, Nick would be damned if he'd allow it. Once he'd saved her ass from this ruckus today, he'd make sure he never got within a football field's length of her again. If only he knew for sure she *was* OK.

She'd looked rather pleased with herself when she'd left, but he seriously doubted she'd ever been on a bike like that. She could be frightened now, wondering if she'd get off the bike alive. He groaned and pressed his hands to his forehead, staring blindly across the road at the garage, wondering if—

He stopped. That looked like—but it couldn't be; how had she— *Was that Roxie?*

He rubbed his eyes. A woman had ambled out of the garage, barefoot and laughing as the sunlight glinted off her blonde hair.

Roxie wasn't weeping in fear. Nor was she lying on the side of the road with her pretty neck broken. Instead, she was sipping a soda and flirting with the mechanic at Joe Bob's Lube and Arcade.

Irritation grew, and Nick drove across to Joe's, pulling into the lot and stopping with a jerk.

"Sheriff!" Joe walked toward him. "How you doing? Squad car giving you problems?"

"No," Nick said tersely. He grabbed the sandal from the seat and tossed it to Roxie. "You forgot this."

She caught it and then grimaced. "I wish I knew where the other was."

"You lost that one, too?"

"Somewhere by the hardware store. Ethan went to see if he could find it."

Joe Bob grinned. "If anyone can find it, Ethan will. I'll send Daryl to get that flat tire off your car, Miss Treymayne. We'll patch her up and get her back in drivin' shape in no time."

"Thanks!"

Joe Bob nodded and headed off to the garage, leaving Nick with Roxie.

Silence reigned while he tried to think of what to say. Should he begin with how irresponsible it was to ride without a helmet? Talk about how close her bare feet were to the exhaust pipe, which was hot enough to cause serious burns? Lecture her on the impropriety of riding with men she didn't know? His gaze narrowed. "How long have you known Ethan Markam?"

"About ten minutes. We'd never spoken until he offered to help with my flat tire." She frowned. "Though he's not as nice as he seems. He made me get off the bike."

Nick's disbelief must have shown in his face, because she added in a sulky voice, "When he realized I didn't have the helmet on, he pulled over and ordered me off." She scowled. "He was actually a little rude about it. Sheesh, who would have thought a man who looked like that would be such a granny?"

"He's just watching out for himself. Something he *should* do if you're around."

"That's not fair!"

"No? For your information, Treymayne, Markam is already on probation for reckless driving."

"He seems to drive just fine to me."

"Not at one hundred thirty miles per hour."

She looked impressed. "Really?"

"Really. Though you seem too hell-bent on having a good time to worry about things like that."

She stiffened. "At least I *have* a social life. Unlike other people who are too stuffy to enjoy anything *fun.*"

Nick bent down so close he could see the dark flecks in her pale blue eyes. "I do lots of fun things, Roxie. Just none of them with women who only think about themselves."

"You—"

The roar of a motorcycle blocked her answer and she spun and marched away from him, her back ramrod straight. The motorcycle's rumble also muted Nick's curse when Roxie, after a furious glance his way, rewarded the biker for returning her shoe with a kiss that seemed to go on forever.

Afterward Ethan looked bewildered and thoroughly smitten, and who could blame him? Even dressed in Sunday clothing and sitting primly in church, Roxie was a sight to incite full-blown lust. Wearing short shorts, her long legs lengthened by ridiculously high heels, her hair wind-tousled from riding a motorcycle, Roxie was enough to incite a full-blown riot.

Scowling, Nick returned to his squad car, refusing to watch another moment. From this moment on, Roxanne Treymayne was completely off-limits.

The clock struck three. Roxie turned over in bed and stared at the ceiling. Again. Sheesh, was she never going to fall asleep? She was beginning to get a headache from trying not to think.

Every time she closed her eyes, she found herself facing Nick's concerned gaze as he pulled into the parking lot at the garage. He'd been worried—genuinely worried. It had surprised her and given her just the tiniest twinge of guilt.

Still, riding on the back of Ethan's bike had been a thrill. *That* was what fun should feel like—wild, free, unfettered. It would have bene a perfect memory except for Nick's dark scowling presence at the end of the ride.

It seemed that no matter what she did, she rubbed Nick the wrong way. She hated that and yet . . . could it mean something? Perhaps he wasn't as immune to her as he'd like to be.

Roxie smiled. That would be nice. Not that anything could come from it; she wasn't staying in this town one day longer than she had to. Still, it felt good to be wanted, if that was indeed what he was feeling.

She stretched and then sat up. If she couldn't sleep, then maybe she could at least read. She grabbed her robe from the end of the bed and slipped it on. Bare feet padding quietly on the cool wood floors, she made her way downstairs, avoiding the two creaking steps just below the landing.

Roxie passed the kitchen without a second glance; it was a pity Mother didn't believe in spirits because a glass of wine would be just the thing. The living room rug muffled her footfalls. She had just started to reach for the lamp switch when a movement by the door caught her eye.

A man's figure was outlined in the doorway.

"Mark!" she whispered. "What are you doing up so late?"

He walked toward her, his shoes making no sound on the rug.

Roxie sighed. "I couldn't sleep either, and now I've a headache."

The streetlight coming through the front blinds fell across Mark, only . . . it wasn't Mark.

This man was too tall. His shoulders too broad.

And he was coming far too fast for her to get away.

Run! her mind screamed. She whirled in the dark, but it was too late.

Something whooshed through the air and her headache exploded into shards of glass-pointed pain.

chapter 15

"*I* NEVER WANT TO LIVE through that again!" Mother sat beside the couch, holding Roxie's hand.

"Me, neither!" Tundy sat in a chair across from them, eyes blazing, her freckles stark against her pale face. "When I came in here and found Miz Roxie on the floor, blood all over the place—"

Roxie lifted her head. "All over the place? I just scraped my cheek."

"It was bleeding more before Doc Wilson put that bandage on it. It's a good thing that attacker was gone by the time I got down here. I thought I was gonna have to whoop some ass."

"You certainly screamed loud enough." Mother beamed at Tundy. "I'm sure you scared him away. He was probably after my good silver."

"Oh, no. He was here to rape us all," Tundy swore, her eyes wide.

"Actually," Mark said as he walked into the room, "you're both wrong. If anyone was going to be raped it would have been Roxie, who was alone and unprotected. And Mother, as much as you prize it, no one is going to break into the house to steal your silver. You only have a cream pot and a sugar bowl."

She sniffed. "They are *very* high quality."

"The thief or attacker had the perfect opportunity to steal them and didn't bother. All he took was one lousy box." Mark met Roxie's gaze. "Nick thinks it must have been a teenager out for a lark."

Roxie managed a faint nod, though it made her head ache all the more. Darn it, why had the idiot hit her so *hard*?

Tundy gave an outraged sniff. "I can't believe that box is missing. And after you were so nice as to bring me them kosher cookbooks, too! I hadn't had a chance to so much as look at a one of them."

Roxie pressed her fingertips to the bandage on her temple, where her head still pounded. She'd awakened to find Doc Wilson taking her pulse and admonishing her to lie still while he completed his examination. Mother had been hovering anxiously in the background while Mark had stomped furiously through the house, Nick following him, looking dark and forbidding as they'd searched to make sure her attacker had indeed left.

Roxie had tried not to cry, but when Doc Wilson had insisted on flashing a light in her eyes, she hadn't been able to hold back her tears. Once unleashed, they'd quickly reached flood strength. Doc Wilson had hurriedly concluded his examination and, patting her shoulder awkwardly, had handed her a box of Kleenex and left. Mother gave her a hug and then went to fetch ice for Roxie's head.

She'd subsided to the dubious comfort of her pillows until, seconds later, Nick had entered the room. Despite her hiccupped protest, he'd scooped her up, placed her snugly in his lap, and held her to his broad chest. For some reason, that little gesture had done it. She'd wrapped both hands in his T-shirt and sobbed for all she was worth on his shoulder.

He'd held her there, stroking her back and murmuring nonsense into her hair as she'd slowly regained control. Finally, a wet, hiccupping mess, she'd released her hold on his shirt.

Nick hadn't said a word, but had kissed her forehead, his lips warm and comforting. Then he'd stood, settled her back on the couch, and placed the Kleenex nearby. "I'm going to leave for now, but I want to talk to you tomorrow. Roxie, I—" He'd raked a hand through his hair, looking furious, his gaze hard. "We'll find that son of a bitch; I promise."

Before she'd been able to ask anything, Mother had returned. Nick had asked, "Roxie, where's your cell phone?"

"On the table by the door. Why?"

He had crossed to it, picked it up, and punched a few buttons. "I put my number in. Call me if you need me, any hour, any time."

Tears had welled again as Roxie had nodded.

Now she sat on the couch, her phone tucked under

her knee. Though Nick had left more than half an hour ago, she could still feel the warmth of his arm about her shoulders. She ached anew, wishing he was still here.

Mark came to sit beside her. "How are you feeling?"

She gave him a small smile. "Other than a splitting headache, I'm fine."

"No, you're not," Mother said. "I don't understand any of this. Why did someone break into the house just to take a box of cookbooks? That doesn't make any sense."

Roxie bit her lip. Whoever it was wanted Doyle's notes, and they wouldn't rest until they got them.

"Whatever the reason, Roxie needs to rest," Mark said. "I'll sleep on the pullout couch in case the intruder returns."

"Good idea!" Tundy wriggled out of her chair, and left to rummage in the linen closet in the hallway.

Mother sighed. "I don't know how I'll sleep."

"Try some whiskey," Mark offered. "It always helps me."

She frowned. "I don't like your levity. This is a serious situation."

Mark's expression darkened. "You don't think I know that?"

"Mark," Roxie interjected hastily, "I'm going back to bed." She stood, taking her phone with her. The metal warmed her cold hands and calmed her thudding heart.

Mark put an arm around her shoulders. "I'll walk you upstairs."

Mother stood. "I'll bring her some milk and cookies."

"Thank you, Mother."

Smiling, Mother swept from the room.

Tundy came in carrying sheets and blankets. "Go on, now. Take Miz Roxie on up to bed while I make up the fold-out bed."

"Thanks, Tundy." Mark walked with Roxie to the steps. As soon as they were out of hearing, he said in a low voice, "Nick thinks the intruder was after Doyle's notes."

"That's what I think, too."

Mark slipped his hand under her elbow as they climbed the stairs. "Nick doesn't think they'll return. Still, he said to let you know that he's right outside if you need him."

She looked up at her brother, surprised. "Outside?"

"He parked his squad car across the street. He'll be there until sunrise."

The knot of tension in Roxie's chest loosened. "That's nice of him."

Mark shrugged. "It's his job."

Disheartened by that blunt statement, she managed a nod.

She was grateful beyond words to reach her comfortable bed. She pulled off her robe and sank into the mattress, wincing as she lowered her aching head to the pillow.

Mark tucked the sheets in and kissed her forehead. "There. Go to sleep. Nick and I will keep an eye on things."

Roxie obediently closed her eyes. "Thanks, Mark." *And thank you, too, Nick. Wherever you are.*

"WHERE DO YOU THINK you're going?"

Roxie jumped guiltily, and her hand dropped from the Mustang's door handle. "Good Lord, you scared me to death!"

Mark scowled from where he was seated in an old lawn chair under a tree at the end of the driveway. He placed his book face open on the grass and stood. "You should be resting."

"I rested all morning and now I'm tired of resting. Besides, I can't stop thinking about last night. Mark, who would want Doyle's notes bad enough to break into our house?"

"You need to leave all of that to Nick."

She stiffened. "*I'm* the one who got attacked. I think I have a right to investigate this now."

His scowl deepened. "Leave it alone, Roxie."

"No. I spent my whole life behaving and I have nothing to show for it. I'll be damned if I sit idly by while some—some *fool* tries to scare me into going away. I will *not* go away. Especially not now!"

Mark gave an exasperated sigh. "Oh for the love of— Roxie, please. Nick will tell you the same thing."

"Then it's a good thing I don't plan on asking him. I won't just walk away." She hoped Nick would understand that, too, though he was so cautious now. And concerned. *Concerned is good. You have to care for someone to be concerned. At least a little.*

Mark picked up his book again, a sulky turn to his mouth. "You're every bit as stubborn as Mother."

Roxie eyed Mark's strategically placed chair, and realized it wasn't visible from Mother's window. "Mark, are you hiding?"

"Yes." His gaze flicked to the car. "Are you running away?"

She leaned against the car and raked a hand through her hair—wincing when her fingers brushed the knot on her forehead. "I can't stand another hour cooped up inside. Doc Wilson said I'm good as new, but Mother won't let me out of her sight."

"How did you escape?"

"She went to the bathroom. I wedged a shoe under the door, so it'll take her a couple of minutes to get out."

He laughed. "She'll be mad."

"I know, and I don't care. I'm going to The Pig and get some brats. I'm about koshered out." She opened the car door and threw her purse inside. "Wanna come with me?"

He grinned. "Sure. I'll drive."

She tossed him the keys and went around the car to

the passenger seat. As they pulled out of the driveway, she caught sight of Mother running down the porch stairs, waving madly, Tundy hard on her heels.

Neither Roxie nor Mark said a word until they were at the end of their street.

"That was a close one," Roxie finally said. "Mark, was Mother always like this? Exaggerating everything and so—*dramatic*?"

"Lord, yes, She's never been any other way that I can remember."

"I never used to see it. I thought people were just unfair to her, always saying mean little things. Now I can see where they were coming from. She's constantly criticizing everyone. Thank goodness Tundy has skin as thick as a rhino's."

"She's never been easy to get along with." He shrugged. "Every kid thinks their parents are perfect when they're young. It's part of the growing-up process to realize they aren't, and our mother is very far from perfect. I don't doubt that she believes she has strong motives for what she's done, but that's not enough. She's hurt a lot of people. At any given moment, she has half the town pissed off at her. It's been that way for years."

"Life hasn't been easy for her. She's taken care of us since Dad died. That had to be tough, returning to his hometown alone with two small children, not knowing a single soul."

Mark said in a guilty tone, "You're right; I forget that. She seems like a rock, acts like a rock, demands she be treated like a rock . . . so it's hard for me to remember she's really just a mushroom hiding under a rock."

Roxie chuckled. "That explains her exactly."

Mark rubbed his chin thoughtfully. With his chestnut hair mussed, his lean frame dressed in a loose T-shirt and shorts, he appeared much younger than his thirty-seven years. "Roxie, I wonder if Mother's just scared."

"Of what?"

"You know how she rolls. She likes to control things and people if she can. Death is the one thing she can't control. Maybe that's why she's even more strident lately. Maybe she thinks she can shout down death."

"She's not going to die."

"We know that, but she might not. She has a hell of an imagination."

Roxie sighed. "You may be right. All I know for sure is that I need a break."

"Me, too. I've been jonesing for a cold beer all afternoon."

She settled back in her seat. "I wish you and Mother got along better."

Mark sent her a surprised glance. "Why?"

"Because it's a strain on me."

He shrugged. "I don't know why. It doesn't concern you."

"Yes, it does. Mother gets upset, and then I have to deal with it."

"Roxie, you know what's wrong with you? You care too much. You care too much about what people think, how people feel, what people are doing—you need to just let it go. Pay more attention to what *you* think and how *you* feel."

"I'm trying to do that," she said, miffed. "You don't understand how it is for me."

"Yes, I do. Mother gets upset and you rush to fix things." Mark shrugged. "You've been doing that since you were little."

Maybe he did understand. At an early age, Roxie had become an expert at cheering up Mother whenever she'd gotten into a furor from whatever person or event had set her off. Which happened often.

As Roxie had grown older, she'd found the whole thing wearing, and by the time she'd left for college, it had been a relief to enjoy a day without a "horrible event."

Perhaps that was why she had stayed in her peaceful, placid marriage for so long. Some might have called it boring and lacking in passion, but to Roxie, it had seemed like the perfect relationship.

"Speaking of Mother," Mark said nonchalantly, "she's pretty upset about seeing you kissing Nick the other day. God only knows what she'll say when she hears about you taking a wild motorcycle ride through town without a helmet or shoes."

"How did *you* hear about that?"

"In Glory, any secret is *everyone's* secret."

Roxie groaned. "Great. Just great." Still, she didn't regret it—she'd had a lot of fun. She would happily have had more, too, if Nick hadn't been such a killjoy.

Well, it was his loss.

Her phone rang. Was it Nick? She'd looked for him this morning when she'd first awoken, but he'd already left. She supposed she shouldn't have been surprised; it was almost ten when she'd managed to crawl from bed, exhausted from the events of the night before. She found her phone in the bottom of her purse. "Hello?"

"Miz Roxie," Clara's voice crackled over the phone, "it's me, Clara!"

Roxie held the phone from her ear. "You don't need to yell, Clara. I can hear you fi—"

"We got us an emergency!" Clara shouted. "Where are you?"

"Driving down Hamilton Road, why?"

"You got to get here and get here quick! Rose and I are in lockdown and they're threatening to call my nephew!"

In the background, Roxie could hear furious pounding on the door. "Clara, what do you mean 'lockdown'? What's—"

"It's Pumper," Clara yelled. "He saw a cat out the window and about lost his mind!"

"Pumper actually *chased* a cat?" Surely that was one of the signs of the apocalypse.

"He was goin' to, but he got tangled in the blanket and fell off the bed."

"Is he OK?"

"He's fine. Got that nice Mr. Paulie from the gift

shop to drive us to the vet's, and now poor Pumper's leg is in a cast. But when we got back, that mean director, Mr. Fostwith, said the dog had to go."

"Oh no!"

"Yup! Rose and I fought 'em; we still are, but we've been in the room for two hours now and we're down to our last Doritos, so we can't hold out much longer. Roxie, I hate to ask you this, but . . . do you think you could take Pumper? Just until we find someone to adopt him that don't have no cats?"

Me? Be Pumper's foster mother? Roxie blinked. *Why the hell not? One narcoleptic beagle couldn't be much trouble.* "Sure I'll take Pumper for you. I'll be there soon."

"Good! Can you bring some food when you come? Rose and I are starving. I think— Wait! Drat them, they're trying to take the door off the hinges. *Rose, I'll get the Taser, you move that chair—*"

The line went dead.

Taser? They had a Taser?

Mark was already turning the car around. "I *have* to see Mother's face when you bring that mutt home."

Roxie flipped him the bird. Mark laughed.

They reached the center just as a janitor was replacing the hinges on Clara's door. Pumper was quite a sight, poor thing, one leg in a cast, his tail wagging at the sight of Roxie.

Mark wrapped Pumper in a blanket and carefully carried him out to the car.

As he left, Roxie bent down to Clara and whispered, "You were just kidding about the Taser, right?"

Clara's grin widened. She slipped a hand into her housecoat pocket and, looking right and left, slipped out a Pepto-pink Taser.

Roxie groaned.

Clara cackled and dropped the Taser back into her pocket. "It's a dangerous world out there. Heck, you know that, since someone beaned your noggin last night."

"How do you know about that?"

"Nick stopped by this morning. Surprised you didn't see him on your way out. He hadn't slept all night, because he was keepin' watch outside your house."

"I—I—That was nice of him."

"Didn't think he'd leave you unprotected, did you? But don't you worry none. While you're here, I've got you covered." Clara patted her pocket. "Saw one of these in a movie and ordered it off the Net. Cheap as hell, compared to the cost of bullets and a real gun."

"Clara, you don't plan on really using that, do you?"

"'Course I do! Rose and I gave one of the gardeners a bottle of our special bourbon if he'd let us practice Tasin' him." She cackled. "I don't think he believes we have a real one, but hoo boy, he's gonna find out!"

Roxie thought fast. "Clara, would you mind if I borrowed your Taser for the next few days? I'm afraid of being attacked again. As soon as Nick figures out who broke into my house, I'll give it back to you."

Clara was clearly waffling, so she added, "I *am* taking Pumper for you."

Clara scowled. "Well . . . okay. You'll bring it back soon?"

"Yes. I promise." Though it wouldn't work by then. A good dunking in a pan of boiling water should take care of that.

Clara reluctantly handed the Taser to Roxie, who immediately turned on the safety and tucked it into her purse.

An aide appeared to take Clara to her physical therapy class, and Roxie headed out to the car, where Mark was waiting.

"Still want to go to the store?" he asked.

"Still want a beer?"

As Mark drove toward The Pig, Roxie closed her eyes as the wind ruffled her hair and the sun warmed her face. After last night's excitement, she welcomed the moment of peace. She just wanted to let the breeze take her away, away from the stress and fear from last night. Away from Glory and Mother and Nick.

Nick? Why had she included him? After all, he'd sat outside her house all night, watching and protecting her.

But he'd have done the same for anyone else in town, too. Their mutual attraction was going nowhere; another reason to leave Glory as soon as possible. Mother was doing better every day and would be able to resume her life soon, then it would be time to leave for Paris and other exotic locales. She wouldn't stop until she'd sunbathed nude on the Italian Riviera.

She tried to imagine herself sunbathing nude with a half dozen handsome, adoring Italian men, but she kept seeing Nick's hard body—his tight, ripped stomach, the strong arms and shoulders that had comforted her the night before.

"Here we are." Mark parked the car between two huge old Buicks.

She'd been coming to this store since she was a child, riding in the bottom tray of the buggy and trying to grab cookies when Mother hadn't been looking. All these years later, some of the exact same cars were still pulling into the parking lot. It must be senior citizen day at The Pig.

Mark handed Roxie a twenty. "Get me some of the good stuff."

"Aren't you coming?"

"And leave Pumper alone?" Mark settled down in his corner and settled his chin against his chest, his eyes closing. "I'll stay here and watch the mutt."

"Lazy ass. You two deserve each other."

Mark grinned but didn't move.

As Roxie entered the store, she saw a young mother with two small children begging for cookies ahead of her.

Her own mother had done so much for Roxie and

Mark. Maybe she'd pick up some orange sherbet for Mother. That might help ease the shock of Pumper, too.

Everything in The Pig was comfortingly the same as it had been ten years ago. The aisles were exactly the same and it took her only a few moments to zip through the store to find what she wanted.

Moments later, she made her way out the front door.

As she pushed the door open with her elbow, one of her bags, perched precariously on top, fell to the ground.

"Are you going to eat all of that yourself?"

The deep voice stopped her in her tracks, and a quiver raced over her skin. Slowly, she turned.

Nick Sheppard stood by a gleaming black Camaro. And not just "a" Camaro but "the" Camaro. It was polished and gorgeous, the top peeled back to reveal black leather seats. Despite the car's appeal, it did nothing to distract from the man leaning against it. Every bit as dark, lean, and muscled as the car, he appeared the more lethal of the two.

Oh *yeah!* her pulsating libido yelled gleefully. Nick Sheppard in a uniform was hot, but Nick Sheppard in worn jeans and a T-shirt was a sight to make ice cream melt—which hers would, if she kept standing here, staring at Nick as if she'd never seen a man before.

She cleared her throat. "I was getting supplies. For Mark." Her gaze fell on the Little Debbies and ice cream. "And Mother."

Nick pushed away from his car and walked toward her with athletic grace. "I think that some of that's for you, and you plan to enjoy it all on your own." His gaze dropped to her mouth. "You always were a little greedy."

Her skin tingled in an alarming way. She couldn't help but notice the way his T-shirt stretched tautly across his broad shoulders and draped over a trim stomach that was as rippled as the tide at full moon.

Roxie immediately sucked in her own stomach. It wasn't fair that men never seemed to gain a pound over the years, while women attracted fat like little magnet dogs.

Did Nick think a woman of her size shouldn't eat ice cream? Well, too bad for him. After last night, she deserved ice cream. "Yes, I am going to eat all of this. Every last bite."

An amused glint entered his eyes. "My mom always said that only a fool would come between a woman and her chocolate, so I'm not even going to ask if you'll share."

"I'd share the beer; that really is for Mark. But your mother's right: the ice cream and Little Debbies are all mine, and you can't have any."

His gaze dropped from her lips. "No? What if I decide to—"

"Roxie!" Mark called from the car.

Nick sent him an annoyed glance before turning back to her. "Before you go, I need to ask a favor."

"A favor? From me?"

He flashed her a lopsided grin that made her stomach tighten. "Yes, from you."

She realized he had the faintest hint of a five-o'clock shadow. It looked good on him, too. *Really* good. "Sure. What do you need?"

"I've been thinking it over and—" He took a deep breath. "Roxie, will you help me with Doyle's case?"

She dropped her bag.

Nick caught it with one hand just before it hit the ground. "Mark would be ticked off if you broke his beer."

"Forget the damn beer. Nick, you've been telling me to forget this case since I got to town. Why do you want me to help you now?"

"I wanted to protect you from things like this." He lifted a hand to brush her hair from the knot on her forehead, his expression grim. "That looks brutal. Does it hurt?"

Not when you're touching me. For a terrified moment she thought she'd said it aloud. Cheeks heating, she said, "Just a little."

He dropped his hand to his side and she saw that he'd balled it into a fist. "Since whoever feels threatened by Doyle's investigation has obviously decided that you're involved, you might as well be. Roxie, someone broke into your house looking for Doyle's notes. People think *you* have them, not me."

"So what do we do? Make a sign that says, Doyle's Notes Are Not Here?"

He grinned. "No, the Stuff 'n Fluff."

"What?"

"You heard me." He gave her that adorable, you're-the-only-woman-for-me smile. "You wanted to help the investigation, and now you can."

"By making a hair appointment."

He nodded. "And while you're there, you'll announce that I came to your house today and forced you to give up Doyle's notes. Make sure that people know that I took them all into custody but will allow you to see them."

She narrowed her eyes. "I still want to see those notes. *All* of them."

After a moment, he nodded. "All right. Come by the office and we'll discuss the case. Since you're helping me, the least I can do is let you know how things stand."

"Thanks. I'm flattered."

"Don't be. If I could think of another way to keep you safe, other than linking you firmly to the Sheriff's Office, I'd do it."

"So this is for my protection?"

He hesitated. "No. It's also because I could use the help." At her surprised expression, he shrugged. "Look at old Pastor Rawlings's widow. As soon as she saw my uniform, she clammed up. Then you and Aunt Clara waltz in and she spills all of her late husband's secrets. I could use someone less—" He hesitated.

"Conspicuous?"

"Professional."

"I can be professional," she said in a lofty tone.

Nick looked her up and down, his eyes glinting with an appreciation that warmed her. "Fortunately for me, that's not the look you've been going for since you got back to town."

She tilted up her chin. "What's wrong with my look?"

His eyes slid across her, arrogant and masculine. "Not one damn thing."

She liked how he said that. Liked it a whole lot more than she should.

He crossed his arms, his stance a challenge. "Well, Treymayne, are you going to help? The secrets in Doyle's box are stirring up this sleepy town, and we need to put it back to bed."

Roxie noted the faint shadows under his eyes and felt a twinge of guilt. He'd stayed up all night just to watch over her.

Her throat tightened. She'd have been glad to help under any circumstances; she just wished it could be on a more even footing. "OK. I'll call Teresa at the Stuff 'n Fluff and make an appointment for tomorrow, if she has room."

"That's my girl."

Only she wasn't his girl, although some part of her whispered how much she'd like to be, at least for an hour . . . or two. Oh yes, at *least* two hours.

He returned her grocery bag. "Better get this to Mark before he decides to come and get it himself."

Roxie took the bag, her fingers brushing his. An instant tremor flashed through her, up her arm and across her chest. What was it about him that made her quiver like a Jell-O mold? "Thanks," she mumbled, deciding to leave before she said or did something she might regret. She took the bag and headed toward the Mustang.

"What were you two talking about?" Mark asked, his eyes bright with curiosity.

"Business." She tossed the bags into the car and slid in.

"What business?"

"None of yours," she returned.

"Sheesh. Ask a simple question . . ." Mark turned on the car and backed it out of the parking spot.

As they drove past him, Nick called out, "Hey Treymayne! Don't forget—" He touched his hair.

Roxie nodded but gazed straight ahead.

Some things were better left in the past. And Nick Sheppard was one of them.

chapter 16

Dear Bob,

My fiancée works at a public works office here in Glory. Last year, at the annual Christmas Party, her boss tried to sneak a kiss in the copy room. I wanted to hit the guy, but she talked me out of it, saying it could put her job in jeopardy.

Now that I'm sober I'm determined to do something about the situation, but my girlfriend says the guy was drunk and to just let it go.

What do you think?
Signed,
Madder Than Hell

Dear Madder Than the Big H,

Someone needs to tell Mayor Harkins that a gift exchange doesn't include the swapping of spit.

Meanwhile, have your girlfriend file a complaint. With elections coming up, Harkins can't afford to get involved in a wrongful firing case.
Signed,
Bob

The Glory Examiner
Aug. 25, section B3

〜◝

*R*OXIE WHISTLED SILENTLY. *The Glory Examiner*'s myserious Dear Bob wasn't afraid of putting the big smackdown on Mayor Harkins. She'd love to put her own smackdown on her attacker, as well as bring Doyle's killer to justice.

She tossed the paper to the car seat, and flipped down the visor mirror. The only evidence of the attack was a bump on the top of her head, an ugly bruise, and a faint scrape that she'd covered with a thin coat of makeup. Other than that, and a desire to keep a light on at night, she was as good as new.

She locked the car and headed across the street for the Stuff 'n Fluff. The place was packed, as always, and it looked as if Teresa had added five or six more chairs.

Amid the bustling cacophony of women's voices, hair dryers, and running water, a woman she didn't recognize looked up from the front desk.

"Can I help y—"

"*Roxie!*" Teresa came running across the room to envelop Roxie in a bone-cracking hug.

There was a momentary lull in the hum while everyone registered who she was. Then every hairdresser in the place immediately bent down to whisper in their clients' ears, no doubt recounting Roxie's every move since she'd returned to town.

Teresa held her at arm's length. "I can't believe

you're here! I was wondering when you'd stop by and say hello."

Roxie laughed. "I'm just lucky you had an opening when I called yesterday. This place is packed."

"We're doing pretty well," Teresa said with a grin. A petite, pixie-pretty blonde with generous curves and wide brown eyes, she didn't look a day older than she had when she'd been on the cheerleading squad, except for some faint laugh lines. She looked Roxie up and down. "Look at you! You are as gorgeous as ever, of course. How's Brian?"

"Brian and I are divorced, as I'm sure you already know."

Teresa wrinkled her nose. "I just thought you might want to make the announcement yourself. I always thought you two were the perfect couple."

"We make even better individuals, believe me."

"I'm sorry to hear that. Unless you're glad, in which case I'm not sorry at all. Do you want to talk about it?"

There was a breathless quality to the question, as if Teresa couldn't wait to hear the gory details.

Roxie smiled tightly. "No."

Teresa pouted. "Very well." She peeped at Roxie from beneath her lashes, a dimple appearing in her cheek. "At least stay long enough for me to tell you all of *my* news. If it's not about you, you, you, then you can listen to me, me, *me*!" She slung an arm around Roxie and turned her toward the row of chairs that lined the back of the shop. "So, what do you want done with your hair?"

"I'd like it much shorter. Something young and fashionable."

"Why, Roxanne Treymayne, are you ready to piss off your mother? 'Cause if you are"—Teresa took both of Roxie's hands in hers and said earnestly—"I'm the woman to help you do it."

Roxie laughed, relaxing. "Mother's ticked you off, hm?"

"Between telling me how I should run my business and critiquing my children, there have been days when it was only professional courtesy that I didn't bury my best shears in her throat."

"Mother has that effect on people."

"You don't know the half of it. Come on back and we'll get you washed."

Roxie sat in the chair at the first glossy black sink while Teresa whisked out a black cape and fastened the Velcro around her neck.

"I didn't expect to like you blonde, especially after hearing your mother's description, but you look like a young Marilyn Monroe."

"Thanks." Roxie gazed down the line of hair dryers. Under one sat a stuffed raccoon, its teeth gnashed in a snarl. "I see Ricky's still doing his taxidermy next door."

Ricky ran the "Stuff" portion of the Stuff 'n Fluff, much to the delight of the male residents of Glory, who were able to hang out at his shop while their wives were getting their hair done.

"Oh, he's full-time with it now," Teresa said proudly. "Business has been going gangbusters and he's won all kinds of taxidermy awards. Why, I just added another chair to my shop last month and—Where are my scissors?" She let out an exasperated sigh. "Just a sec." She walked to the wall and thumped on it.

Moments later, the adjoining door opened and a stocky, brown-haired man with a round, friendly face peeked around the corner. "Yes, dear?"

"Did you take my scissors?"

Ricky had the grace to look sheepish. "Sorry. I was trimming the whiskers on a mountain cat." He disappeared, then returned carrying a pair of professional shears. He saw Roxanne this time, his eyes widening. "Roxie! I'd heard you'd come back and—is that a navel ring?"

His wife followed his gaze to where Roxie's T-shirt had lifted a bit.

Two women sitting under dryers nearby watched with interest, their magazines forgotten.

Teresa gasped. "Roxanne Treymayne, you *slut*! I'm so proud of you!"

Roxie said wryly, "I don't know that 'slut' was what I was going for, but it's better than Stepford Wife."

"I like it," Ricky said. "Teresa, you should get—"

"Don't even say it! I haven't found the nerve to get

my ears pierced, so what makes you think I'll let anyone near my stomach with a needle?"

Ricky chuckled. "Too bad. You'd look sexy."

Teresa blushed and flicked a hand at him. "Get out of here! Can't you see I've got customers?"

Ricky grinned. "Roxie, it was good to see you." He shut the door behind him.

"He's still sweet on you," Roxie said wistfully.

Teresa sighed happily. "Twenty years later, and he still makes me smile. I'm one lucky woman. By the way, do you remember Tiffany MacLean? Well, she married Noah Baxter, and . . ."

Teresa prattled on about who'd married whom and still lived in the area, and who'd moved on. As she talked, she escorted her to her station, past a row of interested faces.

When they reached Teresa's station, Roxie sat down while Teresa stood back and looked at her like a sculptor regarding a block of marble.

"Hm." Teresa's eyes narrowed as she regarded Roxie for a long moment. "How much of a change do you want?"

"A lot."

Teresa leveled a hand at Roxie's jaw. "Right here. With your eyes . . . yup, that's it. I'll give you a sense of it now." With an expert twist, Teresa secured Roxie's hair to the back of her head with a clip.

Roxie looked at herself in the mirror. Teresa was

right; with her hair shorter, her eyes looked bigger.

She met Teresa's gaze in the mirror. "Cut it short."

Teresa grinned. "Thatagirl! I'm also going to suggest a few lowlights to give your hair more depth. Maybe a little honey blonde and a caramel strand here and there."

Honey and caramel? Why not? "Done."

Teresa took her scissors to the sink to scrub them. "You are going to *love* this! I'm going to angle the front toward your chin and—"

She chatted on while Roxie waited, noting that the shop had filled even more since she'd come in. Women were talking in the lobby, chatting by a watercooler, standing by dryers discussing life and love and all the things that made life worthwhile.

And someone here was going to pass important information to the real bad guy or gal. All Roxie had to do was casually bring up Doyle's murder and announce that Nick had taken the box of notes to process them. How could she do that so that it didn't seem contrived?

Moments later, Teresa was busy cutting Roxie's hair. "So, tell me about this Murder Mystery Club."

Roxie couldn't help grinning. "How do you know about that?"

"I see Clara and Rose every Wednesday. They've done nothing but sing your praises since you got back in town. They're both quite fond of you, especially Clara."

Clara would like anyone who drank bourbon with her before noon. "She's quite the character."

"Don't you know it." Teresa laughed, snipping hair here and there. "So tell me, do you think Doyle Cloyd was murdered?"

Strands of blonde hair landed on the polyester cape and slid to the floor. "I don't know what I think," Roxie said casually, though she spoke very clearly so that the women and hairdressers to either side of her could hear. "I suppose they told you about the black-mail notes?"

"Lord, yes! I was talking about that to Mrs. Gannon the other day and she said she wasn't surprised about the mayor, but the preacher? What could Doyle have known about the preacher?"

"Mrs. Gannon? Our high school English teacher?"

"That's the one. She's completely white-haired now, but just as mean as ever. Never tips me more than a dollar and is forever correcting my grammar when I talk." Teresa made a face. "I hate that."

"I would, too." Under the cape, Roxie rubbed her hands on her jeans. "It's a pity the sheriff took all of Doyle's notes into custody."

"No! All of them?"

"Yup." Roxie thought quickly and said in what she hoped was a disgruntled tone, "I wanted to keep them and decipher them for the group, but Nick—I mean, the sheriff—insisted on taking them."

Teresa met Roxie's gaze in the mirror and said just

a bit too casually, "So, you've had a chance to run into him?"

"Yes." Seeing that Teresa expected more, Roxie added, "He hasn't changed much."

"He's even yummier." Teresa sighed dreamily. "When I was in high school I'd have given up cheer-leading for one date with him, though he never looked my way."

"If I remember right, my brother was the one who chased you all through high school."

Teresa grinned. "Yes, he did. I hear he came back with you."

"He's dog sitting for me right now. I took Pumper for Clara."

Teresa laughed. "Oh, did they finally get caught? I knew it was only a matter of time."

"I arrived just in time to stop Clara from Tasing the center director and rescue poor Pumper from being tossed into the street."

"Clara has a Taser?"

"Had. I took it."

"Good for you." Teresa clicked her tongue. "I swear, you never know what that woman might be into. She once told me—"

"Ouch!"

Teresa paused, her comb at Roxie's temple. "What's wrong?"

"Sorry, I have a bruise there."

"From the attack the other night? Did Nick ever

figure out who it was? I heard he'd decided it was a juvenile prank."

Just what Nick wanted everyone to think. The Glory Rumor Mill was fast and surprisingly accurate. Now, if they could just stop it from also being potentially deadly. "That's what we think; that it was just a kid."

"You didn't see anything?"

"Nope, not a thing. But it's no biggie; now I have Pumper for protection."

Teresa laughed and finished up the cut. "A wet dishrag would be more protection than that mutt. The only useful thing that dog's ever done was growl at Robin Wright every time he had the chance."

"Pumper *growled*? I didn't think he had it in him. I bet Robin liked that."

"She hates the dog, and everyone else for that matter." Teresa made a face. "Every time she comes in here, she brags about what new bling she's managed to suck out of the mayor. Last time it was a pair of teardrop diamond earrings. She kept saying they 'look so rich,' as if that was *the* thing to call something sparkly." Teresa shrugged. "You can take a girl out of Pine Hills, but you can't take Pine Hills out of the girl."

"I bet that was pleasant for you."

Teresa grinned. "Oh, I didn't mind. I just added a dollar to her cost every time she said the word 'rich.' I charged her twice what she normally pays, and when she asked why, I told her I'd used my 'richest' products on her hair."

Roxie laughed.

Teresa tossed her shears back into the blue disinfectant. "I'm going to get your color. Back in a few."

Finally, after the color was set under a dryer and a quick wash and blow-dry, Roxie was escorted back to Teresa's chair for styling.

"There!" Teresa turned Roxie's chair so that she faced the mirror.

Her mouth opened in a silent O.

Gone was the silver-blonde ponytail. In its place was a studiously messy mop of wispy gold and caramel curls clinging softly to her cheeks and forehead. It was sheer elegance and made her eyes look huge.

Teresa leaned against the chair and smiled sassily. "Not bad for a country stylist, hm?"

"It's perfect!" Roxie said truthfully.

Teresa unhooked the cape and pulled it off, blonde hair falling to the ground.

Roxie stood, the cool air tickling her ears. She felt light and weightless and free. She stared at the mirror, still amazed. "I can't believe that's *me*."

"Believe it." Teresa led the way to the register at the front of the store. "All you really needed was a dash of color and a bit of a shape-up."

Yes, she had. More than Teresa realized. "I love it!"

"Good!" Teresa hit a button on the cash register. "Your mother called last week and said to use her credit card, once she managed to talk you into coming."

"She didn't talk me into coming; I did that myself."

"I'd still let her pay. Make her feel as if she's done something for you."

Roxie grinned. "Don't forget to put in a good tip."

"You got it! I'll—"

The door jangled as it opened, and Roxie turned and found herself standing face-to-face with Nick.

Dressed in his uniform, he seemed to fill the entire front of the shop. His gaze slid across her and made her heart leap before he turned to Teresa. "Sorry to barge in, but Susan asked me to do this last week and I forgot. She wants to know if you'd come to her house sometime and cut her father's hair."

"Sure!" Teresa said cheerfully, marking it in the appointment book. "Tell her I'll be there around eight on Tuesday. I have to stop by Mrs. Clareton's first." Teresa put the book away and finished ringing up Roxie. "Tell your mother thanks for the tip."

Roxie tore her gaze from Nick to grin at Teresa. "I certainly will."

Nick couldn't look away from Roxie's smile. It wasn't right that a simple smile should affect him the way hers did, but it always had. Her smile was especially alluring with her new haircut. It was hard to ignore the bewildering array of silky curls that clung to her face and neck so sexily. No matter what she did—wore jeans or a silk dress, wore her hair long and brown or short and blonde, wore makeup or went fresh-faced—she was the most beautiful woman he'd ever seen.

She turned from Teresa and caught his gaze, her grin

transforming instantly into a polite smile, the glow disappearing.

It was like seeing the last vestige of light sink out of sight on a cold winter's night, and all of the warmth went with it. He'd delivered Susan's message and there was really no reason to stay, but he heard himself ask, "Have you been out to see my aunt Clara today?"

Roxie nodded, turning over her shoulder to wave good-bye to Teresa, who watched with bright, interested eyes.

Nick caught the avid interest on Teresa's face and gave her a warm smile. Then, to really get tongues wagging, he took Roxie's elbow and walked her across the street to her car.

To his surprise, she allowed him to do so, though the moment they reached her car, she adjusted her purse and freed her arm in the process. Nick glanced back at the hair salon and surprised Teresa and two of the other stylists peeking out the window at them. All three waved, and not one had the grace to look embarrassed.

He turned his back on them as Roxie unlocked her car.

"I did it," she said, glancing up at him through her lashes. "I made sure plenty of people heard me talking to Teresa about how you had all of Doyle's notes now."

"And the break-in from the other night?"

"Teenagers." She shrugged. "For all we know, that's what it could have been."

"They left the DVD player and took a box of kosher cookbooks. It was either someone after Doyle's notes or the Jewish mafia."

She chuckled as she opened the car door and tossed her purse inside. "Perhaps someone tasted Tundy's matzo balls and decided to take pity on us."

He laughed.

Roxie glanced at the hair salon. "So now that the whole of Glory is about to find out that Doyle's notes are in your office, what's next?"

His gaze traveled to her mouth. There was something about it that made his body react in all the right ways. "Beginning tomorrow night, I'll stake out the office, hoping for a glimpse of your visitor. This is all confidential, of course. I don't want you to tell anyone, not even Mark."

"I won't breathe a word. Will you . . . will you be there all by yourself?"

"I might ask old Sheriff Thompson to come and help out. He's still a reserve officer and occasionally drops by when I need an extra set of hands. He's going to start coming by your house, too. Just to check on you and your mother."

"Do you—do you think whoever it was will come back—"

"No," he said firmly, hating the tremor in her voice. "I *don't* think he'll come back, but it's better to be safe." He glanced back at the Stuff 'n Fluff. "I'd better get to City Hall. I'm meeting the mayor about the budget.

Roxie, why don't you stop by my office later on. I want to talk to you about Doyle's case."

For a moment she looked speechless, then her eyes shone. "Nick, I—thank you!"

He shrugged. "We're partners, aren't we?"

Color stained her cheeks though she said calmly, "Sounds good. I'll stop by this afternoon."

She slid into her seat and Nick closed her door, then he stepped back and watched her drive away.

He glanced over at the Stuff 'n Fluff. Only Teresa remained at the window, but he had little doubt she was reporting every nuance of his and Roxie's body language during their conversation.

Good. He wanted people to think Roxie was with him. It might keep any other crazed housebreakers away.

As Nick walked toward City Hall, he saw Mayor Harkins on the front portico, an ugly sneer on his face.

Nick followed the mayor's gaze and caught sight of Roxie's red car as it sped out of sight.

chapter 17

Dear Bob,
  There's this girl I've been meaning
to ask out, but every time I go to
do it, she's already got a date with
someone else.
  How should I take this?
Signed,
Wants a Chance

Dear Wants,
  You should have signed your question
as Snoozer and Loser, because that's
where you're headed. If you want to
ask this girl out, then do it and stop
fiddle-faddling around!
  Here's a clue on how to interpret her
answer: if she wants to go out with
you she will, and if she doesn't, she
won't.
Signed,
Bob

The Glory Examiner
Aug. 26, section B3

⁓

"*S*USAN, DID YOU TAPE another 'Dear Bob' to the announcement board?" Nick demanded as he stopped in her office.

Susan smiled smugly as she closed a file drawer. "Yes, I did. I thought you might find something relevant in Dear Bob's sage words."

"Well, I didn't."

"Then read it again, because that could be written directly to you. If you snooze, you lose. Words to live by."

Nick set down the box he was carrying. "Take it off the announcement board. That's for felons, Amber Alerts, and other important things."

"I like 'Dear Bob.' It's the best part of the paper now that Ty took it over and started running more ads than articles." She pointed to the box. "What's that?"

"That is what we call a 'decoy.'" After lunch, when the town square had been the busiest, Nick had carried the large box to his squad car. Saying hi to the postman and waving at Mrs. Haverland, who owned the flower shop, he'd made sure everyone had seen him. He'd even stopped by the Stuff 'n Fluff to make an appointment to get a haircut.

Everywhere he'd gone, people had stared at the box. It was empty, but he'd written across it in large black block letters, EVIDENCE—DOYLE CLOYD.

Once he'd reached his car, he'd tossed the box in the

backseat, when a sharp "Sheriff!" had brought him up short.

Robin Wright had jogged across the street and panted to a stop, pressing a hand to her overflowing breasts, barely contained in a small exercise top. "Goodness, I can't catch my breath!"

Probably because she'd ordered breasts that were three sizes too large for her narrow rib cage. "Did you want something?"

Robin's eyes had flashed at his dismissive tone, her bow of a mouth tightening.

When he had first returned to Glory, Robin had made up to him in a very unmistakable manner. He'd considered taking her up on what she'd been offering, because she was reasonably attractive. And if her eyes were a little narrow and her temper uneven, well, he could ignore those in bed.

But she made it clear that though she'd wanted to hop into Nick's bed, it was to have been on the sly only; she relished her position as the mayor's girlfriend and hadn't been about to give it up. Nick had no desire to make a cuckold out of his own boss, or any other man for that matter, so he'd turned down Robin's numerous offers.

From then on, Robin had lost no opportunity to make his life in Glory a little less rosy, using her influence with the mayor to cut his budget, question expenses, and add duties to his already overflowing plate.

Nick didn't trust the witch as far as he could spit.

Her gaze had immediately locked on the box. "What's that?"

"What's what?"

She'd frowned, her narrow eyes glinting hostility. "The box you've got in your backseat."

"Oh, that. It's an old case. Something my aunt Clara's Murder Mystery Club turned up by chance."

"There hasn't been a murder in this county in a hundred years."

"That's exactly what I said. But they're determined to prove that old Doyle Cloyd died under mysterious circumstances."

Robin's gaze had lit with sudden interest. "Did he?"

"Not that I can tell, but you never know. I got the box from Roxie Treymayne, who was holding it for my aunt, and now I'm going to investigate."

"Good."

Nick's surprise must have shown, because Robin had given a cold, brittle laugh. "You may not know this, but after his sister died, I'm Doyle's last living relative. And it wouldn't surprise me if someone had murdered him. He was a bitter old man. I couldn't stand him."

"Most people couldn't."

"A lot of people could claim to want him dead, the old blackmailer, although . . ." Robin had pinned Nick with a hard look. "You know who wanted him dead the most? Lilah Treymayne."

"*Lilah?*"

Robin had tossed her head, her gaudy diamond earrings glittering against her dark hair. "No one is going to make me believe that woman doesn't have something to hide."

Nick had been careful to keep from showing any more interest. "I never thought you the amateur sleuth type."

She'd shrugged, causing absolutely no movement in her breasts. Like two solidly carved pieces of art, they'd stood at arrogant attention. "I keep my ear to the ground. By the way, if any money is found from Doyle's blackmail letters, it should come to me."

"I sincerely doubt there's any money lying around."

"There could be. Doyle never did the expected." Robin had looked at her watch. "I'd better get back to the office. Charlie will be waiting on me." She'd flicked a glance back at Nick, her gaze tracing over him until he'd shifted uncomfortably.

She'd purred, "It's a pity you aren't more friendly to me, Nick. I could make things so much easier for you with the mayor!" When Nick hadn't responded, her eyes had hardened. "Have it your way, then." She'd turned on her heel and had sprinted across the street and to the front steps of City Hall.

What in the hell had Robin meant about Lilah having a reason to want Doyle Cloyd dead? Roxie's mother might have been as loony as ten loose nuts in a box, but she wasn't capable of murder.

Still, in his years working undercover, he'd learned

that just when you decided human nature was predictable and let your guard down, you got your teeth kicked
in by an innocent-looking little old grandmother.

The phone rang now, and Susan answered it. She
motioned him to be quiet and gave a wry grimace as she
spoke into the receiver, "Yes, Mayor Harkins. I'll tell
him to call you as soon as he returns. Yes. I will! OK.
Sure. I will. Right. 'Bye." She hung up the phone with
a decided slam.

Nick went to pour himself a cup of coffee. "Let me
guess; the mayor's on the warpath."

"You have no idea." She leaned back in her chair and
stretched her long arms over her head.

Had the old guy seen him talking to Robin? "Was he
complaining about me?"

"No, about your aunt's Murder Mystery Club."

"What's she done now?"

"Nothing. But he feels things are getting out of hand
because everyone in town is talking about Doyle's blackmail letters." Susan grinned. "Your aunt's stirring up a
mess, isn't she?"

"I think Rose is the brains of the group. My aunt is
just the fetch-and-carry guy."

Susan chuckled. "They are characters, the both of
them."

"As are half of the town's residents."

Susan gathered some papers and stacked them neatly
in a tray. "Did you get a chance to speak to Teresa at the
Stuff 'n Fluff?"

"Yes. She said eight on Tuesday would work."

"My shaggy father and I thank you."

"Sorry it slipped my mind. I kept forgetting to ask."

"That's OK. It's been a busy week." Susan opened a drawer, pulled out a few new pencils, and filled the cup on her desk, asking casually, "Did you see anyone else while you were at the Stuff 'n Fluff?"

"No," he said. When Susan gave him a flat stare, he said, "All right, I saw Roxie. She got her hair cut."

"Oh. Was she alone?"

"She was with Teresa."

"No, I meant—" Susan colored. "Never mind."

Nick eyed Susan's flushed face. "If you're asking if I saw Mark, the answer is no."

She turned a brighter red. "I didn't say a word about Mark; you did. Back to your aunt's club, it's surprising that the newspaper hasn't done a story on them."

"Ty's probably squelched it. He avoids anything faintly controversial."

"He's a fool. If he wants more ad revenue, he needs to increase circulation, and the only way to do that is with good reporting. And a geriatric club investigating a possible murder is a great human interest story. It has it all: strong characters, mystery, suspense, and a great setup."

"Sometimes I forget you majored in journalism."

"I'd love to do investigative reporting someday. Meanwhile, I compiled the research you requested on Doyle." She opened a drawer and pulled out a thick folder.

Nick took it and flipped through it, his brows lifting as he noted the amount of information she'd put together.

"Is it what you wanted?"

"Yes. More, in fact." He closed the file and tucked it into the box. "I've never seen anyone with a stronger gift for investigating."

She pinkened. "There was a lot of info to be found. Nick, do you believe Doyle was murdered?"

"No. I'm sure my aunt and her club are ready to call this a mob hit or something just as sensational, but I can't swallow that." Nick added some creamer to his coffee. "Is the mayor expecting me soon? I spent an hour there this morning and I'm about mayor'd out." Far more onerous was the fact that Nick couldn't forget the expression he'd surprised on Mayor Harkins's face as he'd watched Roxie drive out of town after her visit to the Stuff 'n Fluff.

Susan shook her head. "When he called earlier I told him you were out serving warrants on deadbeat dads until this afternoon. It was one of his campaign promises and he's determined to see some action on it, so he didn't demand that you trot over to City Hall immediately, as he usually does."

"Good girl."

She arched a brow.

"I mean, 'excellent job,'" he amended hastily. Susan never got mad, but she *would* get even. "Thanks, Susan."

Nick balanced the box against his hip and, carrying his coffee, disappeared into his office. Soon, he was settled at his desk and sorting through the file. Susan had done a terrific job: every page was dated and referenced, and she'd scoured not just the local papers but some national publications as well. Better yet, she'd also accessed public records to find birth and marriage certificates, land deeds, wills, and other materials all neatly printed out and labeled.

He pulled out a yellow notepad and spread out the papers. First was a copy of a rather decrepit birth certificate for Doyle Floyd Cloyd. Poor Doyle. No wonder he'd had problems.

Following were two marriage certificates, neither to women Nick had ever heard of, and two sets of divorce papers. No children seemed to have come from either union.

Then came a welter of land deeds, tax records, and more. Nick's coffee grew cold, and he refilled it twice and let it grow cold again. Susan made another pot and brought him a refill, which he also forgot to drink.

He was lost in a sea of numbers and letters, his yellow pad filled with scribbles, when a feminine shadow darkened his door. Nick glanced up, expecting to see Susan, and promptly lost his train of thought.

Roxie stood framed in the doorway, a huge pair of sunglasses covering her eyes, a pair of white shorts setting off her tanned legs, while a tiny—*very* tiny—pink shirt outlined her best assets. He remembered those breasts, remembered their shape and feel, the way her nipples would pucker at the slightest stimulation. Seeing them now, and so lushly framed, made his mouth go dry.

He leaned back in his chair and linked his hands behind his head. "Come in, please." He nodded toward a chair.

Roxie didn't move. "I can come back later, if you need to go. Susan said you have a meeting with the mayor."

He eyed her shoes. High heels with shorts. It wasn't a look one often saw in Glory, which was a damned shame.

"The mayor can wait." Nick grinned. "Every time I go to see him, he makes me wait exactly fifteen minutes. He can do the same for me once in a while."

She stepped inside the room, a faint smile touching her kissable mouth. "He does it on purpose?"

"He read a self-help book on being a power broker, and there was a chapter entitled 'Making Them Wait.' I saw it in the men's room at City Hall."

She slipped the sunglasses off and her eyes twinkled, light blue and irresistible. "You're making that up."

"Nope. Read it myself the last time I was waiting on the mayor."

She giggled, which made Nick feel very good.

"So, Treymayne, can I interest you in a cup of my gourmet dollar brand coffee?"

"Dollar brand is not what I'd call 'gourmet.' "

"It's how you make it, not what you make it with."

He rose, taking his own cup with him. "Cream and sugar?"

"No, black."

"I'll be right back." He went into the outer office, Susan's brows rising when he appeared. For some reason, his face grew hot. "Roxie wants some coffee." The words sounded defensive, even to him.

"Then Roxie shall have some coffee," Susan replied, flicking him a smile.

He hurried to the pot and poured two cups, then headed back to his office. "Roxie and I are going over Doyle's files, and—"

"Nick, you and Roxie are both adults. Besides"—she closed her file drawer and gathered her things—"would you mind if I took off now? It's an hour early, but I have some comp time coming and I need to pick up my father's dry cleaning."

"Sure. No problem. I'll see you tomorrow. Roxie and I'll just, uh—We're going to discuss Doyle's case."

Susan rolled her eyes. She fished something out of her purse and, as she walked past Nick, tucked it into his pocket and gave it a pat. "I'll expect a full report tomorrow."

As the door closed behind her, Nick looked into his pocket and saw a small foil condom packet.

Grumbling, he tossed the condom in Susan's top drawer, then picked up the coffees again and returned to his office. Roxie was still standing in front of his desk, her hands clenched at her sides.

So she was as nervous as he was. That was a good thing, wasn't it? He handed her the cup.

She took it, then sat in the chair in front of his desk. That almost undid him, for her white shorts slid up and revealed her smooth, tanned thigh at an intriguing height. She had the most deliciously curved legs this side of the Atlantic.

Flooded with an instant image of those legs clasped about his waist, he hurried to sit back behind his desk to disguise his reaction.

She took a sip of coffee and grimaced.

"That bad?"

"No, it's just hot." She blew on the coffee, and Nick was mesmerized.

No other woman had lips like Roxie. Soft and the most tantalizing pink, her bottom lip was just a touch wider than the top and deliciously full. It was agony watching her pucker and gently blow across her coffee cup. His body tightened, as if she'd been blowing on him.

She blew once more, then took another sip. "Much better. So, you have the new information about Doyle?"

He dug through the papers on his desk, then handed a file to her. "Here's the case file. I made you a copy, so you can keep that."

"Thanks." Roxie paged through it, trying to focus on the words and failing. When Nick had looked up and recognized her in the doorway, he'd looked so happy to see her.

But he'd clearly managed to contain his pleasure, if that's what it had been. Now, he was looking at her without any discernable expression at all.

Well, she could do the same. She put the file on her lap. "Nick, I did some research on the mayor and I thought you might be interested in what I found out. I used your aunt Clara's investigation techniques, and they worked pretty well."

Nick's lips twitched. "What exactly *are* Aunt Clara's investigation techniques?"

Roxie counted them off on her fingers. "Badgering, eavesdropping, character assassination—oh, and bribery."

"That's quite an arsenal. I'll have to ask her to give a workshop for the rest of us."

He clasped his hands on the table, his gray gaze locked on her. "Well, Treymayne? What did you find out?"

She reached for her purse, found C.J.'s notebook, and flipped through the pages. "Here it is. The mayor is having some financial troubles. Serious ones."

"How do you know that?"

"Does it matter?"

"It might."

"I looked in his mailbox."

Nick winced but didn't tell her to quit, so she continued. "Mayor Harkins hasn't checked his mail in at least a week and there were four envelopes from a mortgage company. One was stamped Foreclosure Notice."

Nick leaned forward. "Go ahead."

"There were also notices from a slew of credit lenders and the IRS."

Nick whistled. "That sounds pretty bad."

"I think so, too. Since he hasn't gotten his mail, I think he's in denial."

"Seems to be a way of life for him."

Roxie flipped to another page. "He also asked his ex for a loan."

"That's class."

"That's Mayor Harkins. I got that information from the ex–Mrs. Harkins herself. She was very eager to talk."

"I bet she was. What did she say to his loan request?"

"She said that once he caught up on her alimony payments, she'd consider it."

"Ouch!"

Roxie flipped to another page. "She also told me that the mayor recently sold his bass boat and the pocket watches he'd inherited from his father."

Nick nodded. "You've gathered quite a bit of information. Good job. There are detectives who wouldn't have been so thorough."

Roxie went hot with pleasure. "Thanks."

He flashed her a look of appreciation, which made her even hotter.

His gaze flickered over her, resting on her hair, her eyes, and her breasts. The intimate look reminded her of the kiss in her driveway and of other, long-ago kisses in the back of a red-hot Camaro.

She shifted a little uncomfortably, her hormones wakening at the memory. They'd been hungry then, starving for each other, and just a look across a room could set them both aflame. It was a good thing she wasn't affected in such a way now.

"Did you—" Her voice cracked, and she cleared it before continuing. "Nick, thanks for sharing the report. At first I thought you didn't want me involved in Doyle's investigation because you didn't trust me."

"Trust had nothing to do with it." His gaze flickered to her forehead, where her curls hid the bruise. "Safety was my only concern, though that's a moot point now. Someone in this town definitely wants the investigation into Doyle's blackmail schemes to disappear, and they aren't shy about it."

"So what are you going to do, besides hope in the next week or so that someone comes looking for that box?" She nodded to the evidence box on a table in one corner.

"I'm trying to learn everything I can about Doyle." He gestured to the piles of papers on his desk. "That's what all of this is for."

"And then?"

"And then I'm going to start tracing leads, including the one you just gave me about the mayor." His chair creaked as he leaned back. "So what do *you* think of all this? I could use some help."

Her heart warmed. "There's one thing that I keep wondering about. While Doyle had the intelligence to glean information useful for a blackmail scheme, he doesn't strike me as a person capable of putting such a thing together. So perhaps—"

"Someone else was behind it? That's what I think, too." Nick looked through the papers and pulled out a neatly stacked set of documents. "Copies of Doyle's bank statements." He handed them to Roxie.

She flipped through them. "There's nothing here."

"Nope. His government check was direct deposited into his account and that was it. Not another penny."

"Did he have more than one account?"

"Not that Susan can discover, and she's very thorough. But I did find this." He went to another table, pulled back two boxes of copy paper, and brought out Doyle's box. He took a folder off the top and carefully hid the box again, then brought the folder to the desk. He opened the file, took out a paper, and handed it to her.

She looked at it. "A ledger of the blackmail notes. Did you decipher all of them?"

"All but two." He tapped the paper in her hand. "The person who paid is listed on the left, the date follows, with the amount in the final column."

She looked at the final total. "That's a lot of money."

"Four hundred twenty thousand dollars over a three-year period. You could live well in Glory with that kind of money."

"Or buy someone a lot of baubles." Roxie thought of the diamond earrings Teresa had mentioned Robin showing off. "What a tangle. No clues where there should be, and clues where you'd never think to find them."

"That's why they call it a mystery." His gaze flickered to her forehead. "How are you feeling today?"

She looked up, her cheeks pink. "I'm fine. Mark told me you sat outside my house the night after the attack. Thank you for that."

"That's what I'm here for." He gave her a rueful smile. "Old Sheriff Thompson said something interesting to me the other night. He said I wasn't in Atlanta anymore, and that things were different in a small town. Well, they are. I need to catalogue all of this information, and as I said, I need some help."

He handed her a yellow legal pad covered with strong, bold writing. "I've been reading through each document, making notes on anything that might be of interest."

Roxie looked through it. "How do you decide what's important?"

"By looking for connections."

She was silent a moment, flipping through the pages. Finally, she said, "I have an idea. When we've condensed all of this, we can cut the paper into slips and use each as a point of interest in the case."

"A point of interest?"

"A fact that may or may not be relevant." Her gaze

found the bulletin board covered with Wanted posters. "We can use this and then group the papers according to their connection—reasons for blackmail, Doyle's history, his relationship to people in town—that sort of thing."

"Makes sense. We could color code them, too. Pink highlighter for gossip and unsubstantiated information, and green for known facts."

She grinned. "I wonder if Gil Grissom from *CSI* knows this method."

"Probably not. I don't think it would film well; it's pretty simple and not very sexy."

She shot Nick a look from under her lashes. He was complex and completely sexy, every big, lickable inch. "It will help us see what we have, and what we need to find."

"You've got great organizational skills."

"It's how I planned big events for Brian. When he made partner we had a dinner party for over four hundred people, including two state senators and the mayor."

"It's a damned useful skill." He pulled another legal pad out of his top drawer. "If we want to get out of here before midnight, we'd better get started."

chapter 18

*T*HEY SPENT THE NEXT three hours sorting through the information. When they got through, they had over fifty strips of paper tacked to a big board that covered the far wall. They stood in front of it now.

Roxie rubbed her back. "Doyle had connections to almost every person in town. He'd either worked for them, or was related to them, or *something*."

Nick nodded, his gaze slipping from the board and flickering over Roxie. Over the course of the evening, she'd raked her hand through her short hair a hundred times, and it was now a tumbled mess, wild and out of control, and oh-so-sexy. It framed her face, making her look both delicate and sensual at the same time.

She crossed her arms. "We'll have more information once Pastor Rawlings's widow gets his bank records together. She's supposed to give Clara a call when she's collected them."

"That's a beginning." Nick looked at his ledger and circled two more names. "I'll interview these two before tomorrow evening. Can you go back over your notes from your conversation with Widow Rawlings and see if there is anything we missed there?"

She nodded and leaned forward to look at the ledger list a bit closer. As she did so, her hip brushed Nick's and the clean scent of her shampoo tickled his nose. Damn, she was tempting.

The evening shadows were lengthening and had softened the light in the room. Roxie's hair, no longer a bold gold but a more subtle, seductive blonde, drew his gaze to her kissable mouth.

Something deep inside him flickered to life, his body hardened, and a fierce urge welled through him. Without a word, he slid his hands about her waist and pulled her back against him, her ass tucked against his thighs, her back to his chest. She gasped and stood rigidly, though she didn't pull away.

Nick rubbed his hands up and down her arms, his cheek pressed to her silky hair as she shivered and pressed back. The air about them grew thick and heavy, desire sizzling between them.

Then Roxie turned her head and pressed her lips to Nick's, and every thought he had fled. He turned her in his arms and kissed her the way he'd been dreaming of kissing her since the day he first saw her, the way he'd kissed her in her driveway, the way he wanted to kiss her now and forever.

She moaned and lifted her arms to his neck, pulling him nearer. She rubbed her hips against his, causing him to grit his teeth in delicious torment. She was sprite, siren, and temptress all wrapped up in one delicious package, and he couldn't resist her any longer.

He ran his hands beneath her short top to cup her breasts in her lace bra, and she arched against him as he brushed his thumb over her nipples, the thin scrap of lace easily pushed aside. She filled his arms so well, and the scent of her drove every thought from his head.

He pushed her top up, exposing her bared breast, then ran his thumb over her nipple and flicked it gently. She gasped, writhing in place. "Nick," she breathed, pressing her breast into his hand.

He bent and took her nipple in his mouth, laving it with his tongue. Her hands threaded through his hair as she held him there, a prisoner of intimacy and desire. He needed to have her beneath him; his body was aflame.

He pulled her shirt over her head, then unhooked her bra. She pulled him down for another deep, mind-blowing kiss as he dropped it to the floor.

When he finally came up for air, she was in his arms, naked except for her shorts and heels. He reached for her waistband, but she shook her head, her gaze smoky and sensual. "Now I get to take off *your* shirt."

It took every ounce of control Nick possessed to step back and allow her to unbutton his shirt and tug it off, but he managed. The second it was gone, he slipped his arms about her once more, and her bare skin rubbed against his, deliciously soft and warm.

He kissed her as he undid her shorts, then eased them down her long legs and over her heels. She impatiently kicked the shorts out of the way, and her lace panties soon followed. When she bent to undo one of her high heels, he stopped her. "Leave them on," he whispered in her ear.

Roxie shivered. She couldn't think, couldn't talk, couldn't do anything but feel, and she ran her hands over Nick's chest, greedy and impatient.

He lifted her onto the edge of the table, then undid his belt and dropped it to the table behind her. He was just about to take off his pants when he suddenly turned and left the room, returning swiftly with a silver packet. "God bless Susan," he said in a fervent tone. "Everyone should have a dispatcher with a rowdy sense of humor and a box of condoms in their desk."

"She has a whole box?" Roxie placed kisses up his neck and across his chin.

"She buys everything in bulk."

Roxie grinned wickedly and put her hand on the telltale bulge in Nick's pants. "There's only one bulk item *I'm* interested in."

His lips quirked, and in a few seconds he was naked.

His muscular chest was covered with just the right amount of hair, his washboard stomach was hard, and his thighs the most bitable she'd ever seen. And the best part of him stood proud and at attention. Just looking at him made Roxie burn in anticipation.

Nick placed the condom over his hard cock and quickly rolled it into place, then stepped between her legs and kissed the sensitive spot on her neck, his hands caressing her everywhere, sending rich shivers across her bare skin.

His breathing was coming harsh, matching hers. She burned for this, had yearned for it, dreamed of it. As his cock pressed against her, she hooked her legs about Nick's back.

Looking deep into her eyes, with a thrust of his hips, he sank into her.

It had been so long, so very long, and with that one deep stroke, her body exploded.

Nick held her as she cried out, wave after wave of pleasure washing over her. Gasping for breath, she finally released his shoulder, realizing he was still buried deep within her, rock hard and ready.

Panting, Roxie tightened her legs, pulling him further inside. Nick's strong arms supported her as he began to move, stroking her deep inside, filling her fully. She tugged him even closer, moving with him as his thrusts reached a fevered pitch and, with a husky cry, he came.

Roxie held Nick close, her legs tight on his hips, his warm breath on her neck as they savored the lingering heat of their passion.

Nick's breathing slowly returned to normal.

During their tryst, it had grown dark. The only light was from the streetlight.

Roxie sighed, wiggling a little.

He immediately lifted her from the table and set her on her feet. She wobbled for a moment and he laughed, the sound warm and welcoming. "I forgot you were still wearing your shoes. How on earth did they stay on?"

She smiled sultrily. "Talent."

He let out his breath in a rush. "*I'll* say."

She shivered a bit, and Nick said, "Stay here and I'll get your clothes." He bent to retrieve them and handed them to her. "Can you see well enough to get dressed?"

"Of course."

They were silent as they dressed.

Nick buttoned his pants and put on his utility belt. The silence stretched, and suddenly it was no longer warm and friendly.

Roxie finished adjusting her top and smoothing her hair. "Nick?"

"Yes?"

"Is . . . are you OK?"

"I'm fine. It's just—" His shirt still open, he pulled Roxie to him, nestling her against his shoulder, his hands warm on her hips. "I shouldn't have allowed this to happen. But with you, I can't seem to keep my perspective. I keep wanting more, needing more, and this—" He slipped a hand behind her neck and looked down at her. "—this was madness."

Roxie's throat tightened. "Are you saying you wish this had never happened?"

"No! I've been wanting you since the day you drove back into town. It's just that I should have waited until—" He froze.

"Ni—"

He placed a finger over her lips, his arm on her waist tightening.

Then she heard the stealthy opening of the door in the outside office. Roxie's gaze flew to the fake box of evidence. Someone was taking the bait.

"This way!" Nick whispered urgently. He hustled her behind his desk, pushing her underneath. "I didn't think anyone would bite this soon."

"Should I—" she whispered back.

"Don't do a thing." He planted a firm kiss on her lips. "Whatever happens, do *not* come out. Do you hear me?"

The doorknob to the office began to turn.

Nick unclipped the safety lock on his gun and silently drew it.

Roxie held her breath. *Please God, don't let anyone get hurt!*

The door opened.

Roxie heard the faint scuffle of footsteps moving toward the fake evidence box. Pulse pounding in her throat, she watched from under the desk as small feet in black tennis shoes walked past her.

Nick crouched, ready. As the thief reached the table, Nick stood. "Halt! Police!"

The figure froze in place.

"Put your hands up—"

The lights in the outer office flooded on. "Nick?" Susan called from the hallway. "Are you still here?" She came to the door.

"Susan, no!" Nick yelled, lowering his gun.

The thief grabbed Susan and thrust her at Nick. Susan stumbled forward into Nick's arms as their suspect ran out the door.

SUSAN PRESSED A FRESH cup of coffee into Roxie's hands. "Here. And if you'd like a slug from my special stash, that'll stop the shakes faster."

"Yes, *please.*"

Susan reached behind her desk and pulled out a small bottle, then sloshed a good amount into the cup.

Roxie took a sip. It warmed her through and through, calming some of the internal quivering. "It's been a heck of a night."

Susan's eyes twinkled. "I'll say! Nick's poor shirt was so frightened, it actually came untucked."

Roxie choked, as her drink went down the wrong pipe.

"Easy, there! The hooch too strong for you?"

"No," she gasped.

"Nick's searching around the building and said we're to stay put until he comes back." Susan shook her head.

"The next time I leave my house keys at work, I'm just going to break a window to get in."

Roxie heard a male voice in the hallway. "Mark?" she called.

Her brother walked in with Pumper under one arm, wrapped in a blanket.

"What are you doing here?" she asked, setting down her coffee. "And why'd you bring Pumper?"

"Mother's afraid of him. She said he growls at her when no one's in the room."

"Baloney. That dog never growled at anyone; it would take too much effort."

"Is it alive?" Susan asked.

"Sort of." Mark placed the dog on the floor and looked at Roxie. "What happened? Nick called and said to get down here as soon as possible."

Nick entered the room—his shirt now tucked in—and nodded to Mark.

"Did you find anything?" Susan asked.

"A few possible footprints, but nothing else." Nick frowned at Pumper. "What's that mutt doing here?"

"Mother's afraid of him." Roxie sighed.

Nick locked the door and crossed to his office. "Susan, I'm going to search the scene. Don't let anyone in here." He disappeared into the office.

Mark sat down beside Roxie. "You OK?"

"I'm fine. I was never in any real danger. Susan was the one the thief shoved."

Mark's brows lowered. "Someone could have been seriously injured."

Suddenly Nick appeared in the doorway and held up a small object.

Shiny and bold, a large diamond teardrop earring dangled from his fingers. "Anyone recognize this?"

chapter 19

*I*T WAS MUCH LATER when Roxie and Mark finally got home. Roxie opened the car door so Mark could pull Pumper out and carry him back inside. Roxie followed them up the sidewalk, her mind whirling.

It seemed as if her interlude with Nick had never happened, overshadowed and weighted now by the attempted break-in. Nick had been different afterward. He hadn't looked at her directly, either.

Perhaps he'd just been distracted by the break-in. Yet the thought rang hollowly and she frowned. More than likely he was concerned that their little tryst meant more to her than he wanted it to. Roxie's gaze narrowed. As soon as she could pin him down, she was gong to have a long heart-to-heart with Nick and clear the air.

She followed Mark inside, where he deposited Pumper on a pile of blankets by the door. "Mark, there's a light on in the kitchen. That's odd." She walked toward the kitchen door, where she could hear the low murmur of voices. Light streamed into the hallway, and she could hear Mother's laugh. But it sounded . . . flirtatious?

Roxie was just about to push on the door when Tundy came flying out.

"Tundy, wh—"

Tundy clamped a hand over Roxie's mouth and pulled her toward the den. Mark followed, looking as surprised as Roxie.

"What's going on?" Mark demanded as Tundy released Roxie to close the door.

"I'll tell you what's happenin'! It's a miracle, manna from heaven, the second coming, the—"

"Tundy!" Roxie snapped.

Tundy pointed to a window that looked off the front porch. "Didn't you see that big Lincoln parked across the street?"

"No," Roxie and Mark answered together.

"Well, old Sheriff Thompson has come callin' on yo' momma, and you should see her! Why, butter wouldn't melt in her mouth! She's oozing niceness and smilin', even giggling like a fourteen-year-old on her first date." Tundy clasped her hands together. "It's a sign from above!"

Mark shook his head. "Thompson came over because Nick asked him to. He's to keep an eye on things."

Tundy's beatific expression froze. "He's not here callin'?"

"Nope."

"But . . . he tol' yo' momma she took the shine off every woman he knows!'"

Roxie shrugged. "Maybe he's just gallant."

Tundy scratched her head as she considered this. "No. I don't believe that. I think if you all saw them together, you'd be thinking the same thing I do—that they're sweet on one another. Mr. Mark, you go on in the kitchen all casual like and fetch a drink and see what you think."

Mark exchanged a glance with Roxie. "OK. I'll be right back." He left.

While he was gone, Tundy turned to say something to Roxie, but her gaze suddenly narrowed. Then she grinned big enough to light the whole room. "Why, Miz Roxie, yo' momma ain't the only one with a beau!"

"What?"

"That shirt. The tag's done moved to the outside."

Roxie touched the back of her neck, and sure enough, her tags were on the outside. Darn it! She hurriedly yanked off the shirt and got it back on before Mark returned.

He appeared dazed. "I'll be damned. Mother has a beau."

Tundy nodded, her red curls bouncing. "Miz Treymayne's just beaming! I shouldn't leave them alone too long. Something raunchy might happen, and I'll be sorry I missed it. So I'm gonna go start cookin' this new recipe I found called Yentil Lentil Soup." Grinning as if she'd been the one to make the match, Tundy scooted out.

"Well, I'll be," Roxie said.

"Me, too." Mark stretched, yawning. "Lord, what a long day! It's only ten, but it feels like it's three in the morning."

"No kidding." Her mind raced with everything that had happened—especially the hot sex with Nick in his office.

Mark regarded her suspiciously. "If I didn't know better, I'd say Mother wasn't the only one with a beau. You're smiling like a loon, and I noticed that your shirt was on inside out when I picked you up at the police station."

Roxie's cheeks heated.

Mark flickered a smile. "Once Nick's caught whoever is after those blackmail notes, you should give him another chance. I know you've been doing a lot of thinking since the divorce, but sometimes you have to stop trying to analyze every thought and emotion and just jump in there."

"I don't overthink things."

"Roxie, you do it worse than any woman I've ever known." His expression darkened. "Well, except one."

"Who—"

"It doesn't matter." His expression softened. "Just let go for once, Roxie. Stop waiting for the perfect moment and the perfect man. They don't exist. Trust your instincts—they're good."

"Mark, I'm not looking for any man, perfect or otherwise." Though if she were, Nick came pretty close to fitting the bill. *Easy, Treymayne. That sort of thinking can be dangerous.*

She firmly put the thought away and patted her brother on the shoulder. "Thanks for your advice, though. I appreciate you taking the time from your regimen of napping, eating, and carrying things for little old ladies."

"OK, blow me off. You'll regret not listening to my sage words when things get all mucked up."

Her lips twitched. "There's nothing to muck up. I'm not looking for a relationship."

"Perhaps you should be."

"No, thank you. I already gave at the office."

Mark shook his head. "Roxie, do yourself a favor. At least remember the Mark Treymayne Credo." He assumed an expression of great worldly wisdom. *"Before leaving the scene of true love, make sure all tags have been returned to their proper location."*

"Uh-huh. That ranks right up there with the time you told me all good Christmas presents come from the hardware store."

"Feel free to embroider either of those on a pillow." Grinning, Mark stretched. "What a day! I'm going to bed." He gave her a quick hug and left.

As he climbed the stairs, Roxie could hear Mother's slightly breathy voice reply to something Sheriff Thompson was saying, and the soft thuds of Tundy opening and closing cabinet doors.

It was a peaceful moment, and she should have been happy and content. Yet she wasn't. Instead, she felt uncertain, wondering what the explosion of passion between her and Nick actually meant. She didn't have a lot of experience in the passion department. Her relationship with Brian had been a friendship more than anything, and other than her time with Nick in high school, she hadn't had the opportunity to experiment.

Now that she had, it was heady, addictive stuff. A woman could get used to hot, wild sex like that. She could even come to crave it.

That was one danger of living life on the edge: she might like it a little too much. She had no intention of getting singed by passion; she needed to keep her heart disengaged from her physical reactions, and learn to live in the moment.

Surely she could do that. Suddenly exhausted, Roxie slipped past the kitchen door and up the stairs to her room. She threw on her pajamas, brushed her teeth, climbed into bed, and fell fast asleep.

ROXIE PARKED HER MOTHER'S car across from the sheriff's office. She was going to waltz into Nick's office and clear the air. Better yet, she was going to just let life happen. She was going to say whatever she wanted to say, and do whatever she wanted to do.

She smiled. What she wanted was for Nick Sheppard to kiss her again, and much, much more.

She flipped down the sunshade and opened the mirror. "You," she told herself severely, "need to relax. You're to go in there, say hi, and stop trying to control everything that happ—" She frowned at her reflection. *What in the world happened to my lipstick? I can't let him see me like this!*

She grabbed her purse and began rummaging for her lipstick. Hmmm . . . Pearly Pink was too froofy. She wanted to look authoritative but sexy, and Pearly Pink was not it.

She fished around again and found a tube of Passion Heart Red. That sounded good. When Roxie applied it, the color brightened her up and warmed her light tan. That done, she fluffed her new curls, looked at herself from all angles, then headed into the reception area of Nick's office.

The door was open, but no one was in sight. "Hello!"

Roxie jumped and spun around.

Susan stood in the doorway in a red T-shirt and jeans, her auburn hair in a ponytail. "Sorry, I didn't mean to scare you." She walked past and dropped a bakery box beside the coffeepot. "Feeling better this morning?"

"Much. You?"

"Bit of a headache, but that's all." Susan walked to the desk and kicked the bottom drawer, which shot open. She dropped her purse in, then shut it with a practiced shove of one foot. "Shall I tell Nick you're here, or do you just want to go on in?"

"I guess I'll just go in."

"Want a muffin and some coffee? The muffins are whole wheat from Micki & Maud's Diner. Connie started an organic bakery to augment the restaurant sales and they're as good as anything from those fancy organic bakeries in Asheville."

"No, thanks."

"All right, but you're missing out." Susan sat at her desk, pulled a stack of mail over, and began opening it. "Tell Nick there's breakfast if he wants it, will you?"

"Sure thing." Roxie went to the office door. *Be yourself. Just be natural. Say what you want to say. Do what you want to do.*

She stepped into the office. Nick was sitting at his desk, leafing through a stack of papers, his brows lowered into a frown.

Faint shadows rimmed his eyes. "Roxie! This is unexpected."

"Susan said to tell you there's breakfast if you want any."

His eyes lit, some of his wariness disappearing. "Sausage biscuits with gravy?"

"Whole wheat muffins. Organic."

He crinkled his nose.

"They smelled pretty good."

"Don't let that fool you. Susan's a health food nut, and sometimes she'll bring in something that looks decent but will still kill your taste buds if you accidentally ingest it."

"That sounds pretty dire. By the way, I have some

new information. Widow Rawlings is dropping off her husband's bank records to Clara this morning." She smiled. "It's not much, but it could be another point of interest for the board."

Nick leaned back in his chair, the wood creaking with age. "I appreciate that."

He truly did—though it was difficult to think about the case when Roxie was so close by. She looked fresh and rested, no shadows beneath her eyes. He looked like hell; he hadn't been able to sleep a wink. Yesterday the unthinkable had happened; he'd allowed his common sense to be overcome by plain, simple desire. He couldn't allow that to happen ever again.

It would be tough, though. Even when searching his office for clues last night, he hadn't been able to clear his mind of her. Roxie invaded every waking moment and most of his sleeping ones. Now she came waltzing in wearing sexy-as-hell heels, a pair of tight jeans that made her legs look a mile long, and a top better designed for a woman with less . . . everything.

Nick shifted uncomfortably in his chair. He had to keep things under control. He would not trade his professional integrity for a relationship of any sort, and he'd come perilously close to it last night.

He'd made love to her right here, in his office. What was it about Roxie that sent all of his good intentions flying? The sooner this case was solved, the better. The second it was, he had plans for Roxanne Treymayne.

Roxie's alert gaze rested on his face. "Have you interviewed Robin?"

"Not yet. She called last night, about an hour after you left, and reported a theft. Said someone had broken into the mayor's office and stolen several things from her desk, including her earrings."

"As if she'd keep them in her desk at the office."

"It could be a cover-up; we don't know. But if that's true, then she sure did a number on the mayor's office. It was ransacked, top to bottom."

"Was anything else taken?"

Ah, that's my girl! He nodded. "Some files. The mayor seemed upset, but then whoever did it broke his Babe Ruth commemorative vase."

She chuckled, low and rich, the sound washing over him, taking him back to the day before. His gaze flickered to the table in the corner where they had—Nick's pencil snapped.

Roxie didn't seem to notice. "I don't buy Robin's story."

"There's something not right, that's for sure. Roxie, you said the person who attacked you in your house was male. Could you have been mistaken?"

"No. He was tall—way too tall to have been Robin Wright. Plus, I saw him outlined against the window, and it was definitely a man."

"OK. I wondered." About that and a lot of things. Like what she wore to bed. If she liked to snuggle in the mornings, or if she jumped out of bed to make coffee.

The thought of Roxie in his kitchen wearing one of his shirts and her sexy high heels made his knees curiously weak. *Easy, Sheppard. Lee failed when he let his attraction to a woman interfere with his job. Don't make the same mistake.*

"Roxie, I owe you an apology."

She blinked. "For what?"

"For last night," he said. "I assumed that it would be a few days before anyone came for the decoy evidence, and I certainly thought they'd wait until later at night."

She colored. "You couldn't have known when they'd—" She frowned. "I hadn't thought about that, but it *is* odd they would take a chance and come before midnight, at least. Why would someone do that?"

"I don't know either, and it's now a point of information on our board." He nodded toward the board. "Your method has been working great. I was able to put a few more pieces of the puzzle together. It's very useful to see all of the info pinned in one spot.

"In a large agency, there's a definitive division of labor. I wasn't a detective but a street cop, so I never saw how they put things together." He shrugged. "One of the problems with being the only cop in town is that you're expected to know it all. I do pretty well, but a full-fledged investigation is new ground."

"Aren't there national standards?"

"Yes and no. Because of society's historical suspicion of authority, our criminal justice system is very splintered. You have county and city agencies, local and state and then federal. They all have their own methods and procedures and, depending on the case law in that state, different ways of dealing with evidence and arrests."

"Surely there are some basic tenets?"

"There's a framework, but it can change with every legal decision made. It's difficult to keep up with."

"That's complicated." She was quiet a moment, then said, "Last night, I thought of a few more points for the board. For example, Doyle was supposedly hit at The Pig, yet no suspect was found."

"So?"

"In this community, someone would notice if someone's bumper had a new dent the day after an incident like that. I may not have a degree in criminal justice, but I do know Glory."

Nick linked his hands and placed them behind his head, his dark gray gaze considering. "And?"

"I'll bet you money that the town gossips scoured the town and every car for weeks after Doyle's death. When we were in high school and someone backed into Joy Granger's car at the Methodist Quilt Showing, Clara and Myrtle Estep sat out in their front yard and took Polaroids of every car that went by, hoping they'd figure out who did it and get their name in the paper."

Nick's lips twitched. "That's pretty thin as far as evidence goes. But," he added before she could protest, "you make a lot of sense. It's something to be considered, and I'll add it to our board." His gaze swept over her. "You ever thought about going into law enforcement? You'd make a hell of a detective."

It took a whole minute before the compliment registered. "Thank you. I hadn't thought of a career, just about traveling and getting away."

"Maybe you should think more about going *to,* rather than going away *from*."

As tantalizing as Nick was, she couldn't picture herself in Glory, at Mother's beck and call, being watched by the town gossips and critiqued constantly.

Some of her thoughts must have shown in her expression, for his gaze darkened. "Even if you don't do it here, you should do it somewhere. You have a gift for deduction; it would be a shame not to use it."

"Thank you."

He shrugged. "It's just my opinion."

Warmth flooded through Roxie; he trusted her instincts. It mattered, too, that he cared enough to worry that he'd put her in danger because of their impromptu lovemaking.

"Treymayne?"

She realized Nick was still watching her, his gaze narrowed. "Yes?"

"I never thanked you for taking that mongrel for my aunt. I spoke with her this morning, and she said she's not going to be able to take it back, now that they're onto her."

"I didn't think she would."

"I have a year-old beagle, one of Pumper's cousins.

She's a great dog, but too lively to be alone every day. She's ruined every throw pillow in the house. So if you don't want Pumper, I'll take him. He might do Jezebel some good."

Roxie laughed. "Jezebel?"

"It's a fitting name—trust me on that. I've got her signed up for obedience classes, but I doubt they'll take."

"What's wrong, Sheriff? Afraid you won't win re-election if your dog doesn't toe the line?"

He laughed. "I'm not an elected official. I'm appointed. But if you tick off any more of the city council members, I could well be looking for another job."

"You wouldn't like that?"

"No, I wouldn't." His smile faded. "When I was a teenager, I couldn't think of anything better than getting out of here. I just wanted some peace. But now . . ." He paused, his fingers resting on the desk beside an antique inkwell marked Buncombe County Court Clerk.

"Now?" she prompted.

"I've been here for almost two years, and I've grown to love it. When I worked in Atlanta it was drug deals and murders, carjackings and domestic violence. In Glory, there's been only one suspicious death in the town's two-hundred-year history. The town's safety is one of the things the city council's been playing up to attract people from Asheville. They also approved an ad campaign to try and attract some small industries, too."

"Why would they do that?"

"There are fewer and fewer jobs every year. Look around, Roxie. Most of the people we knew in high school moved away, like you and Brian did. If the city council doesn't bring in new jobs, young people will keep moving away and Glory will suffer. That's why some people might be very upset if Doyle's case suddenly drew a lot of attention."

"How upset?"

"Upset enough to perhaps wish a certain box of evidence would disappear."

She frowned. "That really increases our suspect list. Not only do we have every person on the blackmail list, but now also we have every businessman and -woman in town."

"That about sums it up." Nick leaned back in his chair, the ancient oak creaking loudly. He looked so tired that she wished she could slip around behind the desk and give him a good backrub. She could knead away some of his cares, and the contact would reassure her that all was well. Ever since she'd arrived in his office, she'd felt separated somehow, and not just by his desk.

"Nick, can I—"

"Sheriff?"

Roxie and Nick looked toward the door. Pat stood in the door, her reporter's notebook already open. She eyed Nick and Roxie with interest. "Came to see if you had the crime sheets for the paper."

Nick frowned. "Susan sent those over to you yesterday."

The woman's smile didn't slip a bit, nor did her overly inquisitive gaze move off of Roxie. "Must be in my In Box. I should have checked that before I came over." The woman's gaze flickered over the desk, and then around the room, brightening when she saw the faux evidence box.

Nick stood and crossed to the door. "I'm sure Susan will give you another copy. There wasn't much on there: two reports of citizens locked out of their houses, a missing hoe off Elm and—"

"Ho?" Pat echoed, her eyes widening.

"H-O-E," Nick said slowly. "The kind you use to weed a garden."

Pat looked crestfallen. "Oh." She stepped to one side and said to Roxie, "I'm glad to run into you. I'd like to do a story on your attack for *The Glory Examiner*."

"I'm afraid—"

"I promise not to ask anything personal, like what you were wearing at the time of the attack." The woman smiled, revealing buckteeth that made her look uncomfortably like a beaver. Her gaze searched the office again. "How about we do the interview right here in the sheriff's office? Oh, my, what's that?" Pat walked toward the board where Roxie and Nick had pinned all of their evidence and theories.

Nick slipped a hand under her elbow and steered her away from the board and toward the door. "Thank you for coming, Pat."

Pat struggled to free her elbow. "Sheriff, I'd like to ask Miss Treymayne about—"

Susan appeared in the doorway, looking harassed. "Sorry, Nick. I went to the powder room and she slipped in on me." Susan took Pat's other arm and pulled her toward the door. "Come on, Pat. I've got copies of the crime sheets, if you'd like."

"Yes, but I want to talk to Miss—"

Nick closed the door behind them. "Sorry about that. Pat thinks she's some sort of ace reporter, but she can't keep her opinion out of what she writes. Worse, if she doesn't know something, she's not above filling in the blanks with erroneous information."

"I'm surprised Ty keeps her."

"He doesn't have a lot of choice in who he can hire. Pat's not just a reporter but also her own copy editor. She writes the front-page news, the garden and yard pieces, and a heavily inaccurate political op/ed page that's the delight and frustration of many."

"Sounds like she's a one-woman band."

"Pretty much. Just be careful. Pat doesn't have a mean bone in her body, but she's not above poking around people's cars and houses when she thinks she might find a story. Frankly, she wants a piece of the action and is willing to do anything to get it."

"I'll watch out for her." Roxie glanced at the clock. "I'd better go. I'm supposed to meet with the club later on, and I need to run a few errands for Mother."

He gave a dramatic sigh. "All business, aren't you?"

She nodded, though she knew it was a lie. Her body was screamingly aware of Nick, of how close he was, of how with one step forward, she could throw an arm around his neck and kiss him.

Then why don't you? She blinked at the thought, her gaze locking on his mouth. God, he had a beautiful, masculine mouth, all hard curves. She knew the feeling of that mouth, of the delicious pressure, of how her body heated and flared just at the thought—

"Roxie, if you keep looking at me like that—" Passion flared in the depths of his eyes and she shivered.

Roxie stopped thinking. She stepped forward, looped her free hand around Nick's neck, lifted up on her toes, and pressed her lips to his.

For one agonizing moment, he didn't move. Then he gave a low growl and yanked her to him as he returned the kiss, hot and passionate.

Roxie reveled in the feel of Nick's strong arms about her. She grabbed a handful of his shirt and—

He released her and stepped back, breathing hard. "Damn it, every time I'm with you, I forget."

She blinked, dazed. "Forget what?"

"Everything! I forget where I am, and that I'm in uniform." He shook his head, his mouth thinned with frustration.

She knew exactly what he was feeling; her body screamed for her to latch back onto him and taste him once more. *Easy, Treymayne! You'll disintegrate with thoughts like those.*

Or would she? Perhaps this was what emotional honesty felt like—incredibly alive, and excited, and *thrilled*. This felt good. So, why not?

That question was answered by the firm set of Nick's chin and the frown that now rested on his brow. "Roxie, I thought we could maintain some distance while we're working on the case, but apparently that's not possible."

"Surely we can—"

"No." His lips thinned and he said in a harsh voice, "I'm disappointed in myself. I can't let anything get in the way of this case. I promised myself when Lee messed up that—" His frown deepened. "I refuse to be distracted from my job every time you come traipsing in here with—"

"Traipsing?"

His face reddened, but he continued doggedly on. "Or shimmying, or whatever it is you do."

She plunked her fists on her hips. "I *walk*."

"Fine. You walk. It's just that when you do it, I—" He fixed a grim look on her. "Your—the way you do things—it makes me—" He clamped his mouth closed.

"Nick, what in the hell are you saying?"

"I'm saying that— Oh, damn it, I don't know." He rubbed a hand over his face. "I should never have suggested we work together."

"You said you *wanted* my help."

"I do! I just didn't expect— Hey! Where are you going?"

Roxie didn't even look back. She just kept walking. She walked out of his office, past the reception area without even answering Susan's surprised greeting, down the stairs, and through the parking lot to her car. She slammed the door hard, revved the engine, and didn't stop until she'd driven all the way to the assisted living center, speeding the entire way. *That* was what she thought of Nick Sheppard and his stuffed-shirt attitude.

She found a shady tree in the center lot, parked the car, and sat fuming. She knew he'd been more upset with himself than her, but it still hurt. She'd been helping, damn it!

Slowly, her breathing returned to normal. She supposed she had her answer as to how Nick felt about their tryst last night. She'd been right, too, to think that his manner wasn't as warm as it had been. *She* might be sophisticated enough to separate the physical from the emotional, but apparently Nick wasn't. She sniffed in disdain. "How dare he *reject* me like—like—like—"

That was what made her so furious: she'd offered him so much of herself, and he seemed to easily brush it away. "Can't let anything get in the way of the case, Treymayne," she mimicked with a snarl.

She was *not* used to rejection. Still, if that was the way Nick wanted to play the game, then fine, that was how she'd play it, too. She'd be frozen, unemotional, and untouchable, the exact woman she'd been for Brian.

The thought clutched at her throat and wouldn't let it go. For a moment, Roxie was afraid she might cry, but instead, she snatched up her phone and dialed.

Tundy answered. "Hello?"

"Hi, Tundy. Is Mark there?"

"He left a few minutes ago for the church."

"Damn it!"

"Oooweee, Miz Roxie. You sound madder than a spit-upon wasp. What's wrong?"

Everything was wrong. Absolutely everything. "I'm fine, Tundy, I just need to let off some steam."

"At the Bigger Jigger?" Tundy said hopefully.

Roxie lifted her brows. Why not? At least those men had the good sense to appreciate her. "That's the best idea I've heard all day. I've got errands to run, but I should be home by four."

"Perfect, 'cause happy hour starts at five. Finish up and get home; we got some partyin' to do!"

THE FISHING LINE WHIRLED as Nick cast it across the still pond. He settled into one of the rusty folding chairs on the dock and tried to calm his galloping mind. The sun was already down, the mosquitoes just beginning to buzz, the faint breeze ruffling the bottom of his T-shirt.

He'd spent all day interviewing potential suspects and witnesses, going methodically through the chart.

Mayor Harkins had been in a late meeting with the tax assessor in Asheville, so he had an alibi. So did most of the town, if everyone was to be believed.

Except Robin Wright. According to her, she'd been home reading at the time of the crime. She'd also been suspiciously red-faced at the sight of her lost earring.

But what could Doyle have known about Robin to drive her to such extremes?

Out in the middle of the pond, a fish broke the surface. "Stop mocking me," Nick muttered. He reeled in his line and cast it in the area the fish had just vacated.

What a long, long day. And it had started poorly when he'd stuck his foot into his mouth so deeply, he was sure only surgery would remove it. He hadn't meant to send Roxie packing, just to put some distance between them so they could get this case over and done with. And then—well, he hadn't really decided what would happen then. It all sort of depended on Roxie.

He sighed and jiggled his line, waiting for a fish to nibble. He'd reached for his phone a dozen times today, determined to call Roxie and explain himself, but each time, he'd chickened out. What a mess he'd made of it. Maybe he should drive to her house and—

A pickup turned down the dirt lane leading to the pond, and Nick grinned as Tom came ambling out, carrying a red tackle box and a shiny black reel.

"That's a new rod?"

"Yup. Old one broke."

"Caught that fifteen-pound laker?"

"Nope. Shut the truck door on it like a fool." Tom dropped into a battered chair beside Nick and opened the tackle box. "Any luck?"

"Not today."

Tom shot him a sharp look. "One of *those* days, eh?"

"Yep. I did as you suggested and let Roxie Treymayne in on the investigation."

"And?"

"She's a natural."

Tom pulled out needle-nose pliers and fixed some weights to his line. "Not surprising. She's a sharp one. So's her mother."

"I hear you've been keeping an eye on her?"

"As much as she'll let me," Tom said. "Which isn't all that much. Still . . . it's been fun."

"*Fun?*"

Tom cast his line, which landed neatly beside Nick's. "Lilah's got a heck of a sense of humor. She can mimic that maid of theirs like no one."

"I daresay Tundy mimics Lilah pretty well, too."

"That wouldn't surprise me, either." Tom stretched out his legs. "How's the Doyle Cloyd investigation going?"

"It's going. I've narrowed the suspect list down to eighty-three."

Tom chuckled. "What was it before?"

"Eighty-eight."

"At least you're going in the right direction."

"I hope so." Nick hesitated, then said, "Roxie and I had a bit of a falling out."

Tom sent Nick a measured gaze. "Oh?"

"Tom, I have a problem. Well, not a problem really, but an *issue*." Nick reeled his line in and then recast it, wondering how to explain things without saying too much.

Tom jiggled his line. "Things between you and Roxie not as professional as you'd like?"

"How did you know?"

"She's a looker."

"Yes, she is," Nick said fervently. "I can't keep my hands off her."

"That could be a problem."

"In this line of work, it could be deadly."

Tom considered this. "Sometimes," he agreed. "But sometimes not allowing yourself the freedom to express yourself can be deadly, too."

"What do you mean?"

"Our profession is not known for promoting stable, healthy relationships. We have one of the highest divorce rates out there. I think that's because we learn to be so guarded about everything. You can't turn a thing like that on and off. Don't tamp down those feelings until they don't exist. They're precious. While you shouldn't get jiggy in the office, you most certainly should be able to do so elsewhere."

"I can't believe you used the term 'jiggy.' "

"I listen to popular music, you know. That Will Smith is something else."

Nick grinned reluctantly. "I tried to explain things to Roxie; the need for professionalism—"

"How did she take it?"

"She stomped out. It was my fault; it didn't come out the way I wanted it to."

"Hm. I just came from Lilah's and saw Roxie headed out for the evening. That must be why."

Nick turned to Tom. "Where was she going?"

"The Bigger Jigger."

"That dive? They have more bar fights there than anywhere else."

"She wasn't alone. She had Tundy with her, and they were both dressed in skirts up to here." Tom made a motion at mid-thigh. "Actually, more like here." He moved his hand higher. "Roxie had red boots, too, and—" Tom frowned. "Is that your phone ringing?"

"Yes, damn it." Nick crossed the dock to his tackle box and fished out his phone. "Sheriff."

"Nick, thank goodness!" Susan said. "Where are you?"

"Fishing at Tom's pond. Where are you? I can barely hear—"

"Good, that's not far. You've got to get over to the Bigger Jigger as soon as possible," Susan replied, almost shouting over the ruckus in the background.

Nick shot a look at Tom. "What's up?"

"Roxie came out for the night, and some beefy truck driver bought her a pitcher of margaritas and—"

Then Nick heard a man yell, *"Take it off! Take it* all *off!"*

"Good God, what's she doing?"

"She's—"

A loud crash sounded, and he heard Tundy yell, "That's it, Miz Roxie! Shake that groove thang!"

Nick snapped the phone closed, shoved it into his pocket, and tossed his fishing rod to Tom.

Tom deftly caught it. "Off to the rescue, I take it?"

Nick nodded curtly.

Tom grinned, casting his line again. "I'm glad I retired."

Nick grabbed his tackle box and headed for his truck. "I wouldn't let anyone else handle this job, anyway. It's all mine."

chapter 20

THE BIGGER JIGGER, LOCATED three miles outside of Glory, wasn't in Nick's jurisdiction. Tonight he didn't give a damn.

He parked his truck by the front door of the honky-tonk and strode in. The place was like a thousand others—plank floor, heavy wood bar, pool tables, beer signs lighting up the dark room, with a CD jukebox blaring everything from new country to old rock.

As he strode across the empty dance floor, he saw Roxie right away. She wasn't dancing on the bar, as he'd feared. But Tundy was—much to the delight of two very old, very drunk men.

Roxie was perched on a nearby barstool, her short skirt accenting sexy knee-high red leather boots, her bountiful breasts displayed in a blue top that dipped way too low. Men surrounded her like sharks in a sea of testosterone.

And he had to get her out without starting a riot.

"Thank God you're here," Susan said.

Nick glanced over. She was dressed in jeans and a

low-cut top, her long auburn hair pulled back in a pony-tail. "How long has this been going on?"

"I got here at five. She and Tundy arrived soon after."

"That's a bit early for a drink."

Susan's gaze narrowed. "In the civilian world, it's called 'happy hour.' But Roxie's barely had anything to drink—only two margaritas, but it was more than enough."

He noted how Roxie swayed on her stool. "They must have been big margaritas."

"Or potent. I wouldn't put it past anyone in the crowd to pay for the good stuff just to get her tipsy. It's a good thing I was here when she came in. I knew something bad would happen."

"Why?"

"It was like Moses parting the sea. She walked in the door, and everything but the music stopped. Then the crowd gathered, and the mood has been getting uglier since. I don't think she realizes it, but she's not going to be allowed off that stool without picking one guy over the others."

"And that's when the fighting will begin."

"Exactly."

Nick sighed as Roxie laughed at something someone said. "She's a beautiful woman."

"She's an angry woman, if you ask me. She came in just looking for trouble. Nothing drives a man mad faster."

Tell me about it. Nick eyed the distance between Roxie's stool and the door.

"Take it off!" one of the old men yelled to Tundy, who was down to her bra and velour pants.

"Can you get Tundy out of here?" Nick asked.

"Sure. I'll just tell her there's a party at my house. I'll sober her up and then drive her home."

"Thanks." He started toward Roxie, but then stopped. "Susan, what are *you* doing here?"

"I come here all the time. The chips and salsa are free and the beer is cold. It's an OK place, if you don't stay too late. After one A.M., it can get rowdy."

"I know," he said grimly. "I've seen the police bulletins." Nick flexed his shoulders. "I'm going in."

He made his way to where the men clustered around Roxie. Most of them were big guys, beefy and tattooed. It took a bit of finesse, but with a shift of his shoulder here and an elbow there, he made it to Roxie's side.

He meant to quietly take her arm and lead her through the throng, but she blinked up at him fuzzily and then gave a delighted squeal. *"Nick!"*

Every male eye now turned to Nick with suspicion and dislike.

Roxie threw her arms around his neck. "Nick! I didn't know you came here, too! First there was Susan, and now you and—"

He slipped an arm around her waist and lifted her off the stool. "Lucky for you, I got thirsty." He glared around at the crowd of men, looking each of them in the eye. "If you all don't mind, my *wife* and I would like to go home."

"Wife?" A tall, red-haired man with a beard eyed Nick up and down. "She didn't say nothing about being no one's wife."

"Well, I did," Nick said in a calm voice, tucking Roxie securely under one arm. "You got a problem with that?"

The men shifted. A few on the outer rim drifted away. One or two mumbled something under their breath, then made their way back to the bar. Only three were left facing Nick.

He could take three.

Roxie snuggled against him, sliding one hand into his back pocket and one into his front. She smiled up at him. "Good ole Nick. I'm glad to see you, Nick."

He looked down into her eyes and found the first smile of the day. "Let's go."

She smiled. "OK! I think Tundy—" Roxie blinked. "Where is Tundy?"

"Susan's taken her home already. C'mon, Roxie, let's go."

He turned her toward the door and, together, they made it to his truck, ignoring the few men who straggled along behind them, muttering to one another.

"This isn't your Camaro."

"No, it's not." He opened the door and held her arm to steady her as she climbed in.

She made it halfway, then giggled. "I'm stuck."

Her lush ass was only a few feet from him, rounded and barely covered by her skirt. Swallowing hard, he put a hand on her ass and pushed her the rest of the way into the truck.

Roxie settled in place, her skirt way too high on one side. "Much better," she announced loudly.

He reached over to buckle her seat belt, achingly aware of how his arm brushed her breasts.

As he snapped the buckle into place, she slid her hands around his neck and threaded them through his hair. Her breath brushed his neck as she whispered, "I've always loved your hair."

He went hard instantly, and it took every ounce of willpower not to respond to her invitation. "Not now, Treymayne. We need to get out of here."

He closed the door and climbed into his side of the truck, noting that a few of Roxie's admirers had gathered outside the bar, watching him. He slammed the door, made certain Susan's car was already gone, then took off.

Roxie put her head back and stretched her arms over her head, arching seductively. "Nick, Nick, Nick. You told them I was your *wife*."

"So?"

"They had to know that wasn't true."

"How?"

She splayed her hand. "No ring."

"I didn't specify if you were a good wife or a bad one."

Her smile faded. "I was a good wife when I was one."

"I bet you were," he said softly.

"I was. I was better'n good. I was the best in all of the subdivision."

"I don't doubt that. Once you put your mind to something, you usually do it."

"I do, don't I?" she said in a pleased voice. After a moment, her hand slid over his on the steering wheel. "Nick, can I ask you something?"

Her fingers were cool against his. Nick turned the truck up the road to her house. "Sure."

"When we were in high school, why did you dump me for Sandy Talent?"

"*What?*"

"You heard me." Roxie pulled her hand from his. "How could you have done that?"

"I didn't dump you, Roxie. You dumped *me*."

She sniffed. "We had one tiny, little argument and you ran off with the next girl who walked by."

"We had a *huge fight,* and you told me you never wanted to see me again."

"I didn't. Especially after I saw you with Sandy." She almost spat the name.

He turned into her driveway and parked beneath a streetlight.

Roxie turned toward him, her hair tousled about her face, her shirt pulled dangerously low, her skirt riding up one hip.

Nick cupped her chin so that her gaze met his. "Let's review this, for clarity's sake. Our huge fight was over your mother. She hated me, so you refused to be with me in public."

Roxie blinked, her long lashes shadowing her eyes. "I warned you about that when we first started seeing each other. It had to be a secret."

He released her chin. "Yes, but after we got—" He hesitated, then said, "—closer, I thought things would change. They didn't."

"I wanted them to change, but Mother would have had a cow. I was afraid of her back then."

"She knew how to make a person miserable, I'll give her that."

She looked hopefully at him. "So you understand?"

"At the time, no. But now I do." He shrugged. "I cared too much. After we'd been together, seeing you in secret wasn't enough."

Her brows lowered. "It wasn't enough for me, either. I just didn't know how to deal with my mother then."

"Do you know now?"

A mischievous smile lit her eyes. "Oh yes. I plan on moving to Paris as soon as I can."

"How is that dealing with your mother?"

"Easy. She doesn't speak French." Roxie giggled.

Nick sighed. "Running away is not 'dealing with' things."

"It works for me."

"No, it doesn't. Roxie, you have to face your problems and fix them."

"Like you fixed our little problem this morning, when you told me I wasn't to help with the investigation anymore."

"Roxie . . . I owe you an apology for this morning. I didn't mean to suggest we couldn't work together at all; I just meant we shouldn't be alone. At least, not in my office."

"That's what you meant to say?"

"Yes. But I mangled it, and then you got mad and left and I—I was going to come by tomorrow and explain everything, but then I ran into you tonight and—" He shrugged.

She unbuckled her seat belt and slid forward to place her hands on either side of his face. She pulled him close until his mouth was inches from hers. "Nick?" Her breath was sweet with mint and margarita, her eyes shimmering with undisguised need.

The slow heat he'd been fighting fanned into flames. He couldn't stop looking at her, the way her soft blonde hair, tousled and wavy, framed her face, how her blue eyes shimmered as if lit from within, at the trembling moist lips that he ached to taste again. "Damn it, Roxie, what do you want?" he groaned.

"I want this." With that, she kissed him. She kissed and was kissed, writhing against him as she opened her mouth beneath his, her tongue delving, pleasuring, teasing.

It was a hell of a kiss, long and sensual and wildly passionate, and Nick couldn't get enough, wanting more even as he received more.

"Put the seat back," she gasped as she broke the kiss. She leaned over him, lying in his lap as she reached for the lever, her breasts pressed against his leg.

"Roxie, we can't—"

The seat snapped back and with a growl she straddled him, unbuttoning her shirt with eager hands.

She tossed her shirt aside, then reached behind her and undid her lacy bra, stripping it off with amazing speed.

Nick couldn't believe his eyes. Sitting astride his lap, topless and laughing softly, her full breasts within mouth's reach, was the woman of his dreams. He slid his hands around her waist and captured a lush nipple between his lips.

She moaned and arched against him, her hands threading through his hair insistently as she pressed forward, offering herself.

Nick slid his hands up her back, lifting his hips so she could feel his raging erection. He tangled his hands in her silky hair and pulled her to him, invading her mouth with hot possession and stealing her breath.

She broke the kiss like a swimmer emerging from the water, back arched, hips pressed to his, writhing on his lap. He looked at her straddling him, the streetlight limning her hair with a nimbus of gold.

In that second, Nick realized he had a choice. He

could make love to a passionate but drunk Roxie in his pickup and assuage his blatant desire for a few hours. Or he could stop this now, before he lost the tiny thread of control still in his possession. *Is this what I want? The way I want it? I settled before with Roxie. Can I afford to do it again?*

It was the most difficult thing he'd ever done. Over the blood pounding in his ears, he slipped his hands about her waist and slowly held her away from him. "Roxie. Please. We can't do this."

"Yes, we can." She cupped his face and pressed soft, eager kisses to his lips and chin. Her hair brushed his face, soft and silky and driving him mad.

"No," he said louder. He lifted her and placed her on the seat beside him, then found her bra and shirt and handed them to her.

She looked at her clothes, her head bowed. She was so still, he reached for her.

She jerked away. "*No.* Don't—" She dressed as quickly as she could.

Roxie sagged with disappointment. She wanted him, damn it, and *now*. While her blood was hot and she felt sexy and desirable. A tear welled.

"Roxie, don't." Hands grasped her arms and Nick hauled her against him. "Listen, you beautiful, frustrating pain in my ass: I want you more than I've ever wanted *any* woman in my whole life."

She thought about this, before saying in a tiny voice, "*Any* woman?"

"Hell, yes."

"But then why—"

"Because I'm not a kid anymore, and neither are you. When I make love with you, I want something better than the front seat of my truck. It's not enough."

He wanted her. He really, *really* wanted her. Her eyelashes wet, she smiled, as gloriously happy now as she'd been sad a few moments ago. "We could sneak inside—"

"No more sneaking." His words snapped like ice tossed into a hot pan. At her wounded look, he groaned. "Roxie, the next time you and I decide to be together, I want it to be on a bed, with rose petals and . . . damn it, I want it to *mean* something."

"This means something to me," she said softly.

"Ah, Roxie." Nick rested his forehead against hers. "I hate to say this, but you're drunk."

"Tipsy."

He shook his head. "I don't want you to wake up tomorrow and wish you'd made another decision."

"I won't. I *swear* I won't."

He sighed, his breath warm on her lips. "Roxie, don't push this. I don't have the willpower to say no again." He gave her a quick kiss, then helped her dress. After, he went out to open her door and help her out into the cool night air.

He looked at his truck and gave a rueful laugh. "My windows are so fogged, I'll have to drive with my head out the window to get home."

She giggled. "Watch out for stop signs."

He rested his arm across her shoulder and walked her to the door. "What are you doing tomorrow?"

"Let's see. I have to visit your aunt and then take Mark to the church to—"

"Tomorrow *evening*?"

"I don't know. Why?"

They stopped at the door. "Roxie, I am asking you out on a date."

She blinked. "A date? With you?"

He laughed. "I'll make it even easier. Come to my house and I'll cook something."

"You have a house?"

"I bought my mother's old house when she moved to Asheville. You probably won't recognize it, but you know where it is."

She considered this, her mind still fuzzy. Finally, she cocked a suspicious brow in his direction. "You're sure you can cook?"

He grinned. "Say yes and find out."

She wished she hadn't had that second margarita. She wanted to be clever and funny, but all she could manage was a wondering, "OK."

"That's my girl! Bring Pumper with you. I want to introduce him to Jezebel." He opened the front door, told Pumper to be quiet when the dog growled from his bed in the corner of the entryway, and kissed Roxie on the cheek. "Do me a favor, will you?"

"Anything," she replied fervently, hoping it would be something carnal.

"Go on inside and lock the door. I won't leave until I hear it bolted."

She sighed. That wasn't what she wanted to hear. "Very well. Good night, Nick."

"Good night, Roxie."

She went inside, shut the door, and snapped the dead bolt into place.

Through the door, she heard Nick's muffled, "See you tomorrow."

Miracles *did* happen. Nick Sheppard had asked her out on a date.

Roxie grinned and went upstairs to her room, thinking about the evening, lingering on their hot kisses in his truck. She really would have liked to have made love to him there, and she was pretty darn sure she wouldn't have regretted it in the least bit.

Feeling ridiculously happy, she changed into her pajamas and went to bed.

chapter 21

*R*OXIE PARKED THE MUSTANG across the street from Nick's house and gaped. Two stories and painted white, it was every bit as large as Mother's, if not larger. But while Mother's house had a bit of Miss Havisham's moldy wedding cake happening, Nick's house portrayed solid strength. From the large columns holding up the porch roof to the wide, inviting stone steps leading to the veranda, the house beckoned.

He hadn't been kidding when he'd said he'd been updating his mother's old house; he'd added an entire floor. Honestly, where Nick Sheppard was concerned, she never knew what to expect.

All day long—through her errands, visiting Clara, listening to Mother's gushing comments about "that nice Sheriff Thompson"—the realization that she'd be seeing Nick soon had kept buzzing in the back of her brain. She hadn't even minded when she'd run into the mayor at the post office and he'd tried to kill her with a Gaze of Death.

She turned off the car and looked over at Pumper,

who occupied the passenger seat. "Look at us—on our first double date." Pumper lifted his head and wagged his tail.

"You like the ribbon, don't you?" She adjusted his green bow to a jauntier angle, then reached for the car door just as Nick's front door opened. Silhouetted against the inside light was a trim woman. Nick came up behind her and she turned, then lifted on her toes and kissed his cheek.

Roxie sat frozen, one hand on the door handle, her gaze glued to the scenario. What was he doing, moving women in and out on a schedule? Was someone going to show up after she left?

As the woman tilted back her head and laughed, light caught her dark hair and the curve of her cheek. Good God, was that *Robin*? What was *she* doing here?

Roxie watched as Robin turned gracefully on one red heel and sashayed over to the driveway, where her blue BMW sat. The ho's hips had more swing than the one on Nick's damned porch.

As Robin pulled into the street, her headlights swung in an arc and fell fully on Roxie.

Robin gave her a self-satisfied smirk, and Roxie hoped Robin and her fancy car slid into a ditch on the way home—or she at least got a flat tire just as it began to rain.

Robin's car disappeared, and Roxie realized she was still gripping the door handle. She forced her fingers to relax, but even when she let go of the handle, she couldn't seem to unclaw her hand. *Easy, Treymayne. Don't overreact. This is just a date. There's no law that says he can't see other women.*

Yet somehow that didn't make it easier. Couldn't he have at least scheduled his dates oh, say, twenty minutes apart and not back-to-back? Should she be watching to see who came strolling up the walkway as she left?

No. This wasn't for her. She'd had enough of men and their inconsistencies. She was going home and to hell with Nick Sheppard and his overactive libido. He could go to—

A sharp rap startled her. She found herself looking out the window at a Fitness Forever T-shirt, a pair of muscular arms crossed over the upper edge of the logo.

Damn it. She'd waited too long. Grumbling to herself, she rolled down the window.

Nick bent over, his warm gray gaze fastened on her. "Were you going to come in or just hang out here in the street?"

"I haven't decided yet," Roxie said stiffly. "I wasn't certain if I'd gotten your Visiting Women Schedule wrong and had perhaps arrived early."

"Nope. You're right on time. In fact, I was hoping you might show up early."

"Why? So you could make your girlfriend jealous?" Roxie hated herself for sounding so petty, but she couldn't seem to help it.

Nick's smile widened. "Roxie, I am not dating Robin.

Not that she wouldn't mind if I checked her oil now and then, but I'm not that kind of guy. Not anymore."

Odd as it was, Roxie felt both a stab of triumph and a stab of pure, blinding jealousy. "She kissed you. That seemed quite chummy to me."

"Yeah, I was surprised by that. Or I was until I saw you out here. Robin's the sort of woman who likes it when everyone's pissed off. I don't know what Mayor Harkins sees in her."

"Short skirts, long legs, big fake breasts, and youth."

"That could be it. A pity he also likes petulant behavior, outrageous demands for attention, childish possessiveness, and enough drama for three daytime soaps." Nick leaned down a bit closer and grinned. "So you brought Pumper. He's all dressed up, too! Want to come in?"

"I suppose we should."

"That would make eating dinner a lot easier. I was just getting things started when Robin arrived so unexpectedly. She said she wanted to talk to me about a problem. I'm sure you can imagine what it was."

"She lost an earring?"

"And wanted to know if she could get it back, as she fortunately found the other under the edge of her desk."

"How convenient."

"And interesting. She's just put another point on our board."

"I'm surprised she didn't also complain about three

elderly people wearing black and carrying binoculars. Clara traded a bottle of her special bourbon to the gift store clerk at the center in exchange for a foray to watch the mayor's house this afternoon."

"I heard all about it. I also heard how their sassy, troublesome bandleader, a very attractive blonde with blue eyes that can stop a train, arrived later and made them all go home." He reached through the window and unlocked her door, then opened it. "Let's go inside."

"Now?" Her voice squeaked and she wished she could take it back.

His gaze narrowed. "Afraid, Treymayne?"

Her back stiffened. "Of course not. I'd like to see your house."

"Good, because I want to show it to you."

Why? So he could get her into the privacy of his house for another of those bone-melting kisses and more? The thought sent a jolt of pure adrenaline through her.

He held out his hand.

She put her hand in his and let him help her from her car. He saw her outfit, and his eyes widened appreciatively. "And to think Pumper got to sit beside this all of the way here." He looked at the dog. "You lucky bastard."

Roxie grinned. Her outfit said "nice girls can be fun, too," rather like a very naughty Jackie Kennedy. A light pink cotton cardigan stretched over a white silk blouse unbuttoned just one button too low. Her flared black skirt ended several inches above her knee and flipped a bit as she walked. And her black satin pumps were decorated with ornate silver tassels reminiscent of a stripper's pasties.

She held out one of her feet and let the light catch the tassel. "You didn't say if our date was formal or not, so I tried to cover all possibilities."

Nick was definitely imagining *all* the possibilities. He didn't usually pay much attention to how a woman dressed, beyond the usual appreciation for a well-fitted pair of jeans on a tight ass or a low-cut top that looked as if it might fail to perform its duties. But Roxie didn't need such obvious help; she looked just as sexy in this as she'd looked the first day he'd seen her in barely there shorts and a halter top.

His gaze drifted over her now, resting on the delicate curve of her ass. He wanted to see that tattoo. It had been perched on the table in his office just two nights ago, and he'd missed his chance. He wasn't going to miss it tonight.

"Well?" Roxie asked, startling him.

"Huh?"

She pointed to her shoe. "Isn't the tassel nice?"

Not as nice as tracing her tattoo with his tongue. He grinned as she turned her foot this way and that. "You have lovely tassels."

"I think so, too," she said in a voice of deep satisfaction.

He chuckled. "Let me get Pumper and then I'll give you the tour." He reached across the seat and collected the dog. "Good God, what have you been feeding him? He must weigh ten pounds more!"

"I know," Roxie said, sending Pumper's plump stomach a guilty glance. "I thought Tundy was slipping him tidbits, but it turned out it was Mother. I think old Sheriff Thompson has been good for her. She seems to be softening."

"He's a good man. I hope she appreciates that."

When Nick carried Pumper inside, they were instantly greeted by an adorable young female beagle that barked until Nick admonished her.

Pumper sat on the floor, his cast at an awkward angle as he watched Jezebel frolic. The sight apparently exhausted him, for, with a heavy sigh, he slid to the floor and lay in a heap.

Jezebel took this as an invitation to grab his ribbon. She yanked it free, then scampered about with it dangling out of her mouth.

Roxie laughed. "She has enough energy for both of them."

Nick nodded as Jezebel ran by. "You have no idea."

Roxie looked around, and Nick saw the flicker of appreciation that crossed her face. Suddenly the days and days he'd spent refinishing the old wood floors and ripping down the cracked plastered walls seemed worthwhile.

"Nick, you did all of this yourself?"

"Most of it. I hired some help when I framed in the second floor."

She shook her head and walked around the room, pausing by the fireplace. "This is beautiful!"

"I bought the fireplace front from an antique store, but I made the mantel. It's the same walnut as the floor."

She trailed her fingers over the mantel in a way that made Nick's mouth go dry. "It's beautiful."

"Thank you." The words were hard to say. Roxie Treymayne, in *his* house. "The dining room is to your right. That used to be my bedroom, before I redid the house."

She walked through the arched opening and paused on the threshold. "Wow! This is gorgeous. The wainscoting is perfect, and the chandelier—surely that wasn't from your bedroom?"

He laughed. "No. My mom found it in a yard sale when the old Poleston House went up for sale. Do you remember that house?"

"The one that was empty for years?"

"It's gone now. They bulldozed it and built a small car repair shop."

"I'm glad you rescued it." She crossed to the far window. "Was this where your bed used to be?"

"Just about." He watched her smile, the golden gleam from the chandelier tracing over her smooth skin, twinkling across her golden curls, and tracing a line across the top of her breasts.

Suddenly, he was back in high school and yearning for her like a dying man yearning for water. He didn't just want her; he *needed* her. After all of these years, one smile from her still had the power to make his concentration falter, lock his breath in his chest, and freeze him in place. *I used to dream about you, Roxanne Treymayne. Every night.*

I still do.

She slowly turned to look at him. "What did you say?"

His face heated. Damn it, he hadn't meant to say that out loud. But since he had, he repeated stubbornly, "I said I used to dream of you being here. In my house. I still do."

She made a helpless gesture with her hands. "Nick, I'm no dream. I—I've made some colossal mistakes, including marrying someone I didn't really know." She winced. "I've realized that I married Brian just to get away from my mother, and that's not a very honorable thing to do."

"I know your mother, and it makes perfect sense to me."

She managed a tremulous smile. "That's just the beginning of it. I'm short-tempered, have a horrible time remembering people's names, I hate doing dishes, and the only thing I've found that I'm good at doing is asking people all of the wrong questions at the wrong times."

"I'd disagree that the last one is a shortcoming." He laughed. "Roxie, I have a temper and tend to be short with people. I'm sometimes too judgmental for my own good, and I hate doing laundry. None of us are perfect. I don't know why it would be any different for you."

She bit her lip, and the sight of her even, white teeth

closing over her plump lower lip broke the last thread of control.

He closed the three steps that separated them and kissed her. He kissed her to stop her from thinking, from finding reasons to worry and reasons to think she was less than she was. He kissed her to keep his mind from exploding with the wild, crazed realization that somehow, in building this house, he'd done it with the distant, secret hope that one day she might return and walk in his door. He kissed her because, just as it always had, it felt so right.

Her soft mouth beneath his, her full curves under his hands—they all belonged right there, to him and to no one else. He ran his hands down her back, to the swell of her hips, and then cupped her ass with both hands.

Damn, she was a sexy armful. This was exactly where they were supposed to be, and it felt damn good. It felt *right*.

She moaned against his mouth, and he slipped a hand beneath her silky shirt to her full breast. He rubbed his thumb over her nipple, which popped to life beneath his touch.

He pulled her tighter, and her moan changed to a sound of pain.

He lifted his head.

Her brows were lowered, though her eyes seemed glazed. "Something's pressing into my back."

He pulled her forward. "Sorry. It's the railing to the upstairs."

Roxie peeped at him through her lashes. Her body ached with desire. "Nick . . . I want to see the second floor."

His gray gaze locked on her. "Really?"

"Yes."

He scooped her up and swiftly headed upstairs.

Roxie clutched her arms about his neck.

She put her lips to his ear and whispered, "I want this, Nick. I want you."

His lips curved into a grin. "That, Roxie Treymayne, is the nicest thing you've ever said to me."

Roxie twined her arms more tightly about his neck, and suddenly she was in his bedroom. She had a whirled impression of warm golden wood floors, deep red rugs scattered here and there, and a large fireplace in one corner before Nick spilled her over a large, bleach-fresh bed and followed her onto it.

After that, there was no more thinking. Nothing but feeling. She yanked her shirt off and tossed it, the white silk floating to the floor. He stroked and touched, kissed and tasted. All throughout, he whispered the sweetest of nothings into her ear, making her even madder to have him.

She was naked first, her silk panties falling on top of her shirt. She helped Nick remove his shirt and growled when she saw he wore jeans fastened with a short line of buttons.

He laughed as she attacked them, then he kicked his

jeans to the floor, slipped an arm about her waist, and flipped her to her back.

She pressed a hand to his chest, panting. "Nick, we need—I'm not taking—"

"We need a condom."

She nodded, her body primed and ready. "And hurry!"

He reached for the nightstand, and hunted for a moment. "Aha!" He held up a silver packet, feeling as if he'd just single-handedly won the World Cup.

"Yesss!" She plucked the shiny silver packet from his hand and smiled mischievously. With her hair tousled, her red lips curved so lushly, he watched enthralled as she lifted the pack to her mouth, nipped the corner with her white teeth, and ripped the packet open.

Every cell of his body stood up and took notice, from the hair on the back of his neck to his cock.

She grinned, the sliver of paper still clipped between her teeth. "Ta da!"

She covered her mouth and coughed.

Nick lifted up on his elbows.

She gripped his arm. Her smile had disappeared, and in its place was a strange expression, her lips parted, her eyes wide. Before his bemused gaze she dropped the opened packet and pressed her hand to her throat, an odd gasping noise slipping from her parted lips.

Nick had her on her feet in seconds. He grabbed her around the waist, tucked her back against his chest, made a fist, and gave a sharp Heimlich thrust.

She made a choking sound.

He pressed again more sharply.

A thin piece of silver wrapper flew to the floor and Roxie gasped, coughing and sputtering.

Nick sat down on the edge of the bed, pulling her into his lap. She slumped against him, breathing hard, a hand pressed to her eyes.

Her body shuddered against him, and he tightened his hold. Was she crying? Maybe he'd hurt her when—

She pushed away from him and bent over, laughing so hard she couldn't speak.

Nick grinned and started laughing with her.

Finally, she wiped her eyes and said with a watery chuckle, "I bet that's the first time in the history of seduction someone has choked on the condom wrapper."

He pulled her back down on the bed beside him so they were side by side. "We can only hope it's the last."

She grinned, her face flushed, her eyes watery from laughter. Nick had never seen a more beautiful woman in his life. "Are you sure you're OK?"

"I'm fine," she said in a husky voice. "Humiliated, but fine."

He brushed her hair from her brow, the soft curls clinging to his fingers. "It was nothing."

She smiled and threw an arm over her head, exposing her breast. "I sort of killed the moment, didn't I?"

"Roxie?" He took her hand and placed it on his still firm cock.

Her eyes widened, and her mouth formed a perfect O. Then, her eyes bright once again, she leaned forward and kissed him.

chapter 22

SOME MOMENTS DIDN'T REQUIRE explanation but action—and with Roxie, Nick was learning that action was the most important skill of all.

He stroked her lush skin, lingering on the smooth curve of her breasts, the flat plane of her stomach, the silken line of her thighs. She sighed and pressed to him, as eager for him as he was for her.

She was so sensual—she came alive with every touch, clung to him and opened for him without realizing she did so. It was almost more than he could stand.

He lifted himself over her and rubbed his hips against hers, teasing her even more.

A low moan escaped her throat and she pressed against him. He could feel her need, taste her excitement as he captured her lips again. She wrapped her arms about his neck and urged him on with her tongue and hips.

It was tempting to just delve in, to thrust home and sink into her heated softness, but Nick wasn't about to let this long-waited-for moment—to have Roxie here, in his bed, where she belonged—slip by without making it mean something.

He gently untangled her arms from his neck, nibbling her ear and making her gasp. Then, he slipped down to her round breasts, capturing her nipple and gently sucking it. She gasped and grasped at his shoulders.

Oh yes, he'd make her beg for it. The passion they'd shared in his office had been but a taste of the pleasures to come; he'd see to that.

He trailed a line of kisses from one breast to the other, laving them both to turgid peaks. She writhed beneath him, her hands grasping fistfuls of sheet.

His own body was on fire, his cock throbbing with the desire to take her. It took all of his resolve, but he slipped even further down, pressing light, eager kisses down her stomach to her navel. He ran his tongue across the jeweled navel ring that moved with her every gasp, and then slipped down to the juncture of her thighs.

Her sweet scent made him ache all the more. He rubbed his chin over her tight curls, the dampness making his mouth water. She was so hot, her hips quivering, bucking at the lightest touch. Her eyes were closed, her legs apart, her teeth clenched as she quivered beneath him.

In this moment, she was so vulnerable, and yet so powerful. He would do anything for her. *Anything.*

He bent and pressed a gentle kiss to her center. A

deep shudder ripped through her, then another. He pressed his mouth to her, laving her clitoris with his tongue, teasing and tormenting, daring her to come for him.

Roxie clutched the sheets tighter, fighting for control. She had to fight the urge to thrash her hips, to lift up and meet his eager tongue, to press against him, begging for more. Suddenly, she was awash with greed, with endless need, and the desire to envelop him completely. "Please, Nick," she whispered.

He stopped.

Her body tightened. *"Please."* She lifted her hips, her hands tight on the fistfuls of sheets.

He didn't move.

Roxie writhed. *"Please, Nick. Please!"*

He slid forward, dragging his warm body across hers. Her skin was so flushed with need that the feel of the crisp hair on his chest made her gasp with renewed longing.

His face came into view, his gray eyes so dark they appeared black. "Open for me," he whispered. "Open for me, sweet."

She lifted her legs and locked them about his hips, dragging his mouth to hers as she kissed him desperately.

He leaned to one side, and for a heart-wrenching moment, she thought he was sliding off the bed to leave. Then, to her relief, she heard the drawer open on the side table and realized he was getting another condom. She released him as he rolled to his back and opened the silver packet and rolled it into place.

The second he had it tight, she raised up, threw a leg over him, pressed him to the mattress, and lowered herself onto him.

He filled her so well, flooding her body with instant gratification, instant pleasure, the feeling so intense it bordered on pain. She grabbed his shoulders and rocked forward, noting with pleasure how his face was taut with fevered desire, his body rigid with the same fever that heated her.

He grasped her hips and moved with her, intensifying the pressure of his cock inside her. She ground against him.

Nick couldn't take his eyes off her. Roxie sat on him, her head thrown back, her lips parted, her knees to either side of his hips as she rode him, her face alight with sensual pleasure. Her breasts bounced enticingly with each stroke, her skin flushed a rosy hue.

He couldn't hold back any more. With a groan, he thrust deeply into her, hanging onto her hips, her warm wetness pulling him closer and closer to the edge of control.

He pulled himself up, gathered her in his arms and, never allowing her to break contact, he rolled her to her back. This moment wasn't for him; it was for Roxie, and he was going to make certain she felt every second of it. When she left his house, he wanted her to know that she'd been well loved.

He captured her lips with his as he thrust into her, building his speed to match the eager tempo of her hips. She locked her legs about him and urged him on. Their breath mingled as, with a loud cry, Roxie arched against him. That was all it took for Nick to release his tenuous hold. Moments later, he collapsed on his forearms and buried his face in her neck, breathing as hard as she was.

For a long moment, neither moved. Nick soaked in the luxurious feel of her naked skin on his, the warmth of her arms loosely clasped about his neck, the shivery sensuality of her breath as it brushed his bare shoulder.

With a deep sigh, he rolled to one side, gathering her to him and tucking her against his shoulder, still unable to think clearly.

Roxie snuggled against him, her body quivering with fulfilled passion. She buried her face in Nick's shoulder, marveling at how well she fit against him, as if she'd been made for this one place. She rubbed her cheek against his bare shoulder, smiling as he stroked her arm, his breath warm in her hair.

"Roxie?" Nick whispered.

She knew she should say something, but she didn't want to break the moment.

He pulled her closer and settled deeper into the pillows. Soon, his breathing slowed and deepened, and she could tell he'd fallen asleep.

Smiling to herself, Roxie closed her eyes and snuggled into the covers.

Roxie awoke with a start. She was wrapped in a cocoon of warmth, a sheet tangled about her legs, her chest weighted by . . . a man's arm? She blinked in the darkness and ran her fingers over Nick, memory returning in full force.

She smiled as the lovely feeling of fulfillment settled into her. There was something to be said for just going with the moment, especially when that moment was Nick Sheppard.

She gently turned her cheek so that it pressed against his hard arm. His skin was warm against hers, and she inhaled his scent. His long legs were twined with hers, holding her hostage against the mattress.

She and Brian had never had this type of passion, not even in the beginning.

She shrugged the thought away, the memory not hurting so much anymore. The longer she stayed in Glory, the further away Brian seemed.

Funny, but when she'd come to Glory, she hadn't thought to spend it recovering from Brian; she'd been certain she'd need a more exotic location and the help of someone exotic and unfamiliar. Instead, returning to Glory had started feeling like . . . home.

Beside her, Nick stirred, then stretched. "Roxie?" he whispered.

"Yes?"

He rolled up onto his elbow, his face visible from the street light. "I'm sorry I fell asleep."

"I did, too. I just woke up."

He lifted a hand and brushed a curl from her forehead, his touch feather-light. "Roxie, I didn't plan on this happening so quickly. If I had, I'd have never put that damned lasagna in the oven."

"Is it burnt?"

"No, it's on a timer and turned off—" He looked at the clock. "—over an hour ago. It's probably cold."

She chuckled. "We seem to have a habit of leaving food in ruins. Do you remember when we were in high school and ordered that pizza?"

He nodded. "And then forgot about it because we were—"

"Not paying attention."

He grinned wolfishly. "Exactly. So it got cold and when we tried to warm it up in the oven, we forgot to ah, pay attention again, and it burned to a crisp."

She smiled. "I can't believe you remembered that."

His grin faded. "I remember it all, Roxie."

"So do I." She was silent a moment, then she said, "I didn't think it was possible, but this was even better than when we were in your office."

He kissed her shoulder. "We're good together."

"We weren't when we were in high school. Nick, I never explained what happened—"

His finger touched her lips. "I know what happened."

She tilted her head to one side. "Oh?"

"I was a nineteen-year-old fool." He gave her a rueful smile. "I didn't realize then what I know now: anything worth having is worth working for. We met, fell for each other, and I thought you should throw everything aside and focus on me. When you didn't, I got mad and tried to hurt you—and succeeded. I was a damn fool, and that's all there was to it."

"There was more."

He raised his brows.

"I thought you were the kind of guy who got bored as soon as you'd made a conquest, and I wasn't about to be the one left behind. So I left first."

He was silent a moment. "I don't blame you. I had a track record for that sort of thing. I guess I just thought we were different."

"Perhaps we were. I don't know." She lifted her knees and tucked her arms around them, looking just as vulnerable as she'd looked at nineteen. "Mother said you'd never stay in Glory; that you'd leave it, and me, at the first opportunity."

He shrugged. "She was right about one thing; I didn't want to stay here."

"Neither of us did."

Her teeth sank into her lip, the sight making him harden again. He hadn't meant to seduce her as soon as she'd arrived, but he hadn't been able to stop himself. And as he looked at her now, her hair a mass of mussed curls, her lips rosy from all the kissing, he felt the primitive urge to grab her and take her again.

He ran a hand through his hair. "I am surprised at us."

She flashed a rueful smile. "Me, too, but I'm glad this happened."

"That's my girl," he said, his voice warm with approval. "The Roxie I used to know wasn't afraid of anything."

"Ha! The Roxie you used to know was afraid of everything—failure, embarrassment, being alone, saying the wrong thing, doing the wrong thing, and doing it with the wrong person."

"You always seemed so sure of yourself."

"I've always been a good actress." She leaned back against the pillows. "Even with Brian. I sometimes felt I was playing a role: the Good Corporate Wife. I'm tired of acting. And when I'm with you, I don't feel like I have to—I can just be me."

Something inside Nick's heart shifted. Those weren't the words of a bent-for-hell temptress, though Roxie was the most tempting woman he'd ever known. If he hadn't recognized her when she'd arrived with blonde hair, he'd have known her once he saw her rear end; he'd spent hours in high school admiring it from afar.

A clock chimed in the living room and Nick groaned. "My poor lasagna!"

Roxie chuckled. "We can warm it up."

Downstairs, they heard Roxie's cell phone ring.
Nick sent her a disbelieving look. "The theme to *Love
Boat?*"

"It came with the phone." She reached for her shirt.

"I'll get it." He was gone before she could say another
word. She took the opportunity to hop out of bed and
dash to the bathroom. She quickly washed and pulled a
large robe from a hook by the door.

She came out just as Nick entered the room with her
purse.

She dug out her phone. "It was your aunt Clara. I
wonder why she's calling at this time of night?"

"The last time she called me, she wanted me to
bring her some chocolate ice cream and Doritos." He
frowned. "She never used to eat Doritos, and now it's
all she wants."

"I'd better call her back."

Nick watched as Roxie dialed the phone. His robe
barely reached below his knees, but on Roxie, it almost
dragged on the floor. Better yet, the front didn't close
properly, and he could see the smooth curve of her
breast.

"Hello? Clara? It's me, Roxie—yes, yes. I know,
but—" Roxie's eyes widened. "Who did—"

Something in her voice locked Nick's attention on
her face.

Roxie shook her head. "Clara, you have to talk slower
so I can— Yes, I know her, but what's that got to do
with— *What?*"

Nick moved closer. He could hear his aunt's voice rattling on a mile a minute.

Roxie lifted her gaze to his, shock plain on her face. "Clara, that's *illegal*!"

Nick took a step closer.

Roxie held up a hand to ward him off. "Clara, you have to tell Nick about this." Clara's voice babbled on. Roxie shook her head. "If you won't tell him, I will. In fact, he's right here with me now."

A long silence ensued, followed by a barrage of fast talking. Roxie listened, rubbing her forehead with one hand. "But Clara—I know, but—don't hang up! Let me just—" Roxie lowered the phone. "Someone broke into Doyle's room at the assisted living center, and they caught the thief."

"They?"

"Clara and her friends. They have the person locked in a closet."

Nick swiftly gathered his clothes and dressed. "Clara must be terrified!"

Roxie, who was already yanking on her clothes, shook her head. "Not at all. She asked if I could find some clothespins and duct tape so they could interrogate their suspect."

Nick removed a gun from the nightstand. "You're kidding, right?"

"They've decided this is their big break in the case." Roxie pulled her shoes on and joined Nick at the door. "We're not going to rescue your aunt, Nick. We're going to rescue the person they've got locked in Doyle's closet."

"You know who it is?"

"Yes." Roxie went down the stairs, Nick hard on her heels. "So do you."

"Oh no," he groaned. "Not Mayor Harkins!"

"No, it's someone worse," she said, heading for the front door. "Your aunt Clara has captured Pat Meese, Glory's one and only investigative reporter."

chapter 22

SOME MOMENTS DIDN'T REQUIRE explanation but action—and with Roxie, Nick was learning that action was the most important skill of all.

He stroked her lush skin, lingering on the smooth curve of her breasts, the flat plane of her stomach, the silken line of her thighs. She sighed and pressed to him, as eager for him as he was for her.

She was so sensual—she came alive with every touch, clung to him and opened for him without realizing she did so. It was almost more than he could stand.

He lifted himself over her and rubbed his hips against hers, teasing her even more.

A low moan escaped her throat and she pressed against him. He could feel her need, taste her excitement as he captured her lips again. She wrapped her arms about his neck and urged him on with her tongue and hips.

It was tempting to just delve in, to thrust home and sink into her heated softness, but Nick wasn't about to let this long-waited-for moment—to have Roxie here,

Clara rolled her wheelchair over. "The case is really moving now! Mrs. Rawlings brought us their bank records so we could look for clues, *and* we got us our first witness to interrogate. Did you bring the tape and clothespins?"

Rose rubbed her bony hands together. "We were going to water board her like the president likes to do, but we don't have enough towels."

Nick banged on the door even harder. "Clara? Open up!"

"You're not going to take us alive!" Rose yelled.

The closet door rattled. "Rose Tibbon!" Pat Meese called. "I know you're out there. I recognize your voice. Now open this door, before I decide to write a story about you and that crazy gang of yours—"

Bam! The door to the room flew open and Nick strode in.

"That was pretty good," Clara said admiringly. "Just like in the movies."

Nick scowled and went to the closet. He tried to open the door, but it wouldn't budge. "What's wrong with this thing?"

Clara gave a prim sniff. "I could tell you, but I'm not going to."

Nick leaned against the door and said in a loud voice, "Pat, are you OK?"

"I'm fine. I just want out."

"Damn it, Nick!" Clara said. "I wish you'd let us interrogate the prisoner on our own."

"Clara, Pat's a reporter, not a prisoner."

Rose wagged a finger. "No reporter I ever saw broke into an assisted living center. She's after our st—"

"Stuff!" Clara interrupted, sending Rose a warning glare.

Roxie winced. "Clara, we have to let Pat go. We'll all be in trouble."

Clara jutted out her chin. "We didn't do anything wrong; she shouldn't have come breaking into our club room!"

"How did she get in?" Nick asked.

C. J. pointed to the window. "She broke the glass and unlocked the window."

"*And* cut the screen," Clara said, indignant.

Nick went to the window and looked at the broken glass. "Did any of you touch this?"

"Of course not!" Rose said. "Do we look stupid?"

Roxie thought that probably wasn't the best question Rose could have asked as she was wearing a flowered muumuu and a pair of running shoes with no socks.

Nick crossed to the closet door again. "Pat, how did you get in?" he called through the door.

"Through the window. I came to see what was going on with—oh, just get me out of here!" Something inside the closet rattled, glass on glass.

"Hey!" C.J. yelled. "Careful with the st—!"

"Stuff," Clara finished.

"Pat?" Nick spoke calmly. "Are you standing back from the door?"

"I am now. Are you going to break it down?"

"Yes, as soon as I call for backup. I don't usually process breaking and enterings solo."

There was a long silence.

"Nick, I didn't come in here to steal anything. I just wanted to see what was going on, and visiting hours were over."

"So you just broke in?"

"Yes."

"Pat, do you know that everything you're saying can be heard by everyone in the room?"

Again, there was a long silence. Then Pat said, "Let me out! People will notice I'm missing."

Clara sighed grumpily. "Damn it, Nick, you're spoiling all of our fun. Though I don't have my Taser no more, I could have used some coins in a sock to—"

"Taser?"

Roxie dug in her purse and pulled it out. "Clara got it online, but she let me borrow it for protection."

Nick took the Taser and pocketed it. "Clara, you need a keeper." He turned back to the closet. "I'm letting Pat out. You all stand back."

"You can't let Pat out!" C.J. said. "She'll tell everyone about our still!"

"Still?" Nick asked.

Clara turned an accusing gaze on Roxie. "I told you not to bring the fuzz!"

"Pat, step away from the door." Turning away,

Nick kicked the closet door. It splintered, and Pat stumbled out, blinking in the light.

Wearing black jeans, a black AC/DC T-shirt, and a black kerchief tied around her gray hair, she looked like an aging goth housekeeper.

Nick started to speak and then stopped, looking past Pat into the open closet.

Roxie caught his expression and took a step forward. "What is it?"

"Clara, come here."

She wheeled her chair to his side.

He pointed into the closet. "What's that?"

"Doyle's still." She scowled up at him. "Makes the best bourbon you ever tasted."

"Makes?"

"Well, no. It *flavors* it, doesn't it, Rose?" She turned to Rose. "Tell Nick how it works."

"I know how it works," Nick said abruptly. He stepped into the closet and pulled out a large contraption that looked like—

Roxie blinked. "*That's* the still?"

Rose nodded moodily before saying in an undertone to Clara, "Bet he takes it with him. Stills are illegal."

"They are," Nick said briskly, "but this isn't a still."

Clara frowned. "Then what is it?"

"It's a bong."

Suddenly, it all made sense to Roxie—the club's

urgent need to snack on Doritos, how the nurses had commented that Clara and the others were in a better mood, the faint whiff of weed Roxie had attributed to the cleaning service.

Nick carried the bong into the room. "I take it you've been pouring bourbon in here and pulling smoke through it?"

Rose's jaw tightened pugnaciously. "I don't have to tell you all of our secrets."

"I guess not. Where's the pot?"

"There isn't a pot," C.J. said. "We just use—"

"The tobacco. What you burn in this."

"Oh." C.J. came across the room and rummaged in the closet. He came out with a large shoebox. "Here's some."

Nick's brows rose. "Some?"

"There are seven boxes of it."

Nick flipped open the box. Inside, neatly bagged, was enough pot to keep a sixteen-year-old boy happy for a month. Perhaps two if it was during the school year.

From behind Nick came a voice quivering with excitement. "That's marijuana!" Pat reached into her back pocket and flipped out a notebook. "This is going to be some story!"

"Wait," Roxie said. "Pat, this is only part of the story. If you want all of it, we're going to have to get you to swear an oath of secrecy."

"Oath of secrecy?"

"Yes. Do you just want *this* story? Or a really, really big one? One that might get picked up by the AP?"

Pat's eyes gleamed.

"If you wait until Nick says it's OK, *and* if you promise to protect the identity of the Murder Mystery Club, then we'll cut you in when we solve the case."

"You mean Doyle's death?"

Roxie nodded. "And you'll be the only newspaper to have access to the club. If you mention what's happened now, though, you'll not only endanger the case, but every newspaper for miles around will flock to Glory to scoop your story."

Pat didn't look convinced. "I was locked in that closet for hours, subjected to threats of Tasing, and—"

"Hold on." Nick spoke from where he was removing boxes from the closet. "Aunt Clara, do you want to press charges against Pat for breaking and entering?"

"I can do that?" Clara asked, as Pat gasped, "She can't do that!"

"Oh yes, she could." He placed another shoebox by the door. "Going to be hard to write a story from jail."

Pat swallowed. "It would never stand. It's not even Clara's room! Besides, I could explain how—I mean, if people knew what was here, then—I suppose I should—" She turned to Roxie. "I'd get an *exclusive?*"

"Exactly."

"Yup," Clara said, chiming in. "A real story on how we solved a murder. Wouldn't surprise me if they made a TV movie out of this. I hope Angelina Jolie plays me."

"I bet they have Angelina Jolie play Pat," Roxie suggested. "It's a more pivotal role."

Pat considered this. Finally, she nodded. "OK, done."

Nick sent Roxie a thankful glance. "I've got to get this back to the office. Roxie, you and Pat help me carry this to the car and we'll lock it up in the evidence locker."

"I get to help, too?" Pat looked pleased.

"Absolutely," Nick said. "I'll even let you report that I obtained it in an exciting, unspecified raid, if you keep Clara's and the others' names out of this." He looked at the boxes. "It was sort of a raid. I did have to knock the door down."

"That'd make a hell of a story right there," Pat agreed, looking as pleased as if she'd found gold. "Do I get to ride in the squad car?"

"Why not?"

Clara looked at the bong and boxes stacked by the door and sighed. "Nick, you're my favorite grand-nephew, but I'll be damned if I can come to like this."

"I'm not real happy, either. I was undercover when you called." Nick shot an amused look at Roxie.

She smiled back, and for a moment, it was just the two of them. Aware of Pat's interested gaze, Roxie turned away and collected as many boxes as she could handle. "I'm going to head out to the car."

"I'll see Clara and the others to their rooms. Pat and I will bring the rest."

"Not all of it," Clara wheedled.

"Yes, all of it. *And* Pastor Rawlings's bank records."

As Roxie carried the boxes out the door, Rose yelled after her, "Be careful the mayor don't see you loading up all of those boxes! He might be driven into doing something desperate."

"I'll be careful," Roxie said. She made it to the lobby without incident, thanking Nurse Becky, who came over to open the door for her.

Outside, the cool night air brushed over her. She started to carry the boxes to Nick's car, then realized it would be locked. Instead, she carried them to her own car and dumped the boxes in the backseat beside Pumper, who started awake and looked at her with sleepy curiosity. He looked so cute that she reached in to pat him.

"Need a hand?" came a voice close to her ear.

Roxie stood up so fast that she bumped her head on the car door. "Mayor Harkins! I—You—I mean, no, I don't need anything. I'm fine. Just waiting here.

On Nick. He's inside right now, but he'll be here soon and—"

The mayor waved a hand, an annoyed expression on his face. "Fine, then. I was just visiting Mother."

"Visiting your mother? After visiting hours?"

"The staff knows me, so they let me stay late sometimes."

That was convenient. Had he been prowling the hallways looking for the club, too? "I see. Thank you for the offer, but I'm all set. As I said, I'm waiting on Nick." *And his gun.*

Mayor Harkins frowned. "OK, then. I'll see you later."

He turned, climbed into a car two down from Roxie's, and left.

Roxie pressed a hand to her heart. She'd nearly jumped out of her skin. Really, she needed to calm down and get ahold of herself. The mayor couldn't possibly know how close he was to being discovered.

A car pulled in behind hers. "Need a hand?" came a warm, friendly voice.

Roxie smiled. "Nope! I'm just waiting on someone."

Chuckling, his attractive blue eyes crinkling at the corners, Ty Henderson climbed from his Volvo and looked around. "Maybe the correct question is *why* a beautiful woman like you has been reduced to waiting on someone. It really should be the other way around."

Roxie laughed. "I don't know if I agree with that, but I like hearing it."

Still chuckling, Ty leaned against the car, his gaze falling on the boxes. "What's all of this?"

Roxie shrugged as casually as she could. "Just some stuff for Clara's club."

She looked at the center's glass doors, willing Nick and Pat to arrive. What was taking so long? "You know, I think I'll go and check on——"

Ty slipped an arm about her shoulders and pinned her against him. Something cold pressed into her side as he leaned down, his lips against her ear. *"No."*

With that one word, a shard of fear pierced her heart.

"BECKY, THANKS FOR GIVING us a hand." Nick followed the nurse down the hallway as she pushed Clara's wheelchair while Rose, C.J., and Pat followed.

"You're welcome." Becky's bright gaze rested on the large object C.J. had wrapped in his housecoat. "What's that?"

"This is, ah——" He cast a wild glance at Nick, who answered for him.

"It's 'evidence' for the club's new case."

"We've been keeping it in Doyle's room," Clara said.

"You all aren't supposed to be there after hours, and you know it. I'm going to have to put a lock on Doyle's door if you don't follow the rules better."

"We like it in there," Clara protested.

"We can watch our shows without anyone bothering us," Rose added.

"I know," Becky said, turning the last corner into the lobby. "But bedtime is bedtime."

"Good luck getting these hoodlums to follow rules," Nick said.

Becky grinned. "They sure hate it, don't they?"

"You have no idea." Nick stopped by the lobby door. "Clara, Rose, and C.J., you all get some sleep. I'll be by in the morning to give you an update."

"You going to do chemical analysis on that evidence?" Clara asked eagerly. "Use a microscope and all?"

"Just like *CSI,*" Nick assured her. "C'mon, Pat. Roxie's waiting on us in the car—" He stopped, his gaze locked outside. "Her car is gone."

"She left a few minutes ago."

Nick turned to face Nurse Becky. "Did you see her?"

"I was leaving to hand out meds in the 200 wing and when I went by, I saw her standing outside. I thought maybe she had some car troubles, but then the mayor came up, so I figured he'd give her a hand."

His heart beating unsteadily, Nick unhooked his cell from his belt and hit Roxie's number.

No one answered.

Nick dialed her home phone number. After two rings, Tundy answered.

"Hi, this is Nick Sheppard. Is Roxie in?"

"Hell no, though we've been callin' and callin'."

"When she gets there, will you have her call me?"

"Sure thing, Sheriff. And if you see her, tell her we need some baking powder for the matzo balls."

"Sure thing." Nick closed his phone. "She's not home yet."

"Then where is she?" Clara asked, genuine worry in her magnified eyes.

There was a moment of silence during which every person looked at Nick as if he was supposed to somehow reach into one of the boxes he'd been carrying and magically produce Roxie.

He would have loved to have done that. His voice was grim and tight as he asked, "Becky, are you certain Roxie left with the mayor?"

Becky shrugged. "I suppose so. He was talking to her. He sometimes stays after visiting hours to visit his mother. They like to watch movies together."

Across the lobby, the night nurse called out, "Roxie didn't go with the mayor. She went with Ty Henderson."

Until that moment, Nick hadn't realized he'd been holding his breath. If something happened to Roxie— At least now he could relax. Ty might be a lousy newspaper manager, but he was harmless. "Maybe Roxie got tired of waiting."

As he went to put his phone back on the holder, he dropped one of his boxes. Packets of pot fell to the ground, followed by a handful of scribbled notes.

"More of Doyle Cloyd's blackmail notes!" Clara exclaimed.

Pat reached down and scooped them up.

Nick swiftly shoved the packets back into the box, but not before Becky asked, "What's that—"

"Nick?"

Something in Pat's voice made him turn to look at her.

"Nick, these aren't Doyle's."

"What?"

"I know this handwriting. I see it every day at the newspaper. It's Ty Henderson's. I'm sure of it."

Chapter 24

*T*HEY ARRIVED AT AN old, decrepit house by the lake where Ty used to have parties, a "For Sale" sign now stuck on the dock.

As she turned off her car, Roxie's heart pounded so loud that she was certain he could hear it. "Now what?"

Ty waved his gun toward the house. "We're going to take those damn boxes inside. Get out and no tricks! I'll shoot, and you know I will."

She noticed how his hand trembled and decided it wouldn't be wise to press her luck. As nervous as he was, he was as likely to shoot her by accident as on purpose. She carefully climbed from the car, catching sight of Pumper's questioning gaze over the backseat. "Easy, Pumper," she said.

Ty stared at the dog. "Damn it, why'd you bring the dog with you?"

"He's hurt, so I've been watching him."

"That damned dog might start barking or something." Ty lifted the gun and pointed it at Pumper.

"No," she snapped. "He's harmless. Look, he has a broken leg."

Ty lowered the gun and passed a shaky hand over his forehead. "I don't— We can't—"

"Ty, why don't we just take him with us? All he does is sleep; he won't cause any trouble. And if he's inside, you can stop him if he starts to bark." Roxie tried to swallow but couldn't. If something happened, she didn't want Pumper left in the car where it would get hot once the sun rose. *If something happened . . .*

Please, Nick, please find me. He was her only hope.

"Fine, take the mutt. But if he makes one peep—" Ty pointed the gun at Pumper.

Roxie picked up the dog, staggering with his weight. Inside, she put him in a corner near the front door. Then Ty made her return for the boxes she'd brought from Doyle's room.

Once they were inside, he pointed to an old chair. "Sit and don't make a move. I have to think." His hand was shaking even more, though his finger remained on the trigger.

Half sick, she took the chair. Where was Nick? He'd have realized that her car was missing by now. He'd be worried, but how would he find her? If only she'd thought to leave a clue of some sort—but she'd been too shocked to do anything.

God, please help me. Please. There are so many things I haven't done yet. She'd never get to Paris now . . . but found that she really didn't care. With startling clarity, she suddenly realized that her hunt for an identity was over. She'd thought she wanted to live a wild, untrammeled, unfettered life of pleasure but now that she'd tasted a bit of it—from riding shoeless on Ethan's motorcycle to drinking margaritas while thronged by admiring men—she'd discovered something. Though it seemed that selfish, pleasure-pursuing people got all of the perks in life, the truth was, what *she* wanted was something much simpler. She wanted peace and fulfillment, good friends, and a home of her own. Most of all, she wanted what she'd never had with Brian: a relationship based on love and respect.

And she wanted to find those things with Nick.

Why did I have to realize that now, *when I might never get to tell him?*

It was more than friendship and hot sex. She *loved* him—with every ounce of her being.

She blinked away tears. "Ty, can't we just—"

"Shut up! I'm trying to think." Ty paced back and forth, raking a hand through his hair and mumbling to himself.

Roxie watched him for a moment, trying to calm her racing heart. He looked horrible; disheveled and mussed, as if he hadn't been sleeping well.

"Ty, you don't look good. I know this whole thing is just a horrible misunderstanding, and—"

He gave a shaky laugh. "You have no idea! None! I can't believe this has all come back to haunt me." He went to Widow Rawlings's box and flipped it open. He pulled out a document, then another, throwing them on the floor as he searched yet more desperately. Finally, with a curse, he slapped the box closed. "What in the hell is this?"

"It's Pastor Rawlings's bank records."

"Damn it, I thought this was the box that—" He closed his eyes. "It's still in the sheriff's office, isn't it? I saw you with this and thought it might be another box from Doyle. Damn it! What was I thinking?" Ty wiped a hand over his face, his lips trembling. "I *told* that asshole to burn those damned notes, and he swore that he had. But he kept them. Now that boyfriend of yours has them, and it's only a matter of time."

"A matter of time before what?"

Ty's gaze flickered to hers and held. "Before he figures out it was me, not Doyle."

"*You* were the blackmailer?"

A flicker of surprise lit his eyes, followed quickly by satisfaction. "You didn't know!"

Roxie shook her head. "I thought it was the mayor."

"Does Sheppard think that, too?"

"Ty, what's all of this about? Did you—" She had to swallow before she could speak again. "You killed Doyle, didn't you?"

His face tightened. "No, I didn't. I did a lot of things, but I've never killed anyone!"

She looked at the shaking gun.

His expression grew harder. "Not yet, anyway. Doyle's death was an accident. He used to walk at night all the time; hell, I almost hit him a few times myself. He'd come to the field late at night and—"

"Field?"

"The weed. It was all about the weed." Ty slumped against the wall. Pumper wagged his tail, but Ty ignored him. "People think it's so easy being my father's son. He was the town's most impressive businessman and everyone respected him. No one knew the truth: he was broke."

"But . . . everyone said he was the richest man in town!"

"That's what he wanted them to think," Ty said bitterly. "He was broke his entire life, but he was too proud to admit it. When he died, he left me with nothing but a run-down newspaper, a mountain of debts, and stuck in this town of losers. I didn't have any money. Nothing to keep me going."

"Ty, I'm so sorry. I always thought you were so lucky."

"Oh no. See, I not only inherited my father's debts, but his pride as well. When I was in college, I grew a little weed to make enough money to eat and to pay my fraternity dues. I got pretty good at it, too. So when Father died and I saw the way the things were at the paper, I decided to take what I knew and make it bigger."

"So you became a full-time drug dealer."

"I only grow weed," he said sharply. "Never anything else."

Roxie didn't answer.

He scowled. "You don't understand."

"Probably not. So how did Doyle come to be involved?"

"He was always wandering around—you know how he was. And once he found the field, I couldn't get him out of it. He was like a big aphid, coming to steal all of my good stuff. I had to do something, so I—"

"Killed him."

"No, damn it! Will you stop it with the killing? I *hired* him."

"*What?*"

Ty gave a mirthless laugh. "You didn't know that, either, did you? You didn't know a thing and now I've—" He groaned and leaned against a table, his shoulders slumped. "I suppose you might as well know it all, then."

"No, no! You don't need to tell me more—"

"What difference will it make now? Doyle helped me with deliveries, sales, everything. Eventually we came up with our blackmail scheme so we could expand. He did all of that, too. A lot of people thought he was stupid and mean, but he wasn't." Ty's mouth trembled. "He was better to me than my father ever was."

Roxie didn't know what to say. All her life, she'd believed the picture Ty's father had presented to Glory—that of a respected businessman with a disappointing son. "Ty, I'm so sorry. I wish I'd known you better."

He shrugged. "It's just the way things were."

She realized she was no longer trembling. She caught Ty's gaze and said quickly, "Did Doyle collect the information for the blackmail by eavesdropping at the assisted living center?"

"Yes. Those old farts can't keep their mouths closed. They were spewing family secrets right and left. It was very lucrative. At one time, I was blackmailing everyone important in this town: the mayor, his little bimbo, even the old preacher."

"You were blackmailing Robin?"

"Yes. She left town after graduation, went to Orlando, and became a stripper. She didn't want the sweet old mayor to know about it. Guess she's under the impression he'll eventually marry her if he doesn't know her sordid past."

That explained why Robin had broken into Nick's office; she'd been afraid her past was about to be revealed.

Ty gave a tired shrug. "Funny, isn't it? This tiny town and all of those secrets. It's amazing."

Roxie looked down at her hands, clenched together in her lap.

"Doyle and I were good partners. I paid him with weed, and he liked that. Liked it a lot. After a few years, I'd made enough that I'd paid the old man's debts and had a little for myself. I was just seeing my way clear when Doyle died. Now, I—" Ty's voice broke.

Pumper stirred and Roxie saw the dog looking past

her to the window. She glanced over and saw the flip of a cat's tail. Her heart stuttered. *Not a cat! Of all things—*

Ty took a nervous turn around the room and wiped a shaky hand over his face. "Everything was going so well until those crazy old coots found those boxes in Doyle's room."

"Ty, I wish I knew what to say. I'm sorry. So sorry."

"Sorry enough to keep this a secret?"

Roxie didn't answer.

Ty gave a bitter laugh. "I didn't think so. Now I'm forced to take action." Regret flickered through his eyes. "Damn it, I didn't want it to come to this. I thought it was finally over when—"

A crunch sounded in the driveway. Ty gave a muffled curse and went to the window. "That's Pat's car. What's she doing here?"

He turned from the window and began to turn off the lights. Pumper gave a grumbled growl.

Ty wheeled on the dog, but Pumper either thought better of it or fell back asleep, because he didn't make another sound.

Roxie looked for the cat, but no sign of it showed. Relief swept through her. She wasn't certain Ty would shoot her, but she was sure he wouldn't mind using his gun on Pumper.

A car door slammed and Ty wheeled back toward the window.

Roxie sat up a little straighter. "Is she alone?" The lights from the car shone directly through the window, making it hard to make out the shape of the person approaching.

"Yes." He tucked his gun into the back of his waistband. "She's been poking around here lately, trying to find out why I put the place up for sale."

"Maybe she wants to buy it?"

"Or maybe she suspects something."

He went to a side table and pulled out some duct tape. "Roxie, don't make a sound. I'm going to have to tie—"

Footsteps neared. The car lights gleamed through the window, nothing else visible.

Ty's hand clamped on Roxie's shoulder. He bent to whisper in her ear, "Not a word, Treymayne. She snoops around town all the time. If she doesn't hear anything, she'll just leave."

Roxie nodded, wincing as his fingers cruelly bit into her. *Please God, don't let anyone get hurt!* She could smell the stale odor of sweat coming from Ty's damp shirt, feel the almost-out-of-control tremble of his hand.

Ty dropped the tape, grabbed his gun, and pointed it toward the door.

"Ty—" she whispered.

"Be quiet," he snapped. His face was drawn, his skin waxy in the reflected light. A faint sheen of perspiration shone on his forehead.

Across the lighted window the slinky form of a cat appeared, outlined by the bold light. It took two steps, then paused, poised in a perfect arch.

Pumper stumbled to his feet, a deep growl lifting from his throat.

"Shut that dog up," Ty whispered harshly.

"Pumper!" Roxie said in a hushed voice, her gaze flickering between the dog and Ty's shaking gun.

The footsteps halted outside.

Bam! The back door flew open, and Nick stepped into the room. Ty whirled, startled.

Zzzzzzzzzt! Nick fired off a shot from a hot pink Taser.

Ty fell to the floor, dropping the gun, then struggled to get up on his knees.

"Don't move!" Nick ordered. In the distance, sirens wailed.

Ty slowly reached for his gun, his hands shaking mightily.

"Don't do that, Ty. I'll shoot again." The quiet purpose in Nick's voice brooked no argument.

Ty continued to reach, his entire body quavering. His fingers grazed the gun—

Nick squeezed the Taser trigger again. *Zzzzzzzzzzzt!* Ty flopped to his back, his body rigid. Nick kicked the gun out of the way and turned on a light.

It was over.

Somehow, Roxie's mind didn't work, though her body seemed to know what to do. She climbed to her feet and got the duct tape for Nick, who wasted no time securing Ty's arms. Then he turned on the rest of the lights and tucked Ty's gun into his own belt.

The sirens grew louder. As Roxie watched the distant flash of lights through the woods, a huge quaking ripped through her, stealing every bit of strength from her legs. She almost fell, but Nick had her in a second, easing her back into the chair. "Sit."

As soon as her butt hit the cushion, he bent her head down between her legs. She gulped air as he rubbed her shoulders.

"Easy, Treymayne. The worst is over. The highway patrol will be here in a minute, and I'll take you to the office and get some coffee in you." He pulled a lap blanket off the couch and tucked it around her, then tipped her face to his.

A tear ran down her cheek. Nick gently wiped it away. His own eyes were damp. "Damn it, Roxie, when I thought that bastard had you and might hurt you—" He wiped a hand over his face.

The warmth from his arm and the blanket were slowly stilling her shivers. "Nick? Are you OK?"

"OK? Am I *OK*? The woman I love was just abducted by a desperate man who—" He ranted on, but Roxie couldn't hear another word. *The woman I love. Had he really said that? Out loud?*

She put a finger over his lips.

He closed his eyes and cupped her hand over his cheek, reveling in the feel of her. He'd been so frightened. "I'm sorry. You don't need me yelling when—"

Her voice trembled a bit, her blue eyes wide. "Nick, did you say 'the woman I love?'"

"I may be three times a fool, Roxie, but I love you. I loved you in high school. I loved you when I tried to forget you in Atlanta. I loved you all of those years I was learning to be a cop, someone you might be proud of. But most importantly of all, I love you now."

Her face was tear-streaked, her hair was dusty, but it didn't matter. She was Roxie, *his* Roxie, and no woman had ever been more dear to him.

"Are you sure, Nick?"

He laughed. "God, yes. I love your hair. Your laugh. The way you try so hard to be better, when you're already perfect." He shook his head. "I even love your tattoo, which I *still* haven't managed to get a good look at. But I plan on examining it closely as soon as possible."

He took her hands, his gaze locked on hers. "Roxie, I want this—*us*—to work. If you're willing to give it a shot, so am I."

She smiled, a glint of amusement in her blue eyes. "A shot?"

He grimaced. "Bad word choice. How about we give this a go? Take things one day at a time, see where it leads. I know you can't say you love me right now, but maybe in a few months you'll feel—"

"Nick?"

He took a shaky breath. Damn, why had he pressed things this far? Outside, three squad cars roared into the drive, parking behind his. There was no time, no—

Roxie took his face between her hands. "Nick, I

didn't realize it until tonight, but I love you, too. When I thought I wouldn't see you again—" A sob caught her, and the tears finally came.

Gently, Nick kissed her.

Roxie slipped her arms around his neck and kissed him back.

Outside came the crunch of footsteps on the gravel drive, followed by the arrival of another vehicle.

Nick reluctantly broke the kiss to look out the window at the new approaching lights. "That's not the— damn it, I told them not to come! I'm going to kill whoever is driving that van."

Roxie grinned. "Aunt Clara?"

"The whole damn posse. With Pat driving, it looks like. Great. The paper, too."

Roxie peered out the window. "There's another car behind them. That's . . . that's Mark! And he has Tundy and Mother with him."

Nick tucked the Taser back into his pocket. "Let's go. I'll tell Mark to get your mutt." With the evil cat gone, Pumper wagged his tail but remained on his side.

Roxie glanced back at Ty, who was slumped in his chair, taped tight, a blank look on his dazed face. "What will happen to him?"

"If he's smart, he'll come clean to the DA."

"He didn't kill Doyle. They were working together. Doyle was collecting blackmail money all over town for Ty in exchange for all of the weed he could smoke, and—"

Nick kissed her again. When he finished, she swayed against him, her arms tightening on his neck. "Ooooh, yes. Nick?"

"Yes, my love?"

She smiled. "One day at a time sounds perfect."

He chuckled and kissed her forehead. "Good. Just don't be surprised when it lasts for the rest of your life."

Epilogue

NICK TUCKED AN ARM around Roxie and pulled her close as they sat on the front porch swing.

Roxie sighed and put her bare feet up on the wicker table. "What a week!"

"Um-hm," Nick murmured, nuzzling her ear. "What a week."

She smiled and snuggled deeper against him, enjoying the comforting weight of his arm. "Did you think Ty would confess everything to the DA like that?"

"I wasn't surprised. He got in over his head and just didn't know how to get out of it. I think he was actually relieved when it was all over."

"I suppose so. I never thought he was that sort of person."

Nick's brow lowered. "I went crazy when he put you in danger. I should have given him a warning before I Tased him, but I was frantic to get to you." He leaned down and kissed her deeply, then smiled. "Besides—when you're the only cop in town, sometimes you have to play by the seat of your pants instead of by the rule book."

The door swung open and Susan stormed out, Mark hard on her heels. She took the steps two at a time, stopping at the bottom to swing around and face Mark, who almost ran into her. "Stop right there!" Her voice shook with anger. "No matter what you say, I am *not* going to change my mind."

Mark crossed his arms. "What's wrong, Susan? Are you afraid?"

"Afraid? *Me? Afraid?* Why—you—I should—" She spun on one heel and marched down the walkway.

Mark watched her, glowering, then stomped back inside.

Nick watched, bemused, as Susan threw herself into her car and slammed the door so hard that the entire vehicle rocked. "I wonder what that's all about?"

Roxie sighed. "That might be my fault."

"How?"

"I asked Mark to do me a favor, and it had to do with Susan."

Nick frowned. "Treymayne, you're not making sense."

"I ran into Mayor Harkins at the center this morning. He mentioned that Ty was going to sell *The Glory Examiner*." She looked up at Nick. "I have all of that money from the divorce settlement, and I need to do something with it."

"Wait. You're thinking of buying *The Glory Examiner*?"

"And having Susan run it."

"What?"

"I know you'll have to find another dispatcher—but Susan would be perfect for the paper. I asked Mark to audit it so I'll know what's a fair price."

"I'm surprised he's still here. Doesn't he have to handle his clients?"

"He employs more than twenty CPAs to do that. He doesn't have a business; he has a *Business*."

"I had no idea. He must be making a fortune!"

"He is. And he seems to think the newspaper would be a good investment for me, but only with some changes. He's been reading up on it for the past week and thinks he knows everything."

"What sort of changes does he want to make?"

"Oh, how the accounts are managed, the balance of ads versus articles, what to do with the 'Dear Bob' column and that sort of thing." She grinned. "You knew Susan's been writing the 'Dear Bob' column for the past three years, didn't you?"

"You're kidding me!"

"Nope. Pat kept complaining about having to do it, saying she was a 'real reporter' and shouldn't have to sully her hands, so Ty found someone else. It gave Susan a little extra money and it turned out she was a natural. A lot of people get the paper just for that. I'd like to expand it, as well as do more coverage of local events and—" She shook her head ruefully. "I'm sorry; I don't mean to go on and on. I'm just excited about becoming Glory's first woman editor."

Nick looked down at her with a smile. "Treymayne, are you telling me that you're going to stay in Glory?"

"I thought I might try it—" She was enveloped in a bone-crushing hug, followed by a ruthless, hot kiss that left her panting and clinging to Nick's shirt. "Wow," she finally managed.

Nick lifted her into his lap. "Wow, indeed. You just stay here in Glory, and I'll fill your world with 'wows.'"

Roxie didn't doubt that. She placed a hand on his cheek and smiled. "I can't promise I'll be happy here forever, but I will try. Even Tundy's going to give it a go. She's been hired by the Pine Hills Assisted Living Center as Assistant Director of Senior Activities."

"Now I'm scared."

Roxie chuckled. "You should be. Tundy took to the Murder Mystery Club like a duck to water. I don't know what they're working on now, but Tundy said it was a big case, bigger than Doyle Cloyd's."

Nick groaned. "Wonderful. Just what Aunt Clara needs: an enabler in a pink sweat suit." At Roxie's laugh, he captured her hand and kissed the palm. "What will your mother do without Tundy? She might turn her attention on you."

Roxie glanced at the living room window, where Mother and Sheriff Thompson were silhouetted against the light. Their heads were bent over the newspaper as they looked for a movie to go see. In the background, she could hear Tundy suggesting one that involved a chain saw and a crazy mental patient.

"Mother has something other than me to keep her busy now. And if she gets on my nerves," Roxie said as she slipped an arm around Nick's neck, "Pumper and I can just escape to your house."

"That's true." Nick nuzzled her neck until she couldn't breathe. "You know, to save time, we could just go on over to my house now, without waiting for your mother to tick you off."

"Pumper would like th—"

Nick kissed her.

When she could breathe, she asked, "What was that for?"

"That's for now. And this one"—he kissed her again, more deeply—"is for later." He grinned wolfishly.

A woman could get used to that. "What happened to taking things one day at a time?"

Nick looked tenderly into her eyes. "This is one day . . . and it's our time. Forever. Sounds pretty wonderful to me."

Smiling, she kissed him back, her toes curling.

One day at a time forever sounded pretty wonderful to her, too.